"Are you as passionate as you are lovely?" wondered Venetia.

"I . . . why, yes, my lord," she stammered, reminding Quinn how pleasantly musical her voice was.

"Perhaps you should show me how much."

Bending his head, he captured that full, kissable mouth the way he had longed to do for years.

She gave a faint gasp at the contact and stiffened in response. Quinn could feel shock ripple through the graceful curves of her body, while his own breath quickened at the enticing taste of her.

Her lips were just as delectable as he'd imagined, he thought, relishing their softness. Lush, resilient, the texture of silk, ripe and warm as her body.

When she tensed further, he increased the pressure, parting the seam of her mouth and slipping his tongue inside to tangle with hers.

Her lips trembled under his. Encouraged, he changed the slant of his head and took her mouth more thoroughly, coaxing her to participate in her own seduction. When finally she opened completely to him, Quinn felt the unexpected impact like a jolt of lightning: heat, pleasure, excitement, sheer satisfaction.

By Nicole Jordan

The Art of
Taming a Rake

The Art of
Taming a Rake

A Legendary Lovers Novel

NICOLE
JORDAN

BALLANTINE BOOKS • NEW YORK

The Art of Taming a Rake is a work of fiction. Names, characters, places, and incidents are the products of the author's imagination or are used fictitiously. Any resemblance to actual events, locales, or persons, living or dead, is entirely coincidental.

A Ballantine Books Mass Market Original

Copyright © 2016 by Anne Bushyhead
Excerpt from *My Fair Lover* by Anne Bushyhead copyright © 2016 by Anne Bushyhead

Published in the United States by Ballantine Books, an imprint of Random House, a division of Penguin Random House LLC, New York.

BALLANTINE and the HOUSE colophon are registered trademarks of Penguin Random House LLC.

This book contains an excerpt from the forthcoming book *My Fair Lover* by Nicole Jordan. This excerpt has been set for this edition only and may not reflect the final content of the forthcoming edition.

ISBN: 978-0-553-39255-5
eBook ISBN: 978-0-553-39256-2

Cover design: Lynn Andreozzi
Cover illustration: Alan Ayers

Printed in the United States of America

randomhousebooks.com

9 8 7 6 5 4 3 2 1

Ballantine Books mass market edition: February 2016

For my dear friend and colleague,
Ann Howard White, with heartfelt thanks
for your priceless friendship and support
over the years. Love you bunches.

The Art of
Taming a Rake

Chapter One

"*Take care, Venetia*. Traherne has a magical touch with the fair sex. If you tangle with him, even *you* may find him impossible to resist."

Her friend's recent warning echoing in her head, Venetia Stratham watched the tableaux across the crowded gaming room. She had run her quarry to ground at London's most notorious sin club and found him surrounded by fawning beauties.

Well, perhaps not *surrounded*, Venetia corrected herself in a fit of honesty. But he certainly wasn't lacking for adoring female companionship just now.

Quinn Wilde, Earl of Traherne, was reportedly a splendid lover, and Venetia had no doubt the gossip was true. In all likelihood, his expertise in boudoirs and bedchambers was a chief reason women vied for his favor and tripped over themselves to earn his patronage. Whatever his sensual attributes, though, he was indisputably a rake of the first order. She had come to Tavistock Court tonight seeking proof of his transgressions to show her sister—and here it was, right before her eyes.

Beware of what you wish for. The cautionary adage came to mind, and oddly, her feeling of triumph was trumped by keen disappointment.

She had hoped she was wrong about Lord Traherne.

An inexplicable, exasperating reaction if she had ever felt one.

Traherne was lounging carelessly in his seat at the Faro table, but she had easily located him among the gamesters upon her arrival some twenty minutes ago. With the striking features and form of a Grecian sculpture—tall, sleek, muscular—he stood out in the company. She could not miss his aristocratic elegance, either, or his gleaming fair hair—dark gold streaked with lighter threads of silver.

The two lightskirts hovering at his shoulder, showering him with attention, were also an identifying clue and put to rest any lingering questions Venetia might have had about his predilection for debauchery.

Her lips pressed in a frown of self-reproach. She should be extremely pleased to find the confirmation she'd sought. To think she had once held Lord Traherne in high esteem. In her defense, her admiration had developed before she'd known the kind of heartbreaker he was. Before she had lost her hopeless naïveté to another seductive nobleman.

For her, "Beware of blue-blooded Lotharios" was a more appropriate admonition than careful wishing. She had learned that particular lesson quite painfully. And most definitely, she didn't want her younger sister falling prey to Traherne's spellbinding temptation.

His other vices, such as gambling for high stakes, did not overly concern her. With his enormous fortune, he could well afford to risk large sums on the turn of a card, especially since he regularly won. It was the carousing and womanizing that gravely troubled Venetia. Clearly Traherne was no better than her former betrothed, intent on only carnal pleasure, no matter who suffered hurt and heartbreak.

Just then another curvaceous Cyprian brought the earl a glass of port and remained to observe the play at his table. When the painted beauty draped herself over his arm, trailing suggestive fingers along the sleeve of his superbly tailored coat, Venetia stifled a sound of disgust in her throat.

Now Traherne had not two but *three* clinging demi-reps eager to serve his every need.

But then, women of all ages tended to tumble at his feet. She herself was not immune to his lethal charm, much to her dismay. His smile was captivating, piercing female hearts with deadly accuracy. And when those clever blue eyes glimmered with amusement . . . well, her pulse quickened each and every time, as if she had sprinted a great distance.

In fact, Traherne's entire family possessed the same formidable charm in extraordinary abundance. The five Wilde cousins of the current generation were the darlings of the ton—

Suddenly his lordship's blue gaze shifted in her direction to scan the company. Quickly Venetia adjusted her face mask and tried to blend into the throng of gamblers and *filles de joie*. She had attended a sin club once before, in Paris with her widowed friend Cleo, and this one was similarly genteel. The gaming room boasted a large gathering, as did the adjacent drawing room, where dancing and refreshments and a lavish buffet supper were offered for the guests' enjoyment. She could hear music and laughter and gay conversation drifting through the connecting doorway.

Except for the risqué apparel of the women present, this could have been an elite artist's salon—the sort of sophisticated assemblies she had frequented during her past two years of exile in France. Yet she ought not have come here tonight. If she was caught in this den of iniquity, it would only cement her scandalous reputation, which could further wound her family. But she had needed proof of Traherne's sins to show her sister just how dangerous he was to any gullible young lady's heart.

As if to prove her point, the earl glanced up at his adoring companion and smiled his brilliant smile. A pang of jealousy hit Venetia with astonishing force.

How absurd—how *infuriating*—to be so foolishly affected, even if her reaction could be blamed on elementary human nature. She well knew that masculine breeding, charm, virility, and stunning good looks were potent weapons against the fair sex. In her case, Traherne's keen wit and sharp mind had impressed her far more.

It was a grave pity that he was such a rake, squandering his exceptional intelligence and talents on dissipation and libertine ways. Ordinarily she wouldn't care how many women he seduced or how many mistresses he kept, but her sister was very dear to her, even if they *had* been estranged these past two interminable years.

And if *she* could not conquer her attraction to him, what chance did her highly susceptible sister have?

Despite the rumors about his budding courtship of the younger Miss Stratham, Venetia could not credit that a nobleman of his stamp actually wished to wed a green girl barely out of the schoolroom. But whether he had marriage—or worse, seduction—in mind, it could not end well for starry-eyed Ophelia.

As if sensing Venetia's scrutiny, Traherne refocused his penetrating gaze through the crowd to stare directly at her. The spark that flared in his vivid eyes at her immodest attire made her breath catch. She had borrowed her evening gown of scarlet velvet from Cleo in order to fit in with the other ladies of the evening. The décolletage dipped much lower than her usual wont, leaving her shoulders and the upper swells of her breasts bare.

The shock of Traherne's admiring masculine perusal caught her off guard. Instinctively, Venetia took a step backward, swearing to herself. A mere glance should not have impacted her so powerfully, no matter how lascivious. He was simply being a *man* after all.

She was also concerned that he would see through her disguise. Lord Traherne had witnessed firsthand the most humiliating, painful event of her life. Not only witnessed but actively *participated*. She was to blame for her own downfall, of course. But his actions had triggered the rash, prideful decision that had changed her fate forever. Moreover, she did not wish to give him the satisfaction of seeing her at such a disadvantage—forced to sneak around clandestinely, an outcast of decent society.

"May-yi have the honor of a dansh, my lovely?"

Venetia gave a start at the interruption. With her thoughts so fixed on the earl's sinful character, she'd been unaware of another gentleman approaching, this one much shorter and somewhat younger than Traherne, with darker hair and more flamboyant garb. The dandy's slurred words suggested that he was already half-foxed.

Venetia hid a grimace at the unexpected annoyance. She needed no complications to divert her attention from her goal of saving her sister from the Earl of Traherne's romantic pursuit.

With effort, she pasted an apologetic smile on her lips before answering sweetly. "Thank you, kind sir, but I will not be staying much longer this evening."

Rather than accept her rebuff, the drunkard slipped an arm around her shoulders and drew her close.

With an inward sigh, Venetia set about the task of extricating herself from this unwanted predicament. She was not afraid of being assaulted in so public an arena. Even a notorious hell had rules of accepted behavior to follow, certainly one that catered to high-class clientele such as this. Any number of nobles and gentlemen of the ton were present tonight, as well as a few wellborn ladies, attending incognito.

But this was simply one more damning demonstration that men were often led by their lustful urges rather than honor or common sense, and she was growing exceedingly weary of having to deal with their peccadillos.

*   *   *

Distracted from his thus-far fruitless Faro game, Quinn narrowed his gaze on the masked beauty across the room. She had endeavored to remain unobtrusive, but she was much too noticeable.

Puzzled and curious as to why she was watching him so intently, Quinn absently played another card. Her familiarity nagged at him. She wore a demi-mask and a feathered silk turban to hide her hair, but her feminine attractions were quite apparent. The graceful carriage, the ripe breasts, the lush mouth—

Quinn abruptly gave a mental start as his gaze shot back to her. She was indeed familiar. Miss Venetia Stratham.

What the devil?

He would have recognized her anywhere. She was the kind of woman a man never forgot. Not least because she had been engaged to marry a friend and peer.

She was one of the loveliest women he had ever encountered—luminous dark eyes, rich brown hair, creamy skin, with the most kissable mouth imaginable. Pure temptation even to a man of his jaded appetites. More than once he had fantasized about kissing those luscious lips. In truth, he'd wanted her from the first moment they met some four years ago during her come-out Season. But he had carefully controlled his lust. Miss Stratham was strictly forbidden to him. A gentleman did not poach, particularly from a friend.

Quinn was taken aback—no, startled—to see her here at an elite gaming hell known more for its sexual sport than high stakes gambling. She was still every inch an elegant lady, despite being gowned in brazen red velvet that complimented her shapely figure and almost regal bearing.

His attention now riveted, Quinn watched as an obviously inebriated gamester tightened an arm around her bare shoulders.

The sight troubled him enough that he barely heard the silken voice whispering in his ear:

"How else may I serve you, m'lord?"

"I want for nothing, thank you," Quinn replied, dismissing the high-flyer at his side with much less finesse than usual.

His mind was fixed solely on Venetia Stratham. Had she fallen so low that she was now offering her body for sale? The possibility fiercely disturbed him. Remorse sent his thoughts winging back two years ago, when he'd last laid eyes on her.

She had shocked the ton by jilting her noble fiancé on the church steps, creating a spectacle by boxing his ears and aborting the wedding ceremony in front of over two hundred guests. She'd then flung Quinn a scathing glance as she passed him on the way to her waiting carriage, no doubt despising him for the role he'd played in her bridegroom's dissipation.

The very public denunciation of her betrothed had been the talk of London for weeks, until another titillating scandal had come along to supplant hers.

Quinn badly wanted to know what the devil she was doing in a high-class brothel. And why was she observing him so surreptitiously?

Her unexpected presence was enough to distract him from the task he'd set for himself—gaining leverage over his current opponent, Edmund Lisle, by winning overwhelmingly at Faro tonight.

And watching a young fop proposition her was downright unsettling.

Quinn voiced an oath under his breath as he recognized the blade. Lord Knowlsbridge was in his cups, swaying as he embraced her. Evidently Miss Stratham was not welcoming his attention, though, for she had pasted a pained smile on her lips while trying to extricate herself from his grasp.

She was ill-equipped to fend off a drunken lecher, Quinn suspected, his protective instincts keenly aroused. And seeing the young lord attempt to kiss her was the last straw.

Experiencing a quiet swell of fury, Quinn tossed down his cards and surged to his feet, scattering the lightskirts surrounding him and surprising the pretty Faro dealer. It was poor-mannered of him to treat the pleasure club's attendants so thoughtlessly, and supremely bad form to leave a game in mid-play. But even had his concentration not been shattered, he couldn't sit still while a soused coxcomb pawed at Venetia Stratham.

With a faint smile of apology to the others, Quinn addressed his opponent. "Pray forgive me, Lisle, but I willingly concede. We must resume our game at some other time."

He could feel Lisle shooting daggers in his back as he walked away. There was no love lost between them, with their contentious past involving a jealous mistress, and now the question of how Lisle had come to possess a distinctive jeweled pendant that might once have belonged to Quinn's French mother.

But solving the mystery of a missing family heirloom would have to wait.

As he weaved his way through the crowd, intent on rescuing Miss Stratham, he saw Knowlsbridge endeavoring to remove her mask while she strove to keep it in place. Quinn doubted she wished her identity revealed, for even if she had joined the muslin company—willingly or not—her family's reputation could still suffer from a fresh scandal. And with a younger sister of prime marriageable age, Venetia would be wise to keep her affairs discreet.

He had nearly reached her when, despite her predicament, she saw him approaching and visibly flinched, whether in surprise or dismay, he couldn't tell. For an instant, she started to retreat, then stood her ground, her chin raised, as if bracing herself for the encounter.

"There you are, my dove," Quinn said easily as he came up to her. "I have been eagerly awaiting your company."

When Knowlsbridge took advantage of her temporary distraction to cup her breast, another sharp wave of anger flooded Quinn.

"I'll thank you to leave the lady alone," he warned an instant before she managed to drive the point of her elbow into the sot's flaccid belly and make him grunt.

"Sheesh not . . . a lady," the young lord complained, wheezing for breath.

"Regardless, she is mine."

Quinn slipped an arm around Miss Stratham's waist and drew her close. "I have missed you, darling. Have you missed me?"

She possessed huge, lustrous dark eyes, which were mostly hidden behind her mask, but even obscured, her gaze held surprise. She was clearly wondering what he was about.

But Quinn knew the jackanapes beside her understood the situation quite well: a more powerful male marking his territory, showing possession.

"Are you not pleased to see me, love?" he prodded Venetia.

"I . . . why, yes, my lord," she stammered, reminding Quinn how pleasantly musical her voice was.

"Perhaps you should show me how much."

Bending his head, he captured that full, kissable mouth the way he had longed to do for years.

She gave a faint gasp at the contact and stiffened in response. Quinn could feel shock ripple through the graceful curves of her body, while his own breath quickened at the enticing taste of her.

Her lips were just as delectable as he'd imagined, he thought, relishing their softness. Lush, resilient, the texture of silk, ripe and warm as her body.

When she tensed further, he increased the pressure, parting the seam of her mouth and slipping his tongue inside to tangle with hers.

Her lips trembled under his. Encouraged, he changed the slant of his head and took her mouth more thoroughly, coaxing her to participate in her own seduction. When finally she opened completely to him, Quinn felt the unexpected impact like a jolt of lightning: heat, pleasure, excitement, sheer satisfaction.

Her taste was keenly arousing and infinitely sweet.

Sliding one hand behind her nape, he pulled her closer so that he could drink more deeply of her.

The crowd fell away so there was only the two of them, man and woman, enjoying an embrace powerful enough to shake them both. Her scent wrapped around him as he savored her mouth.

It was a slow, devastating, spellbinding kiss. When her entire body softened instinctively against him, her surrender only increased his craving for her. Painfully aroused now, Quinn felt a primal male urge to take what he wanted—and an even stronger need to heighten her desire.

When his tongue delved insistently inside her mouth, exploring, she gave a helpless moan and leaned into him. The sharp pleasure of it stabbed him in his loins, a pleasure that only heightened when her hand crept up to twine about his neck.

He felt another measure of triumph when her tongue met his willingly this time. Raising a hand to cradle her jaw, he angled his head even further, the better to devour her mouth.

Her breath faded to a sigh as their tongues mated. The tantalizing promise of her response stirred a searing need in Quinn. It had been a very long while since he'd experienced such a sizzling sexual attraction. Perhaps never.

Stark lust turned him hard and renewed his fierce feeling of possessiveness. The sensation rocked him—and Venetia, too, he had no doubt, aware of her shiver of aroused excitement.

When at last he broke off, he kept hold of her waist to support her as she swayed weakly.

Her eyes fluttering open, she raised her face to stare at him. Despite her demi-mask, he could see those lovely eyes were dazed. Her hand rose to touch her lips in wonder, as if feeling the burn there.

She was profoundly shaken, he knew. He felt her trembling as she returned his gaze speechlessly.

Quinn was at a loss for words himself. He couldn't recall ever feeling such intense, unreasoning desire . . .

The sound of nearby laughter served to break the spell.

Venetia visibly shook herself and pressed her hands against his chest. Reluctantly, Quinn released her and cleared his throat, quelling the urge to adjust his satin breeches in public. He couldn't remember a time when he'd lost control of his urges so blatantly.

When he heard another nearby sound, this one an admiring male scoff, he realized the other man was watching with resentment and envy.

"You have all the damnable luck, Traherne," the young lord mumbled almost soberly. "'Tis a pity."

"Pray take yourself off, Knowlsbridge," Quinn ordered in dismissal. "You can see we are occupied."

His voice was husky with passion but held enough authority that the drunken gamester did as he was bid and ambled away, leaving Quinn in sole possession of Venetia.

She was still flustered from his kiss, yet she recovered her tongue readily enough. "I should have expected you to act so outrageously, Lord Traherne."

He raised an eyebrow. "What was so outrageous?"

"You did not have to kiss me."

"It seemed the easiest way to prevent Knowlsbridge

from pulling off your mask. I presumed you would not want to be recognized. Was I wrong?"

"No," she answered reluctantly. "But I am not your *dove*."

"You and I know that, but for his benefit, I needed to stake my claim to you."

When her mouth curved in frustration, Quinn quizzed her. "I thought you would be grateful to me for saving you."

"I did not require *saving*, my lord—"

Her voice had risen noticeably, and she cut off her exclamation upon realizing that they were the object of numerous pairs of curious eyes.

"Shall we take this discussion elsewhere, darling?" he suggested. "Unless you prefer to cause a scene?"

She clearly didn't like his endearment, yet knew he couldn't use her name if she was to preserve her anonymity. And she must have comprehended the wisdom of his proposal, for she nodded briefly.

When Quinn gestured toward the staircase at the rear of the gaming hall, however, she hesitated. "Upstairs, do you mean?"

On the floors above, carnal amusement was the prime entertainment.

"The pleasure rooms are the most appropriate choice if I am to command your services for the evening."

Her lovely mouth fell open, but when he added in explanation, "It will give the appearance of your being my chosen inamorata," she stifled her protest.

Before she could change her mind, Quinn swept out his hand, indicating for her to precede him. After another long study, she turned toward the stairs, the delicate line of her jaw set in a stubborn grimace.

Hiding a wry smile, he followed Miss Stratham. Anticipation lightened his previously sour mood and eased the physical pain of kissing the irresistible but resistant beauty, leaving him with a sense of unfulfilled promise.

His frustrating evening thus far was becoming more intriguing by the moment.

Chapter Two

As Miss Stratham made her away through the crowd, Quinn watched her gently swaying hips with rapt male appreciation. For allure, her form and features rivaled any of the Cyprians present, yet her demeanor was wary.

She stole brief glances at him when they climbed the stairs together. Her expression held determination, as if she was girding herself for a confrontation, yet she also seemed nervous, a suspicion borne out when she faltered upon reaching the first landing. "Where are you taking me?"

"To one of the unoccupied chambers."

"Must we use a bedchamber?" Her tone hinted at concern.

"It is our only alternative if you wish to converse in private."

He took her elbow to guide her up the next flight of stairs, but she immediately pulled away as if burned by the contact. Quinn could sympathize. He still felt the effects of their impromptu embrace in his aching loins.

"You are safe from me, Miss Stratham," he observed wryly. "I don't intend to ravish you."

Her wonderful mouth curved with fleeting amusement. "Given your conduct a moment ago, you will forgive my doubts." She drew a steadying breath. "Very well. I suppose a bedchamber will have to do. Hopefully this will not take long."

She clearly was trying to reassure herself. They climbed to the next floor, and when Quinn began moving down a dimly lit corridor, she accompanied him reluctantly. Her reticence gratified him. He did not like to think her familiar with the sinful sport to be found in the pleasure rooms. But it also added to the puzzle of why she had come here—one of many questions he wanted answered about her.

"Do you mean to tell me what brought you here?"

"I could ask the same of you, but I already know the answer." She responded sweetly, but her tone held disapproval. "Gaming and wenching."

"The two do not necessarily go hand in hand. And my presence here is not the issue. What the devil are you doing in a bordello?"

He could almost see her spine stiffening. "I wished to speak with you about my sister."

So that was her motivation. He should have suspected. "Then you are not here to sell your wares?"

She gave him a startled look through her mask. "No. Whatever gave you that notion?"

His gaze drifted lower to her bodice, lingering on her ripe breasts. "Your attire might have provided a clue."

At his calculated perusal, she gave him a quelling look. "I might have caused a scandal, my lord, but I have not fallen that low."

Quinn was vastly relieved that she was not there to bargain her body. "As scandals go, yours was relatively minor."

"I can see how *you* might think so. You are known for colossal scandals, as is most of your family."

It was true. The Wildes were renowned for their flagrant love affairs, going back many generations. And his own liaisons had provided ample fodder for the gossipmongers over the years, particularly the most recent one with his former mistress.

"I wondered if you might be in financial straits," he prodded. After she dissolved her betrothal, Miss Stratham's parents had disowned her and cut her off without a penny.

"I am not so desperate. I earn a generous income as companion to my widowed friend, Mrs. Cleo Newcomb."

"So I heard."

Wealthy, genteel widow Mrs. Newcomb was a former schoolmate of Miss Stratham's who had offered her a home and employment after the contretemps erupted. They had fled to the Continent so that Venetia could at a distance attempt to recover from her disgrace.

"Did she accompany you tonight?"

"No."

"It is not safe for you to have come here alone," Quinn pointed out.

"The risk is not all that great."

"Knowlsbridge practically assaulted you. What did you expect, gowned as you are?"

She didn't reply right away. They had passed several closed doors, and when Quinn halted before an open one, she peered inside. The lush, dimly lit interior apparently distracted her enough that she answered absently. "I could not visit your home in Berkeley Square for fear of being recognized. And here I could don a disguise."

"That mask and turban of yours do little to conceal your identity." Although they did hide her remarkable eyes and cover up her mass of rich, dark hair.

"I am surprised you recognized me, Lord Traherne."

"I would know you anywhere."

She gave him another quizzical look, but her attention was chiefly focused on the luxuriant scarlet and black furnishings inside the bedchamber.

"You were clearly in need of aid," Quinn continued.

"Actually, I was not. I could have dealt with Knowlsbridge."

He gave a knowing chuckle. "I expected a modicum of gratitude for rescuing you. At the very least, I thought you would want to avoid a public spectacle."

Miss Stratham turned her gaze back to him. "You needn't worry about me, Lord Traherne. I can fend for myself."

"Is that so?"

"Yes. And I have servants for protection."

"Where are they?"

"Waiting with my carriage."

"They won't do you much good out there, will they?"

"I have a knife in my reticule."

She held up the brocade purse whose strings were looped around her wrist.

"Let me see it."

When she drew out a small blade perhaps five inches long, Quinn couldn't help but smile.

"You find something amusing?"

"That is not much of a weapon."

She took issue with his teasing tone. "Do you think I don't have the skill to use it?"

"I trust you do. And I heartily approve of you carrying it. I taught my own sister to defend herself with various weapons."

"I have a pistol at home also, but I did not believe I needed it tonight. I assure you, I could have wielded my knife if necessary. Paris streets can be hazardous for a woman."

Her casual admittance made him frown. After the defeat of Napoleon at Waterloo, the British had flocked to France for the fashion and culture, but decades of war had left the country rather inhospitable, particularly to foreigners and former enemies. "Was your time in Paris so violent?"

She shrugged. "It is wise to be prepared."

"I thought you were residing with Mrs. Newcomb in a fashionable neighborhood."

Miss Stratham shot him another look. "How do you know so much about my circumstances? Oh, yes, my sister must have told you."

He'd made it his business to find out about Venetia long before that.

They had been dallying in the corridor, and when he ushered her inside, her wariness momentarily turned to curiosity. "I have wondered what goes on in a den of iniquity."

"You don't know?"

"No, of course not."

A single lamp burned softly, casting a golden-rose glow around the room. He watched as she took in her surroundings . . . the enormous satin-covered bed swathed in gauzy scarlet curtains, a chaise longue strewn with tasseled pillows, a table covered with an elaborate assortment of carnal equipment.

Quinn was glad for her wide-eyed reception, for it suggested she was still a novice at the erotic arts.

"One would think you have never been to a pleasure club before."

"I have not— Well, I have, but only once, in Paris, and not upstairs."

Her blush was rather endearing. Then she shook herself as if recalling her circumstances and turned the conversation back to him. "It is common knowledge that you frequent places like this regularly."

"I would not say 'regularly.' "

"According to the gossip rags, you do. The society pages follow your movements and report on your whereabouts. That is how I knew where to find you tonight."

"I've made no secret of my patronage of Tavistock's."

"The *Morning Chronicle* speculated that you were meeting Lady X here tonight."

Quinn felt his mouth tighten. His former mistress, Julia, Lady Dalton, was a baronet's widow and went by the soubriquet Lady X. "You cannot believe everything you read."

Venetia did not seem chastened. "The newspapers were not my only source. You know servants are experts at ferreting out information, and Mrs. Newcomb's staff are particularly well informed."

"How resourceful of you," Quinn drawled. He was half admiring of her boldness in tracking him down at a brothel, even if he didn't approve of her being here. It was the kind of action the women in his family would take. Like the Wildes, Venetia Stratham refused to conform or do the expected.

He admired her spirit as well. There was a fire inside her that her elegant, ladylike exterior couldn't hide.

When he closed the door behind him, she glanced back over her shoulder and saw what he had done. "Must you shut the door?"

"Yes, so that we won't be interrupted. The rules are simple. A closed door means the room is occupied."

She digested that without replying but bit her lip in consternation.

"You can safely remove your mask," Quinn said. "Here, let me help you."

When he reached up to untie the strings behind her turban, however, Venetia flinched and drew away from him. "I prefer to leave it on."

He felt a measure of disappointment that he wouldn't get a better glimpse of her beautiful eyes.

She moved farther into the room, gazing around her nervously. He had caught her off guard with their smoldering kiss earlier, and she had quickly recovered her aplomb, but now she seemed flustered again.

Perhaps her fidgets were due to being alone with him in a room designed for sexual pleasure.

With the door shut, Quinn also was more cognizant of the primitive sensations still streaking through him: possessiveness, hunger, desire. Sexual awareness was suddenly rife between them.

She felt it also, he knew. The tension in her body had returned with a new, sharp-edged tautness he could actually sense.

Obviously trying to pretend nonchalance, she cleared her throat. "I confess I am out of my element here."

In an effort to put her at ease, he replied lightly, "You are the one armed with a knife, Miss Stratham. Perhaps I should fear for *my* virtue."

He saw an unwilling smile tug at her lips. "I hardly think you are in any danger, my lord. From what I have heard, you lost your virtue long ago."

Wincing inwardly, Quinn strolled over to the chaise and sat down, casually stretching his arms over the brocade back in an open, non-threatening gesture. In a strange way, her shyness was enchanting. He did not believe for a moment that she lacked courage. She was actually one of the bravest women he knew, including his own sister, Skye, and his cousin Lady Katharine Wilde.

Venetia Stratham had defied society at great personal cost and made herself an outcast by standing up for what she believed, even to the extent of losing the family she held dear. He had to respect that kind of courage.

"So what did you wish to discuss about your sister?" he invited.

"I am highly concerned. The reports say you have taken a marked interest in her."

He'd only stood up with Ophelia Stratham at several balls but already the gossip was rife that he was courting her. A nobleman with his reputation didn't show marked interest in a well-bred young lady without stirring a whiff of matrimony, which indeed had been his intent.

"So you rushed home to save her?" he asked.

"As a matter of fact, yes."

"You feel protective of her."

"Certainly I do. She is my sister. You are very close to your own sister, are you not? I'm certain you wish to protect Lady Skye."

"Naturally." He'd been responsible for his younger sister since he was seventeen years old, but Skye had wed the Earl of Hawkhurst last year, so he needn't worry about protecting her any longer. Hawk had assumed that role quite effectively.

Venetia bit her lip again. "It is my fault that Ophelia's marital prospects are so poor. If not for the scandal I caused, she would have ample legitimate suitors for her hand."

"And you don't consider me a legitimate suitor."

"No, my lord. You may be extremely eligible, but you are not at all suitable for her. You are not the marrying kind."

It was true, he had no interest in marriage. He had good reason for avoiding genteel ladies who not only expected matrimony but connived for it.

When he didn't immediately answer, Venetia pressed him. "I cannot believe you mean to propose to Ophelia."

"Why not?"

"Because you are a rake—" She cut off the word, then went on, obviously choosing her words more carefully. "I mean . . . because of the sort of man you are . . . the excessive lifestyle you lead. You don't truly want to marry her. Come, admit it. She is as different from you in temperament and situation as a young lady can be. And she is far too innocent for you."

On that point he agreed entirely: Ophelia was too young and innocent for him. She most certainly was not his match.

He frankly had wanted nothing to do with the girl, but his cousin Katharine had chosen Ophelia for his future bride to fulfill some absurd romantic theory she'd had since girlhood. Kate firmly believed the five Wilde cousins of the current generation could find true love based on legends of the world's greatest lovers. His tale was supposed to be the Greek myth of Pygmalion—a sculptor who was so enamored of his stone carving that the gods took pity on him and brought his creation to life. Kate thought the younger Miss Stratham was moldable enough to make Quinn an ideal bride, which would have been laughable if not for his cousin's dogged persistence, and Skye's as well. He would be fatally bored within a week of the nuptials, he had told them.

However, sharing his family's schemes and altercations about matrimony was not a conversation he particularly wanted to have with Miss Stratham, so he said merely, "Perhaps the union would not be ideal."

"Are you courting her, then, my lord?"

"I've made no formal offer."

"But you have raised her expectations and those of our parents as well."

In truth, Venetia was the reason he was showing Ophelia such marked attention. Elevating the younger sister in society would reduce the stigma of scandal that hung over the Stratham family. And in small measure make up for the role he'd played in Venetia's broken betrothal. But explaining his feelings of guilt was not something he cared to do just now, either.

Venetia apparently was losing patience with his vagueness. "If you don't wish to marry her, then I can only presume you have seduction in mind."

"I believe you are leaping to conclusions."

"Can you fault me? Accounts of your affairs have traveled all the way to France. I still have friends in England, and even if I didn't, Mrs. Newcomb keeps a regular correspondence with her numerous acquaintances here."

"You have clearly assumed the worst about me."

Her smile was sweetly false. "With good reason. I predicted your debauchery, and this evening I was proved right."

It annoyed him a little that she considered him so dissolute. "I am not as depraved as the gossips paint me."

"I found you here, did I not? When I arrived, there was more than one lady of the evening draped all over you." Her frown expressed censure.

"Appearances can be deceiving."

"Do you deny you are here for the carnal sport?"

"Actually, I do."

"Then you have another purpose for being here? Please, enlighten me."

Divulging his private affairs and discussing family secrets that went back nearly three decades went against his grain. He wouldn't tell her his real reason—that he wanted to unearth information about a treasured family heirloom. The situation was much too complicated and delicate just now, particularly since it involved his temperamental former mistress, which would only be more ammunition for Miss Stratham to use against him.

"Perhaps I came for the cards and the cuisine more than camaraderie and companionship. They serve a good dinner here."

She cocked her head, skepticism rife in her expression.

"I do not have to justify myself to you, Miss Stratham."

"No, of course you do not. And truly, I cared nothing for your dissipation until I heard rumors that you were pursuing my sister. She is not in your league, Lord Traherne. You shouldn't take advantage of young, green girls. You should keep to women of experience who understand the danger you present."

"You assume I am pursuing her and not the other way around."

That gave her pause. "Are you saying that Ophelia is throwing herself at you?"

He'd found Ophelia a bit tongue-tied but earnest and eager to please him—understandable since she was desperate to regain social acceptance. "Perhaps a little. It would not be the first time I have been the target of marriage-minded females. What does your sister say about my supposed courtship?"

Venetia looked uncomfortable. "I haven't spoken with her since I left for France. We have merely corresponded by letter."

"So you haven't seen her in two years."

"Regrettably, no."

He'd heard that her parents still refused to speak to Venetia even now, two years after her rebellion, a true shame. But she seemed to shrug off any vestige of self-pity when she remarked, "I can understand how Ophelia would have stars in her eyes. It is flattering to be sought after by a wealthy, handsome nobleman."

"Your parents certainly seem pleased by my notice."

"No doubt they are," she muttered with a trace of bitterness. "They were distressed that I would not become a viscountess, and you are an even greater prize than Ackland. But you are cut from the same cloth as he."

Matthew Waring, Viscount Ackland, had been a friend since their university days, but the comparison stung Quinn a little. Unlike Ackland, indulging in extended bouts of carnal pleasure was no longer satisfying. His passion now was developing the possibilities that lay within the realm of science and cultivating the innovation that might have changed his parents' tragic fate when they'd perished at sea during a storm all those years ago.

Quinn crossed his arms over his chest, irritated that Venetia thought so poorly of him. "Your insulting me is hardly the way to persuade me to your point of view."

She drew a deep breath, as if forcing herself to control her frustration. "I do not wish to insult you, my lord. I simply came to ask you to please leave my sister alone."

"Have you considered that my attentions might actually be good for her?"

"Not if you seduce her and destroy what remains of her good name."

It rankled that she thought he would stoop so low. Particularly when he was actually attempting to help her sister. His notice would garner Ophelia greater cachet with the ton. And attention from a wealthy earl could go a long way toward making her a desirable candidate for some young buck looking for a genteel wife. "I am not in the habit of ruining young girls."

"No?" Her lips pressed in a line. "You are a libertine of the worst sort."

"Surely not the worst. Your own betrothed was worse." His drawl obviously riled her, but at his added remark, she looked wounded for a moment.

"No doubt you are right." Another tinge of bitterness laced her tone. Then she pulled back her shoulders and drew herself up to her full height. "I hoped to reason with you, Lord Traherne, but I can see it is pointless."

Venetia was staring at him accusingly, and he could almost feel the sparks shooting from her eyes. Her spirit was one of the things he liked most about her. And he applauded her passionate defense of her sister.

In fact, when he'd first begun Ophelia's social reha-
bilitation, he'd hoped that she would have some of
her elder sister's spirit but had quickly realized his
error. Ophelia was sweet and bland with little of Venetia's inner fire. The five-year difference in their ages
also contributed to his preference.

He'd clearly angered Venetia—but then, she had
angered him, making him out to be a villain. She
thought he was lowly scum, dishonorable enough to
harm her sister, when he was actually doing a good
deed. He'd soon regretted embarking on his altruistic
endeavor, but once started, he needed to follow
through or risk leaving her reputation worse off than
before. He knew how to play the courtship game,
even if it thoroughly bored and often irritated him.

"You are maligning me unjustly," he remarked,
"relegating me to the same category as your former
betrothed."

"You were Ackland's partner in crime."

"We were hardly criminals."

"But you were complicit in his lechery. You delivered him to the church, an hour late for his own wedding, drunk and disheveled, straight from the bed of
his mistress."

She had a point, Quinn acknowledged self-
consciously. He'd known of his friend's plans and
hadn't stopped him. Ackland had spent the night before his wedding in the arms of his mistress. Quinn
had found the laggard bridegroom, roused him out of
bed, and driven him to the church where Venetia was
waiting on the front portico.

He could remember the scene vividly: Ackland still
dressed in his previous night's evening clothes, un-

kempt, unshaven, and reeking of cloying perfume; Venetia looking incredibly lovely in a virginal gown of ivory lace and satin.

He could tell the moment she fathomed the extent of her betrothed's betrayal: The man she was promised to had come straight from a prostitute's bed to be united in holy matrimony.

Venetia had deserved much better. She was proud, rightly so, but she hadn't simply been reacting out of wounded pride, Quinn was certain. He was close enough to see the pain in her eyes. No doubt her romantic dreams of a loving marriage had been shattered. She had loved Ackland, or so he'd claimed. Her stricken look had awakened Quinn's protective instincts, especially since he felt partially to blame for not doing more to rein in his friend's dissipation.

He thought she'd handled her humiliation with great aplomb, though. After her very public quarrel with Ackland, she had walked into the church, head held high, and announced there would be no ceremony. While the crowd collectively gasped and burst into conversation, she apologized sincerely to her shocked parents, then turned on her heel and marched out to her waiting carriage, brushing past Quinn on the way.

Ackland was a triple fool—for flaunting his liaison, for publicly shaming her, and for driving her away. How he had chosen his mistress over Venetia was an utter mystery. But it was no mystery why she had felt betrayed by both men.

Still nagged by an uncomfortable measure of guilt, Quinn swallowed his instinctive retort. He might be vexed at her charges, but they were justified. And rather than respond defensively to her accusations and rile her further, he would do better to let her have her say, then disarm her with charm and endeavor to change her poor opinion of him.

That would prove a challenge, obviously, when sparks crackled between them. There was fire in her eyes and frustration as well.

Uncrossing his arms, Quinn leaned back against the chaise longue. "You are right, Miss Stratham. My past leaves much to be desired. But I give you my word, I will not seduce your sister."

Chapter Three

Venetia hesitated, examining Traherne with mistrust and puzzlement. The softer, almost tender light in his eyes was wholly inexplicable. "I don't know if I can believe you. I am no longer the naive, trusting girl I once was."

"I can understand your caution," he said gently.

"Then you can also understand why I mean to prevent Ophelia from making the same mistake I made, falling under the spell of a rake. I don't want her to suffer the way I did."

"You were wounded in love, so you believe your sister also will be." It was not a question.

"If I thought you could love her, I would not be so worried."

Traherne gave a faint grimace, as if loath to discuss the subject of love. "You should return home, Miss Stratham. Where are you staying?"

Realizing he was attempting to dismiss her, Venetia felt her frustration surge. "With Cleo—Mrs. Newcomb. She has a country home on the outskirts of

London, in Kensington. But I am not leaving until I secure your promise to abandon your pursuit."

"I can make no such promise."

Venetia inhaled sharply. She had planned to persuade Traherne with reason, using honey rather than vinegar, but he was making it very difficult for her to remain sweetly calm and in control.

Perhaps it was time for more forceful arguments.

"I wish Ophelia could see you now, sporting with those women. I can still smell their perfume on you." She didn't bother to hide her distaste. "You remind me of Ackland. At least he had only one mistress in keeping at a time, and he never stole another man's inamorata, to my knowledge."

"Nor have I."

"What about Lady X?"

"What about her?"

"I understand she was so outraged when you took up with another Cyprian that she caused quite a row in the middle of Hyde Park. And reportedly, you lured her away from Mr. Edmund Lisle in the first place."

His mouth curved in a sardonic twist. "You should ascertain your facts before making accusations, sweeting."

"What do I have wrong? Was that not Mr. Lisle you were playing Faro with when I arrived? It seemed odd when you are said to be archrivals."

"Our dispute was overblown."

"Granted, I don't know all the particulars, but it hardly matters. Your mere presence here confirms that you are living up to your reputation—or should

I say, living down to it? You could ruin my sister so easily."

Traherne delayed responding while visibly calling on a reserve of patience. "I assure you, my intentions are entirely honorable."

"That gives me little comfort," Venetia retorted. "Even if you were to wed her, you would make her a terrible husband. You will break her heart."

His sigh held exasperation. "I can promise you I will not."

"You cannot help it. My friend Lydia Price learned that to her despair."

His eyebrows narrowed at her.

"Surely you remember Miss Price?" Venetia demanded about her former classmate whose first Season had ended in disaster. "Three years ago when you spurned her love, she was sent home in disgrace and went into a decline from a broken heart."

"Trust me, I never encouraged her. I scarcely knew her. Hers was merely a schoolgirl infatuation."

Venetia could completely sympathize with her friend's captivation. Traherne was dangerously, sinfully beautiful. His physical appeal combined with his enormous charisma and charm made him irresistible to women. She'd always thought him the most compelling man she had ever met, and she now had firsthand experience of his allure: His unexpected kiss earlier had knocked her silly.

"Ophelia is likely to develop the same infatuation for you," she pointed out.

His annoyance was obvious in his expression, but he refrained from replying.

"I will ask you once more," Venetia finally said, "will you please call off your attentions?"

"No."

She sent him a look of sheer frustration.

"It would be ungentlemanly of me to withdraw now," he said in explanation.

"What of it? If Ophelia truly is pursuing you, you could end her aspirations with a single word."

Traherne shook his head. "At this stage, if I suddenly drop my attentions, it can only harm her. The ton will wonder what is wrong with her and the gossips will suspect the cause has something to do with your return to London."

Venetia frowned, examining his rationale. "That is less of a risk than your continued pursuit."

"I disagree. Any withdrawal will have to come from her. You should speak with your sister."

Venetia felt her fingers clench into fists. There had to be a way to make him reconsider. Ophelia would not end his courtship on her own. Venetia had tried to meet with her to no avail, smuggling a message to her via loyal servants and then corresponding several times by letter, but Ophelia was reluctant to heed any warnings. She worried that her marital chances had been severely damaged, and was anxious and fearful that her romance with Traherne would be spoiled.

Hence, Venetia had come here seeking proof of his debauchery to show her sister, hoping to catch him in a lascivious act, as it were.

She took a deep breath, knowing that threatening to expose him was her last resort. "Ophelia will be distressed to learn you frequent a house of ill-repute."

His brows pulled together again as he appeared to

deduce her meaning. "I would imagine she knows. You said it was common knowledge."

"But now I have proof."

"You did not find me in any sort of compromising position."

"The night is still young," Venetia rejoined. "If I wait long enough, I have no doubt you will oblige."

"So you plan to tell her you found me here? You would have to admit you followed me."

"I will if you leave me no choice."

His blue gaze sharpened on her. "I don't take kindly to extortion, darling."

"Extortion has nothing to say in the matter. It is my only leverage against you."

He considered her a long moment. "Perhaps I could be persuaded."

His sudden about-face took her aback. "What do you mean?"

"I will give you the chance to sway me. Come here and kiss me."

Venetia felt a shiver run down her spine. "Surely you are jesting."

"Not in the least. You say you want me to end my courtship. You will have to convince me."

A shock of titillating awareness coursed through her. It was mad even to think about responding to such an absurd proposition. She'd been thoroughly shaken by his kiss—his mere touch was like a lightning bolt streaking through her. She would be wise to avoid any physical contact at all costs.

"What would I have to do?"

"Kiss me, just as I said."

"And then you will give up?"

"I will consider it."

He was merely playing games with her, she decided with disgust. "I won't kiss you, Traherne."

"Then I will escort you to your carriage."

He started to rise from the chaise, but Venetia stopped him. "No, wait!"

His smile was lazy and full of charm as he settled down again. "It is your choice. I have all night. Indeed, I would rather not leave just yet. We should be giving the appearance that we are lovers, and I have a reputation to uphold. It will look as if I cannot keep my woman entertained and only care about my own satisfaction."

"I am not your *woman*," she exclaimed in exasperation.

"No, you are too fainthearted to ever fill that role."

His tone was subtly teasing, which eased the barb. "I am not frightened of you, Traherne."

"No?"

Frightened was not the right description for what she was feeling. Yes, it was unnerving to be here alone with him looking at her in that tender, sensual way, but strangely exhilarating as well.

He was a provocative devil, taunting her, almost daring her to take up his challenge. But she couldn't allow him to know she was the least bit intimidated.

"Only one kiss?"

"Just one."

Surely she could brace herself for the impact.

He patted the brocade seat beside him. "Come, sit here with me."

It was absurd, quivering here like a timorous doe.

Determined to hold her own with him, Venetia crossed to stand before him.

He waited to speak until she sat down gingerly beside him. "Now remove your mask. There is little pleasure in kissing when half your face is hidden away."

When she complied, he studied her for several heartbeats. "That is much better. It is a shame to conceal your most attractive feature."

Venetia regarded him suspiciously. "What feature is that?"

"Your eyes. You have beautiful eyes."

She stifled a scoff. "I am not susceptible to your flattery, Lord Traherne."

"Your beauty is simply a fact, like the heavens growing light when the sun rises."

Inwardly Venetia chided herself for the warmth kindling inside her. Of course his compliments appealed to her feminine vanity. But compliments were the stock and trade of a Lothario. Traherne had females of all ages falling over him, including her own sister. She utterly refused to show the same weakness. The trouble was, the look he was giving her called to some wanton instinct inside her.

"Come closer. You are too far away."

She was perched on the edge of the seat, so she inched a little closer. Shutting her eyes, she tilted her face up to his and held still.

A long moment passed. When nothing happened, she pried one eye open. "What are you waiting for?"

"You must kiss *me*, sweetheart."

Curbing an oath, she leaned forward and pressed her mouth to his briefly. Even that fleeting contact with his warm lips jolted her, making her think of a crackling fire in winter.

"You can do better than a mere peck. Do you need assistance?" A smile loitered about his sensuous mouth, softening his mockery.

"I can manage on my own."

She would comply but on her own terms. When she raised her arms to place her hands on his shoulders, though, her reticule bumped against his chest. Grateful for the distraction, Venetia removed the strings from around her wrist and set the silk bag on her lap, biding for time.

"I am willing to instruct you if need be."

"I know how to kiss," Venetia declared. "I just dislike doing so under duress—and particularly with you."

"You wound me, love."

"Not severely enough, obviously."

He looked faintly amused, as if he were enjoying her discomfiture. He also looked aroused, judging by the expression on his face. He wanted her, she could tell by the sultry gleam in his eyes.

The knowledge made her breathless before she even began, but she had delayed as long as possible. Steeling herself for the renewed shock, she moved closer and touched her lips to his, holding the contact for the space of several heartbeats.

Only then did he assume responsibility. His kiss was soft this time, not taking but offering, yet even that gossamer pressure had the same magical impact as before. All her senses felt assaulted.

Then, parting her lips, his tongue slid into her

mouth. She knew she ought not give in, but his kiss was too enticing. Long moments later his hand cupped her bare shoulder and drew her closer, pressing her against his hard, muscular body, stirring a restless ache low and deep in her feminine center.

Venetia made a sound between a sigh and a whimper. In response, his kiss only deepened. His taste was so delectable. His tongue stroked against hers, tangling in a sensual dance, twining in a long sensuous pattern of withdrawal and penetration.

With consummate ease, he shifted his position, leaning back against the incline of the chaise until she was draped over his muscled, lithe-limbed form. Somehow without her realizing it, she had abdicated control. Warmth radiated up from his chest, infusing her breasts with a delicious heaviness. And he was assailing her mouth with such languor—molding, teasing, tempting, and beguiling. . . .

With the slow awakening of desire, Venetia felt herself yielding, felt her resistance dissolving. Her bones were melting with the heat.

When he shifted beneath her again, one of his knees separated hers. Through her skirts she felt the pressure of his sinewy thigh against her femininity. Venetia tensed. Her heart pounded so loudly, she was certain he could hear it.

She knew a little about what to expect from physical relations. Her friend Cleo had endured a dreadfully unhappy marriage and had wanted her to be prepared. And in Paris, Venetia had explored her long-repressed artistic talent and studied sculpture, including the nude male form. But stone and bronze renderings were a far cry from a live man. And despite her revealing gown, her portrayal of sexual sophistication was largely a pretense.

Then she heard the change in Traherne's rhythmic breathing and realized that certain parts of him had throbbed to life. Venetia shivered. She knew what that male hardness at his loins meant. He was aroused from their brazen intimacy.

His physical reaction instilled an unexpected feeling of triumph inside her. A heady sensation that made her light-headed. She relaxed against him, welcoming the thrilling shocks of heat. He was so vital, so wickedly irresistible. His wonderful mouth held the beguiling promise of answers to a thousand erotic questions.

She never wanted him to stop, but when eventually he did, disappointment flooded her. His lips only moved to her cheek, though. The warm mist of his breath caressed her temple while his hand cradled her throat.

"Sweet Venetia . . ." he murmured, his voice husky and edged with desire.

His thumb stroked the softness of her collarbone before gliding lower. She hadn't worn a chemise, for the straps would have shown beneath her revealing gown, and her corset pushed up her breasts from below.

When his knuckles skimmed over the exposed swells, then slipped down below her bodice to brush her nipple, her breath spiraled away from her. His fingers plucked gently before pulling the velvet down, sending another hot ripple of weakness surging through her. When he cradled one breast in his palm, Venetia whimpered at the feverish surge of pleasure that sensuous caress engendered.

At the soft sound, he kissed her arched throat, then drew back to stare at her. His eyes had grown darker, and she was caught by the hypnotizing heat in the blue depths. Desire shimmered between them, filling the air.

His perusal followed the line of her throat to her bare breasts, his expression intent, powerful, and oh so admiring. She couldn't prevent the shameful tingling of her breasts or the insistent quivering between her thighs.

Her heart thudded harder. She was achingly aware of the soft seduction in those stunning eyes, the play of lamplight on his features, the way the golden blush of the flame gilded his hair. . . .

He bent his head, his lips feathering over her flesh with exquisite pressure till he captured the pouting crest. Venetia gasped at the bright flare of sensation as his tongue circled the areola, laving the taut bud.

Helplessly she raised her hands to slide them into the thick, silky strands of his hair. A tremor shook her. She felt overwhelmed with sensation as his practiced fingers aided his mouth, encouraging her response, coaxing her. When he tasted her other nipple in turn, fire streaked through her, creating an intense yearning inside.

Surrendering, Venetia arched her back against his wicked caress. The brazen need that coiled inside her became a wild, insistent throbbing in her blood. Her breathing was ragged and out of control.

He went on arousing her, teasing the furled bud with his velvet-rough tongue, suckling gently with his warm mouth. A moan escaped her lips at his tantalizing devil's sorcery.

Devil . . . sorcery . . . seduction . . .

What in heaven's name was she doing reveling here in a dimly lit bedchamber with this utterly beguiling hedonist?

With desperate strength, she began to resist the searing pleasure he ignited in her, the powerful urges in her body. She was half sprawled over him, though, which put her at an extreme disadvantage.

With one hand, she groped for the reticule on her lap and finally managed to loosen the strings. Pushing the opening wider, she felt blindly for the handle of her knife in its leather case. Forcibly then, she struggled to push herself up, and in one shaky motion, unsheathed the blade and held it to his throat.

Traherne froze, then blinked at her. His features were heavy and drugged, but the sensuality faded as understanding dawned.

Then amazingly, he chuckled, dismissing the deadly blade at his throat as if it were nothing more than a child's threat.

"Don't force me to hurt you, my lord," she warned in a hoarse voice.

He pressed his forehead against hers and gave another ragged laugh, as if straining for willpower, then caught her wrist and pushed aside the knife.

"You have already hurt me, love. This is twice tonight that you have left me aching."

There was an unmistakable spark of humor in his

voice as he glanced down at his satin breeches and the large bulge there that proclaimed his male arousal.

Venetia lowered her head to follow his gaze, but he lifted her chin with the curve of a forefinger, compelling her to look at his face.

"Never mind. I achieved my objective."

It was Venetia's turn to blink, hers at the tender, amused light in his eyes. Her head was still swimming with the intense sensation of being held in his arms, subjected to his magical kisses, and her dreamlike state had left her weak and unfocused. Thus, it took her a moment to comprehend what he had said.

"What do you mean? What objective?"

"I disarmed you."

"I still hold my knife."

"But I have taken away your leverage. You don't want your sister to know you have been kissing me. Now you will have to tell her, and what will she say?"

Her gaze narrowed. "That was your intent all along—to prevent me from exposing you to my sister."

He had the audacity to look amused. "Forgive me, but yes. Although, I must admit, I enjoyed kissing you immensely."

Her thoughts whirling, Venetia scrambled to sit up and moved to the end of the chaise to put some distance between them. "You are a devil."

"I have been called worse. Straighten your bodice, darling. You don't want to reveal your lovely charms to any of the gentlemen below and have them ogling you the way Knowlsbridge did."

Aghast that her naked breasts were still bared to his gaze, she fumbled to rearrange her bodice.

In her simmering silence, Traherne straightened his own clothing and rose from the chaise, then held out his hand to her. "Come now, I will escort you to your carriage and send you home."

Chapter Four

His declaration left her sputtering and speechless. Ignoring his outstretched hand, Venetia stood but kept her knife at the ready.

"Don't forget your mask, love," Traherne suggested.

She searched around her and discovered it had fallen to the floor during his seduction.

Distracted, she managed to replace the mask and tie the strings behind her turban while chafing at his underhanded methods. He had kissed her into dazed insensibility and imperiled whatever moral standards she once possessed.

Venetia was thoroughly dismayed she had permitted him to go so far. How could she be so weak-willed? All her caution and resistance had been annihilated by warm, hungry desire. Traherne had mesmerized her, excited her, aroused her.

Much worse, he had effectively neutralized her threat to expose him as a Lothario. Although her goals were laudable, she could not possibly tell her sister that she was trying to break up Traherne's courtship of Ophelia and spoil their romance. Ophelia would only think her bitter and jealous because of lingering wounds from her shattered betrothal.

Venetia was disgusted with herself—and her anger showed in her tone when she finally spoke.

"I am warning you, my lord, keep away from my sister. She won't follow in my footsteps if I can help it. I mean to fight for her with the last breath in my body."

"An admirable sentiment but unnecessary. I don't plan to propose to your sister anytime in the near future."

"And you never will if I have my way."

"I will call on you tomorrow at Mrs. Newcomb's home to discuss the situation in depth. For now I want you safe."

His offer took Venetia aback, as did his interest in her safety. Disbelieving, she peered at him through her mask. "You truly mean to continue our conversation tomorrow?"

"Yes."

"Will you swear it?"

"I give you my solemn word. What is Mrs. Newcomb's direction in Kensington?"

His reply mollified her the slightest degree. She might not trust him, but she did not believe he would lie to her face. "It is two miles past Hyde Park, on Melbury Road, Number Twenty-three."

"Come," Traherne urged. "There is a back exit from the club. I will take you to your carriage."

When she stood debating his sincerity, he smiled

that charming, self-deprecating smile that never failed to make her stomach flutter. "If it is any consolation, you struck a grave blow to my self-esteem. This is a first for me, leaving a bedchamber before a lady is completely satisfied."

"It is no consolation at all," Venetia muttered as she returned her knife to its sheath and tucked it inside her reticule.

"If you wish, we can remain here and take our kissing further."

She took a defensive step backward, but his offer settled the issue. "Not if my life depended upon it."

Laughing softly, Traherne escorted her from the room, and together they went downstairs. After gathering her cloak and his greatcoat and tall beaver hat from the majordomo, he led her through a corridor to a rear door. Once again Venetia grew wary, but when she hesitated, he reassured her by explaining: "The stable mews can be reached from this exit rather than waiting to have your carriage delivered to the front door."

She nodded, realizing this was how patrons slipped in and out of the sin club to maintain their privacy.

Outside, they descended a short flight of steps into a foggy mist. The laughter and music grew quieter as they followed a dimly lit pathway toward the rear of the property.

The night air was cool and damp, making Venetia glad for her cloak. When her satin evening slippers made her stumble on the uneven ground, Traherne took her arm to steady her. She tried to pull back from his touch, but he wouldn't release her.

"Be at ease, Miss Stratham. I am merely suffering an outburst of protectiveness this evening."

She gave an unwilling laugh. "What a singular interpretation of events. Is *that* how you exhibit protectiveness, by corrupting me and luring me into lewd behavior?"

He flashed her a grin. "I didn't even begin to corrupt you. You kissed *me*, you will recall."

"Technically, perhaps, but you forced my compliance. And I wound up your helpless victim."

"Hardly." He sent an amused glance down at her reticule, which concealed her knife. "You are one of the least helpless females I know. Besides, I wanted to demonstrate the dangers of your coming to a brothel alone."

"That you did."

He had warned her of the hazard from drunken gamesters like Knowlsbridge, but the greater danger by far came from Traherne himself.

"I would never permit my sister to come to a place like Tavistock's," he remarked.

"Fortunately you are not my brother—or any relation at all."

"I agree, it is fortunate," he said amiably.

"I am *not* your responsibility," Venetia declared, although she had to admire him for championing his sister.

"At just this moment you are."

Seeing the futility of arguing further, Venetia fell silent. Despite her frustration with Traherne, having his tall, solid form beside her made her feel safer as they negotiated the dark path.

They passed through a rear gate and reached the

alley that led to the livery serving this district of London. In the distance, she could see a bustling stable yard illuminated by torches and lamplight, filled with teams and vehicles of all kinds.

As they grew closer, she could hear the male camaraderie of servants waiting for their masters, and make out small groups of coachmen, grooms, and outriders huddling together for warmth and companionship.

"Which carriage is Mrs. Newcomb's?"

"It is a barouche," she said, her gaze searching the crowd.

"There is my landau," Traherne pointed out.

Glancing to her left, she recognized his crest on the door panel. Venetia was vaguely aware of the shadowy figures loitering near his carriage, leaning against the wall of the stable block, but thought nothing of it until a rough male voice called out, "M'lord Traherne?"

"Yes?" he answered.

One of the shadows detached from the group and approached them. It was a heavyset man, his face partially concealed by a low-brimmed hat and dark scarf. He looked to be the sort of prizefighter Venetia had seen at county fairs, all muscle and brute force. She barely had time to register the impression before he suddenly lowered his head and charged forward like an enraged bull, heading straight for them at a dead run.

Venetia was too stunned to react, but at the last second, Traherne pushed her aside, making her gasp. He took the brunt of the impact yet still somehow managed to spin so that the brute went flying face-first to sprawl on the ground.

It all happened too swiftly for her to comprehend, but two more beefy men jumped out of the shadows and rushed toward the earl, cudgels raised, fists swinging.

To his credit Traherne was more agile than his attackers. Raising his own fists, he let fly a punch that felled the second ruffian, then dodged a blow from a third.

Grunts and growls followed as Venetia watched in alarm, unsure if the thugs were attempting to beat Traherne to a pulp or trying to kill him. Either way she was frightened for him.

The scene was surreal, something out of a bad dream. For a moment she stood there frozen, heart pounding, shock making her sluggish. When the first bruiser climbed to his feet to join his comrades in a fresh assault, though, she finally broke out of her paralysis. Wishing she could aid Traherne somehow, she let out a piercing scream to summon help, but knew it would come too late to save him.

"Your knife—give it to me!" Traherne rasped.

A powerful surge of protectiveness flooded Venetia, spurring a fury that these thugs would try to murder him right before her eyes.

Desperately she pulled the blade from her reticule and found the strength to wade into the fray, flailing her reticule over and over again with all her might at their hooded faces, their heads, their massive shoulders while shouting at them: "No! Leave him be! You will *not* hurt him!"

The feminine article might be flimsy, but the unex-

pected onslaught made one lout yelp and scramble to
retreat several paces.

In his haste, he tripped and fell backward onto his
duff. Venetia found herself beside Traherne, forming
a defensive shield, clobbering anything in reach. With
her other hand, she thrust out the knife handle to
him.

He took it and unsheathed the blade as he pulled
her behind him so that he was protecting her again,
then swept the weapon in an arc in front of him.

"Now the fight is more even," he declared with a
humorless grin. "Would you care to have your gullets
slit, lads? Come at me again and you will get a taste
of my skill with a blade."

Clearly they didn't care to test his threat, for they
picked up their fallen comrade and took to their
heels, half limping, half running.

Venetia felt a swell of triumph but was too weak-
kneed to express her relief just then. When she
clutched at Traherne's arm for support, he stepped in
front of her and cradled her chin in his hand so that
he could see her eyes through her mask.

"Are you all right?" he demanded, his voice rough
with concern. "Were you hurt?"

Shock was draining away, giving her enough energy to shake her head and wheeze an unsteady, "No,
I am fine. What of you?"

She was breathless and shaken, but he looked
scarcely winded. He was the worse for wear, however. His hat had been knocked from his head, leaving his dark blond hair tousled, and a wicked cut had
opened on one cheekbone.

Seeing the wound, Venetia inhaled in sympathy. "Your cheek is bleeding!"

"It is nothing."

"It is not *nothing*. It looks extremely painful."

"I have had far worse."

She wanted to touch his face to reassure herself. When she reached up, though, he caught her hand and wrapped his fingers around hers.

Venetia was suddenly captivated by his expression, the inexplicable tenderness in his eyes.

The same tenderness echoed in his husky tone when he spoke. "Thank you, love. I do believe you saved my hide from a trouncing, or worse."

Warmth filled her at his praise, but the spell didn't last. Just then they were surrounded by two dozen anxious people . . . grooms, coachmen, footmen . . . and several issued rapid queries: "M'lord, are you harmed? May we aid you? What of the lady?"

Traherne brushed off their concern. "Our attackers escaped down the alley. Ten pounds to anyone who can follow and report on the direction they fled."

"Aye, milord," someone exclaimed as a number of the younger servants took off at a run in that direction.

Another helpful soul returned Traherne's hat and asked how he could be of service.

"Summon the Watch, Robert, while I escort the lady to her rig," he replied, ushering Venetia forward.

"Was that one of your servants?" she asked.

"Yes—my coachman."

A path opened through the crowd to allow them to pass, and they crossed the stable yard in search of Cleo's coachman.

Glover appeared highly worried for Venetia as he hastened to her side, but he had the discretion not to blurt out her name. "Sweet mercy, miss! Was it *you* those ruffians set upon?"

"Unfortunately yes, Glover. Will you please take me home?"

"Aye, miss, gladly—but do you not want me to pursue the villains?"

"Thank you, no—"

Traherne interrupted in a stern, authoritative voice. "I will handle the thieves. Take your mistress home at once and don't let me catch you bringing her here again."

Venetia sent the earl an exasperated frown but waited until he handed her inside the barouche before saying quietly, "You needn't reprimand him. He only did as I bade him."

"That is no excuse for his folly." When she was seated, Traherne stood in the doorway and leaned in for privacy. "I told you, I want you safe."

"You should see to your own safety, my lord," she suggested tartly. "Those brutes were clearly targeting you, not me."

"Indeed. If I didn't know better, I would have suspected you of setting them after me."

His comment made her raise an eyebrow. "Me? Why would I do such a thing?"

"To protect your sister."

"I am not prepared to resort to violence just yet."

His mouth curved. "What do you call what just happened? You were an avenging angel."

"I was acting in your defense."

"For which I am grateful. Here is your knife back."

She took it from him and resheathed the blade for a second time. "You did not truly suspect me, did you?" she asked a trifle indignantly. "I would never behave in so cowardly a fashion."

"That I have no trouble believing."

Hearing the humor in his tone, Venetia realized he was enjoying himself, or at least his blood was up from the danger he had just faced.

"How can you be so calm? Those brutes could have killed you. You act as if you relished that bloody brawl."

The grin he flashed her took her breath away. "A little peril is good for keeping reactions sharp and provides relief from boredom."

Her exhalation was half scoff, half disbelief. "I for one would have happily remained bored."

"They were likely thieves eager to relieve me of my gambling winnings."

Venetia frowned. "A robbery might explain their assault, except that they never demanded your purse. They attacked right from the start. And they were obviously lying in wait for you."

"Evidently."

"How could they have known you would exit by the rear of the club rather than have your carriage draw around front?"

"I don't know. It's possible they meant to commandeer my vehicle from Robert. But I mean to get to the bottom of it."

Her frown deepened. "What will you do now?"

"I will remain here to investigate and speak to the Night Watch. Someone may be able to provide identification of our attackers."

"Perhaps you ought not stay, my lord. What if they return?"

"Then I will be better prepared for them."

His careless tone vexed her. "I can see I should not have worried about you."

"Were you worried?" he prodded in that teasing tone.

"Regrettably, yes. I want to stop you from pursuing my sister, but I don't want your blood spilled."

"I am gratified to know that."

Venetia bit her lip. In all the chaos, she had forgotten that her problem was the same as it had been when she first arrived. "I meant what I said, Lord Traherne. I will not allow you to harm my sister."

"We will discuss it in the morning. Shall I call on you at ten?"

"The sooner the better. I would prefer an earlier hour if you can drag yourself out of bed."

"Nine o'clock, then, but it may be a late night for me here."

"So you mean to return to the club?"

"Yes. I haven't finished what I began."

"And just what is that?" she asked curiously.

"As I said, I am here for the gaming."

She couldn't resist a taunt. "Not to sport with your latest paramour?"

He contemplated her for several heartbeats. "I feel compelled to mention, darling, that I don't need to patronize a brothel to find female companionship. Not only can I afford someone of a higher class, but my tastes are much more discriminating."

"I don't doubt it," Venetia responded, unable to tamp down a note of bitterness.

He had clearly been enjoying their sparring, but he must have realized that he'd struck a nerve, for his expression sobered.

And then he took her wholly by surprise. Reaching in, he caught her shoulders, drew her close, and planted a slow kiss on her lips that utterly deprived her of breath.

The surge of heat that raced through Venetia was as searing as his two previous kisses, but at least she was more prepared this time. After the initial shock, Venetia pulled back and raised her hand in order to box his ears.

Traherne caught her wrist easily, though, preventing the blow and giving her another sensual smile. "I will see you in the morning, love."

Having stunned her yet again, he stepped back and shut the door, then slapped the panel twice, giving Cleo's coachman the office to start.

As the vehicle drove out of the stable yard, Venetia sank against the squabs, once again left totally speechless. Incomprehensibly, she wanted to curse Traherne and kiss him at the same time.

She raised her gloved fingers to her burning lips, her thoughts whirling. He delighted in setting her back on her heels and keeping her off balance, but her reaction to him was so out of character for her. She was frustrated that she hadn't ended his courtship of her sister, irritated that she was worried for his well-being, and aghast that she not only enjoyed his kisses and tender protectiveness, she actually *craved* more.

Perhaps she had made a grave mistake coming here,

Venetia decided, scarcely believing what had happened tonight. Together they had chased off a pack of thugs bent on malevolence, after Traherne had practically seduced her.

She shouldn't be surprised that he had laughed in the face of danger; he had a brilliant mind but was something of a daredevil who lived on the edge of scandal. And she certainly ought not be surprised at his°rakish behavior. Tonight had left her in little doubt that he would be a marvelous lover. The memory of his erotic mouth would stay with her for a very long time.

Far worse, he aroused a deep, feminine yearning inside her, damn and blast him.

Venetia grimaced. It annoyed her to no end that she could be so tempted by a rakehell. While she was betrothed to Viscount Ackland, she had never permitted herself to acknowledge her forbidden attraction for Lord Traherne, but it was there now, smoldering between them like a banked fire.

And she would have to face him in the morning, making herself vulnerable to him again.

Venetia muttered a low oath. She wasn't certain she could withstand another assault on her senses like the ones he had delivered tonight. In the clash over her sister, she had come out the clear loser. His sharp questions and observations had made her uncomfortable and his seduction had made her melt. She was absolutely not eager to repeat the experience.

Traherne was a cocky, arrogant, outrageous, self-confident, provoking devil, and it was all she could do to hold her own with him.

And yet she had no choice. She would simply have to work harder to persuade him to break off his pursuit of her sister.

And, most important . . . never, *ever* again allow him to kiss her!

Chapter Five

When Quinn's carriage drew up before his Berkeley Square home in the wee hours of the morning, he was no closer to learning the identities or motives of his attackers, since questioning witnesses had yielded no clues. Nor had he won resoundingly at Faro as planned, for by the time he finally returned to the club, Lisle had already departed.

He had also failed to solve the intriguing puzzle of why he'd kissed Venetia Stratham for a third time in quick succession.

He was rarely given to impulsive behavior, but he hadn't been able to resist her temptation. She fired his blood even more than the rush of violent emotion while repelling the assault—exhilaration, fear, triumph.

If briefly he'd suspected Venetia of plotting to incapacitate him to thwart his aims with her sister, her bravery had instantly put to rest that notion. She had come to his aid like a Valkyrie or avenging angel.

Her perceptive questions afterward about his attackers lying in wait for him had no answers, either. The reports from witnesses had proved vague and conflicting and a search of the area fruitless. The possibility that the thugs might be targeting Venetia instead seemed remote, given that they had addressed him by name. If they were set on robbery, perhaps they thought he'd taken possession of the pendant from Edmund Lisle during their Faro game.

As to how they had known he could be found at Tavistock's—

"Are you certain you don't need aid, m'lord?" his coachman asked as Quinn stepped down from the landau.

"Thank you, no, Robert." He ached a bit from his assorted cuts and bruises—sore ribs, scraped knuckles, and a bloody cut on his cheekbone—but nothing worse than he'd endured growing up in a household of three rambunctious boys and two lively girls. "I will need my curricle at half past eight tomorrow morning."

"Certainly, as you wish, m'lord."

Quinn was admitted to the enormous entry hall by a footman, who took his greatcoat and hat. Seeing dried blood, the servant betrayed his impeccable training by frowning and repeating Robert's question. Quinn gave the same reply and dismissed the man to seek his own bed in the servants' quarters.

The mansion was quiet as Quinn made his way upstairs. In truth, the house seemed strangely empty since his sister no longer lived there with him. Skye had a way of brightening his day with her mere presence, and he missed that more than he ever would have expected before her marriage last autumn to the Earl of Hawkhurst.

His bedchamber was prepared for his arrival— lamp and hearth fire lit, fresh water in the washstand basin, and the bedcovers turned down. Quinn had partially undressed, removing his coat, waistcoat, cravat, and shirt, when a soft knock sounded on his chamber door.

At his call to enter, his valet stepped into the room carrying a tray of medical supplies, followed by his middle-aged housekeeper, Mrs. Pelfrey, garbed in a robe and nightcap, although she modestly averted her eyes at the sight of his bare chest.

Quinn couldn't repress a smile at his staff's alacrity. Their network was highly efficient. No doubt the footman had woken the butler, who had roused the housekeeper, who had summoned his valet.

"You should not have troubled yourself to patch my injuries, Mrs. Pelfrey."

"You know Lady Skye would be distressed if we failed to care for you properly, my lord. I made her a solemn promise before she departed."

Mrs. Pelfrey insisted on tending to him, just as she had when he was a stripling lad making trouble with his cousins. She'd been with him for years and had treated many a scuffed knee, becoming even more fussy after his parents' deaths when he was seventeen. In fact, she had helped their bachelor uncle, Lord Cornelius Wilde, raise the five orphaned cousins, primarily at the vast Beaufort and Traherne country estates in Kent, and accompanied them when the family regularly spent the Season in London.

Mrs. Pelfrey felt particularly protective of Skye but

included Quinn in her motherly concern. He suffered her fussing patiently while she applied a liniment to his rib cage that was cool and soothing. His lower right side was the most painful, having caught a punishing blow. When she washed the cut on his cheek, she made a soft tsking sound.

"I did not go looking for a fight this time, Mrs. Pelfrey," Quinn assured her.

"So I heard. 'Tis appalled I am that thieves assaulted you. What is this world coming to when it is not safe for citizens to walk the streets?"

When she was done, he thanked her, then sent her and his valet back to their chambers. By the time he retired to his own bed, Quinn's body was weary but his mind remained unsettled. He lay there thinking back on the evening, alternately pondering the two mysteries.

The attack tonight was the less interesting. There had to be a reasonable explanation, if only he could discern it. Discovering his location would not have been difficult for the thieves, considering how the society pages regularly speculated on his whereabouts, as Venetia had pointed out earlier tonight.

She was entirely wrong about his motives, however. He'd attended Tavistock's in order to track down the family treasure belonging to his mother, Angelique, only child of the Duc and Duchesse de Chagny, who were guillotined during that country's bloody revolution. The priceless collection was thought to be buried at the bottom of the sea off the southern coast of France, but when a distinctive diamond and ruby pendant appeared in London five weeks ago, Quinn wondered if scavengers had found the shipwreck and excavated the sunken riches.

To his confoundment, he'd first seen the splendid piece around the neck of his beautiful former mistress, Julia—or Lady X, as she preferred to be called. Upon recognizing the design, Quinn asked how she had obtained it. And to his irritation, Julia took pleasure in playing coy before finally admitting the pendant was a gift from her current protector, Edmund Lisle, the gentleman who had succeeded Quinn in her affections—if Julia could even be said to *have* affections.

Naturally, however, Lisle was tight-lipped, fearing she still pined for his predecessor. Thus Quinn had altered tactics, challenging the avid gamester at the card table, hoping either to win the pendant from Lisle outright or make his gaming debt so large, he would have no choice but to reveal the jewelry's origins.

Which was what had led Quinn to the club this evening. Not for the carnal sport, as Venetia believed.

Her accusations still stung, particularly her comparison with her former betrothed.

You remind me of Ackland. At least he had only one mistress in keeping at a time, and he never stole another man's inamorata.

Wincing, Quinn rolled onto his side and rearranged his pillow. He most certainly had not stolen Julia from anyone. Precisely the opposite, in fact—although the part about her causing a scene in Hyde Park the previous year was regrettably true.

During the six months Julia was his mistress, her possessiveness had grown rather cloying. Sensing his withdrawal, she'd tried to rouse his jealousy by dallying with Lisle. When Quinn announced he was leaving her, she had hurled a porcelain vase at his head.

Her public rant peppered with vivid invectives in the middle of Rotten Row was the final straw. She'd begun by pleading with Quinn to reinstate her, claiming she had never wanted Lisle, which later had naturally humiliated and infuriated the gamester when he heard the tale. The fact that she eventually took up with Lisle permanently was a testament to Julia's beauty and her wiles. But Quinn was quite glad to be rid of her. Consequently, he'd taken even greater care in choosing his subsequent liaisons.

He was not quite the libertine Venetia thought him, though. For one thing, his responsibilities as Skye's brother and guardian had limited his craving for adventure and excitement and travel.

Granted, his sexual exploits had once been excessive. Bored and restless and jaded with the shallowness of society, he had played at the game of life. Ironically enough, it was the scandal of Venetia's broken betrothal that had started him questioning his rakish lifestyle and seriously changed his focus.

Having been born with a scientific bent and an aptitude for solving puzzles, he'd channeled his energies into a revolutionary endeavor: perfecting the sort of innovation that might have saved the lives of his parents and his uncle and aunt. For the past two years, that one goal had driven him.

Quinn rolled over again, his memories of Venetia further impeding his attempt to sleep. Tasting her delectable mouth had only confirmed his intuition: She was as elegant and graceful as ever—but also pure, luscious woman.

He'd enjoyed himself tonight more than he cared to admit, not least because of the sparks flaring between them in the conflict over her sister. She was much different from Ophelia, who was unfailingly polite, even meek-mannered.

The contrast reminded him of his cousin Kate's theory about legendary lovers and sent his thoughts winging back to a long-ago summer afternoon by the lake at the Beaufort country estate before their close-knit family had broken up so the cousins could attend various universities and boarding schools.

Still grieving their parents' loss, twelve-year-old Kate first began her campaign to find a bride for her brother Ash—Ashton Wilde, Marquis of Beaufort.

"You need to marry and bring us home a mama," Kate insisted.

Ash had practically choked. "*Marry?* Just what put that maggoty notion into your head, minx?"

"If you wed, we would have a mother to raise us, and then we would not have to go away to school in a fortnight."

But her rationale was not so cold-blooded, they shortly learned. "Mama always said someone special is waiting out there in the world for me—indeed, an ideal match is waiting for each of us."

In the intervening years, Kate had never abandoned her longing for true love, for herself or her family. Then, at the beginning of last Season, she'd developed her mad theory about legendary lovers and redoubled her efforts to find them all perfect mates.

"It is up to us to shape our own destinies," she had

argued. "We each must be responsible for meeting our match and making our own particular tale come true."

Quinn profoundly agreed with the need to shape his own destiny. And so he refused to act the milksop, letting his female relatives dictate his future.

He had good reason for being so cynical about love. When he was eighteen, shortly after succeeding to his late father's title, he'd become the victim of a grasping social climber. It was a particularly vulnerable time for him, having lost his parents and left his remaining family to attend Cambridge. Young and impressionable, he'd fallen head over heels for a conniving husband-hunter several years his senior.

Being played for a fool by a woman was one of his least proud moments. Since then he had kept his affairs strictly superficial.

Kate's theory could not survive logical, scientific scrutiny, either. Quinn put faith in physical proof, not romantic fantasies.

And yet . . . over the past year, she had orchestrated a romance for Ash and then her adopted brother and first cousin, Lord Jack Wilde. Skye had pursued her own legendary tale with Hawk last autumn, and as a bonus, had found Uncle Cornelius's long-lost love.

As soon as Skye's vows were said, both women had ardently set their sights on Quinn. He'd fooled them with his overtures toward Ophelia, so they no longer regularly hounded him. But once they discovered his intention to cultivate other suitors for the girl, Kate would be after him again, even if she had to revise her hypothesis.

Venetia would never fit the Greek myth of Pygmalion. Although reportedly she had taken up sculpting during her exile in France, she bore no resemblance to the cold statue of Galetea. To his mind, they were closer to Shakespeare's *The Taming of the Shrew*.

Venetia was far more appealing than her sister, and would make him a better match. She had a lively spirit that intrigued him, unlike the calculating, insipid debutantes who had pursued him for years. And her character was far stronger. She had faced adversity and endured censure and banishment with remarkable fortitude. And even if it made him her foe, he had to admire her devotion to her sister.

In truth, he'd felt a deep attraction toward Venetia from the very first, as much for her warmth and wit as for her beauty.

While he might have desired her then, however, lust did not justify matrimony and he had positively not been in the market for a wife. Instead, his friend and fellow peer Viscount Ackland had courted and proposed to her.

Quinn had thought then that she was too good for Ackland, and he'd always been envious of his friend—not of their betrothal, but of the chance to possess a woman like that. It was the only time he had ever coveted another man's choice.

Tonight he had sampled Venetia's passion, both physical and emotional, and he couldn't deny that he was entranced. The additional irony was not lost on him, either: He was thought to be courting one sister but badly wanted the other.

An utterly inappropriate reaction, given his aversion to matrimony.

When Quinn finally dozed off, he dreamed of Venetia, of taming her and gaining her surrender. He woke hard and aching to the sound of rapping on his bedchamber door.

His valet's entrance abruptly dissolved the pleasurable remnants of his dream.

"You asked to be awakened at eight, my lord."

Rousing himself out of bed, Quinn made an effort to discipline his rash thoughts. Taming Venetia would prove an enormous challenge and lead to paths he didn't wish to go down. The very thought was laughable.

Still, as he dressed and made ready to call on her, he couldn't quell his keen sense of anticipation. It was unwise, no doubt, but he was eager for their next encounter.

As ordered, his curricle awaited him in the front drive, drawn by a pair of sleek bays, with his groom Giles perched behind.

Uncharacteristically, his coachman stood holding the near horse's bridle. "Pray, take care, my lord," Robert bade him. Apparently the servant was still worried, perhaps because the attack had occurred on his watch.

"I will, Robert," Quinn assured the coachman as he climbed into the driver's seat.

When he snapped the reins, the bays took off at a jaunty trot. Behind him, Giles held on to his perch tightly.

The fog had cleared, but the spring morning was cool and cloudy as he drove through Mayfair. At the southwest corner of Hyde Park, the road to Kensington became a rural thoroughfare, but there was a fair amount of traffic in each direction.

Quinn was more preoccupied with his upcoming appointment with Venetia, mentally debating how much to tell her about his courtship of her sister. He had already decided to share his reasons for visiting Tavistock's, in the hope of improving her low opinion of him.

They had driven perhaps a mile when he caught the sound of galloping hoofbeats to their rear.

"Milord," Giles said rather anxiously, "there is a chaise fast approaching from behind."

"Noted, lad." Quinn steered his curricle as far left as possible, planning to give the other vehicle ample room to pass.

Shortly the four-horse team drew abreast at a reckless speed. Quinn caught a glimpse of the driver, whose head was swathed in a tricorn hat and thick wool neck scarf, but concentrated on keeping his own pair steady as the chaise swept past, crowding him.

He had begun to curse the coachman's poor driving when he realized the act was a deliberate attempt to force his two-wheeled curricle onto the verge. In only a matter of seconds, the chaise swerved even farther left, directly into his lane.

His stomach clenching, Quinn drew sharply on the reins to slow his bays and avoid a crash. The chaise pressed him relentlessly, however, and in another moment he felt his near wheel give way. The curricle lurched sideways, causing the bays to plunge off the road into a shallow ditch.

Thankfully, the vehicle remained upright as it bucked

over the uneven ground, but Giles was thrown free of his perch and landed with an audible thud and a cry of pain.

It required all Quinn's skill to bring his frightened horses to a halt. They stood there snorting and trembling as he locked the brake and tied off the reins, then jumped down from his seat to go to their heads.

Hearing the fading echo of beating hooves, he was vaguely aware that the chaise had raced on. He spoke a few soothing words and ran a quieting hand over the necks of both horses. Then he turned to his greater concern, his groom.

Giles, a small slender youth of about eighteen, lay some twenty yards away, facedown in the grass, groaning.

Going to him, Quinn knelt beside him. "Where does it hurt, lad?"

"M-my should . . . er," he gasped.

"Lie still while I ascertain your injuries."

Quinn spent the next few moments conducting a careful examination, feeling for broken bones particularly.

Having participated and viewed numerous wrestling matches in the village near Tallis Court, he could recognize the worst damage as a shoulder wrenched from the socket and a nasty scrape on the forehead.

Gently he helped Giles to roll over onto his back. "I want you to be brave and count to ten . . ."

On "three," the boy let out a scream when Quinn managed to reset the limb.

Giles lay there white-faced and panting, but the

pain was no longer excruciating, as evidenced by his indignation against the perpetrator.

"'Twas a willful crime, milord," he declared. "Would that I could land him a facer."

"I harbor the same wish," Quinn said grimly, glancing around to assess how he would move his injured groom.

Fortunately, a passing farmer stopped to provide them aid. When the lad was carefully settled in the back of the wagon, cushioned by a bed of straw, Quinn was able to check further on his team and the state of his curricle.

Only when he found both fairly sound—a remarkable occurrence, considering the peril they had faced—did he allow himself to dwell on how they had barely escaped grave harm. White-hot fury filled him. Not only had the culprit endangered Quinn's horses, he could have killed his groom or himself.

He would not be able to make his promised call on Venetia, but there was no hope for it. His servant and his horses took precedence and had to be returned home.

Quinn contemplated unharnessing the bays and leaving his curricle there, sending someone to fetch it later, but thankfully more passersby joined in the task of guiding the team and curricle back onto the road.

As he drove them slowly home behind the wagon, he had ample time to consider his new dilemma. Last night's encounter could have been a foiled robbery, but this second deliberate attack had nothing to do with robbery.

Had this been an actual attempt on his life? Clearly

someone wished him harm and had waited for the opportunity to find him nearly alone.

Whoever was orchestrating the assaults could not have known his destination this morning, though, unless . . . They might have bribed his staff to become privy to his private engagements. More likely, they had been closely watching his movements. The driver of the chaise must have followed him from Berkeley Square, Quinn decided.

As to why, he had no idea. To his knowledge, he had no significant enemies—at least not deadly ones.

If it came to foes, Edmund Lisle was the most probable suspect. Perhaps there was something about the pendant or Lisle's relationship with Julia that had caused him to suddenly become vindictive. He was too cowardly to challenge an opponent to a duel, though, and would not have confronted Quinn to his face.

A more dubious possibility was a competitor in his latest enterprise. Some years ago when he'd met an idiosyncratic former sea captain bursting with novel ideas about how to revolutionize sailing, Quinn had become fascinated, perhaps obsessed, by the notion of producing a steam engine for sailing ships. But only recently had he invested significant financial resources, hiring scientists and engineers who could design such a miraculous engine and commissioning a prototype to be built in the docks at Portsmouth.

His two-year project was nearing fruition and could prove lucrative if it actually worked. But Quinn could think of no business rival who would resort to violence to prevent completion of his venture.

One thing was clear, however. Searching for the

perpetrator—or perpetrators—required more expertise than he currently possessed. He would do well to rely on Hawk, who had once worked for the British Foreign Office.

A more immediate problem was Venetia herself. As soon as he returned home and saw to his groom's welfare, Quinn pledged, he would write her with an apology and ask to postpone their meeting till this afternoon.

Meanwhile, he would be more wary in the future and begin watching over his shoulder for whatever enemy he had unwittingly made.

An hour and a quarter later, Venetia's frustration was reaching a boiling point as she waited with Cleo in the green parlor. She had wanted her friend nearby during Traherne's call should he attempt to work his devastating wiles on her again. But he had not even done her the courtesy of appearing.

"I should never have believed him," she muttered from her post at the window. "He gave me his *solemn word,* but it is after ten o'clock."

Behind her, Cleo responded with a consoling murmur as she stitched a pillow cover on her tambour frame. "Watching for his arrival will not make it happen any sooner."

Venetia turned away from the window to resume her pacing. She had slept poorly, which had further depressed her mood and grated on her usually mild temper. Indeed, she had spent most of the night tossing and turning and stewing over her failure to make Traherne see reason, and now he had denied her a second chance to confront him.

"It is obvious he agreed to discuss Ophelia merely to placate me. Well, I am *not* placated."

"Have some more tea, dearest," Cleo suggested.

"I have drunk two cups already."

"Then sit down. You are wearing a hole in my carpet."

"Pacing helps to soothe me while I rant. I should have *known* he could not be trusted."

"*Venetia,*" Cleo said with a smile, "you need to take a calming breath. You cannot let him rouse your anger and blind you to your goal."

Pausing to glance at her friend, Venetia gave a sheepish laugh. "Must you be so reasonable?"

"I have an emotional distance and so can be more impartial. It is not my sister's future at stake. But you must strive for dispassion if you hope to deal with Lord Traherne successfully."

Recognizing her friend's words of wisdom, Venetia forced herself to take a seat on the sofa. "But I feel at such a disadvantage, Cleo."

"I warned you not to tangle with him."

"I know. And I should have listened to you. He is just as dangerous as you predicted."

"You ought not have kissed him."

"I need no reminder," Venetia replied with a sigh. "I am flagellating myself enough for the both of us."

"Very well, my dear, I will cease badgering you. But you will have to determine how better to deal with him when you next meet."

"*If* we ever meet, you mean," Venetia corrected in a tart tone as she picked up her sketch pad and pencil and tried to distract herself by outlining an idea for a new bust. It was best not to dwell on her embarrassingly scandalous encounter with Traherne.

Cleo was her dearest friend in all the world and they had few secrets, but Venetia had flushed hotly when recounting the events of last night. She had also left out the part where Traherne had suckled her breasts, for that detail was just too intimate to share.

But when she complained about his underhanded methods, Cleo had sincerely sympathized.

Understandably, Cleo was even more set against rakes than Venetia, having endured an unfaithful husband for three long years. To aid her spendthrift family, Cleo had made a marriage of convenience and then was widowed at the tender age of twenty-one when Mr. Newcomb was shot in a duel by a jealous husband.

The unhappy experience had left her slightly bitter, and eager for freedom from men. Cleo also longed to see Europe and so offered Venetia a position as her companion, for which Venetia was profoundly grateful.

Two years ago, Cleo had actually been the one to inform Venetia—gently and with much regret—that Ackland had spent the eve of his wedding in his mistress's bed. Rumors that he was still consorting with—and even openly flaunting—his paramour had been floating all the previous day, but of course the bride was the last to know. Cleo, who was much more savvy about men, with servants who adored her and kept her well informed about the ton's doings, had taken it upon herself to investigate.

Venetia's lips tightened at the memory. At first she'd refused to believe Cleo's reluctantly delivered report, and there was no opportunity to confront Ackland before the ceremony, since her repeated messages to his home went unanswered. When he arrived late at St George's church in Hanover Square, where the beau monde held most society weddings, he was still partly foxed and his evening clothes stank of exotic perfume. Seeing his disgraceful condition with her own eyes had forced Venetia to accept the painful truth and relinquish her idealistic naïveté.

Recognizing her dismay, Ackland had employed his roguish charm and attempted to talk his way out of his predicament. He'd sworn he loved her and promised to break off with his ladybird for good, but by then Venetia's trust was irreparably broken. Any man who would betray her so publicly on the steps of a church would never remain faithful to his marriage vows, and she refused to marry an unfaithful libertine.

His deceit had made her sick at heart, Venetia reflected. At the time, she was half in love with Ackland—or at least she'd convinced herself it was love. More likely, she'd been caught up in the excitement of his courtship as well as her parents' expectations, and flattered by the devoted attention of a handsome nobleman.

The scales had been ripped from her eyes that day. She later learned that Ackland had offered for her in order to please his father and gain his inheritance. He was now wed to a young lady and retired to the country, where reportedly Lady Ackland was with child.

No doubt Lord Traherne similarly intended to take a genteel young wife to sire an heir, just as Ackland had done. What other reason could there be for his attentions to so unsuitable a bride as Ophelia, Venetia wondered.

She feared her sweet, gentle sister was even more susceptible than she herself had been, for now Ophelia was desperate to mitigate the damage the scandal had wrought. As was Venetia. She would have done anything for her sister and regretted profoundly that she couldn't make up for ruining her marital chances. It was alarming, though, how her warnings and pleas had fallen on deaf ears during the past week of surreptitiously exchanged messages and letters.

You and I have different aspirations, Venetia. I do not hope for love, merely a comfortable situation.

Venetia suspected she was fighting a losing battle. Their parents had persuaded Ophelia to overlook any possibility of love or happiness in marriage. In fact, their mother was doubtless overjoyed and would want nothing to stand in the way of the nuptials. Helen Stratham wouldn't care that Lord Traherne was a libertine, and not only because of his illustrious title.

Venetia could still hear her mother's furious admonitions regarding her broken betrothal to Viscount Ackland two years ago. Mama had been appalled that her elder daughter refused to marry a nobleman because of such a minor weakness.

"That is what gentlemen *do*, Venetia. You must be willing to overlook their peccadillos. I have done so with your father all these years. You should also."

That somewhat shocking revelation about her father had not changed Venetia's mind. Most of society thought she ought not to have called off the wedding, certainly not in so public a fashion, and instead endured Ackland's licentiousness in silence. Her parents had been furious that she had caused them such scandal and mortification.

Cleo was one of the few people who had taken her side. Cleo cherished her independence from men and strongly encouraged Venetia to follow her example.

And truly, Venetia was earnestly attempting to master the art of repressing her deepest feelings, even if her best efforts had failed her miserably with Traherne last evening. For the life of her, she could not explain why she had reacted so strongly to his provocations, why she had allowed him to rouse both her ire and her sensual longings at once—or why, for that matter, his original transgression had affected her so painfully two years ago.

Inexplicably, she had felt betrayed by Traherne for the role he'd played in her betrothed's duplicity.

The worst, however, was not the personal humiliation and hurt she had suffered at Ackland's hands. The worst was that her family had washed their hands of her. The pain had cut deeply. She missed them terribly, especially her sister. She missed her home and her friends as well.

It had been her choice to leave England, though, and she would likely make the same decision again, Venetia supposed. Her parents might have allowed her to remain hidden away in the country, but exile in France with Cleo was preferable to remaining at home as an outcast, where she would be reminded daily of her sins in defying her parents' wishes.

She was immensely grateful to Cleo for coming to her rescue and offering her a home; she could not ask for a more generous or loyal friend. But even with

Cleo's friendship, Venetia was often lonely, painfully so at times.

Of course she endeavored to repress such traitorous feelings. Attempting to emulate Cleo, she had taught herself to be strong and independent.

And there were benefits to her current situation, Venetia reminded herself. She had far more freedom now, and her life was never dull. She especially enjoyed the salons, the intellectual soirees, the conversation and music and art. A major advantage of being considered a fallen woman was the chance to explore her own artistic talent. In British society, a lady did not pursue art other than charcoal drawings and watercolors, certainly not sculpting.

But sometimes she wondered if her shattered dreams of a loving marriage were worth the price she had paid. She still wanted love, a husband, children—unlikely prospects, given her status as a pariah—

Venetia stiffened her spine. It was past time to banish the wretched sense of longing and deep, abiding loneliness she'd felt all these many months. She defied anyone to catch her indulging in misery or self-pity. She had made her bed, so to speak, and was willing to lie in it, Venetia sternly told herself.

However, she would not let her sister suffer in a similar bed.

When another half hour passed with still no sign of Traherne, Venetia announced that she would not wait any longer. She would not give up trying to convince him, and if he would not come to her, she would go to him.

"Perhaps I should accompany you," Cleo said with a note of concern in her tone.

"No, I don't want to drag you further into my problems."

Because of her notoriety, she could not call at his London home without disguise. Thus, Venetia went upstairs to don a veil in addition to a hat and pelisse.

At the last moment, she searched in her bureau for a more convincing weapon. Traherne had laughed at her knife last evening. Well, she would bring her pistol this time, even if she would leave it unloaded.

If she had to protect herself from him, he might think twice if he had to look down the barrel of a gun.

And as she was handed into Cleo's carriage, Venetia promised herself that no matter what sensual methods of seduction Traherne employed, or provocative diversions he created, or evasive lies he told, or sly manipulations he devised in order to put her on the defensive, she was utterly determined to hold her ground with him this time.

Chapter Six

Lord Traherne's home in Berkeley Square was said to be splendid, but rumors did not do it justice, Venetia decided upon arriving. Elegant and regal, the gray stone mansion was surrounded by terraced gardens that rivaled the royal gardens at Kew.

The earl's butler did not seem disquieted by her concealing veil or insist that she give her name, but politely asked her to wait in the entry hall while he inquired if his lordship was receiving. Perhaps shrouded females visited here regularly.

To hide her nerves and pent-up frustration, Venetia focused her attention on the marble sculptures that graced the hall, trying to identify the artists. The paintings and gilt ceilings hinted at a more feminine touch, and she wondered how much Traherne's younger sister had contributed to the decorating. She had merely a passing acquaintance with the charming Lady Skye, and also with his vivacious younger cousin, Lady Katharine Wilde. Both were older than she by a few years, but she liked them very well.

When shortly Venetia was shown into what looked to be a study, she found Traherne seated at a large desk, writing. He had removed his coat and waistcoat and was informally garbed in cravat and shirtsleeves, which emphasized his broad shoulders and chest to perfection.

Her butterflies soared the moment he looked up and locked gazes with her. He was still one of the most impossibly attractive men she had ever met. His gold hair was tousled, though, as if he'd run his hand roughly through it more than once, while the cut on his cheek had scabbed over and was now surrounded by a dark purple bruise.

The reminder that he was only mortal and not some sort of Greek god served to bolster her determination. This time she would not accept defeat, Venetia vowed.

Schooling her emotions and crushing whatever sympathy she felt for his battered state, she began in a cool tone. "I am surprised to find you here, my lord. You seem to have forgotten our appointment."

Traherne frowned slightly at her declaration but took the time to sand his letter. He seemed distracted when he rose to greet her with a slight bow. "I did not forget, Miss Stratham. I was regrettably delayed."

"Indeed?" she replied, infusing a measure of derision into her voice.

"What brings you here? You could not have received my message so soon, since I just sent off the courier."

She eyed him in disbelief. "I intend to finish the discussion we began last night, of course. When you were tardy by more than an hour, I decided to come to you."

"I was on my way to Kensington when my curricle was run off the road."

She lifted a skeptical brow. Admittedly, his response surprised her. It was not the excuse she had expected—nor was she particularly inclined to believe him. "If you think you can fob off my concerns, you are gravely mistaken—"

"My groom was injured in the accident," he said. "Thankfully not seriously. My physician just left."

Traherne's further explanation took her aback. How could she take him to task if he had a legitimate reason for failing to appear this morning?

Venetia frowned behind her veil. "How do I know you are not just making up tales? Perhaps you were simply too craven to meet me."

His smile was dry. "I assure you, I would not fabricate an excuse that puts my driving skills in such a poor light. An accident of this magnitude only makes me look ham-fisted and inept. Moreover, I would never risk my horses' safety for the sake of assuaging a lady's sense of ill-usage—even one as lovely as you, Miss Stratham."

Venetia held her tongue as she realized the need to reformulate her approach. When she was silent, Traherne expounded.

"Last night I thought the miscreants might be targeting us both, but the incident this morning proved otherwise. You are not the instigator, either, I am convinced."

"Certainly I am not. But regardless of what delayed

your call this morning, you are avoiding the matter of my sister."

"Not intentionally."

"Either way, I would be naive to leave here until we come to terms."

"You are persistent, I will give you that." The slight smile in his voice irked her, even though he quickly followed with a declaration. "I swear to you, seducing your sister is the last thing I would ever contemplate, let alone act upon."

"You swore you would call on me this morning, and that never happened. Besides, a marriage could be nearly as painful to her as a seduction."

"I have no intention of marrying your sister," he stated curtly. "There, is that definitive enough for you?"

"Then why in the devil are you *courting* her?" Venetia exclaimed.

When he glanced at the open study door, she realized she had raised her voice to an unladylike degree. When he strode across the room toward the door, however, she divined his intent and protested. "Please do not close that."

"I presume you don't want our argument overheard by my servants."

"I don't. But I will not be shut in a room alone with you. Not after last night."

"*Now* who is being craven, darling?" he asked, a gleam of amusement in his eyes.

At his long, penetrating look, she found herself flushing. When she refrained from replying, he gave a faint sigh. "You might endeavor to trust me."

"Whyever should I? What have you ever done to deserve my trust?"

A muscle twitched in Traherne's cheek. "You have a point. If it will mollify your sense of propriety, we can take our discussion outside onto the terrace, in public view. That would be less compromising."

She was not concerned about her reputation being compromised—that horse had already bolted the barn two years ago with the scandal of her broken engagement. But the enforced intimacy would grant Traherne an advantage she could ill-afford, given her nonexistent ability to resist him.

When he opened the French doors, she willingly accompanied him out onto the stone terrace, which overlooked his beautiful gardens. Hints of bright color greeted her with the newly leafed trees and early spring flowers. Clearly an army of master gardeners had been hard at work, planting and pruning.

Renewing her vow not to let the earl under her skin, Venetia took a deep breath of the fresh air and turned to face him. "I have made a valiant effort to be reasonable, my lord, and I will try once more. A rake like you is simply not suitable for my sister. You proved that at Tavistock's last evening."

The sigh he gave this time was heavier and held exasperation. "There is only one problem, love. I was not at the club for the carnal sport, as I told you. Gaming was my only purpose. Edmund Lisle is in possession of a priceless necklace that I suspect once belonged to my mother, and I was seeking information about it."

Venetia listened with growing interest as Traherne explained about the shipwreck that had killed his parents, Lionel and Angelique Wilde, along with his distant Wilde relatives, Lord and Lady Beaufort, and his theory that the sunken treasure belonging to his mother's family had somehow been excavated.

"I have initiated inquiries," he concluded, "and sent an agent to the French coast to investigate, but have not yet received any reports. I am still no closer to locating the source of the pendant."

"How did you learn that Lisle had it?" Venetia asked curiously.

Traherne hesitated. "I saw it in the possession of Lady Dalton."

He paused a moment to let that revelation sink in, and when it did, Venetia's tone betrayed her amazement. "*Lady X* has your mother's jewelry?"

"Yes. Lisle gave her the pendant. For obvious reasons, he is reluctant to share any information with me."

"Very obvious," she murmured sardonically.

"Last night was my attempt to force Lisle's hand," Traherne added. "If he were indebted to me for a significant fortune, I could compel him to disclose what he knows."

Venetia shook her head at the irony. "Why didn't you tell me this last evening?"

"I am not one to air family secrets. And had I told you, would you have believed me?"

She gave him a rueful smile. "Probably not. You make it difficult for me to give you the benefit of the doubt."

"But now that I have told you, you can draw the same conclusions I did. It's possible Lisle fomented both attacks to prevent me from reclaiming the pendant."

Venetia considered Traherne for a long moment. "Do you know what I think, my lord? Your sins are coming home to roost."

His eyes narrowed. "What sins might those be?"

"Your debauchery, of course." Humor edged her voice as she couldn't help ragging him good-naturedly. "Doubtless it serves you right if a jealous lover set his thugs on you."

She thought Traherne might take offense, but instead, he smiled that slow, sensual smile that never failed to set her pulse racing. Seeing it, Venetia realized she had allowed him to steer her off track. "But all that really has nothing to do with my sister. If someone is bent on harming you, it could endanger her. And if not . . . Even if your quarrel with Mr. Lisle now is about the pendant and not over your former mistress, you are still very much a libertine and I won't let you hurt Ophelia."

"I repeat, I have no intention of hurting her."

"Perhaps you would not consciously mean to . . . and you may be enough of a gentleman to draw the line at seduction. But with your courtship, you are cruelly raising her expectations, if not actually toying with her affections. And now you say you don't even intend marriage . . . although to my mind, marriage would scarcely be preferable."

When he approached her, Venetia moved backward toward the terrace railing while trying to make her retreat appear casual. Halting his advance, Traherne crossed his arms over his chest and studied her with an air of fascination. "Why do you object so strenuously to my marrying your sister?"

"I want to save her from the heartbreak of having an unfaithful husband. Ophelia is far too vulnerable to a man such as yourself. I shudder to think if she ever came to love you . . ."

"You assume I could not be faithful."

Venetia hesitated. She wanted to be fair, and yet all the past evidence was not in his favor. "I suppose you *could,* but you wouldn't. You will only betray her, the way Ackland betrayed me."

"Actually, I wouldn't. I have more honor than that."

Her eyebrow rose dubiously. "Do you?"

He reacted to her cynicism with a soft chuckle. "I understand the concept of fidelity, sweeting. I don't share my women, and I myself exhibit exclusivity in my affairs."

The scoffing sound she made was half ridicule, half amusement. "Your particular brand of scruples fails to impress me."

"I shall try to do better," he said, stepping toward her again. Venetia was caught off guard when he lifted her veil.

"Don't presume too far, Traherne," she warned. She grasped his wrist, but failed to make him release the filmy black lace of her veil or back down even an inch.

"I want to see your beautiful eyes." He gazed at her steadily, his blue eyes holding a challenge. He was acting contrarily just to see her reaction, she knew very well.

Venetia gritted her teeth. "You have a knack for overstepping your bounds."

He smiled again, and her breath stopped. "True."

He was a provocative devil, but she would not allow him to put her off or distract her this time. Nor would she forget her earlier frustration with him. His charm allowed him to get away with every transgression short of murder, and even that might be possible were he to set his mind to it.

The trouble was, he took a final step closer and bent his head to kiss her.

Tasting the warm satin of his lips, Venetia wanted to curse. Over the past two years she had built up strong defenses, but Traherne was annihilating them once more. When in desperation she tore her mouth away and averted her head, he merely shifted his lips to the sensitive skin of her neck.

"This is exactly what I mean," she protested breathlessly. "You're a rake through and through."

"Guilty as charged."

He made her shiver with desire and excitement, damn him. And he was nuzzling her in broad view of anyone who happened to pass by. Venetia pressed her hands against his chest, irked that he was so careless with what remained of her shredded reputation.

"I can guess . . . what you are about," she rasped. "I've been branded a scarlet woman, so you think you can take advantage of me."

"Never," he murmured. "I am simply indulging in the supreme enjoyment of kissing you . . . and perhaps a little more . . ."

She was startled to feel the cool breeze on her lower limbs. He was raising her skirts, she realized with a thrilling sense of shock. When she managed to forcibly brush them down again, his fingers reached through the fabric at the front of her gown to press against her woman's mound, kindling an even greater excitement inside her.

"Lord *Traherne*!" Venetia exclaimed.

"You are familiar with the adage 'better to be hanged for a sheep than a lamb'? Since you accuse me at every turn of being a libertine, I might as well live up to my dissolute reputation."

The laughter in his tone vexed her as well as his nonchalance. He was trying to get a rise out of her, that was clear. Well, she would foil his plan and give back as good as she got.

Edging backward to elude his embrace, she reached into her reticule and drew out her pistol, aiming it directly at his chest.

When he froze for an instant at her unexpected gesture, Venetia felt mingled relief and triumph. "I brought a more lethal weapon this time, my lord. If I must suffer your company, I plainly need protection."

His genuine amusement was apparent. "You continue to surprise me, love."

When he advanced yet another step, crowding her against the railing, she waved the muzzle at him. "I'll thank you to keep your distance."

"Or what? You will shoot me?"

"I might, if you push me far enough."

He had the temerity to laugh. Venetia's fingers reflexively tightened on the stock. While he stood there, relaxed as ever, she debated whether to cock the hammer.

Of course he was in no danger, since she had not

bothered to prime the pistol with ball or powder. If he were to call her bluff, she would look like a fool. Indeed, she felt like a fool already.

Venetia exhaled a breath in self-disgust. She had let Traherne goad her into threatening to fire when she should have maintained control of her emotions. Normally she was calm and even-tempered, but this maddening man invariably brought out the very worst in her.

While she wavered and considered how to back down from her empty threat, his voice softened.

"I admire the courage of your convictions, Miss Stratham. I should have known better than to provoke you."

Now he was trying to appease her? It wouldn't work, Venetia pledged, even as he continued.

"I suppose it is time to come clean, sweeting. I am not paying court to your sister—"

"So you say."

"You are entirely correct that we are not at all suited. Ophelia is too young and mild-mannered for me. Even so, I am showing her attention, although not for the reasons you imagine."

"Then what *are* your reasons?"

"I am attempting to do a good deed and bring her into fashion with the ton."

His admission made no sense. "What on earth do you mean?"

"With me lending her countenance, she can attract admirers who *are* suitable."

Venetia eyed him narrowly. "Why would you trouble yourself?"

"To compensate in small measure for my actions during your betrothal."

She stared at him in confusion. She could not fully comprehend Traherne's motives, but his declaration took the wind out of her sails.

"You are playing matchmaker for Ophelia?" she asked uncertainly.

"Actually, my sister, Skye, and my cousin Kate are the matchmakers, and I am attempting to avoid their numerous matrimonial traps. But chiefly I am acting for your sake."

"Mine? I don't understand."

"I feel somewhat responsible for what happened to you two years ago."

"You actually feel responsible for my broken engagement?"

"For the scandal that resulted from your rift. Don't look so astonished. Had I not brought Ackland to the church in such a dissipated state, you might have ended your betrothal in a less public forum."

"I *am* astonished. Count me as shocked."

"It is not so shocking that I would want to protect you. You have no man to fill the role since you jilted Ackland and your father disowned you, so I can honorably step in now. You are the weaker sex, after all."

Venetia clenched her teeth at his bald claim, but then faltered. From the glimmer in his eyes, she understood his intent. He was deliberately riling her in that highly provocative way of his—and clearly enjoying it.

"I doubt you believe that women are weak," Venetia finally retorted. "I am acquainted with your sister and cousin, and from everything I have observed, you think very highly of them both."

He nodded thoughtfully. "The women in my family are not weak by any means, and I imagine you are their equal. Most ladies would have cowered in fright last evening instead of coming to my rescue. You threw yourself into the battle like an avenging angel—a very impressive feat."

She gave Traherne another deeply puzzled look. "So when I begged you to end your pursuit of Ophelia, you were simply being ornery by not telling me your plans and letting me think the worst of you?"

"Perhaps a little. As I said, I don't enjoy being extorted. You might aim your pistol elsewhere, darling. Being held at gunpoint is rather discomfiting."

"It is nothing more than you deserve," she muttered even as she let the muzzle fall so that it was pointing at the flagstone. "You should have told me last night what you were about."

"I found it much more pleasurable to ruffle your feathers and demand a kiss in exchange for my cooperation."

He was boasting of his underhanded tactic? Shaking her head in disbelief, Venetia couldn't hold back a reluctant chuckle. How did he manage to make her bristle in one breath, then laugh the next?

He shared her amusement, judging by the laughter in his blue eyes. A moment later, however, his expression changed. He was gazing over the railing at her back, she realized, as if something had caught his eye down in the gardens behind her.

Absently Venetia glanced over her shoulder and saw a figure below. One of the staff, she presumed, since he wore the Traherne livery and carried an implement like a shovel, raised to chest height.

By the time she returned her attention to Traherne, his face had darkened. Then suddenly he lunged at her and pulled her away from the railing. Spinning them both around so that *his* back was to the gardens, he pushed her down.

As she felt herself falling, Venetia gasped, too shocked to react otherwise. She was vaguely aware of the explosive retort in the distance. Then Traherne's body jerked and he gave a soft grunt.

Even though he tried to cushion the impact with his right arm and shoulder, she landed hard, the breath knocked out of her.

It took her a moment to regain her senses and realize that he'd thrown her to the stone floor, behind the terrace rail.

She was pinned partly beneath him, but she recovered more quickly than he did. "What in blazes are you doing?"

"Were you . . . hit?" he demanded in a rough pant.

"Hit? What do you mean?"

Gritting his teeth, he rolled to one side, relieving her of his weight. "That was a rifle shot I heard."

"That man below *shot* at us?" she repeated dumbly.

A surge of fear and fury flooded her veins. Without thinking, Venetia picked up her pistol and struggled to her feet. As she went to the terrace railing, Traherne tried to grasp her skirt but missed. "Keep your head down! The shooter could still be down there."

She started to aim her pistol, for what purpose she wasn't certain since her weapon wasn't loaded and she couldn't return fire.

"He must have fled," she muttered. "I don't see him any longer."

Turning around, she saw that Traherne had been slow to rise and had merely pushed himself up to a sitting position. He was holding his side at waist level, and blood was seeping through his fingers, she realized in horror.

"Dear God . . . were you *shot*?"

"I believe so."

Her shock deepened as a bright red stain spread farther across the pristine white of his shirt.

Alarmed by the sight, she knelt beside him. He was already pulling the tails of his shirt from his breeches in order to examine the extent of the damage.

A coarse gouge scored the fleshy part of his waist, just below his lowest rib.

"It is a flesh wound," he observed unsteadily. "Not life threatening. The bullet missed any bone."

"If you like, I could use your cravat to fashion a bandage until you can send for a doctor."

Wincing in obvious pain, he unwound his intricately tied cravat from around his neck, then gingerly lifted his shirt over his head.

As she watched, Venetia comprehended what had happened. She had been in the direct path of the bullet. Traherne must have seen the threat below and moved to shield her with his body, taking her place at the railing—

Just then she heard the sounds of running footsteps. An instant later several house servants swarmed onto the terrace to find her kneeling over their master, holding a pistol.

When they saw the earl bloodied and half-dressed,

shouts followed. Before Venetia could say a word in explanation, her pistol was seized and she was dragged to her feet by the arms and held prisoner by a mob of angry, loyal employees.

Her reflexive struggle to be set free was cut short when Traherne issued a sharp command to release her at once and return her pistol. "Miss Stratham was not the shooter. The real villain took aim from below and got away."

With skeptical looks on their faces, his servants did his bidding and freed her from restraint. Their conclusion that she had shot Lord Traherne was not surprising, Venetia thought as she stood there catching her breath from yet another shock and rubbing her bruised arms.

A gray-haired man she recognized as the butler hovered over the earl worriedly, but Traherne brushed off his concerns and waved away any help. "I will survive, Wilkins. The shooter is likely long gone, but I need you to organize a search party. Try to ascertain how he gained entry and where he might have gone when he fled."

"As you wish, my lord."

Venetia glanced over the railing. The rear gardens were surrounded by a high stone wall, she could see, but there must be numerous ways a gunman could have entered, including the rear drive and carriage house where the horses were stabled, and the service entrance where tradesmen delivered goods and produce for the household.

Yet the shooter was not her chief concern when Traherne was bleeding so profusely.

"You should also send for a surgeon," Venetia suggested worriedly. "You will likely need to have your wound poulticed or even stitched."

"My lord?" the butler asked, seeking permission to follow her advice.

"Yes, send for Dr. Biddowes," Traherne agreed. "He was just here, seeing to Giles."

One by one, the servants left the terrace. Venetia knelt beside Traherne again. He was pressing the cravat to his side; the white linen had turned crimson.

"You ought to go inside," she said, biting her lower lip in consternation. "Indeed, perhaps you should move to the kitchens so you don't ruin your elegant furnishings."

A wry smile twisted his lips. "A wise suggestion. My housekeeper would have apoplexy to find bloodstains all over my study."

With Venetia's help, he got to his feet. She collected his bloodied shirt, and since she wouldn't leave him injured, she accompanied him through the house, then below stairs to the kitchens.

A half-dozen servants looked aghast when their injured lord appeared in the domestic center of the household. Venetia felt on firmer ground there, however, and asked for linen towels and water for washing, lint for bandages, and a blanket to drape around his bare shoulders.

Then she led Traherne to the adjacent dining hall and instructed him to sit on the edge of a wooden table so she could inspect the gouge in his side. The staff looked on agog from the doorway—until he curtly issued a dismissal and sent them scurrying back to the kitchens.

Alone with Traherne, she carefully washed the drying blood from the skin surrounding the raw gash.

"Does it hurt badly?" she asked, feeling profound sympathy.

"Excruciatingly."

From his light tone, she realized he was exaggerating.

Before she could reply, though, an older woman bustled into the room, her expression fearful and angry all at once.

"Merciful heavens, I heard this . . . person shot you!"

"You heard incorrectly, Mrs. Pelfrey," Traherne replied. "The perpetrator was a prowler in the gardens. Miss Stratham, this is my housekeeper and sometime healer, Mrs. Pelfrey."

Seeing the pistol lying on the table beside him, the housekeeper ignored his introduction. "Why is she *armed,* my lord?"

His hesitation was barely noticeable. "She was carrying a weapon in self-defense because we were attacked last night—"

"Miss Stratham was with you in the alley last night?" Mrs. Pelfrey exclaimed, her surprise and disapproval evident.

Traherne started to reply, then cut himself off—apparently, Venetia guessed, because any attempts at explanation were just making the situation worse.

Mrs. Pelfrey also seemed to realize she had overstepped her bounds, for she changed her focus. "Forgive me, my lord. I am terribly worried for you. May I see the wound?"

"Yes."

When he lifted the towel, dismay claimed her features. The flow had stemmed significantly but the ragged flesh was still seeping blood.

"I fear this is beyond my skills to repair."

"I suspected as much. I had Wilkins summon Dr. Biddowes."

The housekeeper carefully probed awhile, her expression one of grave concern, but she kept throwing angry glances at Venetia.

Venetia, however, was inclined to forgive her since she was clearly acting out of protectiveness for her master.

When the woman made another sound of regret, Traherne stopped her. "Take heart, Mrs. Pelfrey. Of all my injuries, this is my first time being shot."

She sniffed. "This is *not* a jesting matter, my lord."

"There is no point in crying over it, either. My energies are best spent trying to find and stop the culprit before he can cause any more harm. Meanwhile, you should return to your other duties, Mrs. Pelfrey. Giles will be better off with you attending him."

"Poor Giles is sleeping now from the laudanum."

"I don't want you fretting over me."

"Well, if you are certain . . ."

"I am certain."

After giving an acknowledging curtsy, she sent Venetia another censorious look and then quit the dining room.

As he covered the wound again, Venetia heard his faint sigh. "It won't be long before half of London believes that you shot me."

Venetia frowned in agreement. "I suppose there is no hope for it."

His mouth curled. "I would have claimed that I discharged the pistol myself, but no one would believe I could be so clumsy, since I'm a crack shot. I doubt we can contain the damage to your reputation."

"I don't give a fig for my reputation just now. I am worried about you. Mrs. Pelfrey is right—you are taking this far too lightly."

"Not in the least. I simply prefer not to frighten my servants or let them think that a killer might be trying to put a period to my existence."

Perhaps he was right to understate the danger for his servants, Venetia decided. She was badly shaken herself.

Traherne shifted the subject to her skepticism. "Now do you believe that I was run off the road this morning?"

"Yes, I believe you." Venetia hesitated. "I suppose I must apologize for that. I practically accused you of lying."

"It was not the first time you have doubted my word of honor."

"No," she said in a small voice. "I should have trusted you more."

"Yes, you should have."

Looking away from the intent blue depths of his eyes, she leaned over him and gently touched his hand holding the towel in place. "I am so very sorry you were hurt."

Traherne's tone turned curious. "Why such distress? You were ready to shoot me yourself."

She glanced up ruefully. "I could not have done so. I never loaded my pistol."

His eyebrows rose. "It was unloaded?"

"Yes. When I decided to charge over here, I feared I might do you real harm. You are quite skilled at inciting me to mayhem."

He gave a bark of laughter and then winced at the jarring movement to his side.

"Actually," Venetia confessed, "I feel partly to blame." She was frankly appalled at the role she had played, and she felt guilty, even if she hadn't shot Traherne herself.

"Why would you be to blame?"

"You would not have been outside if not for me."

Traherne shrugged. "He would have likely found another vantage point for the shot."

"But perhaps you could have eluded the bullet if you hadn't moved to shield me." He had acted without thought for his own safety in order to protect her. "You might have saved my life by pushing me to the ground."

"Or I might have endangered you more." He looked grim. "It's possible I am being targeted by an assassin. If so, I have put you at risk."

"Who would want to kill you?"

"I have no bloody idea . . . unless it's Lisle."

"Does he despise you enough to *murder* you?"

"I would not have thought so before this. I am not well acquainted with him."

"It is fortunate you saw the threat in time to react. How did you know the shooter was carrying a rifle?"

"I saw the silhouette of a weapon—and after the two earlier incidents, I was watching for danger. A musket would not have that accuracy or range, no matter how skilled the marksman."

"I thought he was one of the gardeners carrying a shovel. He was dressed in your livery colors."

"They were the same colors but not my livery. I don't believe he was one of my staff, but he obviously went to some trouble to disguise himself in my colors, the better to blend in, I presume."

"Whoever he is, he should not be allowed to get away with attempted murder. He could have killed you!" Her angry tone held a note of fear.

"I'm uncertain if he wanted to kill me or scare me away—for what reason I can only guess. What galls most is that he had the temerity to invade my property. He was either superbly confident in his skills or desperate to complete his task."

"Well, whatever his motives, it was a heroic gesture on your part to save me from being wounded or worse."

Traherne's smile was entirely charming. "I'm not certain I can take credit for heroism. More likely it was sheer instinct. But I am happy to have something positive in my column to offset your many grievances against me."

"I haven't *that* many grievances against you. Only where it affects my sister's happiness."

He might have replied had his butler not made an appearance. "What is it, Wilkins?"

"We conducted a search as you ordered, my lord, but there was no sign of the intruder."

Traherne's grimness returned. "I expected as much."

"It is most likely he entered and fled through the east garden gate."

"From this point forward, I want all entrances

locked or guarded. And instruct the staff to be on the alert for strangers or suspicious behavior."

"As you wish. May I be of further service?"

"You may bring me the letter lying on my study desk, along with writing implements. I will finish it while awaiting Biddowes so you may courier it to Lord Hawkhurst in Kent. And have someone bring me a fresh shirt for when I am washed and bandaged."

Wilkins bowed and retreated, then returned a moment later. Since Traherne's hands were still bloodied, Venetia spent the next several minutes taking his dictation at the servants' dining table, explaining about the shooting and requesting Hawkhurst's immediate presence. When she was done, Wilkins carried the missive away to be dispatched.

"Lord Hawkhurst is your sister's husband, but why would you seek his advice?" she asked curiously. "Why not turn to Bow Street or some other authority familiar with murderers and cutthroats?"

"Hawk once worked for the Foreign Office and has experience with matters of this nature. And I want to keep this dilemma in the family for now."

"He has encountered possible assassins before?"

Traherne nodded. "More than once, from what I understand."

Venetia would have explored that intriguing comment, but shortly afterward Dr. Biddowes arrived. "Two incidents in one morning, my lord? Rather alarming, wouldn't you say?"

"You only need to stitch my wound, old friend."

"Let me examine you . . ."

He removed the blanket from Traherne's shoulders and proceeded to investigate the damage to his side.

The two men seemed to share a fond familiarity, but when the doctor took a long look at Venetia, his frowning scrutiny made her flush. He clearly recognized her—perhaps because of her scandalous past—and was not particularly happy to see her. "Is this the young lady who shot you?"

Traherne replied coolly. "You are mistaken, Biddy. She was not the culprit. A lady would not shoot her betrothed so shortly before the nuptials."

Venetia was certain she had misheard—until Biddowes's frown deepened and then turned to a slow grin. "I'll be damned. You are putting your neck in the parson's noose after all this time, Tray?"

"Yes." Traherne sent her an enigmatic glance. She couldn't read his expression, and his succeeding announcement made her gasp. "Miss Stratham and I are engaged to be married. The ceremony will take place tomorrow by special license."

Chapter Seven

The lie was so blatant, Venetia could give it no credence. "You have clearly taken leave of your senses, my lord."

Traherne cast a sideways glance at the doctor, who was engaged in removing medical instruments from a leather satchel. "Will you permit us a moment of privacy, Biddy?"

Biddowes did not seem happy to oblige. "I am short on time, Tray."

"Pray indulge me. It should not take long."

Venetia was unsurprised when Biddowes withdrew from the dining hall. Alone with the earl, she gave him a quelling look. "That was an outrageous falsehood."

"Not in the least. I wish to make you a formal offer of marriage."

Her gaze skewered him. "If this is your idea of a jest, it is in extremely poor taste."

"It is no jest."

"Then you must be mad."

Traherne chuckled without humor. "Desolated as I am to contradict you, it is simple logic. This affair will make your previous disgrace look like child's play. Shooting a peer is a criminal offense, far more serious than merely jilting one at the altar."

"So what of it?"

"Take a moment to consider. What do you think will happen to your sister's marriage prospects if you are mired in yet another scandal? You don't want her to suffer further, do you? If you want to save Ophelia, then you must marry me."

As comprehension dawned, Venetia sank weakly onto the bench. The shock of his words filled her with gut-wrenching dismay. "There must be some other way."

"I can think of no other. And I am not leaving you to face the wolves alone this time."

He was set on trying to protect her? She couldn't help but be grateful for his consideration, but she could not let him make such an enormous sacrifice. "You needn't actually marry me," she murmured. "A betrothal should suffice."

"Not given how spectacularly your last betrothal ended."

She glanced up at Traherne earnestly. "But I don't wish to marry you. And I am certain you don't wish to marry me."

He didn't try to conceal his look of irony. "Granted, I did not wake this morning expecting to offer for you. But we must make the best of a poor hand. Marriage to me is your only course if you don't want to put your sister at risk."

A nauseating, sinking feeling knotted Venetia's

stomach. As much as she wanted to protest, she realized that he was right. A fresh scandal loomed—one that would put her entirely beyond the pale of respectability and ensnare her sister with her. She would be convicted in the court of public opinion without even a trial.

A spurt of defiant anger surged through her. "It is absurd that an erroneous belief should force us to marry."

When she rose to face Traherne in a belligerent stance, he held up a bloodied hand in self-defense.

Venetia gave a start. She ought not take her anger out on him. This problem was not of his making. Indeed, he had acted valiantly to shield her from the shooter.

"You should not have to pay for my blunder. I was the one who drew my pistol on you."

"It makes no difference now."

Venetia shook her head in disagreement. "This is not even the time for discussion. You need to have the gash in your side sewn closed."

"I want your answer now."

"I cannot possibly give you an answer on so enormous a matter!"

"Suit yourself, but I am not budging until you agree to marry me tomorrow."

From the steely look in his eye, she had little doubt Traherne meant exactly what he said. Frustration and despair filled her anew at his ultimatum, even before he prodded her.

"Come now, love, you are delaying the good doctor's practice. Although young, Biddy is one of London's brightest physicians and is extremely busy. He only came to attend me so quickly because I recently donated a large sum to his new hospital."

Venetia nearly ground her teeth. She could simply refuse, but Traherne was likely willing to bleed to death before he gave in. And they could always argue about their alternatives later, after his injury received proper treatment.

"Very well, then, I will marry you."

"A wise choice."

"It is a demented choice," she muttered, pressing a hand to her queasy stomach as myriad emotions assaulted her.

"You may admit Biddy again," he said.

She stalked to the door, exasperated by Traherne's recklessness and the fact that he had so little regard for his own skin. To think that she had once envied his devil-may-care manner and even admired his audacity.

As she moved through the kitchens, Biddowes gave her a curious look but remained silent as he returned to his patient, accompanied by a footman, to aid with the surgery, she supposed.

Her stomach still churning with dread, worry, and guilt, Venetia paced the corridor outside, appalled that her options were so limited. It was unbelievable that her plan to save her sister from Traherne's courtship had only made matters infinitely worse.

And that was not even the gravest problem. Some vengeful gunman was apparently set on killing the earl. She was afraid for his life, even if she frequently felt the urge to throttle him herself. Astonishingly, Traherne aroused her own protective instincts to an extraordinary degree. She felt horrible that he had been shot while shielding her with his own body.

And no matter how shocked she was by his hasty proposal, intuitively she knew he was choosing the only honorable course for a gentleman—which disturbed her greatly. He had already risked his life for her. It also grated that she even needed his protection from society. Traherne did not seem pleased that his hand had been forced, either.

Venetia spent the next half hour stewing and fretting, alternately feeling defiant and totally helpless.

She was already under a cloud of disgrace; more infamy could not hurt her much. But her family was a different matter. She couldn't bear to bring them more pain. She just could not.

By the time Biddowes finally summoned her, she had managed to calm her warring sentiments enough to appear composed. Upon being allowed back in, she found the doctor cleaning the last of his instruments.

Traherne still sat on the table's edge, now with a linen bandage wrapped around his waist, wincing as he donned a pristine cambric shirt with care.

"I am ordering him to rest, Miss Stratham," Biddowes stated bluntly. "His skull is so thick, he believes himself to be invincible. It is the same recklessness he showed when we were lads."

"I am not taking to my bed, even if this blasted wound has left me weak as a kitten," Traherne declared, obviously frustrated by his condition. "My study will have to do. I have too much urgent correspondence to attend to."

"Then lie down on a sofa and dictate your letters,"

Biddowes instructed. "I don't want you breaking open my masterful stitches. You may experience dizziness and fatigue for several days. My willow bark tea should help with the pain. Be alert for signs of fever and have your bandage changed once per day and apply my poultice of flowers of sulphur. I will send 'round more in the morning. If the wound turns putrid, you could die."

"I understand," Traherne grumbled before gruffly thanking his friend with genuine appreciation.

He was able to walk under his own power, so Venetia gathered the writing implements and remained at his side as he retraced his steps through the house and returned to his study.

As he sank slowly onto a leather sofa, a low oath escaped his lips. "How can a simple gunshot be so bloody painful?"

The question only added to Venetia's guilt, but she inhaled a calming breath. "Before we begin writing messages, my lord, I hoped we could discuss this situation like reasonable adults and perhaps find a way out."

He shot her a sharp glance. "Oh, no, I won't let you withdraw from your promise, sweetheart."

"It was not a promise," Venetia objected. "It was a capitulation made under duress."

Traherne sighed. "You cannot back out now without again being seen as a jilt. Not after my announcement to Biddowes."

Her anxiety returned full strength. "Is that why you claimed we were betrothed? So you could force my hand?"

"In part. You should be gratified. You wished to

stop me from pursuing your sister. Our marriage will accomplish your goal in spades."

"But I never envisioned anything like *this*."

"Nor did I," he said with heavy irony. "You realize that if you refuse, you will undo all my noble efforts toward your sister."

Unconsciously Venetia resumed her pacing. "You should have told me of your plans to improve Ophelia's marital prospects from the first. Had I known, I never would have kept hounding you, and we would not be in this disastrous predicament."

"I started to tell you before you threatened me with your pistol and I was shot."

She bit her lip in contrition. "I have said several times how sorry I am."

"So you have. Just as I am sorry for what happened to you two years ago. I mean to make amends. I owe you that much."

"In other words, you feel pity for me. I do not want your pity, Lord Traherne."

"Don't get your back up, darling."

She took another deep breath. "I applaud your chivalry, truly. I am even grateful for it. But you know we would never suit. We could never love each other, and that is not even taking into account your . . . our differing values."

His eyes reflected a gleam of self-mockery. "And that is your chief objection to me? That you could never love me?"

"Among other things. I want love and loyalty and fidelity in marriage. I broke off with Ackland because our goals were vastly incompatible. Marrying you would be leaping from the frying pan into the fire."

"But you would have the protection of my name and title and my fortune at your command."

"Title and fortune are not good enough reasons to marry. If they had been, I would have wed Ackland two years ago."

"You are forgetting that the connection to me would be extremely advantageous for your family, especially your sister. As my countess, you could insure her own superior marriage."

Venetia started to retort, but fell silent. That was the rub. She couldn't forever condemn Ophelia to spinsterhood. She had to save her sister at all costs.

Traherne was correct. Marriage would solve both her immediate problems. She would prevent him from causing her sister untold heartache and avoid another massive scandal at the same time. Best of all, Ophelia might someday be able to wed for love rather than social necessity.

"Sit down, sweeting. You are giving my neck a crick with your prowling the floor."

At his wry command, Venetia sent Traherne a resentful look. "I cannot believe you are so unfazed by this debacle."

"I am hardly that. But there is a simple answer to your objections. We can have a modern marriage of convenience. Once the scandal is over and the danger from my unknown assailant has passed, we can go our separate ways."

That brought her up short. Venetia stared at him. "What do you mean?"

"Ours needn't be a real marriage."

"You are suggesting a union in name only?"

"Precisely. I will need an heir at some point, but

Skye's children can inherit my title. You would be free to return to France with Mrs. Newcomb at Season's end, assuming I catch the perpetrator. I'm not letting you out of my sight until I know you are safe."

"Are you serious?"

"Entirely."

For a long moment, Venetia scrutinized Traherne's handsome features, which held no clue as to his feelings about so momentous a decision. But he could not be as nonchalant as he appeared.

"How do I know you will uphold our bargain?" she finally asked.

"You will simply have to trust me."

In the past day she had gotten herself in big trouble by not trusting his word, Venetia reflected. It was time for her to change.

When she didn't answer immediately, Traherne went on. "Trust or no, we really have no choice. And I won't argue further with you."

She was doing enough arguing for the both of them. For another score of heartbeats, she mentally reviewed the evidence.

The last thing she wanted was to be locked in marriage to a Lothario, especially one as provoking as Traherne. She could not regret choosing to become an outcast two years ago rather than marry her philandering betrothed. She had weathered that scandal and could do so again. And yet this time the damage to her sister would be more monumental. Ophelia would be scorned and spurned, all because of Venetia.

Which was unthinkable.

No, her sister and parents had to take precedence over her own personal wishes.

At the inevitable conclusion, despondency nearly overwhelmed Venetia, but she forced herself to respond.

"Very well, then . . ." she said in a small voice. "I will marry you, Lord Traherne."

"Take heart, Venetia. It is not the end of the world."

There was a gentleness in his voice that surprised her. And when she returned his gaze intently, the blue eyes pierced her. She saw understanding and sympathy there, even tenderness. He must have guessed how distressed she was.

His reaction brought sudden tears to her eyes and a lump to her throat—which made her vexed at herself for showing such weakness.

Whether or not he was giving her a moment to compose herself, Traherne continued as if he had always known what her answer would be. "There is much to be done. I will first have to apply for a special license and arrange for a minister. As for wedding invitations, I have already sent for Hawk. Skye will likely accompany him, if I know her, but I must invite my cousin Katharine as well. My cousins Ash and Jack will be content with a simple announcement, but Kate would never forgive me if she could not attend my wedding."

Squaring her shoulders, Venetia made herself sit beside him on the sofa and start composing a list of immediate needs. She was not one to wallow in despair, or struggle against things she could not change, and this should be no exception. She needed to buck up and face her future with grace and dignity, even if her heart was still resisting vehemently.

It required every ounce of her willpower to join in the planning of her impending wedding, however. She still could not believe this was even happening. The moment seemed surreal, as if another person were inhabiting her body.

While Traherne mused aloud about two other of his closest relatives who would not be present tomorrow—his middle-aged uncle, Lord Cornelius Wilde, who had raised the Wilde orphans and was now enjoying recently wedded bliss in the country, and his aunt-by-marriage, Lady Isabella Wilde, who had returned to her home on a Mediterranean island—Venetia contemplated her own relatives.

"Perhaps I ought not tell my sister and parents of our marriage just yet," she said with renewed gloom. "They will see my actions as a betrayal."

"They won't understand that you are saving them. It is better to wait until our union is a fait accompli. I will send a notice to the papers to be printed the following day."

Venetia nodded. She badly wanted her family present at her wedding but knew they wouldn't deign to come. Ophelia would be unhappy at losing a splendid catch like Traherne and their parents would likely be enraged.

"I would like to invite my friend Mrs. Newcomb," Venetia said.

"Of course. In fact, you should send for her now, since you will be staying here for the night. You will need your friend to act as chaperone."

"Is that really necessary?"

"Yes. I am not letting you out of my sight until I am certain you will be safe. I can protect you better here. I have an army of servants on the lookout for the shooter. Don't fight me on this, darling. I would never forgive myself if you came to harm because of me." From his deadly serious tone, Venetia knew it was futile to protest.

"You should have a care for your own skin," she murmured. "You are the one in grave danger."

"But our villain may target you or my family to get to me. Have Mrs. Newcomb bring you an appropriate gown for the ceremony and enough clothing for an extended trip."

His instruction gave her a jolt. "What do you mean?"

"A wedding journey will provide us an excuse to absent ourselves from town."

Venetia's eyes widened. "You cannot have thought this through."

"It is the best strategy I can devise on short notice. We need to leave London for a while to let the scandal die down. It will also give me a chance to heal and permit Hawk to launch an investigation. We are too vulnerable here in London after three attacks in two days."

His mind had clearly been working while his wound was being stitched, but Venetia did not like where he was leading. "Would it not suffice for us to remain here while Lord Hawkhurst investigates?"

"No. Cowering and hiding away isn't my style, and if I were the only one at risk, I would stay to fight. But I have you and my family and servants to consider as well. Wounded, I make an easy mark. I cannot defend myself or anyone else when I am this weak and helpless. It is not a pleasant feeling, I assure you."

She could well understand how frustrating Traherne would find hiding, as he was a man accustomed to ruling his sphere. But he was not sitting by and doing nothing. Amazingly, he had already contrived the basic outline of a plan.

He also was obstinate about her accompanying him. When he stated outright that he was not leaving without her, for once Venetia made no protest. She would not abandon him now. Not when he was injured. Not when he was attempting to save her family.

"Where will we go?" she merely asked.

Traherne thought for a moment. "I have a minor property in Somerset, near Bath, that belonged to my father. Perhaps that would be the best choice, since few people even know about it. The less public my affairs, the better. I don't want to alert the assassin as to my whereabouts. Regardless, by this time tomorrow we should be on our way."

Evidently he saw the return of her distress, for that look of extreme tenderness returned to his features. Sitting upright, he leaned closer and reached up to cup her face. "It won't be as bad as you fear."

That is what I am afraid of. The unbidden thought unnerved her.

Traherne searched her face. "We should seal our engagement with a kiss."

Venetia drew back with a start. "Surely you cannot be thinking of kissing at a time like this."

"What better time? It will give you something else to think about and distract you from your despair."

Venetia bit back her next argument, realizing he was attempting to ease her dismay rather than bent on seduction.

He must have misunderstood her silence, for he smiled that provocative smile. "Have no fear. I am in no condition to ravish you."

His assertion brought a return of remorse. Venetia glanced at his shirtfront, behind which the bandage was concealed. "You said your wound was not serious."

"It isn't lethal, but pain dampens the amorous mood."

She arched an eyebrow. "Do you mean there is actually something that interferes with your randiness?"

He gave a short laugh. "I am rarely randy. I simply enjoy pleasure, which you will learn about me in time. But enough of the future. At present we have a dozen missives to compose."

Since it was unwise for Traherne to leave the house in his weakened state and give the shooter another opportunity to attack, he asked Hawkhurst to visit Doctors' Commons and apply for a special license. In addition to that and the invitations and announcements, he also wrote a letter to a gentleman in Portsmouth, saying he would be absent for a time and to proceed with testing.

By the time they finished their task and dispatched the messages through his butler, Venetia felt almost a sense of camaraderie with Traherne. Which was absurd. How could she feel the least bit sanguine about having to wed a scandalous nobleman and flee London to avoid a murderous assailant?

Traherne next summoned a disapproving Mrs. Pelfrey and gave his orders to show Miss Stratham to a room for the night.

Before Venetia took her leave with Mrs. Pelfrey, he rose from the sofa in order to kiss her hand. "Tomorrow you will make me the happiest of men."

At his ludicrous exaggeration, she gave what was nearly a snort. There he was again, trying to lighten her mood and make her feel better. An admirable gesture considering how wretched he himself must be feeling. He looked pale and weary, with lines of pain on his face.

Venetia made him promise that he would rest as Biddowes had ordered and left him with peculiar reluctance.

Upon being shown upstairs to an elegant guest bedchamber, she sank into a chair. In general she felt numb and incredulous, but deeper down, her feelings were a welter of confusion. Quinn Wilde, Earl of Traherne, was to become her husband tomorrow. It seemed impossible.

In point of fact, he would not be a real husband to her. They were preparing to orchestrate a deception on the ton with a sham marriage.

She was grateful, however, that he had readily offered her a practical solution. Although she might deplore his rakehell ways, he was making an enormous sacrifice for her sake. More astonishingly, he was willing to let her have an independent life. She could think of no other gentleman who would give up his own future in so heroic a gesture.

And while he could be infuriating, he had also displayed moments of extreme kindness and generosity.

She'd seen his protectiveness of his sister and cousin in the past, and now he wanted to extend his shield of protection to her. In years, no one but Cleo had cared enough to protect her, not even her own family.

Of course, marrying Traherne would be the end of whatever remaining dreams she might still have harbored about her own future. There would be nothing of substance to their relationship. He was offering her no promises, no illusions, no expectations of love or romance, or even physical relations. He had made no mention of sharing a nuptial bed. Even if she could picture him as her lover . . .

Abruptly Venetia shied away from the beguiling image. That way lay danger. It would be difficult enough to keep her attraction under control without dwelling on his superior skills as a lover.

As it was, Traherne not only filled her with frustration and vexation, but also excitement and arousal. More remarkable, a treacherous part of her actually wanted to wed him. It was madness, most certainly. She didn't want to admit her secret yearning even to herself, but some foolish part of her wanted to accept his proposal of marriage for its own sake.

She must be desperate or deranged or both. Cleo would surely think her insane for agreeing to wed Traherne.

She hoped Cleo could come soon. She badly needed her friend's support if not her counsel.

Meanwhile, the oddest bubble of hope was rising up inside her. The morning had ended in utter disaster, and yet . . . she couldn't help but feel strangely, inexplicably, foolishly optimistic.

* * *

Quinn ran a hand roughly through his hair as he returned to his invalid seat on the sofa. He was still dealing with the jolting shock of being shot and proposing marriage in the space of an hour.

The pain in his side, although throbbing, was not too agonizing, he decided. His discomfort came more from the realization that he—a dedicated bachelor— would be wearing chains of matrimony by this time tomorrow.

But he really had no choice. The savagery had already begun. His own congenial housekeeper and his friend Biddy had both leapt to the wrong conclusions. At the accusations against Venetia, a fierce protectiveness had welled up inside Quinn, and he'd made up his mind instantly. It was no more than his duty. She had been hurt too much already.

The irony was not lost on him, though. He'd spent the last decade avoiding serious entanglements, only to be forced to offer a hasty proposal to a beauty who disdained him.

In fact, he should be furious. He'd lost control of his future, when he'd vowed always to determine his own destiny, to govern his own fate. But remarkably, resignation more aptly described his present feelings.

Venetia had fought more against acknowledging the necessity of their union than he had. Quinn frowned as he remembered her expression—her chin locked in a position of pride when she declared she didn't want his pity. Her despairing protests had roused a long-repressed tenderness inside him.

He could actually understand, however, why this particular woman impacted him so profoundly. For one thing, Venetia had true courage. His opinion of her mettle had gone up another notch when she had been ready to charge after the gunman unarmed. She had long ago won his admiration, but she was facing this current turn of events with remarkable fortitude. How many women would make such a sacrifice for a sister, no matter how beloved?

Marrying her would not exactly be a hardship for him, either. She was the sort of bride he would have chosen had he wanted to wed. With her elegance and grace, she would easily fill the role of his countess, and with her intellect and passion, she would certainly never bore him.

She was also one of a few women besides his Wilde relatives who were willing to stand up to him. Nothing like the numerous husband-hunters who had thrown themselves at his head since he was out of short coats. Just the opposite, in fact. Which was highly refreshing. Moreover, Venetia had proved she valued character over wealth and so was unlikely to covet his fortune more than himself.

There were other points in her favor as well. Their raillery amused him, and he felt a palpable desire for her. She was spirited enough to challenge him. Indeed, she would be a constant challenge. Yet there was a sweetness beneath her tart exterior, a vulnerability that called to something deep inside him.

She would never be quietly biddable as Ophelia would have been, though. Her wit, her fire, her independence, her gumption, all had earned his respect. Initially he'd thought Ophelia might possess some of those same appealing qualities as Venetia, but he was mistaken on that score.

He was also aware that he'd created a dichotomy

by suggesting a marriage in name only. Usually when Wildes married, they mated for life.

And Venetia had said she wanted a husband who would love her. She deserved to be loved, to be cherished. But he was not that man.

For him, love was out of the question. He was not about to suffer the pangs and arrows of unrequited love as in his gullible youth. He would never make himself so vulnerable again.

From the time he had fallen victim to a fortune hunter, he had repressed his emotions in favor of cool, scientific logic. He wanted no intimate connections or commitments that would turn him into a helpless dupe.

Oh, he'd expected to wed eventually to gain an heir, but he wasn't certain he even wanted children, since emotional attachments would make him too vulnerable to pain. Perhaps because he had experienced death and loss at an early age, he was not eager to risk more.

Consequently, a marriage of convenience to Venetia seemed the answer. They could both walk away in the end with their hearts intact. Meanwhile, honor and obligation would be satisfied.

He would be uprooting her life in shocking fashion, true, but he would make certain to give her a far better one than she currently endured in exile. A life of wealth and privilege she deserved.

Issues about their future together could be resolved at some later time. For now his first priority was to keep Venetia safe from harm from both his potential assassin and the nearly as lethal knives of the ton.

Chapter Eight

Kate was the first to arrive at Berkeley Square. Despite her genuine worry about the danger Quinn faced, her reaction to his impending nuptials surprised him.

"Poor Miss Stratham," she murmured when she had quizzed him on his marriage proposal and wedding plans.

"Why 'poor Miss Stratham'?"

"It doesn't seem fair that she should be forced to marry you after all the turmoil she endured with her last betrothal. You must admit you will not make her an ideal husband."

He narrowed his gaze on his cousin. "Whatever happened to family loyalty?"

"Of course I am supremely loyal to you," Kate declared.

"I thought you would be pleased that I finally succumbed."

"Not like this. I am pleased you have the good sense to choose someone of her character, and I like her prodigiously. But a ceremony hastily cobbled together in this haphazard fashion? Ash and Jack and Uncle Cornelius won't be celebrating with you, either, as they should be."

"I explained why."

"I know. And a possible assassin is terrifying. But could you have offered her a more unromantic proposal?"

"Romance is not high on my list of priorities just now."

"It should be. I always hoped you would have much more than a marriage of convenience."

"Leave off, Kate. It is enough that I am tying the knot tomorrow."

"It is not enough, Quinn." The vivacious, auburn-haired beauty was the most passionately romantic of the five cousins and always led with her heart. "You know I only want your happiness."

"Aren't I the fortunate one," Quinn drawled cynically.

"Don't be snide. You deserve nothing less than a love match, just as most of our ancestors have enjoyed."

He understood her argument. He was a Wilde. Passion was in his blood, and so was love. He had generations of proof of his family's predilection for spectacular love matches. Love led to ardent marriages where devotion, admiration, and respect formed the foundation of unbreakable unions.

"You must try to woo Miss Stratham," Kate insisted. "Given your success with the ladies, it should not be difficult for you to win her love."

She clearly had no notion of his past history with

Venetia or the travails of his own amorous affairs. Wooing Venetia would be the height of folly, since even if it were possible to win her love, he couldn't return it. And he didn't want to hurt her further.

He would ensure that she never regretted taking this step, though. Her happiness would always come first with him. More, however, he could not pledge.

With effort, Quinn brought Kate's attention back to the dilemma at hand. When he insisted that she leave London for a time and join Skye at Hawkhurst Castle, she agreed with surprisingly little protest, which alone gave him cause for suspicion. Kate was rarely so amenable, and absenting herself so early in the Season was not something he expected of her.

"With luck it will only be for a week or two," he said.

She sighed. "Truly, I don't mind, Quinn. These past few weeks have been decidedly dull. Some fresh country air should do me good. It will be no hardship visiting there, especially if I can ride some of Hawk's magnificent horses and watch the new foals being born. Now, how may I help you for tomorrow? I presume you would like me to handle the details of the ceremony?"

With one hurdle down, he turned his attention to other wedding arrangements.

It was the mark of great trust that Hawk appeared an hour later, having already visited Doctors' Commons and secured a special license for Quinn to marry Miss Stratham. Since Skye would not be joining them until later that afternoon, Quinn decided this was an appropriate time to discuss plans with Hawk and invited Venetia to participate.

Hawk agreed it was best if the groom and his new bride disappeared for a time while he attempted to unearth the villain. "And you believe Edmund Lisle is the perpetrator?"

"He seems the most likely culprit. He may be cowardly enough to attack me covertly rather than confronting me to my face."

When Quinn explained the tangled web with his former mistress, Lady X, Hawk seemed amused upon learning that Lisle had given the pendant to her.

On her part, Venetia was trying hard to conceal the twitch of her lips, probably since she believed his sins were finally catching up to him.

Hawk already knew about the Wilde family tragedy at sea, and the possibility that their shipwreck had contained a sunken treasure. When he inquired about the status, Quinn showed Venetia drawings of the unique design of the collection commissioned for his mother's family.

"It was Hawk's colleague Beau Macklin whom I sent to southern France to investigate," Quinn told her. "Hawk, if you hear anything from Macky while I am away . . ."

Hawk nodded. "I will messenger you in Somerset at once. You may leave it to me. Now, however, I will arrange transportation to convey you there."

"I presumed we could take an unmarked carriage to insure we are not followed."

"You will need more than one. Never fear, my coachman is an expert at eluding pursuit."

Mrs. Cleo Newcomb was announced just then, so Venetia excused herself to receive her friend.

Quinn was glad that unlike his female relatives, Hawk didn't press him for personal details about his impending marriage. It was going to be a long enough day as it was.

As Venetia had predicted, Cleo strenuously objected to the nuptials. "I cannot believe you would willingly ally yourself with Traherne," she began.

"You needn't worry, Cleo. I am no longer the gullible young fool I once was."

Unable to convince her to withdraw, Cleo gave her a heart-to-heart talk, warning her about the marriage bed and trying to prepare her in more detail.

Venetia had very low expectations of her marriage. She was resolved to never fall for another rake. If she didn't give her heart, she couldn't be hurt again. In fact, if she didn't have hopes, she couldn't be disappointed. She was determined to put on a brave front and face the collapse of any remaining dreams she'd once harbored.

The trouble was, Traherne's sister, Skye, was as cheerfully optimistic about romance as Cleo was pessimistic. A delicate, almost ethereal beauty with pale gold hair, Lady Skye possessed the most charming manner imaginable.

"Kate wished to speak to you also, but we both thought you might feel overwhelmed if we ganged up on you, two against one. So I was elected to welcome you into the family. Truly, it is a pleasure to have you for my sister, Miss Stratham."

Taken aback by her warm reception, Venetia managed a grateful smile. "Thank you, Lady Skye."

"If we are to be family, you must call me Skye. I would imagine you have a million questions about my brother."

"A million and one, actually."

"Well, it is most important that you understand why he is so cynical."

"And why is that?"

"Because he has always been the target for ruthless husband-hunters, beginning when he was barely out of leading strings. It is not surprising that he would wed you to protect you, though. He is not quite the rake the world thinks him."

At Venetia's skeptical look, Skye went on. "Quinn has always been overly protective of the women in our family. Kate and I were young when we lost our parents. If not for having to help raise me, he would have traveled the world. I could not ask for a better brother, truly, but he has always been too smart for his own good and is easily bored. My uncle, Lord Cornelius Wilde, is a renowned scholar. Quinn shares his intellectual brilliance but never followed in his academic footsteps. He always had too much lust for danger and adventure."

Skye paused a moment to study Venetia's expression. "I was quite happy that he found his life's work recently. For nearly two years, Quinn has been holed away working feverishly on an invention—a design for a nautical steam engine that he claims will revolutionize sailing and save countless lives. You see, it is his own way of changing fate. If our parents' ship had been powered by steam, it would not have sunk."

The revelation about his cause surprised Venetia. Skye must have liked her response for she nodded sagely. "I am very glad Quinn plans to hide out for a time while he heals. If I know him, he's eager to hone his wits on uncovering a murderer. He made me promise to take refuge in my husband's castle, but I worry that he gives little thought for his own safety. Please, will you watch out for him while you are in Somerset?"

"I will do my best."

"Then I can rest easy. Now, if Kate or I can help you in any way, don't hesitate to ask. Doubtless this situation is supremely awkward for you, but we hope to remedy that by making you feel at home with us."

With such a warm welcome, Venetia was not surprised that the evening proceeded far better than she could have hoped. A congenial dinner was followed by music and lively conversation. Even Cleo unbent a little in the face of such determined charm on the part of the ladies Skye and Katharine.

Traherne worried Venetia, however, for she couldn't help noticing he was in pain.

He retired to bed earlier than the rest of the company. Seeing him leave the drawing room, she excused herself and went after him, caught up to him as he was climbing the stairs. "Do you need assistance changing your bandage, my lord?"

"Mrs. Pelfrey will tend to it."

"You needn't go through with this," Venetia offered.

He gave her an arch smile. "If you mean our nuptials, we have had this discussion already, and nothing has changed since then."

She spent much of the night tossing and turning and woke the next morning a bundle of nerves. As she dressed in a gown of pale green satin overlaid with white lace, her dark hair arranged in a braided coronet, Venetia couldn't help recalling her last fateful wedding day.

The ceremony this time was quite small and subdued compared to the lavish wedding at St George's in Hanover Square. When the minister began to recite the vows, Venetia felt her veins fill with ice. She still had difficulty crediting she was standing here plighting her troth to a man who was nearly a stranger.

Traherne's voice was deep and aristocratic and tinged with irony; when it was her turn to respond, Venetia found the words stuck in her dry throat. She was fighting panic—no doubt the same feeling every bride experienced.

Traherne gave her a long, level look and raised an eyebrow, as if to ask if she was thinking about bolting, which somehow had a calming effect.

Shortly after he offered her a brief kiss to seal the vows. His lips were cool and dispassionate but still searing. The contact distracted her until they signed the documents that finalized their union. When the minister addressed her as Lady Traherne, she realized she had just become a countess.

The next half hour went by in a blur and soon enough she was saying her farewells. Cleo took her aside from the others and hugged her fiercely.

"If you need anything at all . . . if you are the least

unhappy, send me word and I will come fetch you at once. If Traherne makes you miserable, I will shoot him myself."

Venetia forced a smile. "I am sure that won't be necessary."

In a few moments more, her new husband was handing her into a plain carriage hired by Lord Hawkhurst and Venetia girded herself for a long journey.

Chapter Nine

Thankfully their departure from London was un-
eventful. Before even leaving the city, they changed
vehicles once more at a busy posting house, which
reminded Venetia unpleasantly of the secretive nature of their flight. They set a rapid pace and har-
nessed fresh teams at regular intervals, since Traherne
wanted to make as much progress as possible. The
drive to Somerset could not be made in a single day,
so he planned to stay at a hostelry that evening.

Despite her anxiety over their improvised marriage
and the danger from his clandestine enemies, however, Venetia felt a curious sense of adventure. They
were in league together now, whether she liked it or
not.

Traherne proved more considerate than she expected, supplying hot bricks for her feet and a woolen
lap robe to ward off the unusually chill spring weather.
He seemed determined to ensure her comfort, yet
they left the vehicle only twice, to use the necessary
and obtain food and flasks of hot tea.

Venetia hadn't slept well the previous night, and by late afternoon weariness overtook her. When she began nodding off, Traherne drew her against his good side so that she could rest her head on his shoulder. "You should sleep."

"What about you?" she asked, raising her gaze to search his face for signs of pain. No doubt the unremitting buck and sway of the carriage was jostling his wound.

"I am fine."

"You don't look particularly fine. You are weary yourself."

"A bullet wound will achieve that."

Before she would let herself sleep, she used her lap robe to make a cushion for *his* head. Although Traherne could likely care for himself, she felt absurdly protective of him, perhaps because she was conscious of the debt she owed him for pushing her out of the path of a bullet.

When Traherne shook her gently awake sometime later, the interior of the carriage was dark. It took Venetia a moment to recognize the lack of motion and realize where she was.

Reflexively she flushed. She was draped against Traherne's strong body, enjoying his warmth.

"We will stop here at The Lion for the night," he murmured as he tenderly brushed back a tendril from her face.

Wincing, she sat up. He could be seductive without even trying, and she sincerely hoped he wouldn't try. When he escorted her inside, however, he raised her misgivings by engaging a single bedchamber.

"It will be safer if we remain together," he explained quietly as they followed the proprietor up the stairs. "I am armed to the teeth and am a light sleeper, so you are better off with me as your guard."

There was only one bed, Venetia noted, which meant they would have to share, unless Traherne volunteered to take the floor, which was unlikely, she suspected, nor could she possibly ask him to do so in his injured condition—

Realizing her scatterbrained thoughts were leaping ahead, she ordered herself to calm down. Her wedding night was looming, but she took consolation in Traherne's promise that they would have a marriage in name only.

They ate supper at a small table and afterward she rummaged in her valise, which Cleo had packed with clothing and books and art supplies, and drew out a novel to read.

Traherne occupied himself with studying a sheaf of documents he had brought with him. For a while, the silence was—remarkably—almost comfortable between them. Wounded, he seemed more approachable, not quite as imposing as the wealthy, powerful nobleman he actually was.

As the hour grew later, though, Venetia found herself growing tense. And when he put away his correspondence and rose from the table, her heart rate increased significantly.

Wanting to put off the moment of reckoning as long as possible, she offered to change his bandage. When Traherne agreed, she helped him remove his coat and waistcoat and then his shirt.

He had a magnificent body, she thought, watching the lamplight play on the wheat gold of his hair and the rippling muscles under his skin. The sight of him sitting there shirtless made her stomach curl with fresh nerves.

She concentrated on unwrapping his bandage and examining the wound. The ravaged skin had dried and tightened, she saw, but all in all it seemed to be healing. "The stitches do not look overly inflamed. Do they hurt?"

"It itches as much as it hurts. This morning Biddy sent me more of his special ointment. Will you apply some for me?"

She opened a jar of yellow paste and was met with a pleasant scent. When she spread a small amount on the wound, Traherne's features relaxed. She was supremely aware of his nearness and her own body's response to touching him.

When she was done, she wrapped a fresh strip of linen around his waist. While she washed her hands, he began taking off the rest of his clothes. Although she kept her back to him, Venetia felt her nerves skittering.

Several moments passed before he spoke again. "Come to bed, love. We both have had a long, tiring day."

She risked a glance over her shoulder at him and was very glad to see that he had donned a nightshirt.

"You should retire alone," she murmured. "I am not in the least sleepy after my nap in the carriage."

A hint of amusement glinting in his blue eyes, he gave her a pointed look, as if to ask, *Is that the real reason?*

He didn't challenge her prevarication, however, and only replied mildly, "You will be more comfortable if you take down your hair. Allow me to assist you."

"I can manage," Venetia hastened to say as he crossed to her side.

She removed the pins from her coronet and combed out the dark tresses with her fingers.

"You have lovely hair," Traherne remarked.

She shot him a quelling look and found herself caught in his gaze. Was he trying to steal away her wits? She wanted to appear sophisticated and unaffected, but with him watching her so intently, it was impossible.

"Do you need help changing your gown?" he prodded, evidently knowing she was dallying.

She shook herself from her enchantment. "Thank you, no." She found her nightdress but hesitated. "Will you put out the lamp first?"

"You needn't be missish with me. I have already viewed your charms."

He had kissed her breasts, he meant.

She felt herself flush, and yet she welcomed the teasing note in his voice. She liked it better when he was provoking her. Indeed, for her own self-protection, she wanted to keep their relationship adversarial so that she could resist him more easily. Yet maintaining their initial antagonism was much more difficult when one had to share a bed.

She waited until he put out the light before beginning to undress. The darkness enveloped them, relieved only by the flames from a lazy hearth fire. She heard the rustle of the bedcovers as he settled in the bed. Venetia felt her tension soar, knowing he expected her to join him. Eventually she climbed in be-

side him but turned her back to him and stayed as far
away as possible on the narrow mattress. Perversely,
the scent of him was alluring while his warmth surrounded her, and both were having an arousing effect
on her.

"Try to relax, love. You are as jittery as a feral cat."

"What did you expect? I have never slept with a
man before." She paused. "It feels strange being married to you, even if it is not a true marriage."

"Trust me, it feels strange to me as well." His voice
was dry with humor. "But I told you, you have nothing to fear from me."

"Why am I not reassured?"

"Because you attribute wickedness to my every motive, regardless of how innocent."

Venetia could not let his comment go unremarked.
"Just how innocent are your motives, Lord Traherne?"

"I am your husband now. Isn't it time we left off
such a formal method of address? My given name is
Quinn."

"Perhaps, but I prefer to use your title. And you are
not truly my husband."

He didn't argue the point, merely offered a different sort of rationale. "Lamentably, your ravishment
will have to wait. I am not in the best condition to
make love just now."

"That is a vast relief," she said honestly.

"You sound happy that I am in dire pain."

Dire pain? He was clearly exaggerating the extent
of his suffering.

"I think," Traherne added when she was silent, "I

deserve more sympathy from you. You said yourself, I was wounded while trying to shield you."

"Yes, and I am profoundly sorry for that."

"Your remorse warms my heart."

The laughter in his tone made her aware how he was playing on her guilt.

"It is small wonder that someone wants to hurt you," Venetia observed. "You are positively aggravating."

"How can you be so heartless after I was shot in your defense?"

Opening her eyes, Venetia almost rolled them at the dark ceiling. "Must you remind me at every turn? You enjoy making me grovel, don't you?"

"What I enjoy is changing your poor opinion of me."

"That would be impossible."

"You were frightened for me yesterday, admit it."

"It was the stress of the moment."

"Is that all?"

"Of course I felt compassion for you, as I would for any wounded creature, but I should never have given in to your extortion."

"Extortion? That is a case of the teapot calling the kettle black. You initiated the tactic at Tavistock's, if I recall."

Just then Traherne reached out his hand and drew his fingers gently down her spine. Venetia shivered with unexpected longing. "I'll thank you to keep your hands to yourself, my lord."

"As you wish."

His hand fell away, and Venetia was conscious of an infuriating feeling of disappointment. At the same time, she felt the strangest sense of regret. This was nothing like the wedding night she had once imagined. She had expected to love her husband and give herself joyously. She'd hoped for sweet words and whispered secrets and expressions of undying affection and devotion. Not this sparring exchange.

She closed her eyes and willed sleep to come, but failed utterly. There was something too intimate about sleeping while Traherne was awake. It made her too vulnerable. She was excruciatingly aware of her own body and the heat building inside her.

Apparently he was having as much trouble sleeping, for although she listened for the sound of his even breathing, it never came.

When she shifted her position restlessly for the fourth time, he sighed softly. Then he started to speak gently.

"Venetia, love, I have promised to keep you safe. That means from myself as well. I am not the sort of man to attack virgins, in any case. And I have never in my life hurt a woman or taken one against her will."

Venetia felt the tension ease inside her fractionally. She knew enough about Traherne to believe his claim. Whatever his vices, he would never hurt her, at least not physically.

Despite his reassurance, however, it was a long, long while before she fell asleep.

Quinn lay awake for much longer. His own body was on fire, and not just from his bullet wound.

No doubt it was a mistake to share a bed with Venetia. He had always lusted after her, and her proximity was trying his forbearance to the limit.

Amusing, really, that he finally had her in his bed but couldn't honorably do a damned thing about it.

Far less amusing, however, were all the conflicting urges warring inside him.

One was Venetia's response to him tonight. Her rebuff had pricked his pride, yes. Rejection was a first for him, since women usually craved his touch, but her skittishness downright offended him. He had never had a woman fear him, especially since he gave his lovers only deep pleasure.

Another was his own inexplicable response to their nuptials and the vows they had taken just this morning. Venetia had made a stunning bride—elegant, graceful, beyond lovely. *Your wife now,* Quinn reminded himself.

The acknowledgment roused a powerful possessiveness inside him.

A possessiveness he didn't want to feel.

It hadn't helped that in the firelight tonight, she had looked perfectly enchanting. Her skin glowed with a luminous quality, while her enormous eyes drew him in with their limitless depths. And her hair . . . long, lustrous, dark. He could easily fantasize about those silken strands skimming over his skin as she bent over him and used her satin lips to bring him to climax.

Regrettably, for now the picture would remain strictly a fantasy.

It was also odd how the most desirable woman he had ever encountered was also totally inexperienced.

Venetia's innocence was endearing, perhaps because he was unaccustomed to consorting with virgins.

Lying next to her barely clad form now, Quinn felt the same rush of hunger he'd felt at first kissing her at Tavistock's, only this was even more forceful. He could readily imagine what lay beneath her nightdress . . . the luscious body, the ripe breasts, the long slender limbs.

He wanted Venetia badly, more than any woman he'd ever known.

Yet his strongest urge had nothing to do with the physical. Most of all, he wanted to win her trust. A challenge that would be difficult at best.

And his strongest internal conflict had everything to do with his own past. Venetia not only stirred his blood but aroused long dormant emotions inside him—excitement, fascination, anticipation, to name a few. Emotions that he had worked hard to crush over the past decade and ardently wanted to repress now.

His most dangerous feeling, though, was *enjoyment*. Even in pain, he was finding unreasonable pleasure in her mere presence and even more pleasure in their verbal battles. Quinn very well knew he needed to keep his distance from Venetia, and he'd thought riling her was one way to do it. But deplorably, their sparring was like an aphrodisiac for him.

Trying to ignore the sleeping beauty beside him, he gingerly shifted his position to lie on his back and shut his eyes while preparing to endure a long night.

It would be damned hard to sleep with the aches in his side and loins, and keeping his feelings for Venetia under strict control might prove futile.

* * *

Venetia woke to the most enchanting sensations. Warmth. Contentment. Sweet arousal. She had been lost in a captivating dream. Traherne was kissing her, making exquisite love to her. . . .

Her eyes fluttering open, she recognized the inn bedchamber. It was early morning, with golden rays of sunlight filtering beneath the window curtains.

Behind her, Traherne lay unmoving, his front cradling her back beneath the covers, one arm draped casually across her waist. From his slow, even breathing she thought he was still asleep, but his body was hot enough to stoke a furnace.

Or perhaps the heat came from *her*. Her derriere was snuggled against his loins, her softer curves pressing against his hardness.

She knew enough about sexual relations to realize that he was fully aroused, even in his sleep. His desire was instinctual, of course, the result of primal nature, but Venetia couldn't help relishing the sinful thrill of being captured against his muscular male form.

Then again, savoring his embrace wouldn't be sinful if they were truly man and wife.

A strange longing swept over her. For a moment she found herself wishing this was their nuptial bed.

She let her eyes drift shut, pretending for now that Traherne was her husband in more than name. Amazing how the fantasy made such a vast difference in her feelings toward him. She would have no thought of resistance. Instead she would surrender willingly. Better yet, she would turn over and slowly kiss Traherne awake. If he were hers, she would embrace the role as his wife and lover and respond with every ounce of ardor she possessed. . . .

The rush of longing increased. She was quiveringly aware of him, enveloped as she was in his warmth and scent.

When she felt the slightest shift in his position, Venetia went very still. Traherne had awakened, she realized.

In another heartbeat, his hand began lightly stroking her belly through the thin cambric of her nightdress. His lips were very near to her ear. As she debated how to respond, he pressed even closer to nuzzle her hair with his face, burrowing deeper. His mouth was warm, his breath moist at her nape.

When his hand shifted slowly upward to cup her breast, her pulse spiked. His palm molded to the curve of her breast, massaging gently in a slow, languid motion that was unbelievably sensual.

She ought to stop his caresses, Venetia knew. She had no business indulging in fantasies when she desperately needed to keep her defenses strong. But she didn't want this wonderful intimacy to end. Not just yet.

Heat swelled inside her as he discovered her nipple beneath her bodice. His long fingers gently squeezed the peak, making her arch reflexively into his palm.

He must have taken that as an invitation to proceed, for soon his hand glided downward, sliding over her rib cage, his fingers burning her thigh. . . .

"Traherne . . ." she murmured.

"My name is Quinn, love," he urged, his voice rusty and low.

She couldn't reply, not when this breathless languor

had overtaken her and sapped all her willpower. Her body tingled, while her feminine center throbbed with warm yearning. His touch was magical, his strong fingers stroking delicately over her bare skin where the skirt of her nightdress had ridden up.

Her eyes remained closed as she rode a dreamy wave of pleasure. When he raised the hem farther and covered the soft mound of hair at the juncture of her thighs, she gave a shuddering exhalation and grasped at his forearm to stay him.

Despite her response, though, his fingers went on sliding over her already slick flesh, probing her moist secrets with a deliberate pressure. At the same time his knee pushed hers apart from behind, exposing her further to his caresses.

Venetia abandoned any thought of protest. Instead, her senses feasted on the shivering sensations he was stirring in her. She forgot everything else but the erotic feel of his ministrations, forgot even how to breathe. Her body quivered, pleasure racing through her veins.

Then he slipped one finger inside her cleft and fire sparked in her. Venetia gasped softly as another shudder rippled through her limbs.

A second finger joined the first, opening her a little wider. The feeling of his penetration was indescribably glorious. She felt herself melting.

His thumb rubbed the nub of her sex in a repetitive glide while his finger teased her, moving in and out, lingering and withdrawing from her weeping flesh. Of their own volition, her hips strained wantonly to get closer as the coiling tension grew. The gossamer friction was a delectable torture. Her fingers clutched at his arm as her body grew tighter, hotter. The pleasure built and built with his gentle thrusts.

Her hands fisted in the covers and she heard her own shallow, ragged pants as he brought her to the peak of arousal. Suddenly, she could bear it no longer.

Venetia gave a soft cry and shattered. For a dozen heartbeats she shook and pulsed with sweet spasms.

His attentions left her weak and dazed for a long while. The soft caress of his breath stirred wisps of hair at her temple as she lay cradled in his arms, wondering at the novelty of passion.

His voice was low, intimate, when he finally spoke. "Did you find that pleasurable, sweeting?"

She couldn't utter a denial for it would be a lie. The explosive fire had been exquisite, better than she could ever have imagined.

"You know I did," Venetia eventually managed to say, her voice a hoarse rasp.

"There is far more I want to show you."

"That would be extremely unwise."

With a light touch on her shoulder, Traherne rolled her toward him, so that she lay on her back, gazing up at him. "Not at all."

He stroked her cheek with a finger. In the pale morning light, with his gold hair ruffled and a shadow of stubble roughening his jaw, he looked very male and oh, so sensual.

His eyes had darkened to sea blue. She saw lust there and desire and unmistakable need. His palm cradled her face with infinite tenderness.

"Kiss me, sweet Venetia . . ."

She wanted desperately to obey. Venetia watched, spellbound, as he bent toward her.

His breath fanned warm against her lips before his mouth settled on hers. Another heated rush of feeling assaulted her. His kiss was languid but took her breath away.

She tangled her fingers in his gilded hair as his teeth nipped at her lips. When he increased the pressure and kissed her more deeply, she opened to his exploration. His tongue penetrated her lips in an intimate invasion, meeting hers, playing in a leisurely dance, coaxing, enchanting her again. She was thoroughly bewitched when, to her surprise, his mouth left hers.

However, his attentions had only moved lower, his lips brushing over the column of her throat, her bare collarbone, the cambric covering her breasts, her belly . . . as if driven to explore further.

He paused briefly at the apex of her bare thighs. Venetia stiffened at the shocking realization that he planned to kiss her there at her center.

When he parted her curls with his tongue, she gasped at the blatant carnality of it.

His tongue stroked her gently, probing her folds. And then he drew her swollen flesh between his lips.

A soft moan escaped her at the unbelievable things he was doing with his mouth. The sensations were incredible. His mouth moved on her, slow and erotic and extremely thorough. He was driving her mad with his caresses. Yet it was his tenderness that stunned her most. She had never felt anything like this captivating man's assault on her senses.

An aching torment rose inside her, burning through her body. When he sucked more powerfully on the sensitive nubbin, she jerked, lifting her hips halfway off the blanket.

His hands moved to her thighs to hold her down. "Be still, darling. Let me taste you. . . ."

The soft command was a reminder of her shattered willpower. As her head shifted feverishly back and forth on the pillow, she could feel him reveling in her body's heated response.

Forcing her eyes open, she glanced down to see Traherne's golden head between her thighs. She was giving him far too much power, Venetia knew. She was already a melted puddle of desire. If she let him continue, she would surrender completely.

Her hands blindly found his shoulders. "Enough . . ." she rasped. "Please . . ."

For a moment he continued his brazen ministrations, until her voice grew stronger.

"Quinn!"

At her plea, he left off and raised his head to look at her. For a moment he remained still, poised above her. But then he gave an almost imperceptible sigh and shifted his weight.

He settled on his side again so that he lay watching her.

Venetia rolled over to face him. She had a greater chance of fending off his advances that way—and more control over her own traitorous desires. He was undeniably wicked, and he made her long to be wicked with him.

When Traherne reached out his hand as if to touch her, she flinched and instinctively drew her knees up in a defensive posture. When she contacted his body accidently, he flinched as well and shut his eyes in obvious pain, his breath hissing through his teeth.

Instantly repentant, Venetia issued a sincere apology. "Oh, did I hurt your wound? I am so very sorry!"

"Not my wound," he rasped, gritting his teeth. "Just my loins."

Easing back, she glanced down and saw his swollen manhood thrusting out below the hem of his nightshirt. His member was long and thick—much larger and darker than she thought it would be.

Her gaze fixed on his hard male flesh; she bit her lip. "I did not mean to hurt you."

"I believe you. Give me a moment and I will recover from the blow, if not from my hunger."

Her mouth turned down in puzzlement. "Hunger?"

"For you."

Her gaze rose again to his face. "Your randiness, you mean. Cleo says randiness is in a man's base nature."

"Cleo says?"

"My friend Mrs. Newcomb."

"I know who Cleo is. I am merely curious about her perspective."

Venetia made a face. "My mother never saw fit to explain to me what happened in the marriage bed, so I have had to rely on Cleo for my education. She has told me a great deal about carnal relationships."

"Is that so?" He sounded amused.

She felt rather indignant that Traherne was ragging her on so intimate a subject. "Forgive me, your lordship, if I am not as sophisticated as your other lovers."

"Easy, love. I did not mean to prick your sensibilities. You know much more than is typical of a young English lady."

"I have studied male anatomy for my art. We drew and sculpted nudes in class."

"Indeed?" His eyebrow rose.

"The French are much more liberal than the English and more accepting of women artists."

"But art is different from real life."

"Clearly. You are . . . much larger than I expected."

"What did you expect?"

Realizing that he had noted her intent scrutiny, Venetia felt herself blushing wildly, which was absurd, given the carnal intimacies they had just shared. "I don't know exactly. I have little firsthand knowledge."

"Your innocence is appealing."

Both of her eyebrows lifted. "To a man as experienced as you? You astonish me. Given all your numerous lovers, I should think you would prefer skill."

His mouth curved. "You vastly overestimate my promiscuity."

"Do I?"

"Yes, and you vastly underrate your appeal."

"I hardly think so. You don't want me specifically."

Traherne gave a pained laugh. "Of course I want you. I would have to be dead not to want you."

"What I *meant* was that you would lust after any woman. I am not so special."

"You are wrong. You are very special. And I want you very badly."

Venetia stifled the wistful longing that coursed through her and replied with a laugh. "Flattery comes as naturally to you as breathing, doesn't it. You use pretty words as tools of seduction."

"My desire is not mere flattery. Male arousal may be a natural reaction to sleeping with a beautiful woman, but that doesn't explain the intensity of what I feel for you. Shall I show you how much I want you?"

At his provocative question, her heart leapt in her chest. The absurd thing was, she wanted Traherne to want her. How contrary was that? Perhaps it was womanly pride, or perhaps it was much more personal.

She shied away from that rebellious thought and swallowed against the sudden dryness in her throat.

When she remained silent, he gave a faint smile. "I know you want me, too."

"I do not," she lied.

"Your body says differently. Your breasts are swollen. Your nipples are puckered. . . ." He raised a finger to brush her throat. "Your pulse is very rapid. See? You shiver at my slightest touch. You can't honestly say you don't want me."

No, not honestly, Venetia reflected. She was keenly aroused, she admitted.

Traherne was still thoroughly aroused as well. His voice was husky and low when he pressed her. "You feel heat at your core. That is sexual craving, my love."

He shifted his hand to touch her mouth with his fingertips. The sensuality in even that light contact was like a lightning bolt, but it was his gaze that had the greater impact. She stared into his eyes and felt herself being drawn in.

He was mesmerizing her again, she realized to her dismay.

Inhaling sharply, Venetia visibly pulled back from the spell that held her, and forcibly steeled herself. His confidence was intimidating, and she very much disliked feeling intimidated. Even more, she despised feeling defensive and powerless.

Venetia took a deep breath. It was time she turned the tables on Traherne. She wanted to be his equal, not a victim of his skilled seduction. Somehow she had to prove that she could stand up to him, or he would forever use his knowledge of her weaknesses to trample all over her.

"I understand," she said slowly, "that unrelieved arousal is extremely painful for a man, but I don't want to worsen your injury or increase the pain of your wound."

Surprise lit his eyes. "I could manage if I lie on my back and if we are slow and careful. If you were to straddle me, I could show you how to move."

"That was not quite what I had in mind." Her heart thudding in her chest, she reached down to cradle his shaft in her fingers. "I imagined something more like this. . . ."

She had an instant to savor his shock as he drew a ragged breath. "So you mean to service me with your hand?" he asked rather hoarsely.

"That is my general plan. You said you were in pain. I am willing to provide a cure for your lust."

She had caught him off guard, but his body obviously welcomed her fondling. While she stared, his stiff erection stirred eagerly between his thighs and thrust against her palm.

When brazenly she began to stroke his swollen flesh, Traherne clenched his jaw, yet amusement tinged his tone. "I should have expected you to act in so novel a fashion. Let me guess. Cleo told you how to proceed."

"Well, yes. She wanted me to be prepared for the marriage bed and warned me how painful it could be. Therefore, she advised me how to expend your sexual urges so I would not have to submit to you."

Some of his humor faded. "Your friend does not think much of men, does she?"

"No, not much. Her marriage was sheer misery. It was how she dealt with her husband so that he would leave her alone."

"And you mean to follow her strategy."

"It seems sage to. If I assuage your carnal needs, you won't want me."

There was more than a touch of irony in his muttered reply. "It would take too long to disabuse you of that daft notion." In a louder voice, Traherne made an observation. "Cleo's wretched experience is regrettable, but she has given you a warped perspective. You would find great pleasure in my lovemaking. I would make certain of it."

Venetia hesitated. "Thank you, but I am not inclined to test your claim."

"So that leaves us at an impasse."

Grasping her wrist, he drew her hand away from his loins. "I cannot believe I am saying this, but tempting as it is, I must decline your sacrificial offer."

Venetia blinked in disbelief. "But why?"

"First of all, there is a great deal more to lovemaking than climaxing. But more important, I am not interested in pleasure if it is one-sided. If there's to be any lovemaking, we both need to enjoy it. Until then I will suffer in silence."

Rolling gingerly onto his back in deference to his injured side, Traherne threw off the covers, then rose from the bed. "We need to be on our way if we are to make our destination by midday."

Surprise flooded her, followed swiftly by disappointment. She was also strangely disgruntled that he had not allowed her to regain some small measure of power.

Before she could respond, though, he delivered another declaration. "Rest assured, Venetia, when we make love, the pleasure will be wholly mutual and reciprocal."

When, not *if,* he had said, Venetia realized.

Frowning, she followed suit and rose from the bed in order to wash and dress. Traherne was far, far too confident for her peace of mind.

Chapter Ten

As they traveled the final few hours, Venetia took great care to stay on the opposite side of the carriage and avoid Traherne's touch, but the taste of passion he'd given her was impossible to forget. She could still feel the heat of him pressed against her back, his hand caressing her breast, his mouth moving on her sex.

When we make love . . .

She shook herself roughly. They would be thrown together for heaven knew how long, so she had best control her traitorous urges.

Fortunately, Traherne took it upon himself to tell her about this area of Somerset south of Bath, which had been famous since Roman times for its warm mineral springs and where the ton flocked to bathe and drink the waters.

"The cottage where we will be staying has a hot springs welling up from the ground. Biddy approved my coming here because of its healing properties."

Venetia viewed the attractive landscape with interest. The charming villages they passed boasted thatched cottages and stone houses interspersed with woodlands and orchards and rolling meadows full of grazing sheep and cattle.

Around midday, they drove through a wide gate. Eventually the wooded grounds gave way to more manicured lawns. On a rise overlooking an ornamental lake stood an enormous Tudor manor with gabled roof and mullioned windows.

"The estate has been rented out for years," Traherne informed her, "but the family doesn't make use of the cottage."

"Why not?"

Traherne hesitated a moment before his mouth curved. "Because of its history. One of my Wilde ancestors built the cottage for his mistress."

Venetia didn't know whether to laugh or to wince. "You are taking me to your love nest?"

"Not *my* love nest. I have never occupied it before. I inherited the property from my father."

She couldn't help but rag him. "So your father brought his ladybirds here?"

"Not that I'm aware of. Certainly not once he met my mother. The current tenants are responsible for the upkeep. I wrote them two days ago and asked that the cottage be made ready for our arrival."

He opened the small panel and conferred with the coachman as to the direction. They drove for another ten minutes, around the lake, to a more hilly area.

At the end of a secluded lane, they drew up before a large stone house surrounded by a lovely walled garden.

"You call this a cottage?" Venetia said. "It is large enough for a mansion."

"It should prove comfortable enough for a week or two. I wanted to make up for putting you in this unfortunate position."

"Oh," Venetia said lightly, "you mean compelling me to marry you and flee London for a life on the run, in danger of being shot at any moment?"

Traherne flashed his most disarming smile. "Yes, that unfortunate position."

Concern for him welled in her anew. "Is it safe for you to stay here, do you think?"

"I believe so. Few people know about this property. My father certainly never advertised his ownership. An elderly couple serves as caretakers of the cottage. No doubt they will hire extra servants from the village if necessary. I trust they have at least cleaned it by now and made it presentable."

As predicted, when they dismounted from the chaise and made their way inside, several staff of varying ages lined up in the entryway to welcome them. The eldest man and woman identified themselves as Horton and Mrs. Horton. There was also a newly hired chambermaid, houseboy, and ruddy-faced cook.

They all seemed in awe to be serving an earl and his lady, for they bowed and scraped to the point of discomfiting Venetia.

Mrs. Horton seemed particularly nervous and eager to please. "Pray forgive the musty smell, my lady. We only removed the holland covers yesterday."

Venetia smiled to put the housekeeper at ease. "It is

quite all right, Mrs. Horton. You were just informed we planned to descend upon you abruptly."

"Thank you, my lady. We have arranged for a cold luncheon and a hot supper, if that is acceptable," Mrs. Horton added.

"Yes, of course."

It felt odd to be addressed as "my lady" and be asked to approve the menu. Venetia glanced at Traherne, who was watching her with a glint in his eye, as if wondering how she would handle her new role.

When they toured the house, she noted the luxurious appointments and gilt furnishings done in expensive velvets and brocades. She was very glad to know they would have separate bedchambers. Perhaps newlyweds should share a bed, but the aristocratic class often slept apart, which suited her perfectly.

Traherne left her to change out of her travel gown and wash. When she joined him in the small dining room a half hour later, he rose to hold out her chair for her.

"I trust the accommodations meet with your approval," he said lightly as he seated himself beside her.

"I did not expect such elegance for a house of ill-repute. Apparently your ancestor spared no expense for his *cher amie*."

"It was designed as a bower of bliss."

"But a gold chamber pot is rather extravagant, don't you think?"

"We Wildes rarely do anything by half measures."

They were interrupted just then by servants who carried in platters of ham and cold duck, with cheese and fruit for a second course.

Alone with Traherne once more, Venetia returned to the earlier conversation. "I am surprised the Hortons were able to hire a staff on such short notice."

"Wealth has its advantages."

"Evidently. It feels rather awkward, however, being addressed as 'my lady.' "

"You will grow accustomed to being my countess in time. You aren't living in exile any longer."

Venetia arched an eyebrow and gestured with her hand at their surroundings. "What do you call this if not exile?"

"Hopefully Hawk can track down information on my mysterious assassin and our time here will be short-lived."

She shuddered at the reminder.

Seeing her gesture, Traherne frowned. "I have not yet properly apologized for putting you in danger."

"I suppose it was not strictly your fault that I was caught in the crossfire. And you didn't deserve to be shot. I understand why Edmund Lisle would resent you if he believed you were trying to win back Lady X, but rake or no, you ought not have to die for stealing his mistress."

"Your support is touching." He smiled lazily, then distracted her by changing the subject. "What shall we do this afternoon? If you like I can take you to explore the grounds."

"Is it wise for you to be tramping around the property? You could break open your wound."

"I refuse to remain bedridden. Biddy said that an easy soak in the spring would be good for my wound, but I think I will wait another day before testing the waters. I may need your help bathing tomorrow, though." At her hesitation, Traherne's blue eyes flickered with amusement. "The sooner I recover, the sooner I can protect us myself and we can return to London."

Venetia started to decline but changed her mind. She wanted to help him heal quickly so they could end their enforced intimacy quickly. "Perhaps I will," she said noncommittally.

"In any case, we ought to make the best of the situation," Traherne said. "A week or two in Somerset will be deadly dull—unless we find some other form of entertainment to occupy us. How do you feel about fishing?"

"Fishing?"

"There are several streams and lakes nearby. The sport should be adequate to pass the time."

"I have never fished before, but I enjoy the outdoors. I will be happy to take my sketch pad and try my hand at drawing the countryside while you do battle with the fish."

At the completion of their meal, he found a fishing rod and line in the gardener's shed behind the cottage, then led her along a footpath through the woods to a meadow scattered with wildflowers.

And so it was that they spent the lovely spring afternoon beside a rushing stream. The climate was significantly warmer here than London in recent days, and Venetia was comfortable in a pelisse and bonnet as she settled on the grassy slope. Traherne stretched out beside her, half reclining on his elbows, and idly dipped his line in the water while she sketched the pretty landscape with a charcoal pencil.

Her gaze drifted to him frequently, though. She kept wanting to sketch his handsome profile instead of the country vista. Sunlight played with the elegant planes of his face and heightened the gold glints in his hair and the shadow of stubble on his strong jaw.

It would have been a companionable silence, except that she was far too aware of him and her regrettable lapse in judgment this morning. Her lips still tingled and burned from his kisses; her skin felt the imprint of his body against hers.

Whatever had possessed her to allow his caresses to go so far?

She was asking herself the same question later when he interrupted her wayward thoughts. "May I see what you are drawing?"

When she passed over her sketch pad rather reluctantly, he studied her rendering of the meadow scene with interest.

"You show talent."

His praise warmed her, even if it was not strictly warranted. "Thank you, but I am still a rank amateur. My ability to portray inanimate objects and landscapes is rather mediocre at best. I am actually better at depicting people. For some reason, I have a knack for capturing facial expressions."

"Is that why you took up sculpting?"

"That, and as a way to occupy myself. When I first arrived in Paris after the . . . debacle of my broken engagement, I had a great deal of time on my hands. I dislike lazing around, feeling useless with no purpose."

He gave a short laugh. "I can well understand *that* sentiment. Our interval here will be the longest I have ever gone with nothing to do. I would imagine sculpture is a very different art form than sketching or painting."

"It is. But I discovered that I like working with my hands. I have concentrated primarily on learning how to make busts. I start by fashioning a model out of clay, then create a final version in stone or bronze."

It was hard to explain the joy of creation, shaping and carving the clay, replicating a specific facial expression. Then choosing the best stone and deciding on each chisel stroke. Her hands would be covered in clay, her apron smeared and spattered as she became lost in her work. When it came time to convert the model to stone, a fine sheen of dust would replace the bits of earth.

"Fortunately the academy I attended had some excellent tutors who were not averse to training ladies." She made a wry face. "Had I attempted to sculpt here in England, it would have tarnished my reputation even further. As you know, female artists are not welcomed by society and in fact shunned in most circles. Having the freedom to explore my artistic talents was one of the few benefits of the scandal."

"A pity women are so limited in their choices—as my sister and cousin regularly remark."

"Yes it is—"

His fishing line jerked just then, and Traherne turned his attention to his catch, but by then her nervous tension had been broken. When ironically he hailed his triumph over the small carp wriggling on his hook, Venetia found herself laughing with him.

The amiable mood continued for the remainder of

the afternoon. Indeed, she felt more comfortable and in tune with Traherne than she ever thought possible.

Their camaraderie even lasted into that evening when they returned to the cottage. In keeping with his wish to remain informal, Venetia kept on her gown of blue kerseymere. When she joined him in the parlor before supper, she noted that Traherne had donned a comfortable-fitting coat but that he had shaved for the occasion. They dined together on three courses this time—beef consommé and braised lamb, followed by rhubarb tarts for dessert.

After dinner they again retired to the elegant parlor, where a cozy fire now burned. Once again Traherne spread out his sheaf of papers on the small writing desk while Venetia read on the sofa.

When the tea tray was brought in, he joined her on the sofa. To distract herself from his nearness, she ventured to make conversation.

"What are those documents you have been studying so intently?"

"Specifications for a new ship design."

"Your sister mentioned your endeavor with a steam engine for sailing ships."

He shot her a glance. "Oh, you spoke to Skye about me?" There was a slight note of provocation to his voice.

"I was curious in a general sense. I know so little about you. It is only natural to have questions about the man I was about to marry."

"What did she say about me?"

"That you are driven to pursue this design in an effort to save lives."

His lips pressed together. "It grates that I cannot be

present for the final stages of construction. The engineering can proceed without me, of course, but I like to be kept abreast of our daily progress."

So he was not as sanguine about his confinement as he appeared. On the contrary, a moment later he confessed to being impatient with his injury and more than a little restless.

"I despise feeling weak and dependent, but I detest even more feeling impotent. It seems cowardly to be forced to hide in the country."

Indeed, Venetia thought, more than most men, Traherne would dislike feeling helpless and vulnerable, but she disagreed with his characterization. "It is not the least cowardly to withdraw from the battlefield while you recuperate," she countered. "A wise general would say to marshal your resources and regroup and live to fight another day."

A faint smile twisted his mouth. "How obliging of you to champion me. Will wonders never cease?"

She formed a retort, but Horton appeared just then to inquire about any further needs they might have. Traherne dismissed the caretakers and servants to return to their own homes. When they took their leave, Venetia became highly conscious that she was alone in the house with her new husband.

Traherne continued sipping from his glass of port while she took a large swallow of tea. Suddenly the parlor seemed far too intimate. And yet she couldn't prevent herself from watching him, admiring how the firelight found the threads of gold in his hair and illuminated his blue eyes, his sensual mouth. . . . His sensual, magical mouth . . .

When a quiver ran through her, she tried to cover up her weakness by rolling her shoulders.

"Are you cold?" Traherne asked. "Shall I stir the fire?"

"No, I am merely stiff from the long hours of travel."

"Come here," he commanded and caught her arm to draw her closer.

"Why?" she asked warily.

"So that I can massage your shoulders. Have no fear, I won't proceed any further without an invitation."

He turned her sideways so that her back was to him; she held herself rigid as his hands gently began moving on her shoulders. It was deplorable how his simplest touch made her breathless . . .

"Relax, love," Traherne admonished. "I intend to keep my promise to protect you."

Oddly enough, she believed him. *Why is it that this man can make me feel so safe, so secure, and yet so flustered by his very nearness at the same time?*

He began kneading more deeply, working out the tight knots in her muscles. When he found a particularly sore spot and brought her relief, she almost sighed with bliss.

At the soft sound she made, his hands suddenly stilled. A moment later his touch became lighter. For a heartbeat, his fingers played on the bare skin of her neck above her gown.

Then slowly he bent his head to kiss her sensitive nape. Venetia gave a start and pulled away. "Traherne!"

When she gazed over her shoulder at him accusingly, he held up his hands innocently. "Mea culpa, I couldn't resist. Your skin is too lovely."

His gaze drifted lower to her breasts, as if he was recalling their lovemaking this morning.

Silently cursing her response, Venetia set down her cup and rose to her feet. He had only to look at her and she felt desire flood her. "I believe I will retire to my room."

"As you wish. I mean to remain here for a while longer and cool off. Pleasant dreams."

She felt herself flush as she made her way from the parlor. She sincerely hoped her dreams would not be as erotic as the one that had awakened her that morning. If they were, she would never survive this confinement.

To her gratitude, she passed a fantasy-free night and woke somewhat refreshed. Traherne must be an early riser, for he was already at the breakfast table when she came downstairs.

As they began their meal, he proposed they explore the grounds afterward. "I fear I can't ride without further damaging my side but I can traipse about well enough."

"I would like that," Venetia agreed readily, eager to see more of the countryside and escape the isolation of the cottage.

When they set out, the spring morning was crisp and fresh; morning sunlight quickly burned off the slight mist that hung over the meadows. Out of concern for his injury, they strolled the footpaths at an easy pace, beside a meandering stream.

When they reached a charming stone bridge, Traherne pointed toward a gully in the distance and explained about the geography of the district.

"The hills to the southwest of us are riddled with limestone caves, some quite large. Our underground spring here carved out a smaller cave aeons ago. I mean to wait until this afternoon to risk bathing. The water is hot enough, but it will be more enjoyable once the air is warmer."

Venetia wasn't certain then if she would accompany him, but it was one of the most pleasant mornings she could remember, certainly since her banishment from England.

Another surprise awaited her when they returned to the cottage. No sooner had they entered than the estate's tenants came to call.

When the middle-aged couple introduced themselves as Colonel Randall Langford and his wife, Marie, Mrs. Langford practically gushed with joy at having an earl and countess staying on her back doorstep. She went on and on with embarrassing effusiveness about how honored she was to meet her ladyship, and she was not too old to try to flirt with Traherne.

"There will be many a broken heart among the fair sex," Mrs. Langford declared, fluttering her eyelashes at him. "I follow London society with great interest—the papers are delivered to us monthly—but I had not heard the news that you had tied the knot, my lord. You have long been considered the biggest prize on the Marriage Mart."

Unexpectedly, Traherne slid his arm around Venetia's waist and drew her close. "I am fortunate to have won the biggest prize, madam," he said, sending

Venetia an intimate, adoring look, evidently meant to convey the message that they were madly in love.

"Well, it is a sad day for the other ladies, I am sure," Mrs. Langford replied with a sigh, her cheery friendliness suggesting that she hadn't made the connection with Venetia's scandal two years ago. "We wish to invite you to dine with us one evening and hope you will grace our humble circle with your attendance at the local assembly on Friday evening."

"You will understand if I want to keep my bride all to myself."

Colonel Langford stepped in. "Of course, of course. We recall what it is like to be newly wedded. Come, my dear, we are interrupting his lordship's nuptials. They are likely eager to return to their boudoir."

At the images of them remaining abed indulging in sexual romps, Venetia felt herself flushing. However, when their visitors had left and Traherne released her, she felt an unmistakable pang of disappointment. Naturally she saw the wisdom of maintaining the pretense of being happily wed since it increased the likelihood they would be left alone, but for a moment she couldn't help wondering how wonderful it would feel if her husband's adoration were real.

He must have seen her expression for he raised a quizzical eyebrow. "You didn't wish to accept their invitations, did you?"

"No, they were kindly meant, but I would rather not be the object of so much avid attention."

"Nor would I. I don't want to advertise our presence here."

Perhaps it was his casual manner that swayed her, but after luncheon when Traherne asked her to accompany him to the hot springs to bathe, Venetia went willingly. In truth, she was concerned about him reopening his wound and thought he might need help rebandaging it.

Or at least that was what she told herself. It helped that he carried only one towel, which suggested that he didn't expect her to bathe with him.

His manner remained friendly and nonchalant as he guided her along the footpath to the gully and helped her down the rocky slope. The entrance was little more than an irregular hole in the wall, and they both had to bend to squeeze through the low archway.

Once her eyes grew accustomed to the dimness inside, she saw they were in a domed hollow.

"The pool cave to the rear of here," he explained, "is high enough for us to stand upright, but we will need a light to make our way there."

To her left, an old, rusty lantern sat on a narrow wooden shelf, and when Traherne struck a flint and lit the wick, the flame lit the walls and roof with a welcome glow. Taking her hand, he led her across the grotto to a passageway. "It is not far to the pool, but step carefully."

She wore sturdy half boots, but the sloping ground was wet and she had to stoop the entire way. The tunnel widened at the end and opened up to a much larger chamber. The air seemed warmer here and gave off a mineral smell that was not unpleasant.

This cave was darker, with no daylight filtering in from above. The lamplight illuminated shadowy walls at the rear and ragged stalactites in colorful hues of orange and green and white dripping down from the vaulted ceiling.

"How pretty," Venetia was surprised into saying.

"Yes," he agreed, holding the lantern higher, the better for her to see.

In front of her was a roughly oval pool some twenty feet long set at an angle. The black surface reflected a gold sheen, but when she followed Traherne to the edge, the dark green water looked clear as it lapped at banks of smooth rock. The bottom looked to be smooth as well.

"Is it very deep?"

"Perhaps three or four feet. The spring flows from the far end and empties there to your left. At some recent point in time, the course of the stream must have shifted, or the entrance would have been more hollowed."

She could hear the musical trickle as the overflow disappeared into a crevasse in the wall. When Traherne set the lantern on the ground and began to undress, Venetia waited while he removed his shirt and unwound his bandage. Then she inspected his wound.

"The flesh does not look as angry as yesterday. You will live, I suspect."

"Biddy's miracle salve must be working. Now let's see if his prescription of a mineral bath is similarly effective."

While he finished undressing, she sat down on the stone bank at the pool's edge and averted her gaze. She heard him slip slowly into the water, then the hiss of his breath.

Concerned, she jerked her gaze back and found him grimacing. "Are you all right?"

"Yes. The heat just stung at first."

He submerged himself completely for a moment and came up again, slicking wet hair back from his face.

Venetia watched as water cascaded over his torso. His wet skin shimmered in the golden lamplight, accenting the power and grace of his lean, muscular form.

Beautiful, she thought rather breathlessly. He had a magnificent body that put the classical statues to shame, with broad shoulders that tapered to a narrow waist and hips. . . .

Her gaze skittered away. The pool was higher than waist-deep but did little to conceal his lower extremities and the dark hair that arrowed over his groin.

Before she could do more than swallow the dryness in her throat, he sank down again in order to float lazily.

"You should join me," Traherne suggested. "The temperature is pleasant, no warmer than a hot bath." When she hesitated, he added mildly, "There is no reason to be prudish, love. It is not as if we haven't slept together."

It was precisely because they *had* slept together that her senses were on full alert, and his brazen nudity was only making matters worse. But she thought she had an appropriate retort: "Forgive me if I am not a *femme fatale* like your mistress, Lady X."

"Former mistress," he said, unfazed. "You can at least take a risk and dangle your legs in the water."

He was right, Venetia acknowledged. She was only denying herself by letting her reservations dominate her inclinations.

Raising her skirts to her knees, she pulled off her boots and stockings, then swung around on the stone bank and lowered her legs up to her calves. Venetia sighed with pleasure. The silken caress of the water felt divine.

"I told you so," Traherne said with satisfaction. "You would enjoy a full bath even more."

"Thank you, but I am content where I am."

A few moments later, he stood upright, his body glistening. He was closer now, near enough that his male attributes were clearly visible beneath the surface. She could see his manhood thrusting hard and proud against his belly.

Venetia felt herself blushing hotly at the sight.

"Your modesty does you credit," he commented, which made her eyes narrow.

"Are you mocking me?"

"Never."

"I don't believe you. You are trying to goad me again."

"Is it working?"

His mouth twitched into a crooked grin, which ignited a deep need in her to smile back. "Could you please turn around, Traherne?"

He let out an exaggerated sigh but obliged, giving her his muscled back. The change of view was not particularly helpful, however. Venetia couldn't prevent her gaze from drifting lower. His buttocks looked hard as well, and firm to the touch.

Apparently he wasn't willing to leave off provoking her, either. "You can see that I am in urgent need of a nurse," he remarked casually.

"What do you mean?"

"My loins are in a state of acute pain. If you were to fondle me, it would serve to distract me."

"I offered yesterday morning. You declined."

"I have changed my mind."

"Well, so have I."

Traherne cast a glance over his shoulder. "It is your duty as my wife to succor me."

"We have only a marriage of convenience," Venetia retorted. "Duty doesn't apply."

"Then take pity on me. I am wounded and weak, as helpless as a babe."

She laughed outright at that. "You are as helpless as a tiger."

"Perhaps 'babe' is not accurate. But my self-esteem has been sorely damaged by my injury. Employing my skills as a lover will give me the opportunity to prove my manhood. It is the least you could do."

She had no ready reply, but she was enjoying herself immensely, Venetia realized. Bantering with him was not only exhilarating, it was delicious and tantalizing. If she didn't take care, it could become addictive.

"You are not luring me into the water, my lord. And I am not falling prey to your charm. No doubt you have enchanted half of England's female population, but I prefer not to join their ranks."

"Only half?"

The blatant sensuality in his sultry blue eyes was impossible to ignore. The way he looked at a woman was utterly sinful.

"Three-quarters, then. You cannot count children." She shook her head. "You are too accustomed to having your own way. I feel I should oppose you on general principal. Besides, I have scruples about surrendering to a shameless libertine."

Eyeing her reproachfully, he slid back into the water. "I should make allowances for your mistrust. Your antipathy toward men is excusable, given your history."

"I don't harbor antipathy toward all men."

"Just rakehells."

"Deceitful rakehells in particular. Can you blame me? I nearly wed one. It is not at all heartening to know your betrothed preferred a prostitute to a marriage bed with you."

His gaze turned strangely tender. "No, I cannot blame you. But not all rakehells are deceitful."

"I suppose not," Venetia agreed grudgingly. "All the same, I refuse to succumb to your blandishments."

He arched an eyebrow. "You do realize what an irresistible challenge that is."

Venetia's pulse suddenly leapt as she locked gazes with him. When Traherne turned fully to face her, she stared mutely, feeling the fresh sizzle of heat between them.

As she floundered for a retort, his voice softened to a murmur. "I'll wager I could make you want me if I set my mind to it."

He was arrogant and outrageously self-confident, yet for good reason. "That is one wager I don't intend to make," Venetia hastened to say.

"Why are you so set against lovemaking? I can safely predict you would enjoy carnal relations."

"I am perfectly happy without."

"I doubt that. You clearly don't know what you are missing."

Except she did know. Or at least she had a strong inkling. Just yesterday morning Traherne had given her a powerful taste of what his lovemaking would be like. "I will forgo the opportunity to discover it, thank you. Furthermore, our marriage is not a true one, so there should be no consummation."

"We needn't consummate our union to enjoy ourselves."

Venetia's lips curved. "Is everything about pleasure for you?"

"Certainly not. But pleasure is preferable to the alternative. And you deserve some pleasure in your life after the past two years."

"Oh, so now you are thinking about me?"

His slow, lazy smile was absolutely devastating. "Not entirely. But I do have your best interests at heart. You are my wife now. My countess. I have an obligation to ensure your well-being and happiness."

"I hereby relieve you of the obligation."

"What if I don't wish to be relieved?" He considered her thoughtfully. "Before our union, you were resolved on becoming a dried-up spinster. Is that still your aim?"

Venetia eyed him narrowly, taken aback by the seriousness of his question. For a change, she sensed he was not trying to bait her. Even so, she had no immediate answer for him.

When she remained silent, he posed the question a different way. "Do you intend to remain a virgin for the rest of your life?"

"I have not given it much consideration."

"You should. I know for a fact you are not passionless."

Her flush was instinctive. "How did we come to be discussing my passion or lack of it?"

"Because you strike me as someone in need of reassurance. Trust me, you have no earthly reason to feel insecure in your appeal. You are one of the most desirable women I have ever known."

"Ackland did not think so," she couldn't help but reply, then bit her tongue, ashamed of the hurt in her tone.

Evidently Traherne had taken note of her bitterness, though, for he said frankly, "Ackland was a fool."

She looked at him in disbelief. "He was your friend."

"He was still a fool for giving you up—"

Traherne seemed to catch himself then, for he cut off the remark and his mouth curled wryly. "I've had enough of bathing for one day—and enough sexual torment as well." He waded toward her. "Do you mean to watch me dry off?"

"No." Snatching up her stockings and boots, she scrambled to her feet and backed away.

His soft chuckle followed her retreat across the cave. "Never fear, I promise I won't seduce you unless you wish me to."

Unless you wish me to.

The words repeated in her head like a delicious threat, which disturbed her nearly as much as his unsettling comments. But Venetia busied herself putting on her shoes and stockings while he dressed, and by the time they left the cave, she had willed herself to composure. She even helped him apply a fresh bandage when they returned to the cottage.

And when that chore was done, she congratulated herself. She had faced Traherne's most potent temptations yet and felt almost confident that she could manage to resist him for the remainder of their time here together.

Almost.

He was treading in dangerous waters, Quinn reflected as he watched Venetia leave his bedchamber after seeing to his wound.

Yes, she presented a unique challenge—a woman who professed not to want him, a bride who insisted on sleeping alone. Yes, her resistance stung his pride and brought out the conqueror in him. But regrettably, the issue was far more complicated.

He was being lured in emotionally, damn and blast it. He cared, more than he'd realized.

He also relished her company as much as he'd feared he would. Venetia was . . . strangely comfortable. He needn't treat her like delicate porcelain, eschewing frankness and honesty or withholding barbs out of concern that he might offend her feminine sensibilities. Instead she responded to his teasing with worthy gibes of her own, with humor brightening her luminous eyes. Her directness, too, was utterly novel and refreshing after all the toadying sycophants who had fawned over him since he was in short coats, trying to win his favor.

The truth was, he was delighted by her mind and her body both. Despite the strain on his loins, he felt pleasure simply being with her.

Admittedly he'd never felt so fiercely attracted to any other woman. Nor had he ever struggled so hard against physical need. Since their first night together as man and wife, he'd spent his time in an acute state of arousal, with self-command and desire warring brutally in his midsection.

Remembering the searing pleasure he'd felt bringing Venetia to climax that first morning together was especially stirring. There had been wariness in those amazing eyes of hers, but also curiosity and need . . . and so much vulnerability and wonder in her face.

Her vulnerability drew him in, kindling an instinctive need to protect her that vied powerfully with his desire to possess her. Most of all, he wanted to expose the passionate, sensual woman beneath her defensive, guarded exterior.

She had no faith in her desirability, Quinn was well aware. Her self-esteem had been wounded too deeply by Ackland's betrayal.

He would change that, Quinn decided. He intended to make up for the deprivation she'd endured during her two years of exile. She had suffered too much hurt through no fault of her own.

Pleasure. The word was greatly on Quinn's mind of late. Despite his physical discomfort and the warnings of his conscience, he meant to show Venetia the kind of pleasure she deserved, to make her feel the same pleasure he felt when she was near.

He would have a great deal of work to do to overcome her feelings of mistrust, of course. But he was willing to go slowly. Venetia had to be wooed delicately, enticed like a shy butterfly.

Quinn's mouth curved in a wry grimace. He'd never

envisioned wedding a reluctant bride. He'd never imagined needing to seduce his own wife, either. Ironic, when he was supposed to be such a vaunted lover.

But regardless, he would make Venetia forget her painful memories of her betrothed if it was the last thing he ever did.

Chapter Eleven

The afternoon in the cave set the pattern for their relationship over the next several days. They shared an easy rapport as they came to know each other during their wide-ranging discussions, yet with a powerful undercurrent of sexual tension beneath.

When Venetia quizzed Traherne about his past, she discovered how he had come by his obsession with steam-propelled sailing ships. His distant relative and Lady Katharine's uncle, Lord Cornelius Wilde, was a literary genius, but translating ancient tomes from Latin and Greek was not for him, Traherne admitted.

"I was always more interested in science and mathematics," he explained. "For a time, I dabbled in medicine, which was how I met Biddowes. While still at university, I became fascinated with innovations. Although engineering is not my expertise, I could recognize ingenuity and hire technical experts to bring an invention to fruition, so I began funding various projects and providing capital for minor ventures. It is only in the past couple years, however, that I became involved on a grand scale."

"Your steam engine?" Venetia asked.

"Yes. There are actually several enterprises pursuing the radical notion of steam power at sea, both here in Britain and in America. But mine will be one of the first to actually test the theory in a working model. We hope to launch by summer's end."

"It seems an admirable endeavor," Venetia observed honestly, "especially for a man of your stamp."

The corners of his eyes began to play with a smile. "Did you think I spend all my time in dissipation?"

"Well, yes. Or at least all your nights. You have always led a life of notoriety, and I know for certain that you consort with a raffish set, including Lord Byron, and of course Ackland."

"There was a period in my life when I followed the frivolous vicissitudes of a wealthy nobleman, but I moved on to more productive endeavors."

Venetia pursed her mouth. Traherne continually managed to subvert her admittedly biased conceptions about him. The Wildes were a breed apart—scandalous, hedonistic, passionate—but each time she tried to dismiss him as an arrogant, self-centered rake, he pushed her off balance.

He also acknowledged that his parents' drowning had influenced him significantly. "Had their schooner been powered by steam, they might have been able to outrun the storm that took their lives."

Venetia heard the deep emotion in his voice, the anger and sadness, and so was hesitant to press him further. She could only imagine the shock and grief he'd felt at the untimely death of his parents. It was difficult enough to endure that her parents had renounced her. She couldn't bear to think of them perishing.

"How did it happen? I believe you said they were returning to England after collecting your mother's inheritance that had been hidden since the French Revolution."

"You have a good recollection for detail. My parents, along with Kate and Ash's parents, had set sail from the southern coast of France when a storm overtook them and sank their ship with all passengers and hands on board. Flotsam and pieces of wreckage washed up on shore for weeks afterward, but the site of the shipwreck was never discovered. It was thought that the de Chagny family treasure sank with them . . . until the pendant appeared."

"Yes," Venetia said dryly, "adorning the neck of your former mistress."

Ignoring her gibe, Traherne went on. "I set out to determine how Lisle came to possess the pendant. In addition, I sent Macky to France to investigate any recent news of the shipwreck. I also wrote to my mother's distant cousin in Paris, the Compte de Montreux, requesting his aid in learning about a possible salvage attempt. The tragedy happened fourteen years ago, so Macky's task will be difficult, but I had expected to hear from him before now. I've had no word in three weeks." Traherne gave a testy sigh. "There has been no word from Hawk yet, either."

"It has only been five days since we left London," Venetia reminded him.

He ran a restless hand through his hair. "I know, but I will be glad to return. I cannot cower here in the backwoods of Somerset forever. I need to discover if Lisle hired an assassin to kill me."

"Do you think him guilty?"

"He is the prime suspect, although I have no evidence linking him to the attempts on my life. For all I know, the culprit could be the owner of a rival shipping company, determined to prevent my steam-propelled ship from reaching completion. But if Lisle is the perpetrator, was his motive because I initiated a search for the treasure or something else?"

"Such as eliminating the competition?"

He raised an eyebrow in question. "Competition?"

"For Lady X's favors. I should think jealousy would be a likely reason for Lisle to wish you in Hades. In truth, I cannot fathom how you reached the ripe age of—how old are you anyway?"

"One and thirty."

"Well, I am surprised you managed to survive all your scandalous affairs without some possessive rival or slighted lover attempting to murder you before this. I was prepared to do it myself, albeit for a different reason."

His smile broadened. "I trust I've succeeded in improving your opinion of me."

"Somewhat," she conceded with a grudging smile. "At certain moments, I even find myself admiring you."

Traherne laughed outright at her admission. "I am elated to count small measures of progress."

In return, he probed her own past. That evening after supper, Venetia unexpectedly found herself revealing her deepest feelings about her bitter experience with Ackland.

"I felt like the greatest fool alive, to be so ignorant of his deception. All the while he was courting me and claiming to love me, he was disporting with a demi-rep behind my back. I only suspected the truth mere hours before the ceremony, and didn't truly believe it until he arrived at the church unkempt and reeking of perfume."

"I admired you on the church steps, acting on your beliefs."

Venetia looked at Traherne warily and saw only sympathy in his expression. "My response was actually unplanned. I reacted out of shock and pain and humiliation."

"You should be proud you took a stand. A weaker woman would have gone through with the ceremony or given in to hysterics."

She looked away from his disconcertingly tender gaze. "It is hardly fair," she muttered a long-held grievance. "My betrothed was the libertine, but I was the one punished and branded a scarlet woman. Men are allowed outrageous license to do anything they please, especially noblemen. Take yourself, for example."

"Yes, do take me." His easy tone suggested he was trying to lighten her mood, yet it didn't soothe her.

"Your scandal in the park with Lady X was worse than anything I created. You didn't suffer one bit."

"It helps that I have a title and fortune. Had you possessed the same, your crime might have been mitigated a degree. But you were a genteel young lady who caused a public spectacle."

Venetia sighed. He had punctured her swelling bubble of frustration. "Indeed. My airing soiled linen in public angered my parents immensely. Had I learned earlier about Ackland's long-standing liaison, I might have been more discreet when terminating our betrothal."

She gave Traherne a considering look. "You knew he kept a mistress and yet you did nothing to warn me."

"A man doesn't betray his friends."

"I would have been spared a lot of pain had I known. And I might have spared my family."

She deeply regretted the distress she'd caused her family but not her denunciation of Ackland. "If I could do it over again, I still would have ended our engagement. I could never have been happy wedded to him. He was not the honorable man I thought him. My mother couldn't forgive me, though. She thought Ackland was only sowing his wild oats before he settled down, and could not understand why I objected to marrying an adulterer."

Traherne hesitated. "I might point out that you cannot commit adultery without being wed."

His response was perfectly logical, but her feelings were not driven by logic. "He would have eventually been unfaithful, I have no doubt." Venetia ground her teeth together involuntarily as she rose to her feet and began to pace the small parlor. "I don't believe it is too much to ask that a husband remain true to his holy marriage vows, especially when he claims to love you. But I have learned my lesson. I will no longer trust any man's avowals of love."

"There you are again, tarring all of us with the same brush."

"With good cause." She glanced over her shoulder

at Traherne. "I doubt you would ever practice fidelity."

She could see her accusation nettled him. "You don't know that," Traherne answered slowly. "It's not unknown for a rake to change his wicked ways."

Venetia shrugged. "You needn't bother to try. You promised we could lead separate lives once the danger has passed. I mean to hold you to your promise and return to France as soon as may be."

He cocked his head. "Are you certain you would be any happier living in France?"

"I believe so. I have come to relish my independence. That has been the one major advantage to being an outcast. The scandal liberated me in many ways."

Another smile tugged at his mouth. "You are not so liberated, love. You are still trapped by your past, and you have grave inhibitions about carnal relations."

She quickly rallied. "I *meant* that I am no longer smothered by the same constrictions as before. My art is a prime illustration. In my parents' view, my desire to pursue sculpting is another sin to my credit, or so my sister told me in her smuggled notes." Venetia's second sigh was even deeper. "I regret most disappointing them."

"Your parents don't deserve your consideration after casting you out. Their treatment of you was deplorable."

In a way, she agreed with him. For a moment she was spun back two years to the aftermath of her public rebellion. She had been ruined and socially ostracized and exiled to a foreign country, but none of that held a candle to how hurt, how devastated, she'd been by her parents' repudiation.

Suddenly her throat ached and her eyes smarted with unexpected tears. She had felt frighteningly vulnerable and alone those first few months. Without Cleo, she would have been desperate, forced to eke her own way in the world, living in shabby-genteel circumstances or outright penury.

Venetia stared blindly down at the carpet as she remembered. She had been prepared to endure the unenviable life of a spinster, but it had been such a lonely time, with so little remaining of her dreams. As a childless widow, Cleo was in a similar predicament. They had clung together and developed a strong friendship, to her eternal gratitude.

Just then Traherne rose from his chair and moved closer, startling her out of her sad reverie. When he touched her face, brushing back a tear that had escaped, her gaze snapped up to his.

She saw tenderness there, heart-tugging tenderness. His blue eyes were clear and intent, as if he could see down into her soul—which made her feel raw and exposed.

Despite her innate response to his sympathy, though, a jolt of purely sensual awareness shot through Venetia at his touch. There was no denying the surge of heat she felt standing this close to him.

"You know I don't want your pity," she said finally, with more defiance than she intended.

"Trust me, sweeting, it is not pity I feel for you at the moment. Just now I want to shake your parents, or commit some even more violent act upon their persons."

What *she* wanted just now was for Traherne to put his protective arms around her, to draw her into his warm embrace and simply hold her. But that would never do.

Drawing back, she covered her discomfiture by resuming her place on the sofa and disparaging his tactics. Oh, he was a wily devil. She knew very well he enjoyed undermining her defenses, yet she could feel herself softening toward him almost hourly.

If she was honest, she would admit she greatly enjoyed his companionship. His conversation was scintillating and his sharp wits kept her own honed. Even with the peril they faced—or perhaps because of it—she couldn't deny the exhilaration he had kindled in her. Traherne had yanked her out of her safe cocoon and enlivened her dull, lonely existence. She was never lonely when she was with him. . . .

Venetia swallowed, resolutely pushing away the ache in her chest. She was her own mistress now. She had fought hard to build her new life in France, with a fulfilling pursuit to occupy her time. For her own self-preservation, she couldn't now add a libertine husband who had been compelled to wed her.

When he spoke again, his voice gentled even further. "Let me be clear, Venetia." He waited until she looked at him once more. "I want to assure you, as my countess you can continue to be independent. You will have the means to live whatever life you wish."

Venetia shook her head. "As your countess, I am legally your property."

"I have no desire whatsoever to curtail your freedom."

"Even so, I'm certain you don't want a wife underfoot, hindering your licentious lifestyle. And for me, one rake in a lifetime is more than enough."

Only by the slightest tightening of his jaw could she see that she had struck a nerve, probably the same one as before. He did not like her criticism of his wicked exploits.

But then he seemed to shrug off her disapproval and poured himself another glass of port before lounging in his chair and changing the subject to more pleasant matters.

The next morning brought another fishing excursion. When they settled on the grassy bank beside the stream—Traherne with his rod and line, Venetia with her sketch paper and pencil—she began to draw a collection of wildflowers. After an hour, her concentration waned and her gaze gravitated to the aristocratic lines of his profile.

Her fingers itched to capture his handsome features in clay—the high cheekbones, the sensual mouth, the intelligent eyes. . . . Before she knew it, she found herself sketching Traherne's likeness. In this light, his sunstreaked hair was the color of winter wheat, and she struggled to capture the right shading with mere charcoal.

Frowning at her rendering, she bit her lower lip and glanced back at him, only to discover he was watching her.

"What are you drawing?"

The instant flush on her cheeks at being caught out annoyed her. She ought not feel embarrassed about sketching Traherne when he was the only human subject available. Her interest had nothing to do with her captivation with him—

Knowing she was lying to herself, Venetia hedged her reply. "Nothing of importance."

She abandoned her present sketch in favor of the wildflowers, while Traherne returned to his fishing, and eventually a companionable silence resumed. The sun rose high in the sky till the warmth of the day felt more like summer than spring.

Traherne shed his waistcoat and coat, and Venetia removed her pelisse. A short while later she realized she was perspiring under her bonnet and so removed that article also, along with her shoes and stockings, then moved to sit beneath the shade of a nearby willow tree in order to protect her fair skin.

But she continued to watch his sporting success. By the time another hour had passed, he had an impressive catch collected in a pail of water.

"I plan to hand these fine fellows over to Mrs. Horton to vary our menu," he remarked as he gathered his gear, "even though I would rather build a fire and grill them."

Venetia raised an eyebrow in surprise. "Do you know how to clean and cook a fish?"

"I learned as a boy." He flashed a grin at her skeptical expression. "Why do you look so shocked?"

"I find it hard to believe that a pampered, wealthy nobleman has common talents such as cleaning fish."

Traherne winced. "You do have a habit of cutting me down to size with that uncomplimentary tongue of yours."

His aggrieved tone made Venetia want to apologize for the undeserved criticism. "Forgive me—my remark was uncalled for. I meant merely to say that your aptitude is unusual when you have a large kitchen staff at your mansion in London and countless other servants at your beck and call."

"For your information, I grew up mainly in the country. I spent many a pleasant hour of my childhood having adventures in the woods with my cousins on the Beaufort and Traherne estates. I could live off the land now, if I were forced to. I could even endure privation if need be. I just don't see the need. Have you ever tasted fire-grilled trout?"

The thought made Venetia's mouth water. "No."

"It is one of life's small pleasures. But we will have to make do with the picnic basket Mrs. Horton packed for us."

His comment made her realize she had grown hungry. While he washed his hands in the stream, she laid out the alfresco luncheon of mutton pie and apple tarts under the willow.

When they had finished eating, he lay back on the grass, his hands folded behind his head, and closed his eyes, apparently sated and content.

Venetia felt replete and drowsy as well. She wanted to lie down beside him and nap, yet the last time she had slept beside him, she had woken to his marvelous lovemaking—

"Do you mean to go to sleep?" she asked to distract her wayward thoughts.

"No. I am devoutly attempting to keep my hands to myself." At her puzzled silence, he pried one eye open to regard her. "You have no idea how incredibly appealing you are, do you?"

The rhythm of her heart changed perceptibly. The sexual awareness between them had returned with a vengeance. That same tingling, nervous, exhilarating sensation she had fought for days.

In self-defense, Venetia wrapped her arms around her upraised knees and averted her gaze to look out over the far meadow. "Did you have to go and spoil a peaceful afternoon?"

"Only you would think a compliment egregious."

"Coming from you, it is. Your motives are always suspect."

He sat up and eased closer to her. "I'll have you know I have been at great pains to earn your trust."

She shivered, merely from the soothing, cajoling sound of his voice, and tried to ignore him.

Traherne was having none of her dismissal, though. "Look at me, love."

His touch on her arm sent a small shock of heat plunging through her veins. Against her will, Venetia obeyed. His slow, engaging smile was utterly heart-stopping, taking unfair advantage of her lowered guard. Yet the challenge in his eyes, the dark sparkle in their depths, were even more potent.

She was not sexually experienced, but she had no doubt what she was feeling. *Desire.* For him. Every time he touched her, she felt a sudden, sharp leap of hunger deep inside her.

And she was woman enough to recognize the heated sparks in his eyes. He wanted her, she was certain of it.

A tremor ran through her. She desperately needed physical distance between them, yet she couldn't seem to move. Instead she sat there rigidly, holding her breath, afraid even to breathe the same air he did.

He was so close, she thought surely he could feel the longing thrumming through her body.

Pressing his advantage, he raised a hand to brush the curve of her jaw with the back of his knuckles. Sensation skittered up and down her nerve-endings. "You're so soft and warm and lovely, Venetia."

"No, I am not," she murmured in protest.

"You are. It is not just empty flattery. Repeat after me, 'I am very desirable.' "

"I would feel foolish saying such a thing."

"Then I will have to keep saying it for you. You are exquisitely desirable, sweet, beautiful Venetia."

It was supremely gratifying to think he considered her a desirable woman, and yet Traherne's objective was her surrender, Venetia reminded herself.

Then he bent and pressed a featherlight kiss to the side of her neck. The delicate sensation sent another shiver racing down her spine, but she remained tense.

"You might attempt to cooperate in your seduction," he murmured, breathing laughter against her bare skin.

"You said you would not seduce me unless I wished it."

"I collect that time has come. Can you deny it?"

His fingers lightly cupped her chin and turned her face to his. His eyes were mesmerizing, holding her spellbound. With forcible effort, Venetia lowered her glance, but only as far as his mouth.

A mistake, she realized, for she couldn't help recalling how he'd suckled her breasts with such exquisite tenderness that morning at the inn. How he'd kissed her body and inflamed her to quivering, aching arousal and brought her to a shattering, unforgettable climax . . .

The disturbing promise of his mouth made tension race through her like fire, and suddenly she was unbearably hot, in part because she knew he was remembering the same things.

Then he smiled again, a lazy, dazzling smile that sent a sweet, treacherous stab of longing straight through her body to her heart.

"Beautiful Venetia," he murmured in that same husky tone before angling his head to kiss her lightly. His breath feathered against her lips, warm and soft, while his hand stroked down her arm.

The heat from his palm burned through the fabric of her sleeve, but she fought the sensual sparking of her nerves and the desire flaring to full-blown life inside her.

"Traherne . . ." she warned raggedly.

"Call me Quinn, and I will cease prodding you."

"You will?" she asked, her tone highly doubtful.

"For the time being."

"Very well, then, *Quinn,* pray stop trying to kiss me and leave me be."

He went still, then pulled backed reluctantly. "As you wish, darling . . . but I give you fair warning. Every time you call me by my title, I will kiss you again."

To her surprise, Traherne—Quinn—resumed his position on the grass, as if nothing extraordinary had happened between them.

Venetia lifted a shaky hand to her mouth, still feeling her heart slamming against her ribs, and wondered why he was able to reduce her to such raw need with his shamefully practiced kisses.

The bulge in his breeches, however, suggested she had affected him nearly as much as he had her. And when he spoke, his voice remained husky and low. "Perhaps it's time to discuss the state of our marriage."

Thrown off guard by the sudden choice of topic, Venetia gazed at him with wary curiosity. "What is there to discuss?"

"Might I remind you that there is nothing wrong with enjoying each other now that we are wed?"

Comprehending his meaning, she sucked in an uneven breath. "You know how I feel about consummating our union."

"True, but you ought to reconsider. There is no reason for us to endure sexual pain."

"What . . . exactly are you proposing?"

"A modern marriage, of sorts. We can indulge our cravings and explore the pleasures of the marital bed without further obligations or entanglements."

"You mean purely carnal relations."

His eyes held hers, no longer flirtatious, just unsettlingly candid. "Precisely. It needn't be complicated. Pleasure only, nothing deeper. We both want each other. We have since the first time we kissed at Tavistock's."

Her arrested expression turned flustered. "You are surely overstating the impact."

"Not in my case. Kissing you was like being struck by a lightning bolt."

She stared in disbelief. Certainly she had experienced that staggering, electric feeling at the first touch of his mouth, but she couldn't credit that he had felt similarly. "I very much doubt you felt lightning bolts."

"It is the honest truth. It surprised the devil out of me."

When she shook her head, Quinn went on. "Think about it. We could have the ideal arrangement. We each cherish our freedom—you perhaps even more than I. Once we ferret out the assassin and it is safe, you can return to France as we agreed."

At her hesitation, he added to his rational argument. "Simply because Ackland betrayed you is not ample reason to deny yourself fulfillment."

"It is not only that. . . ."

"I understand. You don't want to be wed to a brute. But I am hardly like your friend Cleo's late husband. The fact that her marriage was so miserable is regrettable, but most marriages are not like hers."

"I am astonished that a consummate rake would defend the institution of marriage," she remarked archly.

"As am I." A dry smile hovered on his lips. "But we are married for better or worse, so we might as well make it for the better." At her cautious look, his tone changed to gentle reassurance. "Never fear, angel. I have hopes of convincing you one of these days, but as I told you, the choice to become lovers must be yours."

A telltale quiver shivered through Venetia. The truth was, she was supremely tempted by his offer. She wanted to know what Quinn's lovemaking would be like. She wanted to explore her feminine longings, to satisfy her yearning for his tender touch. Most of all she wanted an end to the loneliness.

She didn't want to be a barren virgin for the rest of her life, yet that would likely be her future unless she embraced his proposal. Now that she was Traherne's—Quinn's—wife, she could never, ever consider taking any other man for a lover.

Those seditious thoughts and more flashed through her mind momentarily, but Venetia put off answering and began packing up the remains of their lunch. "I believe I will return to the cottage. Will you come with me?"

"Not just yet. I mean to remain here and take a nap. It is exhausting work seducing nubile damsels who refuse to be seduced."

She couldn't help smiling, but as she left her thoughts were preoccupied by his proposition. Once the idea was planted in her mind, it was difficult to dismiss.

Over the following week, she couldn't help listening to the traitorous voice inside her head: What would be the harm in taking solace from her husband sexually, for their mutual pleasure?

When he'd originally promised a marriage in name only, she had expected—hoped—that physical relations would play no role in their marriage. Clearly her notion was a pipe dream with a man as sensual and physical as Traherne . . . Quinn.

His restraint surprised her, though. Surely this was not how he behaved with his usual sexual conquests. He managed to entertain her and enchant her instinctively rather than from obvious calculation.

Of course, enchantment was inherent to his very nature, as innate as breathing, but she would have expected him to be the very essence of devilish seduction. Instead, his attempts to persuade her were not overly overt. He relied on mere looks, the occasional touch, a tender tone of voice. It was almost as if he were *wooing* her.

He was also giving her a glimpse of the real man behind the captivating facade. In addition to fishing and picnics and visiting the cave, they went on long, ambling walks together through woodlands and meadows, where they debated favorite books and artists and food. Quinn questioned her about her art studies and the intellectual salons in Paris. In turn he shared stories about his close-knit family, including his antics as a boy and his sister's and his uncle Cornelius's recent marriages.

Venetia appreciated that he didn't press her about her own family, since the subject was so painful. He seemed sensitive to her moods and feelings, as a world-class lover should be.

And although she struggled with conflicting emotions, it grew easier each day to imagine them becoming lovers.

She was intently aware of the burning desire she felt for Quinn. The fact that he was actually her lawful husband made him even harder to resist. As did sleeping in an adjacent bedchamber with only a door to separate them.

She deplored his masculine beauty also.

Her attraction was not only physical, though. Her feelings were evolving the more time she spent with him.

Her own vanity played at least a small role, undoubtedly. Quinn made her feel *wanted,* made her feel like a desirable woman again, repairing her shaken self-esteem and restoring her confidence in small measure.

Venetia tried valiantly to keep her distance, but by week's end, she knew she was failing. Indeed, she could no longer remember why it was so crucial to oppose him. She couldn't deny the taut awareness, the bone-melting attraction, the stab of longing deep in her belly each time he merely looked at her.

Nor could she ignore a simple realization: He not only was giving her the power of choice, he was waiting for her to seize the initiative. It was up to her to take the next step.

Chapter Twelve

Quinn came slowly awake in his bed, his body hot, his cock throbbing as usual. His dreams during the night had been rife with sexual fantasies of Venetia, derived from scalding memories of their first morning together at the inn.

His mind lingered on those searing images now. Her soft, creamy skin. Her rose-tipped breasts. The stiffness of her nipples as he'd suckled her. Her moans of ecstasy as she writhed beneath his claiming mouth . . .

Murmuring a low oath, Quinn reached beneath the covers and took hold of his aching rod, then brought himself to quick relief. Sated but not fulfilled, he rose to wash while letting his mind wander to the afternoon of their most recent picnic together. How enchanting Venetia had looked—more country beauty than elegant countess.

Images continued to assault him as he shaved. Her hair tousled, bonnet flung aside, her feet bare and showing her delicate ankles and shapely calves. Her amusement at his alleged fish-cleaning prowess, her lovely face expressive, her huge eyes glowing. His compulsion to devour those luscious lips, to plunder that sweet body.

A feeling that was becoming more and more prominent of late, Quinn reflected.

It was sheer torment to keep his hands to himself—and impossible to repress the excitement he felt around her, his keen awareness of her scent, the sound of her voice.

Purposely Quinn shifted his thoughts to her solemn confessions about her broken betrothal. Her admissions hinting at her lost dreams had twisted his heart. And the look crossing Venetia's face—bittersweet, haunting, sad—had sent a surge of pure tenderness pulsing through him. He'd wanted to wrap his arms about her and heal her hurt.

Another prominent feeling that was increasing daily in urgency.

He was coming to care too much, Quinn knew, yet he couldn't summon much regret. Despite his growing frustration at being forced to hide out here, he relished having Venetia all to himself. Even more remarkable, he *wanted* to be closer to her.

He also wanted to share more of himself with her. Normally he kept matters about his life very private from his lovers, but he'd willingly told Venetia about his drive to create some meaningful consequence to his parents' tragic deaths. Not that his goal was a secret. Merely that he'd long ago learned to keep his relationships purely sexual and shallow.

He couldn't maintain that same dispassion with Venetia now.

In truth, he'd meant his offer of a modern marriage. He wanted her to be free to choose her own fate. After insisting that she wed him, he owed her that much. Yet for the first time he wondered what a real marriage with Venetia could be like.

Wondered what it would take to make her want to remain in England with him.

Quinn shook his head in amazement. He couldn't believe he was actually contemplating trying to build a lasting future with Venetia—or at a minimum, give their union a real chance to blossom.

Her issues would not easily be overcome. She mistrusted intimacy even more than he did. He'd almost laughed when Venetia had claimed to be liberated, knowing that she was still shackled by her painful past. He wanted to be the man to set her free, to make her forget her betrothed had ever existed, to ease her hurt and teach her how special she was.

Pondering the challenges he faced, Quinn grimaced wryly. Since the moment they'd met, he hadn't measured up in her eyes and had more than once earned her disappointment. More important, unjustly or not, she felt warranted in questioning his honor and his ability to remain faithful.

He would have to prove he would never betray her, obviously, Quinn reflected. But how to convince her was much less obvious.

Love would be an excellent reason for him to remain faithful, but he wasn't ready to entertain such a drastic step. He had his own problems with trust, admittedly. He was still unwilling to leave his own fate in a woman's possibly callous hands, rendered impotent and helpless, his heart at the mercy of fickle providence.

Even if he couldn't offer Venetia love, though, he'd vowed to give her a good life, to ensure her happiness.

And perhaps there could be much more between them than simple pleasure after all.

He would definitely have to think on it, Quinn decided, since clearly he would never be able to conquer his ever-burgeoning desire for her.

Shortly after midday, their situation changed abruptly. As they were finishing luncheon, a message arrived from the Earl of Hawkhurst. Quinn bade the courier to see to his horse and wait for a reply, then studied the missive intently.

From her place beside him at the dining table, Venetia watched anxiously as Quinn frowned. "What does Hawkhurst say? Did he find evidence linking Lisle to the attacks on you?"

"No. He had Lisle followed and also questioned a number of servants and acquaintances, but uncovered no suspicious behavior. Hawk now believes Lisle is unlikely to be the culprit. But he sent news of greater import."

"What could be greater?"

"A report from Macky in France."

"About the shipwreck?"

"Yes." Quinn's grave expression worried her. "Macky found no indication of a salvage effort or recently discovered treasure. As far as he can tell, my parents' schooner is still there at the bottom of the sea. But there were rumors of a survivor from the wreck. A passenger who lived several weeks before dying of her injuries."

Venetia felt her heart skip a beat. "Weren't all the passengers thought drowned at sea?"

"Yes, but these rumors claim that the day after the violent storm, a woman washed ashore near a coastal village some twenty leagues from the port where my parents embarked."

She furrowed her brow as she tried to calculate the meaning of the news. "Could it have been your . . . mother?"

When Quinn lifted his gaze to hers, she could see the troubled emotion there in the blue depths. "It's possible. Or it could have been Ash and Kate's mother, Lady Beaufort. Or a maid or some other female servant. Hawk warned that it is too soon to draw any conclusions. Macky needs more time to identify the woman and locate those who tried to nurse her back to health. It happened so long ago, though, the trail is ice cold."

Quinn ran a hand through his hair in obvious frustration. "Macky's investigation has only spawned more mysteries, but his report settles it for me. I am returning to London on the morrow."

His adamant declaration disquieted Venetia. "Is that necessary?"

"I want to be ready to sail to France in the event there is any news about my mother."

Of course if his mother had survived for even a short time, he would want to know more about what had happened. Even so . . . "But in London, you will still be in grave danger."

"I have cowered here long enough."

"Can Hawkhurst not continue investigating in your absence?"

"It grates, relying on Hawk and Macky to solve my problems. I intend to take back control of my life."

Hearing the resolve in his voice, Venetia realized the futility of arguing. "What will you do?"

Quinn folded the missive. "I think the time has come for me to confront Lisle directly. Face-to-face, I can get a sense of his desire for revenge and perhaps determine for certain if the attacks on me are related to the pendant."

"And if not?"

"Then I should refocus the investigation elsewhere, starting with my main shipping rival. In any case, my return could serve to draw out the assassin."

A chill swept over Venetia. "Surely there is no need for such haste."

"There is every need. By the time I reach London, I will have been gone a fortnight."

Aware of the queasy knot forming in her stomach, she tried once more. "You do remember that your wound is not fully healed yet?"

"It has healed well enough. You saw that for yourself yesterday when you inspected the remaining stitches. I can ride now, and I no longer feel disgustingly weak. You needn't worry about me, Venetia."

"How can I help it? You could be killed."

"I promise you I will take every precaution," he said lightly, almost jovially.

It disturbed her that he was dismissing the danger so readily.

Evidently Quinn had similar concerns about her,

judging by his next statement: "I want you to remain in Somerset. You will be far safer here."

Her eyebrows shot up. "You must be jesting. I won't cower, either."

"I am not asking you to cower."

"Are you not? What is good for the goose . . ." Quinn was a protector at heart, but she felt the same protectiveness toward him. "Even if our marriage is a sham, I want to accompany you."

"Our marriage is not a sham."

"Perhaps not entirely—which bolsters my argument. You are my husband now. My place is by your side."

His gaze arrested and lit with a sudden glint. "So you are claiming me for your husband?"

She hesitated. "Temporarily, yes. I thought a chief justification for our hasty marriage was that you could save my family from scandal. If I remain in the country so shortly after our nuptials, it will look as if you have abandoned me."

"True." He paused a moment, considering her. "You cannot be eager to return to London and deal with your sister and your parents as regards our marriage."

Venetia felt her heart sink. Her family was yet another reason she would rather postpone her return. No doubt they had been shocked to read the wedding announcement in the papers. By now they would have had time to absorb the news, but they would likely still be furious at having their obedient younger daughter's splendid marital prospects stolen by their traitorous elder daughter.

"I am not looking forward to *that* encounter," Venetia admitted honestly.

"You won't be alone," Quinn said reassuringly. "Particularly since I am responsible for our union."

"I am grateful. But the consequences of our nuptials are trifling compared to the threat to your life."

He pursed his lips pensively. "I might detour slightly to Portsmouth on the way to London. The construction of my steamship is at a crucial stage, and I want to check the progress. Moreover, I can ascertain if my master builder or engineers have seen any signs of sabotage or the slightest evidence that might implicate my business rival, and if not, to alert them to mount a vigilant watch."

The longer he delayed the better, Venetia thought. "You did not answer me, Traherne. If you are returning, so am I."

"I gave you fair warning about using my title, love." He rose from the table and went to her side. "Your slip warrants a kiss." With a forefinger, he tipped her chin up, then bent down to capture her mouth.

Venetia was jolted by his abruptness but found herself melting with warmth. By the time he drew back, her entire body was pulsing with need.

"Quinn, then," she said unsteadily. "I want your answer."

"I like the sound of my name on your lips."

At his amused tone, she gazed at him in flustered exasperation. "You are trying to change the subject."

"Not at all. The discussion is over. We will both have to concede. We leave at first light tomorrow morning." He paused, letting his gaze sweep down her gown to linger on her breasts. "When I have sent a reply to Hawk by courier, I will visit the cave, if you care to join me. This will be our last chance to enjoy the hot springs."

Despite her frustration, Venetia recognized his comment as an invitation and suddenly felt her pulse leap. Quinn was right. This would be their last chance to enjoy the cave pool—and to enjoy each other in such uniquely intimate circumstances as well.

Venetia spoke little as she followed Quinn along the tunnel to the inner cave, but one word was forefront in her mind: *want*.

She wanted to end this unbearable sexual tension between them. She wanted to give in to desire. She wanted to know passion with this man. Yet the paralyzing shyness that had suddenly struck her rendered her mute.

She watched silently as Quinn undressed by lamplight. Her concern about his injury was very real, so when his shirt came off, she scrutinized the healing flesh at his waist. The seam looked puckered and red but no longer quite so jagged. Still, she wanted to press her lips against his wound to soothe away the last of the pain.

Then he shed his boots and breeches and Venetia found it difficult to breathe. Her mouth dry, she stood transfixed. He was beautiful, the most riveting man she'd ever beheld, a golden Adonis. His body was perfectly proportioned, rippling with muscle, long-limbed, well endowed. Her stomach contracted at the sight of his swollen manhood, jutting out long and thick from the nest of dark hair at his groin.

Looking up again, she realized her examination

pleased him. When their gazes touched, locked, a shiver danced down her spine.

Something in him drew her so powerfully, and not just his mere physicality. Swallowing, she dug her nails into her palms, battling a fierce urge to touch him.

In the silence, Quinn turned away and slipped into the pool.

He sank below the surface and came up again to stand facing her, waist deep in the water, his hair dripping, his skin streaming, his torso glistening in the soft lamplight.

"So?" he murmured, waiting for her to decide.

"I want to know what lovemaking is like," she said in a voice barely above a whisper.

The resultant flare in his eyes only fired the sizzling current of awareness that hummed through her.

"Why don't you undress and join me?" he suggested. "The water is a pleasant temperature."

Obeying, Venetia removed her gown, then her half boots and finally her undergarments.

She was thankful that Quinn was not staring at her but had started swimming, rolling and submerging lazily in the water, giving her time to adjust to their mutual nudity.

Hurriedly, Venetia slid into the pool. The heat was a bit of a shock as she ducked to cover herself up to her neck. She was certain that even in the dim light, Quinn could see her blush, and when he spoke, she knew he understood her nervousness.

"You needn't feel shy with me, love. We have been intimate before, remember?"

Of course she remembered. The memory of his

touch filled her with a sweet, aching longing. Given their past encounters, it was foolish to hide her naked body from him.

Steeling herself, Venetia stood up. When her bare breasts broke the surface, Quinn went very still.

"Do you have any notion how damned beautiful you are?"

His praise made her flush, while his tender scrutiny left her trembling with vibrant sensations.

"Come closer, Venetia," he commanded huskily.

As she obeyed, he trapped her in his hot blue gaze. When she halted a foot away, she was intensely aware of the heat emanating from his body, aware of how hard her heart was beating. And his eyes . . . Those intense eyes held her entranced, effortlessly capturing her senses.

He reached for her, the heat of fingers on her bare arms more scalding than the water, and drew her close enough that her thighs brushed his, setting off a new chain of sparks. But then he seemed to struggle with himself.

"Perhaps you should take the lead. I don't trust myself to go slowly."

His admission was made in a hoarse voice. It strangely comforted her, knowing that she was not the only one so powerfully affected. "I . . . am not certain what to do."

A deeper flash of tenderness showed in his eyes, so naked and soft it took her breath away. "You can begin by taking down your hair. I have longed to see it free."

Reaching up, Venetia began removing the pins from her hair. Quinn must have noted how unsteady her fingers were, however, since he moved behind her and took over the task.

He tossed the pins on the edge of the pool and snared a stray lock, letting it drift through his fingers. "Your hair feels like satin."

Gathering the dark mass in both hands, he threaded his fingers through her tresses as if reveling in a treasure. "I have wanted to do this for a very long time. Years, in fact."

Puzzled, she glanced over her shoulder at him. "What do you mean, years?"

"I've wanted you from the moment I first met you. Could you not tell?"

"No . . ."

Angling his head, he lowered his face to hers. His breath fanned warm against her mouth before he gave her the most exquisite kiss imaginable.

Desire replaced the shaky feeling inside Venetia, as undeniable as the need to breathe. Quinn kissed the strength right out of her bones as his hands slid around her from behind to fondle her breasts.

A tremor passed through her. She felt her heart clamoring against her ribs at the glorious sensations in her breasts, in her entire body. When a soft moan escaped her, he pressed closer, making her keenly aware of the hard blade of his arousal nestled against her buttocks. Then his leg slid between hers, bringing the heart of her into intimate contact with his thigh, setting off a fresh firestorm of sensations in her middle.

A short time later, he shifted his lips to the side of her neck, ending his kiss but not his attentions, instead concentrating on her pleasure elsewhere.

"You have the most delectable skin . . ." he said with rapt admiration. "So creamy and soft."

Leaving one hand to attend her tight nipples, he moved the other lower, stroking over her bare skin beneath the water, sweeping across her mound, tangling in the thatch of curls that hid her sex.

". . . and the most luscious body . . ."

He touched her all over, the drift of his fingers so erotic on her skin, she softened against him helplessly. Nuzzling her temple, he slid his fingers between the slippery folds while his thumb found the sensitive nub unerringly, sending jolts of desire through her, the action so completely sensual that she whimpered.

At the sound, he delved deeper, caressing her inside and out with slow strokes. He aroused her until she was quivering, until she felt overwhelmed with sensation, until her hips were undulating with need.

"That's it . . ." he whispered in her ear. "Give in, sweet Venetia. Let me give you the pleasure you deserve."

A great shudder rocked her as her cries echoed in the small cave.

The climax that shook her and carried her away left her faint and weak. Long moments later she realized she was leaning back against Quinn, half floating. His arms supported her while he pressed soft kisses against her hair.

She opened dazed eyes to look up at him. The tenderness she saw on his face was incredible.

A warm lassitude had stolen over her, so it was a very long moment before she could speak. "It doesn't . . . seem fair that I should have all the pleasure."

"Trust me, I feel immense pleasure, making you come apart in my arms."

"Still, there is more, isn't there?"

"Far more. But you will have to control the pace."

He made her feel so desirable, and she wanted him to feel the same way. Her feet finding the bottom of the pool, she turned in his embrace and slid her arms around his neck, then raised her lips to his.

She hadn't counted on his reaction, however. His arms abruptly tightened around her, and his mouth came down hard on hers, startling a moan of surprise from her.

His control was on a knife's edge, she realized with a feeling of elation. His kiss was hungry and lusty and raw, devouring. She returned his passion measure for measure. The heat between them only intensified, stirring the wildness that clamored in her blood. As if he shared her same fever, he kissed her more fiercely than ever before, as if he were starved for the taste of her mouth.

She never knew what made him break off. Quinn held himself a little away from her, his face hard and taut, his breathing heavy. Panting herself, she gazed up into his searing eyes. Deep in them an unmistakable emotion burned: raw need and naked desire.

Gathering her courage, she reached to touch the pulsing crest of his manhood. She heard the harsh intake of his breath as she wrapped her fingers around his rigid shaft—

Quinn caught her hand and held it away. "Stop, or I will wind up ravishing you."

"I wouldn't mind," she said shyly. "I want to touch you."

"Venetia . . ." Her name was a tormented whisper.

"I want to kiss you there, the way you kissed me."

He groaned deep in his throat. "Not just now. You will make me explode. This time is for you."

Stepping closer, she pressed a light, provocative kiss against his chest. "Then why are you waiting? Please, take me, Quinn."

Bending, he leaned his forehead against hers and shuddered. "We need to go slowly for your first time. Your body must be ready."

"I think I am ready now."

His head lifted again so he could see her face. "There is no hurry. I don't want to rush this moment. I want to savor it."

Knowing he had to suppress the violent wrench of exhilaration and anticipation flooding his veins, Quinn inhaled another harsh breath and regained command of himself.

He stood still for a moment, his gaze taking in her creamy nakedness. Her body was exquisitely lovely, not lush but perfectly shaped, even lovelier than he'd imagined. The sight ravished his senses. Moving closer, he cupped her buttocks and drew her hips to his. Her body had been primed for him for days, but he wanted her breathless and pleading for him, so he reached down to press his palm between her thighs.

Venetia stifled a gasp of pleasure, but he heard her accelerated breathing, felt her excited trembling. Her innate sensuality stirred and excited him as well.

He watched the flush of color on her cheeks spread down her throat as his fingers teased her sex. When he judged her ready, he lifted her up and encouraged her to wrap her legs around his waist while he centered his cock at her cleft.

Then bracing her hips with his hands, he pressed the blunt head of his erection carefully upward, parting her folds as gently as he could.

Venetia made no response initially, but when he encountered resistance, she caught her breath and bit her lip.

"Am I hurting you too much?"

"No. Not too much."

"Relax against me if you can."

When she complied, he eased farther into the heat of her and felt the expected obstruction give way. For a fleeting moment, pain flashed across her face at the intimate invasion, but then her features softened.

Quinn drove more deeply into her tight, velvety sweetness and waited for her to grow accustomed to his size. "Better?"

At his question, she moved her hips slightly, testing. "Yes."

He couldn't repress the shudder of hot tension that gripped him. The need to possess her was overwhelming; the raw, primitive urge to join with her, to mate with her, nearly uncontrollable. Yet he fiercely clamped down on his urges and began to move slowly, holding her gaze all the while.

Her eyes were luminous with heat and need. "I want more," she entreated after a moment.

Obliging, he surged slowly in, sheathing himself fully in her melting warmth, until he was seated deep inside her, then pulled partway out.

At his slow thrust and withdrawal, Venetia closed

her eyes and arched her back, straining toward him. Soon she was shifting feverishly against him and panting, her nails digging into his shoulders as she clung to him.

There was something enchanting about how lost, how abandoned, she looked. Something magical at how their bodies merged as one, locked together, moving in a timeless, primal rhythm.

When he felt her first delicate convulsions, Quinn clenched his jaw in an effort to hold back. But when he felt her peaking, all the air left his lungs and his muscles bunched. In another heartbeat, her spasms pushed him over the edge. She was coming for him, melting around him. . . .

At her climax, he groaned as wave after wave of raw desire washed through him. He'd wanted to keep his violence to a minimum, but the beauty of it was too much, the wait had been too long.

His thrusts grew more frantic until he finally exploded. Ecstasy crested and broke over him in powerful waves, leaving him spent and gasping.

In the aftermath, Quinn held her tightly, shocked by the intensity of what had just happened. Their harsh breaths mingling, Venetia collapsed against him and pressed her face into the curve of his shoulder.

After a long moment, though, she sighed, a blissful sound. "Can you die of pleasure?" she whispered.

Perhaps so, Quinn thought as he breathed in the sweet scent of her.

He hadn't expected his powerful, powerless response. Their intimacy had rattled him to the core. He couldn't remember ever feeling such pleasure as taking Venetia for the first time. And still sheathed in the hot wonder of her body, he knew a single time would never be enough.

Yet he needed to consider her innocence.

With regret, he withdrew from her body and lowered her into the water.

She kept her arms about his neck, looking up at him uncertainly. "Did I hurt your wound?"

"Not in the least."

"Then . . . it was pleasurable for you?"

Tenderness tugged at his heart. "It was even better than my dreams."

A strange expression lit her luminous eyes. "You dream of me?"

"How could I not?"

She ducked her head but not before he saw her shy smile.

Quinn was aware of the rippling of tender emotions inside him. While Venetia was still dazzled by the lush mysteries of passion coursing through her body, passion was no mystery to him. This intoxicated feeling, however, was staggeringly unique in his experience.

He'd told himself that her sexual liberation was his goal. But he was fooling himself by pretending there was nothing deeper. He was becoming too involved, he knew. Coming to care too much. And yet it felt natural.

His silent contemplations, however, only served to rouse Venetia's uncertainty again.

"I doubt I could ever measure up to your other lovers," she murmured.

"You can and you did." She was far better than his

other lovers, but she needed more reassurance, he knew. "I have wanted to make love to you for years."

"I never knew."

"Honor prevented me from showing any sign while you were betrothed."

"Do you suppose . . . Could we make love again?"

He couldn't stop his smile at her unique combination of shyness and abandonment. Her eagerness was highly flattering, but he had to think of her.

"It was your first time. I don't want to make you too sore."

Disappointment crept over her beautiful face.

"Never fear, love. I promised you pleasure, remember?"

He guided her backward until they reached the edge of the pool, but there he hesitated. Venetia was looking up at him expectantly, her ripe lips parted.

Returning her gaze, Quinn was suddenly struck by the swift return of passion. He'd thought he needed time to recover, but he had already grown hard again where her hips cradled his.

How could he ever have thought they could keep apart when their desire was so strong? How could he ever have thought he could keep his need under control?

It was fortunate that she'd insisted on returning with him to London despite the danger. He didn't want to leave her behind. For one thing, he needed a great deal more time to woo her, Quinn thought, wondering if an eternity would be enough to satisfy the craving he felt for Venetia just now, if anything could douse the unreasoning desire that seared him.

Giving in momentarily, he reached up and took her

face in his hands, more roughly than he intended. Hunger drove his fingers deep into her hair to bring her luscious mouth to his. Her response was just as passionate and impulsive, though, and renewed all his thoughts of ravishment.

He kissed her ravenously, until they were both breathless. Then with a harsh, shuddering inhalation, he forced himself to break off and step back.

Shifting his hands to span her waist, he lifted her up to sit on the bank.

"Quinn . . . what are you doing?"

He was taking back control of his own riotous, helpless longings. "Lie back, sweeting."

Urging her down onto the flat stone, he nudged her legs apart. Her breath hitched when he leaned forward and splayed his palms over her bare breasts.

With Venetia spread out before him like a sumptuous feast, he stepped between her parted thighs. "I have wanted to do this for years also."

Lowering his head, he lightly kissed her slick cleft, eliciting another soft gasp from her.

The taste of her rekindled the fierce ache in his loins. And moments later, when she whispered his name—his given name—on a husky, needful rasp, the fire that ignited inside him was as powerful as he'd ever felt.

Quinn proceeded to have his way with her, aware that possessiveness had never gripped him so hard. He was also aware of an incontrovertible fact: With the consummation, he had made Venetia his wife. For better or worse, he had claimed her for his own.

And in so doing, they had crossed an invisible bridge and there was no going back.

Chapter Thirteen

Before they left for Portsmouth early the next morning, Quinn suggested once more that Venetia remain safely in Somerset, but she would have none of it. In good conscience, she could not possibly remain behind. What if he were killed while she was safe in hiding, sitting here cravenly doing nothing to help him? If he had to face danger, she wanted to be at his side.

Granted, Venetia reflected as Quinn handed her into the waiting coach, her about-face in so short a time was odd considering that she had wanted to do him bodily harm only a fortnight ago. But she felt linked to him now, in no small part because of the consummation of their union yesterday.

Her body still throbbed with the aftershocks. She had never realized passion could be so magical. Their joining had been like becoming part of him—profoundly intimate not only physically but emotionally as well.

Quinn was the consummate lover, by turns gentle

and demanding, always captivating. Venetia flushed to remember how he had made her writhe and moan and then calmed her afterward with soothing whispers.

His remarkable skill explained why women threw themselves at his feet and lost their heads and hearts over him. Why former paramours tried desperately to hold on to him—Lady X causing a public scene to regain his favor, for example—and why Venetia's own young schoolmate, Lydia Price, had fallen madly in love with him with absolutely no encouragement.

She herself was no less susceptible than those hapless victims of desire, Venetia conceded as she sat next to Quinn in the swaying vehicle. In truth, she realized, she felt decidedly different than she had during the journey that had brought them here. After yesterday's experience, she understood how one could easily become addicted to lovemaking. She also better understood why certain men became rakes.

It was not just the incredible pleasure Quinn had given her with his masterful lovemaking. It was more that he had made her feel utterly womanly and desirable in every part of her being. And when she recalled spending last night in his bed, how the entire time he had held her like a cherished lover . . . the memory of how wonderful it felt made her throat ache.

Dawn had come far too early, to her mind. She had wanted to stay curled against him forever, warm and safe and treasured.

Waking beside Quinn was a newly cherished experience as well. Simply meeting his tender blue eyes made her breath catch. But then, breathlessness was becoming a habit every time he merely looked at her.

And when he touched her—even if the gesture was as casual as assisting her into the carriage—she felt a warm, telltale swelling between her thighs.

Foolish, really, especially since his focus this morning had switched to more serious matters. Venetia had to shake herself from her blissful memories to concentrate on his reasons for detouring by Portsmouth on the southwestern coast of England: He not only wanted to check construction of his steamship but to alert his master builder and engineers to watch out for any signs of sabotage.

"My methods of fabrication are no secret," Quinn expounded, "but if the villain is my main shipping rival, David Huffington, I would expect him to try to prevent our completion. If he hopes to corner the market on ocean steam transport, greed could be his motive. Otherwise, why would he try to kill me but leave my newly designed ship intact?"

His rationale made good sense to Venetia, and for the remainder of the journey, she listened with interest as Quinn explained the rudimentaries and scientific principles of propelling a wooden-hulled, three-masted, schooner-rigged sailing ship by auxiliary steam power.

He was obviously passionate about the subject. As he narrated the difficulties of design and manufacture, particularly the crucial relationship between weight and stability and the enormous scale of the endeavor, it became clear that he was not just the source of funding but was deeply involved in every aspect of the venture. And when they arrived in Portsmouth early that afternoon, she received a firsthand glimpse of Quinn in action.

A soft spring rain earlier had left the air smelling fresh and clean, but the more pungent scents of brine and fish and tar joined the mix when they reached the shipyard.

His construction crew, Quinn had said, was supervised by a master builder and three engineers but relied on seasoned sailors to advise on practical operations. A nearby foundry had made the single-cylinder engine, boiler, and twin collapsible paddle wheels, which had all then been transported by wagon in pieces and assembled on a dry dock.

Upon stepping down from the carriage, Venetia could see the decks swarming with laborers. The moment she boarded with Quinn, a small group of men broke away to greet him with enthusiasm, looking surprised once the introductions were made to learn that his lordship had married.

After that, Quinn became fully absorbed with the challenges and the smallest details regarding the new ship—so much so that he seemed to forget about her. Yet Venetia didn't mind. It was fascinating to see this side of him, his sharp mind intent on solving problems, the intrigued light in his eyes as he interrogated his engineers about gear ratios and flywheels and housing frames for the ten-bladed paddles and inspected even nooks and crannies.

The construction efforts were still encountering obstacles, he was told, and although there had been no obvious instances of sabotage, his crew promised to be on guard during the final two months before launch.

"It is all quite amazing," Venetia said honestly when she and Quinn returned to the carriage.

Her praise made him smile. "Several paddle steamers have served as river ferries here in England in the last decade, and one crossed the Channel to France last year. But none were designed for speed or have proved seaworthy for long voyages. Huffington's steamship construction is six months behind ours and it hasn't the increased capability of weathering storms. But even if I have no evidence to suggest he's the culprit, it's only wise to investigate him, if only to rule him out."

Venetia's expression sobered at the reminder they were returning to danger.

The closer they got to London, the more her nerves felt on edge. Their mission was to find and stop a potential killer, but they disagreed over the best way to proceed. Quinn's plan was to flush out the villain by making himself more visible, which alarmed Venetia.

"I intend to take precautions," Quinn assured her. "Hawk has experienced men I can call upon. I can hire a virtual army for protection if need be. In fact, I want armed footmen accompanying you at all times. If I am at risk, you will be also."

"I trust you will do the same for yourself."

"Yes, but I must be discreet about it. I cannot draw out my attacker while surrounding myself with guards and hiding at home."

She gave a huff of exasperation. "You are supposed to have a brilliant mind. It seems witless and reckless to put yourself out there as a target. I don't like it one bit."

"I am flattered that you are worried for my sake."

"I am not the only one. Your sister thinks you risk your own skin far too frequently."

"In this case it is necessary. I'll call upon Lisle first thing tomorrow so I will have the element of surprise. I will go armed, naturally."

Her gaze clashed with Quinn's. "If Lisle is guilty, he could kill you before you have a chance to defend yourself."

"I promise I will be ready for him."

Venetia bit her lip, remembering the shock of seeing Quinn's blood, her stark fear when she realized that he had been shot. She couldn't bear to think of him being hurt again, or killed.

"Come here, love," he commanded in a soothing voice as he reached for her and drew her against him. He was obviously trying to mollify her, and as she laid her head on his shoulder, she felt an instant warmth.

Although her concern didn't abate, Venetia reflected that she would just have to hope and pray his plan would succeed.

It was nearly midnight when they arrived at the Traherne mansion in Berkeley Square. Despite being roused from their beds at the late hour, the servants were far more welcoming to Venetia than previously, perhaps because Quinn had made it clear that she was now mistress of his household. He suggested, however, that she retire for the night while he checked his study for any messages from Hawk.

When Mrs. Pelfrey inquired if the lord and lady were to have separate bedchambers, Quinn said to give her ladyship the same rooms as before, then made for his study. As she followed Mrs. Pelfrey upstairs to her rooms, Venetia tried to stifle her disappointment at the sleeping arrangements and instead focus on the luxury and taste surrounding her in the beautiful mansion.

The distraction lasted as she washed off her travel dirt and donned her nightdress. To her dismay, though, when she climbed into bed she felt acutely alone and lonely. Rolling over, she punched her pillow, highly annoyed at herself. She had spent only her second night in Quinn's arms and already she missed him.

Although weary from the long journey, Venetia lay awake long into the wee hours, assaulted by uncertain, chaotic feelings. Most likely Quinn was curtailing his pursuit of her since he had succeeded in making her his conquest. It stood to reason that he would no longer want her as ardently. Or perhaps the exact opposite was true: He wanted her to plead to be with him.

Which she would never, ever do. She couldn't afford to forget that he had broken countless hearts, including her young friend Lydia's. She was determined she would never fall in love with Quinn as so many other foolish women had done. Her heart had shut itself away, and she intended for it to remain so.

Still, she couldn't shake her anxiety for him.

Venetia rose early the next morning, bleary-eyed and groggy, and after pulling on a dressing gown, joined him at the breakfast table.

Quinn, already dressed for the day, looked surprised and amused to see her. "Are you checking up on me?"

"No. I only wanted to implore you to be careful."

"I intend to. If it eases your mind any, I plan to conceal a pistol in my greatcoat pocket and carry a sword cane. By the bye, Hawk sent a message saying he approves of my plan to confront Lisle."

"I suppose that will have to suffice."

"Have some breakfast, my love. You must be hungry."

Venetia knew she couldn't possibly eat just now, but she accepted a cup of tea from the footman hovering at the sideboard. The knowledge that Quinn could lose his life filled her with dread. Rationally or not, she would fear for him every time he left the house until the assassin was caught.

When he had finished eating, she followed him to the front door. After donning his coat and hat, he stepped closer to her. Molding a hand to her face protectively, he bent to give her a brief kiss, and for a fleeting moment his lips lingered on hers.

The gesture was casual yet affectionate, no doubt for the benefit of the servants, but it left Venetia flustered and hot and reminded her vividly of his lovemaking. And just now, she was glad for the diversion.

"As soon as I speak to Lisle," Quinn assured her as he accepted his pistol and cane from his butler, "I will return home and give you a report."

"I will be waiting anxiously. Please, take care."

When he was gone, Venetia turned away from the door instead of watching him descend the front steps and enter his waiting carriage. She was firmly resolved to control her trepidation and shake the worry that she was possibly sending him to his death.

She told herself she oughtn't feel ashamed of her fear for Quinn, or disconcerted that she felt such a strong alliance with him, even if they weren't true man and wife. It was only reasonable that the threat of danger bound the two of them together. And it was all right that she wouldn't breathe easily until he returned home to her safe and sound.

It was difficult, Quinn thought as he settled into his carriage, to leave Venetia like that, looking tousled and drowsy and heartrendingly beautiful, having just arisen from her bed.

A bed he regrettably hadn't shared.

As the vehicle began to move forward, a searing memory flashed through his mind of their lovemaking in the cave that last day in Somerset:

Venetia's expression full of dazed wonder and urgency as he moved inside her.

Her soft cries of ecstasy as he released her inner fire, all that long-repressed passion . . .

He could still taste the sweetness of it, the hot stinging need in his body, the staggering intimacy he'd felt, the overwhelming tenderness. Her ability to fire his blood had never surprised him, but he still felt stunned by his feelings in the aftermath of their consummation.

He would find it even more difficult, Quinn knew, to wait for his plan for Venetia to bear fruit. He had forced her to wed him, but he couldn't force her surrender. He had to let her come to him.

Quinn felt his jaw flex involuntarily. He'd long ago learned that there was an art to wooing women. In fact, he had deliberately honed his skills as a lover, his way of controlling his fate in small measure. After being pursued for his fortune and title at a young age, he'd wanted to be desired solely for himself, not his inheritance.

In Venetia's case, he needed to build her desire to a fever pitch so that she would come to him willingly. So that she would *stay* with him willingly.

It would take all of his willpower, however, to curb his impatience.

At least he seemed to be making progress in one respect. She cared enough to be gravely worried for him. He felt similarly about her. Few women would be so stalwart in the face of danger. Venetia was not one to turn away from peril out of fear, he knew. Rather, she would cope with any crisis that came her way, even if it meant braving an assassin at his side. Her courage continued to impress him—and worry the devil out of him as well.

Quinn's fingers closed reflexively around the handle of his sword cane. It would be unforgivable if she came to harm because he'd married her to save her family from ruin, only to make her a target for a killer. He had to solve the riddle of the assassin quickly and put an end to the threat to their lives. Only then would he relax his guard. Only then could he move on to solving the problem of his marriage—gaining Venetia's trust and healing her past hurts.

Another thing was also becoming clear. He couldn't let her conflict with her family continue to fester. She had been separated too long from the sister she cared deeply about.

Quinn tightened his grip on the cane. First he had to confront Edmund Lisle and discover what he could about the pendant. After that, he would see about mending Venetia's relationship with her parents and her sister.

Lisle resided in a newer part of town, near where Quinn's cousin Jack lived, in an elegant, storied terrace house. When Quinn demanded entrance, the sleepy manservant who answered the front door looked properly intimidated and hastily agreed to rouse his master from his bed.

Several minutes later, the master himself came stalking down the staircase. Edmund Lisle was a man of medium build, a trifle portly, with thinning brown hair—and, at the moment, bloodshot eyes, likely the result of a late night gambling. He also boasted handsome features and a vast fortune, which no doubt appealed to Julia.

Lisle was barely civil enough to invite Quinn into a nearby parlor, and in the same gruff tone, ask him to be seated. Before Quinn could state his business as requested, Lisle went on the attack.

"I cannot imagine what has brought you here, but if you are attempting to lure Lady Dalton back, you will fail." His animosity was obvious, as was his defensiveness, and both likely stemmed from jealousy, Quinn knew.

"I assure you I have no such aim."

"Then why the devil are you here?"

Lisle was clearly puzzled by the visit rather than wary and nervous, which was a point in his favor, Quinn calculated. A guilty man would not have seemed so surprised.

"I came to inquire about your motives."

"I beg your pardon?"

"Did you try to have me killed a fortnight ago?"

Lisle first stared, then gave a bark of laughter. "Good God, no. Why would you think so?"

"There have been three attempts on my life recently, beginning the evening we played cards at Tavistock's. Each time assailants tried to end my existence."

"And you think it was I? How preposterous."

If he was acting, Quinn couldn't tell. Lisle's astonishment seemed genuine. Certainly he was exhibiting no sign that he feared retribution for attempted murder.

"Why in blazes would I want to kill you?" Lisle asked in true bafflement. "Granted, I may sincerely dislike you, but my antipathy is not so severe that I wish you dead. Besides, I wouldn't dare challenge you. You are known to be a crack shot and an even better swordsman."

"You could have hired accomplices," Quinn pointed out.

"To what purpose? I am not idiotic enough to risk your wrath. I value my skin too highly."

If Lisle was lying, he was making an expert job of it, but more likely he was innocent of the charges.

Quinn tried another tact. "Yet you blame me for Lady Dalton's scene in Hyde Park last year."

Lisle nodded. "I was livid enough to carve out your spleen, I admit. I was sorely jealous. But Julia and I came to an understanding. She had a change of heart, and I forgave her for her hysterics in the park." He pursed his lips thoughtfully. "Surely I am not the only enemy you have made. There must be others who have reason to want vengeance. A cuckolded husband, perhaps?"

Quinn let the insult slide, not bothering to explain he had never cuckolded anyone. Instead, he decided to move on to the next line of questioning. "Then you won't mind telling me how you came by the ruby and diamond pendant you gave her."

Lisle looked even more puzzled, then narrowed his eyes. "Is this some sort of trick? Or trap?"

"Not at all. How did you acquire the necklace?"

Lisle's gaze remained suspicious. "Why the devil do you care?"

"I believe it once belonged to my mother's family. When I saw Lady Dalton wearing it, I recognized the distinctive design as part of a collection, commissioned by the Duc de Chagny in France, before the Revolution."

"Did Julia know the design was your family's?" Lisle stopped short. "Of course she did. That is why she coveted it. The moment she saw it, she wanted it. Now I know why."

Lisle did not look happy with his calculation, and his mind was obviously still whirring. "Was that why you challenged me to a game at Tavistock's?"

Clearly Lisle was no slow top, and Quinn decided honesty was his best course. "Yes. I hoped to win it from you."

"I am glad you decided to fold that night. I regularly win, but you have the devil's own luck."

He'd ended the game when he'd spied Venetia, Quinn remembered. "Again, would you mind telling me how you came by it?"

Suddenly Lisle's expression softened as understanding dawned. "Do you mean to tell me there is something of mine that you want?" A slow smile stretched across his mouth. "I never would have expected to be in this position in a hundred years."

Lisle laughed with genuine amusement, and oddly Quinn liked him the more for it. In fact, he could see what Julia saw in him. Lisle was affable and generous and indeed honorable, with an ironic sense of humor that Quinn would have appreciated under other circumstances.

"I am willing to pay a handsome price for it. It has great sentimental value, since it was my mother's."

"The pendant is not mine to sell. I gave it to Julia."

"I know. But I would like your consent to buy it from her."

When Lisle hesitated, Quinn added, "Just think of it. I will be in your debt."

"Yes, you will be in my debt. I think I like the sound of that."

Lisle was enjoying having the upper hand for once, but then his mouth curled. "I realize you are throwing me a bone, Traherne."

"Hardly," Quinn answered at once. "You won Julia fairly."

After all the humiliation Julia had caused him, Lisle deserved a sop to his pride. Moreover, there was no point in wounding his dignity further, and there were benefits to making him an ally.

"I suppose I could be persuaded to tell you how I came by the pendant," Lisle said a trifle tauntingly. "Oh, what the devil . . ." Evidently he decided to relent. "I won it honorably, at Faro."

"From whom?"

"A chap named Bellamy. George Bellamy."

Quinn tried to place the name. "I am not acquainted with him. What can you tell me about him?"

"Not much. I am not familiar with him, either. And I haven't a clue how it came to be in his possession. I play cards for the sport, but gaming is his profession, and I suspect his major source of income."

"How do I find Bellamy?"

"I believe he lodges in Belgrave, although I am not certain. I do know he frequents Brooks's Club. You might start there in making inquiries."

"I will, thank you. As I said, I am in your debt."

Lisle grinned again, then sobered. "I give you fair warning, Traherne. Julia is mine and I intend to keep her."

"I promise I have no intention of challenging you for her affections. I agree wholeheartedly. She is yours."

"As long as you and she both know it," Lisle muttered. Then he paused. "It is too early for wine, but would you care for a pint of ale to cement our new understanding?"

Quinn smiled for the first time. "I would very much like that."

Vast relief filled Venetia when Quinn returned home seemingly unscathed. Watching his arrival from the parlor window, she waited anxiously until he joined her and she could confirm for herself that he had suffered no physical harm.

However, she wasn't certain what to feel about his conclusion that Lisle was not the perpetrator.

"Far from being angry and bitter," Quinn said as he settled beside her on the sofa, "Lisle was amused by my suspicions. And he was quite happy to learn I had no designs on his mistress, Lady Dalton."

That revelation made Venetia extremely happy also. She listened earnestly as Quinn detailed the steps he had taken to find the gamester George Bellamy.

"Bellamy has lodgings on Clarges Street. When I called there, his landlord said he had left for the countryside nearly a month ago on a repairing lease. Apparently he was short of funds due to his gaming losses. But he recently paid his rent in full for the next quarter and is expected back in town shortly. I promised the landlord a large sum to alert me the moment Bellamy sets foot in London again," Quinn added with a determined glint in his eye. "And I've tasked Hawk with investigating him in addition to Huffington. It's imperative that we learn more about his background, and quickly."

"It is almost as if you are enjoying the intrigue," Venetia observed, noting Quinn's expression.

He was quick to deny any relish. "I might enjoy solving the mystery if the consequences weren't so serious. Count me angry and frustrated, though, not to mention troubled. As long as the assassin is at large, my family is at grave risk." His gaze came to rest intently on Venetia. "Protecting you and my sister and the rest of my clan is my most important goal just now."

Venetia was grateful that he wanted to protect her. Other than Cleo, no one had cared about her welfare in two long years, not even her parents, who by rights should still have felt some sort of sheltering instincts.

The thought made her throat tighten. What a stark contrast from Quinn, she reflected, recalling how he had sprawled over her, shielding her from a bullet with his own body.

Indeed, he had been concerned for her from the first, even before she returned from France. His ostensible advances toward Ophelia had been altruistic—his attempt to repair some of the damage his friend Ackland had wrought on Venetia and her family with his dissolution. Venetia had certainly misunderstood Quinn's motives. . . .

"Meanwhile we can turn our attention to your family," Quinn was saying. "It is time to mend the rift."

"I'm not sure that is possible," she said uncertainly. "My parents may not even speak to me."

"They will if they are at all wise. I shall write them immediately, informing of our intent to call this afternoon."

When she looked skeptical, Quinn smiled without humor. "They won't dare refuse me admittance."

"Probably not. I, on the other hand . . . They despise me, not only for my rebellion two years ago but now, I'm sure, for stealing you from Ophelia."

"You didn't steal me."

"Even so, I can't help but feel guilty for spoiling her chances to marry well."

"You are accepting too much blame. Don't fret, darling. I am responsible for our marriage. And I will deal with your parents."

Venetia bit her lower lip. "Truthfully, I am not as

worried about my parents as I am about Ophelia. No doubt I hurt her. I very much want to meet with her and explain what happened . . . try and make peace with her, if that is at all possible."

Quinn's reply was a faint scoffing sound. "You care more about your sister than you do about yourself."

"Perhaps. In any case, I need to make amends for my past actions."

"You have more than made amends already. You wed me to spare her from ruin. You could even say you sacrificed yourself. Your family should all be grateful."

"They won't see it that way."

"You don't deserve their condemnation," Quinn returned forcefully.

Venetia had to agree. It still shocked her a little that her parents were so callous and unfeeling as to cast her out for refusing to marry Ackland.

"Allow me to deal with your family," Quinn repeated. "If they continue causing you distress, they will soon regret it."

She sent him a grateful smile. "I don't want them to suffer. I just don't want to be a pariah to them any longer. And it would be beyond my fondest hopes if we could return to somewhat amiable terms," Venetia said wistfully.

"Come here, love," he commanded. Reaching for her, he drew her onto his lap and lowered his face to hers. After giving her a sweet, lingering kiss that left her short of breath, he continued to nibble at her lips, evidently set on teasing her out of her low mood. "Far from being censured, you should be awarded a halo. You saved your sister from a fate worse than death—marriage to me."

She summoned a twisted smile. "I was mistaken on that score. Marriage to you is not worse than *death*."

Quinn chuckled while Venetia brought them back to the conversation. "Ophelia was likely stricken to lose you."

"She never had me."

"But she showed a decided partiality for you. Understandably, she was dazzled by your seductive charm. And my parents expected her to wed you."

"Their expectations were unfounded."

"Were they?" Venetia queried. "From the moment Ophelia made her debut, you were very particular in your attentions to her. According to the gossip rags, you stood up with her at three balls and took her in to supper at least once."

He feigned horror. "A shocking crime."

"Everyone thought you were on the verge of making her an offer. I'm sure my parents hoped to see Ophelia settled at Tallis Court before the year was out."

"They will have to be satisfied to see *you* established there."

Venetia didn't argue that she was unlikely to take up residence at the Traherne country seat, given their specific marital arrangements.

"Your parents won't risk being ostracized," Quinn added. "If they hope to show their faces in London, they will not only recognize you again but embrace your return to the fold."

It was a valid threat, Venetia knew. The Earl of

Traherne and his illustrious cousins in the House of Beaufort could rule London society if they wished.

"My reinstatement is not my biggest concern," Venetia asserted. "I don't want them to force Ophelia to marry for wealth and status. She should be able to marry for love. That was chiefly why I returned to England and sought you out."

"Why you hunted me down, you mean."

"I thought it was crucial to prevent your courtship—a courtship that never really existed." Venetia heard herself sigh. "Mama is set on Ophelia marrying a title, just as she was for me, and she likely won't be put off. I believe the loss of Ackland's title disturbed her the most."

"But now you have an even higher-ranking title," Quinn pointed out. "I've told you before, there are major benefits to being my countess. Your new position wields a great deal of power."

"In what respects?"

"You can now help Ophelia find a suitable match, for one thing. I can safely promise that Skye and Kate will be delighted to matchmake for your sister once the danger is over." Quinn abruptly shook his head. "God help me, I can't believe I am actually considering encouraging their romantic notions."

"Would they really help Ophelia?" Venetia asked hopefully.

"Of course. You have a new family now. Unlike your relatives, we Wildes don't turn our backs on our loved ones."

Somehow that quiet reassurance brought sudden tears to Venetia's eyes. She ducked her head to hide her response, not wanting to appear absurdly emotional.

Fortunately Quinn didn't seem to notice.

"That is one unique advantage to my family," he was saying. "We might commit more than our share of scandals, but we stick together through thick and thin. And you are a Wilde now, whether you like it or not. Now, pray excuse me while I go compose a note to your parents."

With one final, fleeting kiss, he shifted Venetia off his lap, extricating himself from their embrace, and stood.

Venetia watched him go with a chaotic mix of emotions whirling inside her.

You are a Wilde now. Strange how comforting those words sounded.

She wanted to believe them, too. Even if her marriage to Quinn was not on solid or permanent footing. Even if in the near future she would live her own life separate and apart from his.

Most of all, it was wonderful to think she was no longer alone. That she needn't be beset by such painful loneliness any longer.

Even if she was only—foolishly—indulging in wishful thinking.

Chapter Fourteen

Quinn's message received a swift reply confirming a time for their call. Thus, he and Venetia arrived at her parents' home on Henrietta Place some three hours later.

The knowledge that she wasn't alone fortified Venetia as she entered the parlor where Tobias and Helen Stratham awaited. They might not want to acknowledge her existence, but she would insist on it for Ophelia's sake.

Their fawning welcome for the Earl of Traherne proved a sharp contrast to their stiffness with their prodigal daughter.

"Venetia," her father said, nodding his head once in terse greeting.

"It is good to see you again, Papa . . . Mama."

Neither responded, and their exchange of glances indicated how awkward this meeting was for them.

Venetia felt a deep sadness as she gazed upon her parents for the first time in two years, taking in her father's graying hair, the new lines on her mother's face, their lips pursed in displeasure. Evidently they still could not pardon her for the unforgivable crime of bringing scandal to their good name, and worse, refusing to recant her public renunciation of Viscount Ackland and marry him.

Rather than converse with Venetia further, Mr. Stratham addressed the earl again. "I confess we were surprised by your sudden marriage, Lord Traherne."

"Yes, indeed, my lord," Mrs. Stratham added. "We heard there was a shooting."

"The shooting by an unknown perpetrator was incidental to our marriage," Quinn stated brusquely. "I have long admired your elder daughter and was greatly honored when she accepted my hand."

Brushing off any subsequent quizzing, he asserted that the visit was not made to effect a reconciliation but to discuss how to present a united front with the ton, and that he expected the Strathams to support his own family's efforts to bring Lady Traherne back into favor. Venetia had never seen Quinn so cold, and his dictatorial manner clearly intimidated her parents.

He concluded with an indictment of their woeful treatment of her. "Would that you had shown the slightest inclination to shield her from her vicious detractors. For that alone Venetia deserves your abject apologies."

Both Strathams turned red-faced and hastened to stammer contrite apologies, claiming they had merely acted out of concern for Ophelia.

Venetia accepted their explanations graciously, while giving Quinn a grateful glance. It was a novel feeling, knowing he was not only looking out for her and taking her side, but going to battle for her.

Yet her sorrow was only increased. Quinn was right; her parents wouldn't dare refuse him. Her rift with them, however, would never truly be mended, she realized. They had never been effusive or overly affectionate toward her, but they were her flesh and blood. If they had stood by her two years ago, the harsh judgment of society would have impacted her far less, and now they were only relenting due to coercion.

Venetia ached to think Ophelia would feel similarly. She had been protective of her younger sister since her birth and couldn't bear the thought of forever being separated.

"I should like to speak to Ophelia if I may," Venetia said quietly in the uncomfortable silence.

At her father's hesitation, Quinn intervened in a commanding voice that most mortals would jump to obey. "You will make Miss Stratham available to her, Stratham."

"Y-yes, certainly, my lord. I will have Ophelia summoned by a servant at once."

Venetia might have mustered a smile at her father's alacrity if not for the knots in her stomach at the thought of finally meeting her sister after so long. "I would prefer to see Ophelia alone, if I may."

"She is in her room," Mrs. Stratham offered stiffly. Venetia interpreted her mother's tone to mean they had hidden her there, not wanting to expose their younger daughter to the elder's shameful tarnish.

Quinn said he would wait here with them in the parlor, then smiled at Venetia and brought her gloved fingers to his lips in an obvious—if false—display of romantic affection. "Take all the time you wish, my love."

With a forced smile, Venetia excused herself and, with trepidation, climbed the stairs to the floor above. She devoutly hoped it was possible to gain back her former loving relationship with Ophelia.

When she reached her sister's bedchamber door and rapped lightly, she was swiftly bid entrance. She found her sister half reclining on a chaise longue, reading a book.

"Venetia!" Ophelia exclaimed breathlessly. She rose hurriedly but then stood gazing at her, not speaking.

Venetia did the same, drinking in the sight of her. Ophelia was more slender and not as tall as she, with hair a shade lighter than her own.

Then, with a tremulous smile, Ophelia launched herself across the room into Venetia's arms. "Oh, dearest sister, I have missed you so dreadfully!"

Relief flooded Venetia, along with a poignant gratitude that her sister had not adopted their parents' rigid coldness.

Ophelia drew back, her expression mournful. "Can you ever forgive me for shunning you?"

"Of course I can forgive you. You were only obeying Mama and Papa."

"But I was horrid to you. I never even met with you as you asked me to. Mama and Papa were adamant that you were to be cast out of our family. I am so very sorry, Venetia. I should have had the courage to rebel as you did." Ophelia hugged her hard again. "I have missed you so much," she repeated fervently, her declaration almost a sob.

Venetia felt tears well in her own eyes. "And I, you."

"You must have been so lonely."

Indeed she had been. "Yes, but that is all over now."

She returned her sister's embrace fiercely and found herself openly weeping at the release of her great fear.

Realizing Ophelia was now crying inconsolably, though, she fought for control. "This will never do, Phee. Our reunion should be a happy occasion."

"Yes, you are r-right."

With a shuddering breath, Ophelia pulled back and went to her bureau to fetch two handkerchiefs, one of which she handed to Venetia. When they began sniffing and drying their eyes in unison, they both gave watery laughs.

Linking arms, they moved over to the chaise and settled there as they had so many times when they were girls. For a time they spoke of less consequential matters before returning to the heart of their estrangement.

"I feared you might think I had stolen your beau by marrying Traherne," Venetia said tentatively.

"Oh, I was angry for an instant," Ophelia replied, "but not terribly. From your letters, I knew you were worried for me."

"I didn't want you to make the same mistake I made, falling in love with a libertine."

Ophelia smiled. "There was little danger of *that*. I was always nervous around Lord Traherne. He is too clever for me by half and a bit overwhelming. From the first, I could tell he was not interested in romance. He was never the least amorous. But until now, I never understood why he showed me such favoritism. His attentions would make sense if he was only helping me for your sake, Venetia."

"Still, I am sorry to have blighted your hopes of marrying an earl."

"It was Mama who harbored such fanciful dreams for me." A mischievous glint shone in Ophelia's eyes as she sighed theatrically. "It would have been pleasant to live on a great estate with servants and lovely clothes and jewels, but I doubt Lord Traherne would actually have wed me. I am very glad for you, though. But why *did* you marry him, Venetia? I would have thought he was too much like Ackland for your tastes."

"It seemed the only way to avoid further scandal after I was suspected of shooting him."

Her sister's eyes widened. "But you did *not* shoot him, did you? The rumors were many."

"No. His assailant is still at large."

Ophelia frowned. "How disturbing."

"Indeed, it is."

"Does your presence here now mean that you have mended fences with Mama and Papa?"

Venetia responded with a wry smile. "Regrettably, no. I doubt they will ever forgive me."

Ophelia made a face. "Mama especially was outraged by what she terms your public shaming. She believes you willfully sullied your reputation and left us the object of speculation and pity. I understood why you balked, however. Honorable gentlemen do not parade their doxies in front of respectable folk, and certainly they do not flaunt their indiscretions shortly before the wedding ceremony. You would have been miserable as Ackland's wife. I trust you are not too unhappy with Traherne."

"Strangely enough, I am not unhappy in the least."

Venetia saw no point in elaborating just now about her agreement with Quinn to go their separate ways.

"Of course," Ophelia went on, "Mama will disregard her objections now that you are a countess. She will see Traherne as the best way to recoup our social fortunes."

"Luckily, he agrees. And we both believe my new rank should aid in finding you a good match. I promise I will do everything in my power to help you, Phee. And Traherne's sister, Lady Skye, now Lady Hawkhurst, and his cousin Lady Katharine will lend their influence also."

"That would be capital!"

Venetia hesitated. If she succeeded in promoting a match, she would no longer feel quite so guilty for dashing Ophelia's prospects with Quinn, but even more than that, she wanted her sister's happiness. "You ought not be compelled to marry Mama's choice, Phee. You deserve to have love."

Ophelia cocked her head thoughtfully. "Perhaps I do. And now that you have fulfilled Mama's wishes and married an enormous fortune and illustrious title, I may be able to marry for inclination rather than duty."

They spoke for a few moments more before Venetia said with real regret, "I had best return to the parlor. Traherne was kind enough to keep Mama and Papa occupied while I met with you, but he should not be obliged to keep up the pretense for long."

Ophelia accompanied her downstairs, and they entered the parlor arm in arm.

To her surprise, her parents were much more welcoming, even going so far as to invite her to stay for tea. Quinn declined, claiming business matters to attend to, and shortly rose, extending a hand to Venetia so they could take their leave.

After she bid a fond farewell to her sister, Venetia went to her mother, who actually unbent enough to embrace her, albeit awkwardly. Thus, she left far more hopeful than when she had arrived. Venetia and her mother would never resume their former familial relationship or regain a semblance of warmth between mother and daughter, but at least the outright animosity had vanished for now.

Once settled in the carriage beside Quinn, Venetia questioned his methods. "Whatever did you do to win over my parents?"

"I charmed them with my enormous charisma, of course." His slow smile was reminiscent of the devilishly captivating Quinn she had come to know.

"Seriously, what did you say to them?"

"I first used veiled threats, then sweetened the pot with bribes. In short, I promised our support in finding a husband for Ophelia."

"Mama must have been overjoyed."

"She was."

"*I* was overjoyed that Ophelia bears me no ill will. . . ."

When her voice broke on the last word, Venetia ducked her head in embarrassment.

"What is this, tears?" Quinn asked.

Forcibly, she sniffed and brushed away the telltale moisture on her cheeks. "I must thank you again for saving my family from more scandal."

"I believe you deserve the credit. In fact, I impressed upon your parents how much they owe you. At least they now clearly see the benefits of staying on your good side."

He was trying to make her feel better, for which she was also grateful. Not for the first time, she reflected on how amazingly generous and kind Quinn was—a character trait he often hid behind his provoking manner.

Reaching up to brush her cheek with his thumb, he returned to his usual provocative self. "Did I ever tell you I can't abide weepy females?"

His complaint won a faint laugh from her, as no doubt he intended, and yet the emotional relief after so very long was difficult to suppress. Venetia accepted his proffered handkerchief and brought it to her eyes but couldn't hold back a sob.

"I beg of you, love, no more tears."

"I am s-sorry. I am not usually a watering pot."

"How well I know it. You are ordinarily given to confrontation instead."

Her quiet sobs didn't abate, though. With an aggrieved sigh, Quinn pulled her close and wrapped an arm around her. "Very well, you may cry on my shoulder, as long as you don't ruin my coat. This was tailored by Weston, I'll have you know."

It took some time, but Venetia eventually regained

control of her emotions. Then taking an unsteady breath, she gave a shaky chuckle against the blue superfine fabric and responded in his same vein. "It would be criminal of me to ruin your fine coat, you look so very handsome in it."

Holding her away, Quinn captured her gaze while letting his eyebrows shoot up in mock amazement. "Finally a compliment. Will wonders never cease?"

His warm teasing had the same effect as usual, and just like that, the fierce sexual attraction between them returned full force.

He didn't act on it, though. Rather, he retrieved the crumpled handkerchief from her clutching fingers and proficiently began drying her tears while changing the subject to their plans for Ophelia.

"I discussed with your parents the necessity of appearing in public together this week, the better to bolster your sister's prospects. I have faith that Kate will develop a grand strategy for her, but the Season will be over if we don't act soon. We will have to attend some functions, of course. If we vary our schedules and our routines and keep our social events secret until the last moment—and if our armed guards remain vigilant—we should decrease the risk. We need to be accessible, but give no advance warning or easy opportunity to my enemy."

Venetia nodded in agreement. "That seems wise."

"The question then becomes, how do we occupy ourselves in the immediate future? It will not be pleasant being confined to the house for long periods. What do you require to resume your sculpting?"

The question surprised her. "What do you mean?"

"Wouldn't you like to sculpt again?"

"Yes, very much." She had missed her art a great deal.

"What does it entail?"

Her brow furrowed as she mentally reviewed the necessities. "I would need my tools and fresh clay and some proper stone . . . as well as a place to work."

"You can purchase supplies, can you not?"

"Yes. Actually, I brought some implements with me from France, so I can fetch them from Cleo's home. I would like to see her, in any case. I have missed her, and I feel guilty for abandoning her." Venetia's mouth twisted in a faint smile. "Not only was I supposed to be Cleo's companion, she returned to England chiefly for my sake."

Quinn disregarded her lament. "We can build you a studio here in London, I presume."

"That isn't practical. I would need a kiln to fire the clay molds, and a special table with vises to hold the stone in place while I chisel. . . ."

"There must be kilns in town that can accomplish the firing for you."

"Perhaps. But you needn't go to such trouble or expense on my behalf."

"It is no trouble. Indeed, it is the least I can do. If you are able to work, your enforced confinement won't seem so onerous." He paused a heartbeat. "In addition to improvising a workshop here, I could always construct a larger studio at my estate in Kent. Tallis Court is your home now as well as mine."

Venetia wasn't certain how to respond to his suggestion, but she noted how his shrewd gaze was studying her. "Your offer is extremely kind, but truly,

I don't want to establish anything too permanent or become too settled."

Quinn's expression didn't change overtly, but she sensed that he didn't like the reminder that her future was not here in England with him.

In truth, she would rather not even visit Tallis Court. She might fall in love with Quinn's family home and grow too attached. If she intended to return to France, she was better off not risking temptation.

She wondered if Quinn could divine her weakness. His eyes, so sharply intelligent, seemed to penetrate her thoughts.

Yet he didn't argue. He merely stated his intentions: "Then you will have to settle for a makeshift workshop here in town."

Over the next several days, Venetia was astonished by the speed at which Quinn acted. For her studio, she chose an upstairs north-facing room with ample light, and in short order his army of servants had completed the transformation.

Quinn himself took her shopping for proper tables and heavier equipment and looked on as she supervised the placement of various items and supplies, all the while asking curious questions and expressing fascination at her creative process.

As for commanding his staff, as Quinn wished her to, Venetia instructed the butler and housekeeper to carry on as before her marriage. She had never been mistress of her own household, but although the notion was extremely appealing, she did not want to interfere if she was only to stay for a few more months.

On the second afternoon—accompanied by armed footmen and grooms, at Quinn's insistence—she set out to visit Cleo and fetch the sculpting tools she had brought to England with her.

It was wonderful to see Cleo again, even if her friend was still highly critical of her marriage to Traherne and still gravely concerned for her.

Over tea, Cleo quizzed her thoroughly about her time in Somerset. "You are not falling under Traherne's spell, are you?"

"No," Venetia answered, knowing she wasn't being entirely honest but hoping her hesitation didn't show.

Cleo seemed skeptical, even when Venetia explained about her agreement with Quinn and said that her plan was to return to France once the assassin was caught . . . although she was now thinking of remaining here in London until her sister's marital prospects were further along. The thought of resuming her former life in Paris was not nearly as appealing as it once had been, but Venetia didn't like to dwell on her possible change of heart.

Instead, she smiled at Cleo. "Enough about me. How have you been occupying yourself, Cleo? Are you eager to return to France?"

After a pause, Cleo gave a soft, almost secretive smile. "I have been reacquainting myself with some old friends."

"Do I know them?"

Cleo suddenly looked oddly flustered. "I don't believe so. But in any event, I am in no hurry to leave England just yet."

Venetia sensed a subtle change in her friend but couldn't quite put her finger on it.

Two hours later, she bid farewell to Cleo with great regret. "It isn't safe for you to visit me until the assassin is caught, but with all the footmen I have guarding me, perhaps I can come back here soon."

"You know you are more than welcome at any time. I have missed you immensely, Venetia."

"Not as much as I have missed you, my dearest Cleo."

The two women embraced each other fondly. Then Venetia made her way out the entrance door and down the front steps, through the walled garden and out to the curb where her carriage and footmen awaited.

Once settled and on her way, she realized what was different about Cleo. There was almost a glow about her, a contentment Venetia had never seen before. Her friend seemed unusually . . . happy.

Perhaps they were both withholding their deepest, most private confidences just now, Venetia thought wistfully. She could certainly sympathize with the desire for privacy. Some feelings were just too intimate to share. She wasn't yet ready to confess her evolving feelings for her new husband, especially when she didn't fully understand the incipient emotions herself.

She did understand, however, how satisfying it was to apply her skills at sculpting again. Her plan was to present her mother and father with small busts of the entire Stratham family as a peace offering of sorts. When Quinn visited her new studio the following morning, he found her wholly immersed in the joy of creating—elbow-deep in clay, her apron mud-spattered, her hair escaping its knot in careless tendrils.

His observations and questions about her work made her supremely self-conscious, though, especially when he brushed back a wayward wisp of hair from her forehead and tucked it behind her ear.

Barely hiding her flush, Venetia cleared her throat. "I work best alone. Perhaps you wouldn't mind leaving me to myself?"

His blue eyes gleamed with humor. "Are you banning me from your studio?"

"Forgive me, but yes," she replied cordially. "I will never be able to concentrate with you hovering over me."

"If you insist . . . but I am mortally wounded."

Smiling, Venetia watched him leave, feeling thankful, but also with genuine regret. She would have liked to ask Quinn to pose for her, for the challenge if nothing else. It wouldn't be easy to capture his essence in the clay beneath her fingers—to transfer the lethal elegance of his aristocratic features or show the intelligence of his eyes, the sensuality of his beautiful mouth. The distraction would prove too overwhelming. Even worse, she might expose some of the burgeoning, inexplicable feelings she was trying desperately to ignore if not repress altogether.

Instead, Venetia stifled a sigh and returned to the much safer task of depicting her sister's pretty face in clay.

Chapter Fifteen

By week's end, Venetia had finished clay molds of Ophelia and their mother, yet she was still no closer to sorting out her conflicting feelings for Quinn.

At least they were making progress on the social battlefront. Having agreed to attend only select engagements to keep their exposure to a minimum, they chose to make their debut at a grand ball hosted by Lord and Lady Perry, where the cream of the ton would be present, including Quinn's adopted cousin, Lord Jack Wilde, and his beautiful wife, Sophie, whom Venetia was greatly looking forward to meeting.

Lady Katharine's brother Ash and his wife, Maura— the Marquis and Marchioness of Beaufort—would remain in the country with their new baby son, but they sent their fondest well-wishes, and Maura wrote a long letter to Venetia welcoming her into the family.

The Wildes were clearly determined to rally around the Stratham sisters. Not only was Katharine developing a matchmaking scheme for Ophelia and arranging introductions to potential beaus, Skye commissioned her favorite modiste to design lovely gowns for them both. The night of the ball, when Venetia dressed carefully in her exquisite gown of apricot silk with a cream lace overskirt and descended the staircase to the entrance hall, where Quinn awaited her, his blue eyes flared with appreciation.

The admiration was reciprocal. He had a presence that made mere mortals seem insignificant. And garbed in evening clothes—black coat, gold brocade waistcoat, and pristine white cravat that set off his handsome face and dark blond hair—every immaculate inch of him screamed wealth and bone-deep nobility.

"You look amply prepared to face the wolves," he commented as he offered her his arm.

"I hope so. I cannot believe how nervous I am," Venetia confessed, "knowing I will be the target of every gossip and disapproving dowager out there."

"You will be the most dazzling beauty at the ball."

"It helps that your sister has impeccable taste."

"A gown can only accentuate a woman's loveliness, not create it."

"Spoken like an experienced flatterer," Venetia said with a wry laugh.

"If you have any doubts, you have only to watch the faces of everyone you meet tonight. I will be the envy of every man there and you the idol of every woman."

The slow, captivating smile Quinn sent her warmed her inside, so that Venetia actually found herself anticipating their first joint venture into society with more optimism than apprehension.

Her only qualm came when Quinn escorted her to their carriage. They would be accompanied by the requisite number of footmen—sporting pistols, reminding her acutely of the danger. Venetia hated the feeling of being on guard at every moment, but she vowed not to let it ruin their evening.

Upon their arrival, after they made their way through the crowds to the ballroom, Venetia was greeted effusively by both Katharine and Skye, who quickly made her known to Sophie, a dark-haired beauty with an enchanting smile, and Lord Jack, a devilishly handsome rogue who obviously possessed the Wilde charm in great abundance.

Venetia instantly liked them both, but regrettably, she had little time to become acquainted with them, for a steady stream of people began approaching, begging for introductions—or in many cases, reintroductions. It was clear from the first moment, her reception would be far different than she'd feared, for most of the ball guests hailed her return into their midst.

The hypocrisy jarred her a little. The same hoity-toity class that had shunned her so viciously before now toadied to her because she was a countess supported by a powerful, noble family. But for her sister's sake, Venetia smiled and did her best to charm her former detractors.

Quinn played his role extremely well. For the nonce, he was not the rake or celebrated lover that rumors portrayed him, but a protective, attentive, doting husband who gave every appearance of being in love with his new bride.

He showed her family every courtesy as well. When the Strathams joined their party, Katharine made certain their audience knew she had taken Ophelia under her wing, as had the entire Wilde clan, including the Earl of Hawkhurst.

When the orchestra struck up, Quinn led Venetia onto the floor while Lord Hawkhurst did the same for Ophelia. Quinn applied for Ophelia's hand next.

It amazed Venetia to see him dancing with her sister. So much had changed in such a short time, she thought, amused by the irony. She had never dreamed her confrontation with Quinn at the sin club would turn out this way, with her wed to him. Even more unbelievably, she not only wanted to keep watch over him and keep him safe, but felt an ownership she had no business feeling.

Shrugging off her surge of possessiveness, Venetia kept a close eye on her sister instead, gratified to see that Ophelia had a steady stream of dance partners, many of whom were eligible young bachelors, thanks to Katharine.

Some while later, though, an incident threatened to shatter her pleasure for the evening. Her partner—an elderly gentleman—was escorting her to the punch table when she spied a stunning raven-haired beauty staring at her from across the ballroom. Venetia recognized her as none other than Lady X, as the gossip rags had dubbed Julia, Lady Dalton.

Venetia's stomach lurched at the sight of Quinn's former mistress. She busied herself thanking her elderly partner for the refreshment and quizzing him about his family and young granddaughters, but then a sultry voice spoke behind her.

"I wondered when you would be brave enough to show your face in public, Miss Stratham."

Venetia first froze, then turned to find Lady Dalton languidly waving a hand-painted silk fan. Her manner was outwardly amiable for the sake of appearances, but the brittle tone to her voice suggested anything but friendliness.

The elderly gentleman suddenly recalled a prior engagement and bowed himself away. Although her stomach felt weighted by a lump of lead, Venetia pasted a smile on her face, conscious of countless pairs of eyes watching them.

"I don't believe we have met," she managed to say.

"But you no doubt know of my history with your husband," Lady Dalton purred.

Caught completely off guard, Venetia struggled to think of a suitable retort. Evidently the widow saw her as a rival and was staking the advantage by boldly seeking her out in front of an inquisitive crowd. She had to give Lady X credit for audacity, even though she couldn't stop the fierce pang of jealousy raking through her—or seem to make her tongue work.

Before she could deliver a reply, Lady Dalton continued. "I must applaud your cleverness, Miss Stratham. I initially thought you were supremely foolish to shoot Traherne, but I suppose it was the only way you could ensnare him."

"I understand you failed to ensnare him yourself," Venetia said sweetly. "Tell me, do you still covet my husband?"

Lady Dalton shot her an acrimonious look.

Just then Katharine appeared and slipped an arm around Venetia's waist, ostensibly intent on coming to her rescue. "Tsk, tsk, Julia. Your claws are showing—an unbecoming trait when you profess to be a lady of quality. And you seem to have forgotten that Venetia is no longer Miss Stratham, but the Countess of Traherne."

Lady Dalton turned her unfriendly stare on Katharine, who responded with a brilliant smile. "It must nettle you, Julia, to know Venetia succeeded where you could not."

Lady Dalton arched a supercilious eyebrow. "You are mistaken," she responded coldly.

"Am I? Quinn has fallen madly in love. It was so very romantic. He never was the least interested in marriage until Venetia came along."

Venetia noted that Katharine showed no remorse for the blatant falsehood, and she couldn't help but be grateful for her protectiveness—as well as feel a measure of justice and gratification when Katharine concluded:

"I advise you to go lick your wounds in private, Julia, and refrain from making a further spectacle of yourself, as you have done so regularly in the past."

By now the widow's eyes were shooting daggers, but she seemed to realize she had met her equal in Lady Katharine Wilde.

When Lady Dalton spun angrily and strode off, Katharine's gaze followed her retreating figure. "She is fortunate she failed to land Quinn. He would have murdered her before the honeymoon was over. Luckily he saw her true colors. . . ."

Breaking off her muttering, Katharine turned to

Venetia and offered her a conspiratorial smile. "I have longed to tell that woman off for ages. Her scheming makes me livid—" Abruptly Katharine gave a charming laugh. "Oh, I know, I scheme and plot as well. But my intentions are entirely virtuous. My aim is to find true love for my siblings and cousins. Julia, on the other hand, has always been a witch, and she seems set on causing you trouble. She is green with jealousy because you married Quinn. She thinks you captured his heart."

Venetia winced. "I am sure you know that is not true."

"Pah, even if Quinn hasn't fallen in love with you yet, he very well *could*. It is only a matter of time."

"A month ago he was courting my sister," she pointed out dryly.

"But not because he wished to. It is my fault he ever became involved with Ophelia."

"What do you mean?"

"I plagued him to pursue your sister." Katharine sent her a sheepish smile. "I have a confession to make, Venetia. When I was a young girl, I became obsessed with the notion of finding true love as so many of my Wilde ancestors have done."

She paused while Venetia nodded kindly.

"In that vein, I began looking for possible matches based on legendary lovers throughout history. You know of the Greek myth of Pygmalion? Well, I thought Quinn could mold your sister into the bride he wanted. But I see now that he was absolutely right. They would not suit at all. Ophelia is a dear sweet girl, but you are a much better fit for him. Quinn can be stubborn and infuriating, and he needs someone who is his equal, who can stand up to him."

She was indeed better-suited, Venetia agreed. Quinn would have eaten her sister alive—or at least crushed her tender heart.

"You might even be his ideal match," Katharine added. "We Wildes often marry our soulmates."

Venetia's eyebrow lifted. "Quinn very clearly does not want a soulmate. And I cannot see him as mine."

Katharine studied her face. "His past affairs have colored your perception, perhaps for good reason."

Venetia couldn't help a twisted smile. "For *very* good reason, I would say. His affairs are legion."

"If you are worried he will betray his marriage vows, you shouldn't be. Quinn is a man of honor. If he gave his word to you, he will keep it."

He hadn't actually promised fidelity, although he had intimated at such. He was not the libertine Venetia had thought him, however, and she was willing to admit she might have misjudged him on other counts as well.

At her silence, Katharine pressed on. "The thing is, women like us think with our hearts, but Quinn thinks with his head. He sees love as a cruel game, where he is the prize and the intended victim."

Katharine hesitated, as if debating how much more to reveal. Then she lowered her voice. "He was taught to be so cynical. Shortly after his parents died, while Quinn was attending university, a fortune hunter sank her claws into him. That tale is not common knowledge, by the way. I was barely thirteen at the time and my uncle Cornelius was his legal guardian. Quinn asked for an advance of his fortune and the

Traherne jewels to give to his inamorata. It was only years later that I happened to learn the story. I had asked Uncle Cornelius why Quinn was so resistant to my legendary lovers theory, and he let it slip that Quinn had once been in love. I wouldn't rest till I learned the whole of it."

Katharine paused again. "It seems to me that trust will be a chief barrier for you both. Quinn will have to trust you completely before he will ever risk his heart."

Venetia pursed her lips thoughtfully. She had never really considered his perspective. Trust was such an enormous issue for her, yet she hadn't realized it might be just as significant for him.

"But I promise he will be worth the effort, Venetia," Katharine said earnestly. "I have it on good authority that reformed rakes make excellent husbands. My own brother Ash is a prime example. Love makes all the difference in the world. I suspect that is the secret to inspiring a man to embrace fidelity—making him fall deeply in love with you."

"So how do you make a man fall in love, deeply or otherwise?" Venetia asked, intensely curious.

"I wish I knew," Katharine said with a self-deprecating laugh. "I am supposed to be this grand matchmaker, but I've failed spectacularly for myself. I have never found anyone to love me in return. There was one man years ago. . . ." The wistfulness on her face suggested a painful history before she gave a graceful shrug. "In the end, it didn't matter. He was an American who left England when war broke out between our countries. After that, there was no hope. He owned a fleet of sailing ships and fought against

Britain as a privateer, which essentially made us enemies."

Katharine cut herself short. "How I am rambling! I have never told that tale to anyone but Skye. Certainly not my brother Ash."

"I won't betray your confidence, Katharine."

"Thank you." She sighed. "But enough about me," Katharine said amiably. "My point is simply that I am still holding out for true love—although at four-and-twenty I am considered almost a spinster."

Venetia herself was close to being considered a spinster, she reflected before realizing Katharine was still musing aloud.

"So how do you make a rake fall deeply in love? I think you start by first making him want you. Love may very well follow desire, I've always believed. But whatever you do, you cannot be overt about your pursuit. I learned that lesson the hard way. I could not persuade Br . . . my gentleman to want me, even when I offered myself. My attempt was disastrous, the most lowering experience of my life." Katharine gave a mock shudder at the memory before continuing. "And Quinn has more bitter experiences at being pursued than most. He has escaped too many lures of debutantes and determined mamas not to be on his guard. He cannot realize you are chasing him or you will drive him away."

Venetia's initial response was amusement. She was not about to chase Quinn. At any rate, making him fall deeply in love with her would likely be an impossible task. At the same time, she couldn't stifle a tiny kernel of exhilaration at the challenging prospect. . . .

Venetia mentally shook her head. She shouldn't let

herself indulge in wishful thinking. It was purely a fanciful dream, that Quinn would love her so much that he would never stray from the marriage bed.

He felt *something* for her, however, she was sure of it. He made her feel warm and secure and wanted. Surely that was not all mere illusion? And unquestionably her own feelings for him were deepening. Of late they felt new, sweetly raw and uncertain. . . .

No, she would be utterly foolish to consider pursuing him, Venetia scolded herself. And yet . . . she could imagine what it would be like if Quinn were her lover, her love, her joy.

At that novel thought, Venetia was beset by a whole host of contrary emotions, yearning the chief among them. That and the urge for self-protection. If she were to fall in love with Quinn and he betrayed her, she would be devastated.

Yet was the chance worth taking? It was true that she couldn't be hurt if she never gave her heart, but perhaps the possible pain was worth the risk—

"So this is where the two of you have been hiding."

Venetia gave a start as Quinn appeared at her side. Evidently he had come in search of her when the music ceased.

While Venetia was finding her tongue, Kate smiled brightly up at him. "We were not *hiding,* cousin. I was just discussing my theory with Venetia."

He let out a sigh of acute exasperation. "I hoped you would spare her your fanciful nonsense." Shifting his gaze, he glanced down at Venetia. "I'm afraid this is Kate's notion of matchmaking. She has made a nuisance of herself since she was a tot, badgering us all with her demented theory."

"By now Venetia knows I am the romantic in our family," Katharine retorted cheerfully. "And I collect I deserve to crow a little. If not for me, you wouldn't be wed to her now. It all started with my theory."

"But you had the wrong legend for me. Venetia and I have more in common with Shakespeare's *Shrew*."

Katharine laughed. "Perhaps you do. Your ripostes with Venetia resemble Katharina and Petruchio's in the Bard's comedy. I always thought my legend would be *The Taming of the Shrew,* but I can see now how it would fit you better, Quinn."

Just then, a gentleman came up to claim Katharine for a pair of country dances. With a charming smile, she excused herself, leaving Quinn alone with Venetia.

Frowning slightly, she thought back to what she remembered of Shakespeare's comedy. Katharina, the headstrong elder sister of modest daughter Bianca, had scared away all of Bianca's suitors with her shrewish tongue until Petruchio appeared and promised to turn Katharina into an obedient bride.

When understanding dawned, Venetia gave Quinn an arch glance. "So I am the shrew?"

The gleam was back in his eyes, and so was the provocative devil. "You must admit you can be a real termagant when you choose. And you blighted your sister's prospects of marrying me."

"You never mentioned the parallels before."

"Because I knew you would bristle. I was bristling myself at the idea of being Pygmalion. Kate should have known better than to think I would ever want a statue for my wife."

"No, I can't imagine you would," Venetia returned with genuine amusement.

"I would rather have a shrew."

"Would you?" she asked skeptically.

"A shrew is more interesting by far. I am happy with the sister I married."

His announcement startled Venetia a bit, even though she knew he was jesting. For a moment, she stared up at him, wondering if he could divine that she was thinking about the possibility of pursuing him. His eyes were so blue and clear she felt as though he could see to her soul.

Finally he held out his arm to her. "Would you do me the honor of dancing, my love?"

At the endearment, she again felt that foolish, romantic surge of warmth. His tenderness was merely a show for the benefit of their critical audience, yet unbidden another small kernel of hope flared to life.

Quinn could so easily break her heart. But if she had to lose in the end, shouldn't she at least have the satisfaction of going down fighting?

Chapter Sixteen

The warmth Venetia felt lasted throughout the evening and carried over on the drive home as she sat beside Quinn in the carriage. By rights she should be weary at such a late hour—nearly three o'clock in the morning—but her spirits were so light that energy surged through her.

"I believe we can count the ball a grand success," she declared with elation. "Ophelia seems very happy to have so many potential suitors. Indeed, she was glowing."

In the dim interior, Venetia saw Quinn smile. "I told you my original aim was to help her attract more suitable admirers than myself. I trust you finally believe me."

"I do now that I know of your cousin's theory about Pygmalion—and how Kate was pressing you to court Ophelia. But I can't credit that you compared me to a shrew."

"You are an adorably sweet shrew."

With an arch look, Venetia adopted his bantering

tone. "A shrew is precisely what every woman wishes to be called," she complained sardonically. "And if you think you can tame me, Lord Traherne, you should think again."

"Take care, darling, or I will attempt it."

Perhaps it was the headiness of the moment, but Venetia took a deep breath and plunged in before she could change her mind. "I dare you to try."

She could tell she had surprised him, but his answer came swiftly. "Would you prefer your bedchamber or mine?"

It took her a bit longer to respond. She would be wise to invite him to stay with her for the night, Venetia decided, rather than go to his bed, or he might think she was chasing him, as Katharine had warned against.

"You are welcome to come to my rooms."

"I would be delighted."

The air between them was suddenly charged with sexual tension, which lasted as they entered the house and handed their outer garments to a footman, and intensified when Quinn led her upstairs to her bedchamber door.

Instead of accompanying her inside, however, he bent to murmur in her ear, "I will come to you in a quarter hour. That should give you time to ready yourself for me."

The words were ripe with meaning, and Venetia felt her mouth go dry. He meant to draw out her anticipation and leave her hungering.

Entering her room, where her sleepy lady's maid awaited her, she changed out of her beautiful ball gown and donned her nightshift. Then, dismissing the girl with her thanks, Venetia sat at her dressing table, slowly brushing her hair. Her nerves were on edge as she waited for her husband to come to her.

Her husband. If only that were completely true.

Strange, how having a real marriage with Quinn now seemed so profoundly appealing. Moreover, tonight Katharine had started her thinking a great deal about trust and love.

It was not fair to judge Quinn based on her past wretched experience, Venetia conceded. He was strong and admirable, not weak and deceitful as Ackland was. Ackland had deluded her as to his true character, but once her eyes were opened, her disbelief and hurt had been replaced by anger. The truth was, her pride had been savaged far more than her heart.

She couldn't help comparing the two men in other ways also. Curiously, Quinn treated her as a flesh-and-blood woman, not a fragile, delicate flower or genteel damsel to be set on a pedestal. Ackland had wanted her for his own material purposes and hadn't shown her an inkling of the passion Quinn did with the simplest of kisses.

There had never been any spark between them, either. She had never kissed her betrothed with a fraction of the ardor she felt for Quinn—nothing like the explosive fire that had erupted between them from their first moments together at the gaming hell.

And she was willing to trust Quinn in many respects now. She knew he would keep his word and allow her to return to France once the threat was over. And yet . . . she yearned for a different future than her current path. If not for the danger to Quinn's life, she might actually be glad for the excitement and adventure of being his wife.

Furthermore, at heart, she had a deep hunger for love. She'd learned that about herself these past few weeks.

In France, she had made herself believe that her dreams were hopeless. She had been determined to be content with her chosen lot, to accept the great yawning emptiness of her life. Yet returning home to England had forcibly reminded her of her sense of isolation these past two years.

I have been so alone.

Venetia shook off the dark reflection as her mind skipped ahead. If she didn't act now, her future would only hold more of the same. All she could look forward to was a lonely spinster existence.

She wanted to change that dreary fate. She wanted to belong someplace, belong to *someone. To Quinn.* She wanted true love. A devoted husband. A chance at having children, a family. *With Quinn.* She felt a bone-deep longing for those things.

The brush stilled in her hand. What if she could permanently return from exile? What if she could become Quinn's wife in more than name only?

In fact, what if he truly was her life's mate?

The compelling thought aroused a deep ache inside her. She ought not deceive herself, of course. It was mad to think she could ever become his soulmate. She wanted far more than Quinn could give. Apparently he would risk his life long before he would risk his heart.

But I have to try.

Venetia gazed down at the brush, wondering if she

could somehow turn the tables on him. They had jested about him taming her, but clearly she was the one who must do the taming.

So how did one tame a rake? By making him fall in love.

And how could she make Quinn fall in love? He was a pleasure-seeker. What would he want with love? But if that was so, was the way to his heart through pleasure? If Katharine was right, perhaps passion *could* lead to love. . . .

Slowly Venetia resumed her brushing. If she thought she stood a chance, she wouldn't hesitate to attempt a seduction, to tempt Quinn with every skill she could summon, to try and make him desire her beyond reason. And yet . . . he was so much more experienced at lovers' games.

She took a steadying breath. Perhaps for now she simply needed to focus on increasing his desire for her. That much she could do.

Rising, Venetia went to the hearth to stir the coals, then snuffed the lamps so that the room was bathed only in firelight. As she finished her task, her hopes began to rise with her increasing confidence.

Shedding her nightdress, she stood naked before the floor-length cheval glass, her back to the door. She felt herself trembling in anticipation as she waited for Quinn. By the time a soft rap sounded on her bedchamber door, however, Venetia had strengthened her resolve.

Judging by her initiation to passion in the cave pool, when they made love tonight, she knew Quinn would want to make her beg and plead for him. But if she had her way, she would make *him* do the pleading this time.

When she bid entrance, he stepped into the room and shut the door behind him. He wore a crimson brocade dressing gown, she saw in the mirror's gold-hued reflection, and his hair glinted amber in the firelight.

He faltered when he spied her nudity. *Good.* She had surprised him. She needed every advantage she could muster.

He crossed the room to stand behind her. "Are you ready for me?" he asked, his voice low and throaty.

As she met his gaze in the looking glass, a sizzling current arced between them. "Yes," she replied shakily. She was wet and eager for him already.

In response, he brushed her hair aside and nuzzled the back of her neck. As his hands slid down her arms, the heat of his palms on her bare skin distracted her from her intent. She was supposed to be taking the lead here, but she was having difficulty concentrating. Quinn stood close behind her, his hands spanning her waist. His body felt hot and hard against her back, reminding her of his alluring caresses. Her stomach clenched as she imagined him touching her further, stroking her hot skin, tracing the swells of her breasts. . . .

As if he could read her mind, his arms encircled her midriff. His breath ruffling her hair, he reached up to cup her bare breasts. The very air smoldered with seduction as he stared at the ripe mounds cradled in his hands.

"How beautiful you are," he murmured, tracing

the rosy areolas with his thumbs, lightly teasing the peaks, which were distended and hard.

The sight of him fondling her was supremely erotic, as was his brazen touch on her protruding nipples.

Then his hips shifted closer, sending a streaking heat shuddering through her. With her buttocks nestled against his groin, she could feel his arousal through the silk of his robe. Tingles radiated from every place their bodies touched, even before he parted the fabric of his robe to let his arousal spring free and began gently caressing her bottom with his hardness.

"Do you remember how it feels to have me deep inside you, love? How you moaned for me?"

Venetia drew in a sharp breath and arched back to press against his powerful body. The promise of having him inside her stirred a pulsing deep between her thighs.

"*I* remember, beautiful Venetia. I remember how hot and sweet you are. . . ."

His manhood slipped between her thighs, probing purposefully her feminine folds. She shuddered helplessly at the throbbing thrust of him against her most sensitive flesh.

"I want you moaning for me again, sweetheart. I want you writhing in my arms."

When the rush of pleasure intensified, Venetia dug her nails into her palms, fighting to hold on to her senses.

"Quinn . . . not so quickly," she declared hoarsely. "You won't seduce me as easily as you have in the past."

"No?"

Easing away, she turned in the circle of his arms to gaze up at him. "If I am a shrew, you will have to work to win my favor."

He smiled down at her from his wicked blue eyes. Her challenge apparently amused him. "What do you suggest I do to win your favor?"

"Take off your robe."

Without protest, he complied, untying the sash and letting the garment fall to the carpet.

His nudity was enough to take her breath away. With firelight sculpting his arms and shoulders and powerful thighs, he was incredibly beautiful. How was she supposed to make a man like this feel overwhelmed by lust? Especially when she was so hot already. She was filled with tension and wild anticipation—

Take care, Venetia. She had to remember her role as a femme fatale.

Gathering her control, she tossed out another challenge. "I won't make it easy for you to tame me, Quinn."

"I would expect nothing less."

The lightness of his tone told her he was too confident. Resolutely, she reached down and curled her fingers around his hard shaft. At the feel of him, Venetia's stomach tightened. She couldn't stop the wave of remembered desire that mere contact with him aroused.

And from his knowing eyes and sensual smile, he understood her dilemma.

Once more Venetia strove for casualness. "You would make a superb model for a sculpting class," she observed.

He raised an eyebrow. "How many men have you seen nude?"

"Not many. And none were aroused as you are. I never realized a man's . . . member could be so large."

To her gratification he swelled further in her hand. "The credit belongs to you."

"Does it?"

Covering her hand with his, Quinn wrapped their joined fingers around his erection. "This is for you, sweet Venetia. Only for you."

Did he mean his desire, or was he also talking about fidelity?

Knowing it would be a mistake to continue in so serious a vein, she smiled up at him. "I think you are talking too much. You may kiss me now."

His sensual lips and sinful smile were only a breath away, yet he didn't obey. Instead, he reached out to gently squeeze her nipple. "You said there was no hurry."

The brush of his fingers sent another bolt of awareness shooting through her. As usual, one touch was enough to make her breathless and mindless.

With a forcible effort, Venetia maintained her concentration and raised herself on tiptoe so that she could kiss *him*.

Quinn bent his head then to take her lips forcefully. It was the kiss of a man who knew exactly what he wanted. His mouth was hot and hungry, claiming hers and stealing her will. Her body came alive as a flush of heat—of pure, raw wanting—streaked through her.

You cannot give in, Venetia scolded herself.

Quinn kept on kissing her, though, arousing with

silky strokes of his tongue, slowly driving, deliciously plundering, until she managed to pull away.

He merely lowered his head to her breasts. His fingers tightened on one stiff crest, while his mouth attended the other.

When Venetia gave a soft moan, he suckled harder. The pleasure was so intense she felt weak, almost faint.

Then slipping his hand between her thighs, he parted the slick folds and gently buried his fingers inside her. Venetia gasped. She wanted, needed to fill herself with him again—

No, she had to stop him.

Her fingers tangling in his hair, she held his mouth away. "No, Quinn," she rasped. "That is far enough."

He sighed with obvious regret. "Very well. Fortunately I am a patient man."

She couldn't say the same about herself. She felt impatient, restless, needy. She was already quivering from his sensual torment, and he had barely begun. Her breasts felt highly sensitized and tender from his suckling. . . .

Venetia shook her head to clear it. "Lie down on the bed," she ordered.

"What do you mean to do?"

"Pleasure you. Satisfy you."

"Then I am happy to oblige."

Crossing to the bed, where the covers had already been pulled down, Quinn stretched out on his back, leaving room for her to join him. When she moved toward him, he watched her avidly, his gaze raking her body.

His regard thrilled her. She wanted him to see her

as a desirable woman. Her most ardent wish tonight was to be the lover he wanted.

Climbing into bed, Venetia knelt beside him, then stopped to study him. She was captivated by his golden splendor. His sleek, muscular body was beautiful, rawly masculine. And when her gaze dropped to the jutting length of his sex, her breath caught in her throat.

He was watching her in turn, his gaze frankly, sharply male. Venetia wet her suddenly dry lips with her tongue. She wanted to make him hard, as feverish and desperate for her as she was for him, to put an end to this restless, hot longing he'd kindled inside her.

"Now what?" he asked, his tone faintly taunting.

"You must advise me on what you like," she suggested, "since I have never done this before."

His smile was slow and dazzling. "As you wish, sweetheart."

Yet he did nothing more.

"Quinn," Venetia said more insistently, "you will need to show me how to pleasure you."

"I expect you can use your imagination."

The excitement of yearning swept over her. Pressing her hands against his bare chest, Venetia let her palms glide downward, loving the play of light and shadow over his body . . . admiring how his muscles shifted, smoothly rippling under taut skin . . . her fingers skimming over his flat belly, toward his loins. . . .

And there she faltered.

When she made no move to proceed, Quinn urged her along. "You can begin by touching me."

She reached lower to brush the thick, pulsing heat of him with her fingertips. "Like this?"

He remained completely still, yet his voice was husky with desire when he replied. "Exactly like that."

"I suspect I need more detailed instruction."

He closed his fingers around her hand. For the next few moments, Quinn guided and tutored her, showing her how to stroke him with the same erotic rhythm he'd used to pleasure her in the cave, teaching her the points where he was most acutely sensitive. But eventually he released her hand.

"Feel free to take over and explore your natural womanly talents. I won't lift a finger to interfere."

The prospect exhilarated Venetia. When she continued fondling him on her own, the powerful, instinctive thrust of his hips was gratifying. It was a heady feeling, eliciting such a response from such a vaunted lover. And when she cupped the velvety pouch beneath his shaft, Quinn inhaled audibly. His eyes looked as hot as the hearth fire.

Encouraged, she bent to tenderly kiss his healing scar. Perhaps because he was letting her assume the power, she was ready to take her seduction further.

"I like this wanton side of you," he said in an unsteady voice.

"I like it also," Venetia agreed in a whisper.

His body spoke to some primitive instinct inside her, while his virile maleness made her feel wonderfully feminine.

Feeling bolder now, she shifted her position, letting her hair glide across his belly. When she pressed a delicate kiss against the warm skin there, she shivered with yearning. Surely Quinn noticed her shaken response; Venetia guessed that she was affecting him nearly as much, since all his muscles had gone rigid.

Deliberately she fixed her gaze on his manhood. The hot flesh of his member was a temptation, his erection long and swollen and ready . . . She could only think of how he would feel when he plunged into her, how his splendid arousal would fill her.

A fresh curl of desire unfurled inside her. She could feel the pulsing in her core increase, as though he were moving inside her already.

She drew a slow breath then and kissed the satin heat of his arousal. Quinn shuddered, while his fingers threaded in her hair. As she stroked the smooth flesh with her tongue, the faint strangled sound he made in his throat could have been a growl or a sigh. And when she began suckling, his hips jerked.

She had taken him aback again, she realized. In response, she slid her hands beneath his buttocks to hold him still. It made her feel powerful to turn the tables on him, and her confidence grew further at his helpless reaction.

Resuming her seductive ministrations, she let her lips play on his hard rod. Apparently, though, she was driving him to a breaking point, for his hand clenched in her hair.

"Enough torment . . ." he rasped.

She raised her head to gaze up at him in the firelight. His features had become taut, and when he grasped his erection as if preparing to ignite his own climax, she refused to relinquish control. "No, let me . . . please."

Desire dilated his eyes. Holding her gaze, he nodded. His wide shoulders were rigid with tension, the tendons in his neck straining, as if bracing for pain. Yet all she wanted was to give him the same kind of exquisite pleasure he had given her.

With renewed purpose, Venetia bent to him again. No longer tentative, she drew her tongue lingeringly over his arousal, tracing the swollen head with delicate pressure, loving how his breathing had turned ragged, the way his masculine buttocks hardened in her hands. . . .

Surrendering, Quinn gave himself up to her control. When her mouth closed over his aching cock, he shut his eyes at the sublime sensation. Her caresses felt like silk, so soft on his skin, so incredibly erotic.

The innocence of her untutored mouth only heightened his arousal, and when Venetia began to explore him more feverishly, he was ready to claim her then and there. More than anything he wanted to spill himself in the welcoming warmth of her body, yet he resisted the urge.

Instead he let his mind drift into sweet fantasies about Venetia, imagining that he was taking her, surging into her. . . .

The image was almost his undoing. Quinn barely had time to draw her mouth away and replace it with her hand before he gave in to the blissful climax that ripped him. Heat exploded through him, searing in its intensity.

When finally he stopped shuddering and opened his eyes, he found Venetia watching him uncertainly. The endearing insecurity on her beautiful face only compounded Quinn's desire for her.

"You learn quickly," he managed to rasp, his voice hoarse.

He caught the shy, pleased smile that hovered on her lips. "I had an expert tutor."

"I'd say you require little tutoring. Your natural instincts are rather impressive."

She laughed softly at that and pressed a tender, suggestive kiss on his bare chest.

Regretfully, Quinn held her away. "Forgive me, love, but it will take me a moment to recover my stamina."

"I can wait."

Venetia let him dry her wet hand and his loins with a corner of the sheet, then curled her delectable body against him. Quinn pulled her closer, so that she lay with her head on his shoulder, his arm tight around her. He very much liked this side of Venetia. He found her eagerness to please him thoroughly endearing.

Feeling a familiar wave of tenderness, he pressed a light kiss on her hair. Her fledgling power was unexplored as yet, but he'd felt it in her every caress. If she ever decided to wield that dormant power on him in earnest, well . . . he could be in deep, deep trouble.

Admittedly, though, he was to blame for her newfound sexual assertiveness. He'd set out to free her of her inhibitions and he was succeeding.

In fact, as far as he was concerned, tonight had settled the matter for him: He was not letting Venetia out of his arms. Despite how their union had begun, they could have a good marriage. It would take some doing, but he would somehow make her want to stay with him. As soon as the danger was over, he would focus solely on Venetia and dedicate himself to winning her over.

Frustratingly, however, there had been no progress thus far in catching his assailant. Hawk had interviewed various engineers, scientists, manufacturers, and dockworkers at the shipyard, but had found no indication that Quinn's chief shipping rival was in any way involved in the attempts on his life. For now the investigation was at a dead end, and he was losing what little patience he had. As a consequence, he'd spoken to Hawk at the ball earlier tonight about their next steps, and together they had decided to stage a trap for his assailant, using Quinn himself as bait. They would need to plan carefully—

Realizing the decidedly unromantic train of his thoughts, Quinn gave a silent, ironic laugh. Now most certainly was not the time to be thinking of assailants and villains. Not with Venetia so warm and willing in his bed . . . except that they were lying in *her* bed.

"Next time," he remarked lazily, "you will come to my rooms. My bed is bigger and more comfortable."

"You are assuming there will be a next time."

Glancing down at her beautiful face, Quinn returned her gaze steadily. "Won't there?"

Venetia hesitated for a fraction of a second. "I suppose your bed would be better. Very well, next time we will use yours."

Her agreement surprised him a little. "What changed your mind?"

"I realized you are right. We should enjoy each other for the moment . . . for as long as I remain in

England. It need be nothing more serious than pleasure. Meanwhile, we are here, naked, together. . . ."

Reaching up, she wrapped her arm around his neck. "You promised me pleasure, my lord, and I expect you to deliver."

He chuckled at her deliberate provocation. She understood her formal address would result in his kissing her, and from her expressive, dark eyes, she wanted much more than a kiss.

"You know I can't resist a challenge like that," Quinn pointed out.

"I am counting on it," Venetia retorted before raising her sweet mouth to his.

Chapter Seventeen

As luck would have it, the investigation advanced a step the following afternoon when Quinn received a message from George Bellamy's landlord, saying the gamester had arrived in town.

Taking the same precautions as before, Quinn went armed for the interview, while Venetia waited for him impatiently at home. Upon his return, they repaired to Quinn's study, where he shared what he'd learned.

"Bellamy claims to have won the pendant last winter at a Paris gaming hell. He recalled the name of the club but not the French gentleman who possessed the pendant, only that he was elderly and had the manner of an aristocrat."

"Do you believe Bellamy?" Venetia asked.

"Yes. He seemed entirely forthcoming, and I could see no reason for him to lie to me. He also appears innocent of any designs on my life."

"I suppose we should be relieved."

Quinn gave a sigh of frustration. "This new lead

may prove fruitless. There must be hundreds of elderly French nobles who gamble in Paris. And the pendant's prior owner may have nothing to do with my would-be assassin. In fact, I'm almost convinced the two events are unrelated. It stands to reason a French nobleman could have salvaged the sunken treasure, since the shipwreck occurred off the southern coast of France, but why would there even be a connection to my shooter if not through Lisle?"

"Didn't you tell me that your mother's distant cousin is a French nobleman?"

"Yes. Phillipe Rieux, Compte de Montreux."

"Perhaps he can assist in discovering who gambled away the pendant to Bellamy at the Paris hell, or who might have tried to recover the valuables from the ship."

"Perhaps. When I wrote to him two months ago, he promptly replied that he knew of no attempts to locate the treasure."

Venetia pursed her lips. "If the *compte* is related to your family, is it possible he possesses pieces from the collection that weren't lost with the rest of the jewels?"

"It's possible, but he made no mention of it in his letter. And if he did own any of the jewels, why would he hide the fact, particularly when he knows I am searching for ties?" Quinn looked thoughtful. "I will have to write to him again."

"How well do you know him?"

"Not well. I haven't seen him in years, but I remember him visiting Tallis Court when I was a boy. For a short while he and my mother were engaged to marry.

But that was before my father visited Paris and swept her off her feet."

"So your father stole her away from the *compte*?" Venetia asked curiously.

"It was not a love match, merely an arrangement to unite their fortunes and bloodlines. My mother, Angelique, was an heiress, the only daughter of the Duc and Duchesse de Chagny. Although . . . I suppose Montreux could have been in love with her. She was a stunning beauty who reportedly had all of Paris at her feet."

"Love match or not, he could not have been happy to lose her and her fortune."

"Apparently they made up their differences. During the Revolution, he fled France to escape the savagery of Robespierre and his cohorts. Montreux spent several years in exile here in England and only returned home when the French royals were reinstated."

"So jealousy was not a factor," Venetia mused. "He must not have been too heartbroken by your mother's jilting if he remained close enough to be welcomed into her home by her rival suitor."

"And she was highly sympathetic to his plight, since her own parents were guillotined."

Just then Quinn's butler appeared in the doorway, holding a silver salver. "Forgive the intrusion, my lord, but you asked to be informed at once when any correspondence arrived from Mr. Macky."

"Yes, Wilkins. I have been expecting it."

Quinn accepted the letter and dismissed the servant, then settled back in his armchair and stared at the seal for a long moment. Venetia only understood his hesitation upon remembering it could contain information about his late mother's death.

Finally Quinn broke the wax seal and opened the missive, which looked to be two pages long.

The silence that followed left Venetia on edge. With increasing concern, she watched the play of emotions cross Quinn's face . . . foreboding, sadness, puzzlement, and resolve.

"What does Macky say?" she asked anxiously. "Did he learn the identity of the shipwreck survivor?"

Quinn's troubled gaze lifted to meet hers. "Yes. It was Lady Beaufort, Kate and Ash's mother."

"Macky is certain?"

"As certain as he can be after all this time. Macky located the cottagers who cared for her after she washed ashore. She recovered consciousness only a short while before perishing from her injuries, but long enough to divulge her name and the name of the ship that sank. A marker in the church graveyard bears her name, Melicent. And the *Zephyr* was my father's yacht. Additionally, she had distinctive auburn hair like Kate's, and she wore a gold locket with the Beaufort crest etched on the face."

Venetia wasn't quite certain what to say to console Quinn . . . or whether he regretted that the surviving passenger had not been his own mother.

His expression remained grave when he continued. "Macky says there is more news . . . or at least suspicions that a storm might not have caused the *Zephyr* to sink. Melicent spoke of a fiery blast, and sailors in the vicinity reported seeing an explosion and fire— the kind that usually only occurs during military battles at sea. There were other indications of a fire as well—namely burnt wooden ship debris strewn on the beach. Macky speculates that a keg of gunpowder was set alight on board the *Zephyr*. But that begs the question, why would a passenger ship—a private yacht—have gunpowder on board?"

"Perhaps for protection?"

Quinn nodded. "They might have had cannons on board. Piracy is rampant along that part of the coast. If an explosion did occur, was it accident or foul play? The *Zephyr* could have been sabotaged. Macky means to remain in France to see what more he can discover. We may never know the truth unless we can locate the shipwreck."

The silence resumed with Quinn deep in thought.

"Would you rather the survivor have been Angelique?" Venetia asked quietly.

"No, to be truthful. It would be harder to think of her suffering such lingering pain. It is difficult enough knowing that her life was ended so soon."

"I am so sorry, Quinn. It must be horrible to lose one's parents like that, especially at a young age."

"I was devastated, Skye even more so." His mouth curved faintly in a sad smile. "What I remember most is my mother's charm and joie de vivre. She was the most lively, enchanting person I have ever known."

Qualities he had inherited, Venetia thought to herself.

"My father adored her," Quinn added softly, "and she, him. Perhaps it was best that they perished together."

Quinn gave a heavy sigh. "I will have to let Ash and Kate know about their mother at some point.

Ordinarily I would call a family meeting so I could tell them in person. Such unhappy tidings ought not come in a letter or from a near-stranger like Macky is to them. But I must wait until they are no longer at risk." His jaw flexed in anger. "Just one more reason I want to be done with this interminable waiting."

"At least a delay will give Macky time to investigate the possible explosion," Venetia pointed out.

"When this is all over, I may go to France to see my aunt Melicent's grave for myself, and to instigate a search for the shipwreck. But I can't leave in the middle of danger to myself or to you and my family—or, for that matter, until my steamship is successfully launched."

Quinn ran a hand roughly through his hair. Then, rising, he went to the sideboard and poured himself a snifterful of brandy. Downing a large swallow, he grimaced at the burn.

"Are you all right, Quinn?"

"Yes. This just stirs painful memories," he answered, indicating the letter. "It is a grim reminder that I was helpless to save them."

Venetia wouldn't point out that although his regrets were not irrational, he was being too harsh on himself, and that he held no blame for his family's deaths. At the time, he was only seventeen, long before he started on his quest to glean some meaningful results from the tragedy.

Moving across the room, Quinn flung the letter down on his desk, then gazed back at Venetia. "I would rather be alone, if you don't mind."

"Yes, of course." She could understand his desire to mourn his parents in solitude.

"Close the door behind you," he ordered quietly as she rose.

As he tossed back another gulp of brandy, she left him alone. If he needed to drown his sorrows in spirits, then she would not seek to stop him. But that didn't prevent her from worrying about him. Dinnertime came and went with no sign of Quinn. Venetia spent the rest of the evening watching the clock as the hands slowly swept toward midnight.

Finally, she set down her book and returned to the study. She rapped softly on the door in case Quinn was sleeping off a drunken stupor.

When Quinn bade entrance, however, his voice seemed steady enough. He sat at his desk, poring over blueprints of his steam engine—a reminder of his obsession with exerting control over his own fate.

Venetia felt relief that he seemed perfectly sober, but there was a bleak set to his features that twisted her heart.

"Cook kept your supper warm. May I bring your plate here so that you can eat something?"

"I have no appetite."

His grim tone was curt and dismissive, but perversely, a surge of protectiveness and tenderness welled up in Venetia. She wanted very badly to comfort him and ease his sorrow.

"Well then, will you come to bed with me?"

His blue gaze sharpened on her. He considered her invitation for a long moment before he ultimately nodded.

As she took his hand and led Quinn upstairs to his bedchamber, the significance was not lost on Venetia.

They would make love in the master's bed for the first time, almost like husband and wife.

And yet this moment was unlike any other intimacy that had come before. Just now Quinn was not the alluring, seductive lover she had come to know. The firelight sculpting his high cheekbones in shadow exposed something vulnerable and unguarded in his expression that called to her.

His very nearness made her feel safe and cherished, and she wanted him to feel the same way. She needed to hold him, to show him that she cared. She gave no thought to her hope of taming him. This was no time for games. She needed to be there as his friend, his solace.

Silently they undressed each other, not speaking except with touch. Then tenderly Venetia put her hands on either side of his face and pulled his mouth down to hers. Her effort to comfort him, however, failed when he took command.

His passion was hot and insistent, spurring and controlling the rhythm of her breathing. His kiss sought and demanded. Without breaking contact, he scooped her up and carried her to the bed.

A yearning sensation spread in her chest as he laid her down and settled between her thighs. Her breathing sharpened. She felt his heated need, his unsated hunger as he poised above her, on the brink of plunging inside her.

Desire, hot and molten, unfurled in her belly when he slowly began to thrust. Swollen and iron-hard, he filled her, burying himself to the hilt. Then his free hand slid between her thighs, stroking her where they were joined.

At the keen pleasure, Venetia gasped and arched against him. And with that helpless response, his carefulness ended. He turned ravenous, delving into her mouth with gloriously hungry kisses while plumbing her body.

Moaning, Venetia melted under his unexpected assault, loving the fever in his touch, the urgency in his lips. Heat erupted between them, around them. Their joining had never felt so frantic, so essential. Quinn was moving as if a fire raged inside him. He claimed and took and stole her will, his mouth and body possessing hers, fierce and demanding and wildly sweet.

In return, she clung to him, gasping, matching his frenzied movements with abandon. She was beyond needing him. She yearned, she ached. As he drove into her, a cry ripped from her, plaintive and primitive.

Pleasure spiking, she clutched convulsively with her inner muscles, until her entire world exploded in a soul-shattering burst of color.

A heartbeat later, Quinn followed with a savage shuddering, his arms clenching around her until finally he collapsed upon her.

When at last she regained partial use of her senses, Venetia found him splayed over her, breathing harshly. She didn't mind his weight. Instead, she felt exquisitely possessed.

She was only slightly disappointed when he withdrew and rolled to one side, since he gathered her close against him. She relished the naked heat and strength of him, the feel of his hard body cradling hers. Quinn lay unmoving, his legs entwined with hers, as sated and spent as she.

Venetia sighed contentedly and shut her eyes, her thoughts drifting. Her plan to offer him comfort had transformed unexpectedly to something more profound. Tonight had somehow felt different, a laying bare of intimate feelings between them. Both of them were vulnerable but learning to trust. She smiled softly, assailed by the hazy knowledge that this was how true love felt—

Instantly her smile changed to a frown.

Oh, dear heaven.

She was in love with Quinn.

Venetia went rigid as she tried to make sense of the shocking realization. She heard the hushed crackle of the fire in the hearth, the quiet, even sound of his breathing, yet there was nothing hushed or quiet about the powerful emotion that had gripped her in the throes of lovemaking and still gripped her.

Dismay crept over her. Did Quinn feel even a fraction of the ardor she was feeling in such overwhelming measure?

Cautiously she shifted her head to glance at him. Thankfully, he seemed to be sleeping.

Venetia exhaled slowly, vastly relieved that he hadn't guessed her secret. She could never confess the full extent of her feelings, either. She couldn't tell him that he was the most wonderful man she had ever known, or that she had fallen madly in love with him, totally against her will.

Blast her foolish weakness for him. She had warned herself adamantly not to trust Quinn, but her heart hadn't followed that safe, sensible course. She had tried to protect herself, but now it was far too late.

She had exposed herself to an immense amount of pain. If he betrayed her, she would be devastated.

If he betrayed her.

The possibility was less certain than she would have believed even a week ago. Quinn had responded tonight with satisfying fierceness—or rather, his body had responded. At least that was something in her favor. She could take heart in his urgency, couldn't she?

And she ought not give up hope so readily. Yes, it could be disastrous if she couldn't persuade him to return her love, but she refused to accept defeat before she had truly put her pursuit to the test.

Fresh yearning sprang up in Venetia, so sudden and sharp it frightened her. She had no earthly idea how to proceed from here, now that she was willing to acknowledge the depth of her feelings for Quinn.

She only knew that she intended to fight for his love with every ounce of strength and determination she possessed.

Chapter Eighteen

Quinn found himself lingering in bed the next morning, holding Venetia as she slept. It was nearly impossible to leave her side, with her body so warm, so soft, her sleek, dark hair entangling them.

Once again he'd spent a night with her that was different from any in his experience. He could still feel her tight sheath clenching around his cock in a violent climax. Still feel himself sinking under sensation. Still feel the afterglow that was unique with her. Still marvel at how perfect she felt in his arms.

He could so easily lose himself in her—

Quinn felt a constriction around his heart. If he wasn't careful his emotions would be so hopelessly tangled he would never break free. And yet . . . the prospect didn't unnerve him as it should have.

His fingers playing in her hair, he gently stroked back the wispy tresses from her face. He would have to sort out his feelings soon, but now was not the time.

On that resolute thought, Quinn forced himself to rise. He had major work to do this morning.

While he washed and dressed, he took great pleasure in watching Venetia. He left her still sleeping in his bed. Upon descending the stairs, he wrote her a note, saying he would be gone all morning, expending some of his frustrated energy at Gentleman Jackson's boxing salon. Over breakfast, Quinn checked the morning paper and smiled grimly to see that the bit of gossip he'd planted had made the society news.

He wouldn't, however, tell Venetia until the last moment because she would disapprove or would demand to be involved, and he didn't want to put her in any more danger than was necessary. She would likely spend the morning in her studio, and her sculpting should keep her occupied until he could return and put her mind at ease.

At Jackson's, he met with Hawk to set plans for flushing out his assassin. They discussed options and contingencies in minute detail, and then spent another satisfying hour in a bout of fisticuffs.

Upon returning home, Quinn was told that Lady Traherne was indeed in her studio. He started to climb the stairs in order to share his scheme, but just then the butler admitted a visitor. When he saw who it was, he gave a mental start.

"Speak of the devil," Quinn murmured under his breath. Only yesterday, Phillipe Rieux, Compte de Montreux, had been a prime subject on his mind.

Quinn turned around and descended the stairs in order to greet his unexpected guest. Montreux was a slightly built, elegant gentleman, with graying dark hair, olive complexion, and serious features. However, he smiled broadly at Quinn before speaking in perfect English with only the barest of French accents.

"Lord Traherne, it has been some years since last we met. Perhaps you remember me?"

"Certainly, *monsieur le compte*," Quinn replied, accepting the proffered hand to shake. "Will you accompany me to the drawing room, where we can be comfortable? Wilkins will bring refreshments."

"*Merci,* I would like that."

"Would you prefer tea, or something stronger?"

"Wine, if you please."

Quinn nodded at Wilkins, who silently heeded the request.

"I confess to curiosity," Montreux said as he accompanied Quinn down the corridor from the grand entrance hall. "You have many footmen in your employ. I encountered several who were armed. May I inquire as to why?"

"I recently escaped a few accidents that seemed intentional."

Montreux's expression registered dismay. "*Mon dieu,* I trust you are unharmed!"

"Thus far, yes. I am surprised to see you, *Compte.* Only yesterday I was speaking to my wife about you."

"Ah, *oui,* I received news that you had wed. I hope to meet your lovely bride today."

Entering the drawing room, Quinn waved his visitor toward a sofa and took an adjacent armchair for himself. "What brings you here to London?"

"I had business affairs that required my attentions. Also, I confess, you provoked my interest. I received your query about the de Chagny jewels—in particular, the prize pendant of diamonds and rubies. Yet I never heard what progress you made in determining ownership."

Quinn proceeded to tell the *compte* about the pendant being won by an elderly Frenchman, possibly a nobleman, at a Paris gaming club called Le Chat Noir.

Montreux frowned. "But yes, I know of it. I have played there myself upon occasion. But you have no more information about who would give up such a magnificent piece?"

"Regrettably, no."

The *compte*'s expression turned earnest. "I must ask, how may I assist you? I wish to offer my services in any capacity you require. I was very fond of Angelique and was desolate when she died."

"Thank you, monsieur. I will let you know if there is anything you can do."

A slight pause followed. "And what of my dear Angelique's ship that sank with so many poor souls on board?"

Quinn hesitated to mention the sole survivor of the wreck or the rumors that an explosion had caused the *Zephyr* to sink. For whatever reason, it felt wrong. Despite Montreux's genial air, he was nearly a stranger, even though very distantly related and had known Angelique well enough to seek her hand in marriage.

"There is no news of any significance," Quinn said easily just as Wilkins carried in the tea tray.

Quinn dismissed the butler and poured a glass of Madeira for the Frenchman before expounding. "I may institute a search for the wreckage of the ship this summer."

"I see." Montreux eyed his wineglass, then pulled out his handkerchief and wiped his brow. Another moment passed before he inquired after Quinn's sister and cousins and uncle.

"You heard that my uncle Cornelius married last year?"

"*Oui,* I did." Montreux offered a smile. "I have brought you a gift in remembrance of your mother . . . several bottles of my finest cognac, which was produced by my own vineyards. You simply must taste this special vintage as soon as may be. I do not believe I boast overmuch to say it is the nectar of the gods. The bottles are in my carriage. I will have them carried to your wine cellars by my driver."

"That won't be necessary. My servants will see to it."

"*S'il vous plaît,* I insist on helping."

"I would be honored to accept," Quinn responded, "but you will understand why I prefer to have my own staff carry them inside."

The look Montreux sent Quinn showed clearly that he preferred having his own way and didn't enjoy being thwarted, doubtless a product of his aristocratic upbringing. Then Montreux gave a Gallic shrug. "But of course, it will be as you wish, my lord. Angelique would have enjoyed this gift. She was very fond of French cognac." He glanced around the room. "It is sad to think she will never grace these halls again."

A light rap sounded on the open door just then.

"Forgive me, I did not mean to intrude," Venetia said politely as she entered the drawing room.

Montreux was the first to respond. He rose instantly and strode forward to meet her. "A visit by a beautiful lady is never an intrusion."

Venetia did not look taken aback as Quinn thought she might. Instead, she answered in kind. "You must be my husband's charming cousin."

Montreux smiled and demanded an introduction from Quinn, who complied.

"*Enchanté, madame la comtesse,*" the *compte* declared as he kissed her hand.

"Spoken like a true Frenchman," she returned lightly.

"Oh, you know the manners of a true Frenchman?"

"I had the pleasure of spending the last two years in Paris."

"Ahh." The *compte* studied Venetia intently.

She turned to Quinn. "May I speak to you briefly in private, my dear?"

Before Quinn could reply, Montreux spoke again. "You may have his lordship to yourself. I was this moment preparing to take my leave."

Quinn rang for Wilkins, and when the butler appeared, gave specific instructions to collect the bottles of cognac and show the *compte* out.

After Montreux had said his farewells and left, Quinn gave his attention to Venetia. "What did you wish to speak to me about?"

She must have seen him frowning, for she asked a different question than the one he expected. "Did you press the *compte* about the pendant and the shipwreck?"

"Yes. He says he has no knowledge of either. But his timing is curious. Why would he appear in London just now? And there is something odd about his manner."

"Perhaps he is ill?" Venetia mused. "Did you notice the way he was perspiring? Also, his hand when he took mine was cold and clammy."

"You would have noticed those things with your artist's eye. Now that you mention it . . . he made liberal use of his handkerchief during his visit."

"The *compte* wouldn't want you dead, would he?"

"A good question," Quinn said thoughtfully. "He seems too soft to be an assassin. I remembered Montreux as something of a dandy, and he doesn't appear to have changed much in the intervening years." Quinn's frown deepened. "I can think of no reason he would want to kill me. Besides, were I to die, he wouldn't stand to profit. Before my marriage to you, Skye would have inherited my unentailed property and possessions, and now you will." He shrugged. "If Montreux is involved, we will flush him out."

Venetia suddenly gave a start, as if recollecting her purpose. "That reminds me . . . I just saw the *Morning Chronicle*. It says you will attend a professional boxing match in South Hampstead this afternoon."

"Yes."

Her expression turned anxious. "You can't seriously be considering using yourself to bait a trap."

"In fact, I am. Hawk is fully supportive and will provide the personnel. We have it all carefully planned. We mean to set up our villain and encourage him to make a move."

"You deliberately intend to make it easy for him to kill you."

"To *attempt* it, yes. With luck we will expose the culprit this afternoon."

"You cannot depend on luck," she retorted almost angrily.

"There is no call to be upset."

"Of course there is! You are risking your life."

"My life is at risk no matter what I do. This way I hope to have some measure of control over the time and place for an attack."

"I am also upset that you didn't trust me enough to tell me of your scheme ahead of time. I had to read about it in the morning newspaper."

"I knew you would object. Additionally, I didn't want you to become involved."

"But I am involved—"

"Don't rip up at me, love."

She gave an exhalation, clearly torn between exasperation and worry. "You relish danger far too much, Quinn."

"Hardly. I have been cowering behind my armed servants for weeks."

"But you could lose your life."

"Come here, sweetheart." He drew her into his arms, despite her reluctance to be placated. "My demise is very unlikely. But even if it were likely to happen, I must act. We are making no progress as it is."

Venetia shuddered. "I fear for you every time you leave the house. I couldn't bear it if something were to happen to you."

He suspected she had not meant to sound so ardent

and emotional. But he was pleased to think she was more invested in his welfare than she let on.

"I knew it," he murmured, his tone faintly teasing. "You are more fond of me than you admit."

"I have a care for your skin, even if you don't."

"Oh, I have a great care for my skin."

When she started to protest further, Quinn placed two fingers on her lips. "Venetia, you should trust me. I promise to take every possible precaution."

"Oh, very well."

Wrapping her arms about his neck, she raised her lips to his. Her kiss was brief but hard and fervent, conveying her unspoken fears. As she pulled away, something unlodged in his chest, a warm, unfolding sensation.

"Please, Quinn . . . come home safely," she pleaded, looking up at him with her huge, luminous eyes.

He was struck by how badly he wanted to come home to her. A huge wave of affection and tenderness washed over him. "I will try my utmost."

"I suppose that will have to do," Venetia said grudgingly. "At least tell me exactly what you and Hawkhurst have planned."

Settling with Venetia on the sofa, Quinn proceeded to outline the details of their trap. An hour later as he went upstairs to his bedchamber to prepare for the afternoon ahead, he let his mind drift back to her urgent kiss and contemplated how far they had come in less than a month—from Venetia threatening to shoot him to kissing him ardently of her own free will.

He had come a vast distance himself. How far?

He'd started by seeing her as a challenge, but now he wanted so much more.

The thought brought Quinn up short in the middle of tying his cravat. He wanted a future with Venetia.

And yet . . . what *he* wanted wasn't really the question. The question was, could he give Venetia what *she* wanted? He would have to promise her fidelity, which would be no problem. Honor alone would keep him faithful, and with a woman like her, he would never want to stray.

She wanted love, however.

Loving her wasn't beyond the realm of possibility. He was a Wilde after all. Love and passion were in his bones.

He already felt a deepening affection for her. He'd become addicted to having her around, in his life. In truth, he could see himself with her several years from now, even decades from now, having children, growing old together. A bigger truth? He wanted a real marriage with her. He wanted Venetia as his wife forever.

Forever.

Something clutched hard in the region of Quinn's heart. He was falling in love, he realized. He should have recognized the tenderness he felt for Venetia, the need to keep her from harm, to cherish her always.

Quinn shook his head in wonder. He couldn't believe he was succumbing to his convenient bride.

But was his capitulation really so miraculous? Before meeting Venetia, he was determined to remain in control of his own destiny, refusing to become the unlucky victim of unrequited love again, to make himself so damned vulnerable. He'd thought he could escape any deep emotional entanglements with Venetia, yet he was being drawn in more irrevocably each day. She had chipped away steadily at his cool cynicism, thawing the ice in his heart with her warmth and caring. From the first, he had admired her inner fire, her passion, her devotion to her sister . . . and now he wanted that same devotion for himself.

Quinn made a scoffing sound that was part ridicule, part chuckle. He had been lured into his own courtship.

Indeed, it was possible that he could never have escaped his fate. Perhaps Kate was right: Venetia was his ideal match. The kind of perfect fit his sister and his cousins Ash and Jack had found. Admittedly they were content and fulfilled in a way that he never had been.

His parents had known that remarkable contentment. An image flashed in Quinn's memory, the love and devotion in his parents' eyes as they gazed at each other, the pure happiness.

He wanted to have that same happiness with Venetia.

He couldn't force her to love him, certainly. But he wouldn't let her current resistance stop him. He'd grown up knowing the best kind of marriage, and no other sort would do for him. When this was all over, he intended to claim her as his own, and he would let nothing and no one stand in his way.

Even though her heart was not in her work, Venetia returned to her studio. She was already vexed and on edge, and her nerves would be shredded if she had to wait idly all afternoon for Quinn's safe return from the boxing match.

She would much rather have occupied herself by seeking Cleo's advice about winning her husband's love, but she decided against a visit. Not only would the journey to Cleo's isolated country home in Kensington be too risky with the assassin still at large, her friend would not be happy to hear how drastically her feelings toward her marriage had changed. No doubt Cleo would try to dissuade her from her goal.

It was something of a relief, therefore, when two hours later a message arrived from Ophelia, pleading for help standing up to their mother in the matter of prospective suitors.

At least she could be of some use to her sister, Venetia rationalized. And she had armed guards to protect her. Furthermore, her parents lived much closer than Cleo, in a bustling part of town. Helping Ophelia would keep her from going mad waiting helplessly at home for word from Quinn.

When she arrived at her parents' home, Ophelia launched into her complaints at once. "Oh, Venetia, thank you for coming! Mama is being completely intractable. I favor one gentleman, but she objects for no good reason and wishes me to embrace an altogether different choice. I pray you will speak to her and convince her she is mistaken."

Venetia made soothing comments to temper Ophelia's frustration, and once she understood the particulars, agreed to referee their argument and talk to their mother. But she kept an eye on the mantel clock the entire time, and her unsettled thoughts kept drifting as she wondered how Quinn was faring with his scheme to root out the killer.

It was going to be a very long afternoon.

The boxing match had the festive atmosphere of a country fair. Vendors hawked meat pies and ginger-bread and ale near a low wooden platform, which had been roped off to form a ring. Large crowds milled around, betting on the outcome between two professional bruisers.

At the start, the contest seemed fairly even, with the hulking combatants bobbing and weaving and landing bare-knuckled jabs to the shouts and whis-tles of the spectators, then graduating to more pow-erful blows that would have instantly felled lesser men.

Quinn kept one eye on the match, another on the crowd. Occasionally he spied Hawk, who moved among the throng keeping watch. The local cham-pion won, to the delight of the crowd. At the conclu-sion, Quinn managed to separate himself from his footmen as planned, and strolled across the grass field without escort, toward his waiting carriage.

He was halfway there when he recognized the brutes following him. The same three thugs who had ambushed him in the alley behind Tavistock's were now armed with knives and cudgels. Unlike that night, however, Quinn had some advance warning this time. Additionally, Hawk and his men were highly proficient at their assignments.

It was simpler than Quinn expected to subdue the three thugs. Before they could barely blink, they were trussed and gagged and secured in a wagon. Their capture won a few looks from curious bystanders, but no one came to their rescue as they were carted to a nearby tavern and carried down to the cellar.

"Well done," Quinn told Hawk with genuine admiration.

Hawk returned a faint smile and shook his head. "Save your praise until we learn the name of their employer. Their tongues will likely loosen once they have stewed awhile. Let us go above stairs and enjoy an ale."

They left the three louts twisting and fighting to break free of their bonds and returned to find them sullenly protesting their treatment with curses.

By calm reasoning Quinn presented their options. The usual punishment for attempted murder of a peer was transportation to the penal colony at New South Wales, or hanging here in England. The alternative was prison, but he might be willing to provide their release once he had apprehended their employer.

His threats were not idle, and eventually they revealed their own names—Croft, Thackery, and Beck, although at first they stubbornly refused to identify who had hired them.

Finally Beck capitulated, evidently having the most concern for his skin. "I 'ave no wish to 'ang. 'Tis a Frenchie you seek."

"A Frenchman?"

"Aye, a Frog. But we wasn't ordered to kill you. 'e paid us to waylay you to see if you 'ad a certain ruby and diamond pendant on your person."

Thackery chimed in. "'is name was Firmin. Armand Firmin."

Hawk spoke up then. "Are you acquainted with Firmin, Traherne?"

"Not to my knowledge." Quinn had half expected his assailant to be Montreux.

"Who is he?" Hawk asked Thackery.

"Just someone who 'ired us."

"Where can we find this Firmin?"

"I dinna ken."

"But you must have communicated with him recently, since you were lying in wait for me this afternoon."

"Aye," Croft hastened to offer. "At an inn near the Wapping docks. The Arms, on High Street."

"Describe him for me—his age and appearance."

" 'e was younger than me, black 'air and eyes, tall and thin with a beak nose. And 'e had a cold stare. A killer for sure. Made me skin crawl, 'e did."

Quinn questioned them further about the other two attempts on his life—when his carriage was run off the road, and when he'd been shot in his own garden by a man disguised in the Traherne livery colors—but they professed to know nothing more.

Hawk drew Quinn aside. "We will pay a visit to The Arms and scout out the surroundings, but it might not be Firmin's headquarters. Be aware that we may not secure him today."

Quinn had difficulty quelling his disappointment and frustration, yet they were another step closer to identifying his deadly assailant.

Venetia could claim success in championing her sister's cause, for she managed to soften their mother's opposition to Ophelia's favorite suitor. Now she was eager to return home and discover what progress, if any, Quinn had made.

When she descended the front steps of the house and headed down the walk toward the brick entrance gate, however, she didn't see her carriage waiting at the street curb as expected. Her steps slowed as she reached the gate, for another closed carriage stood in its stead, driven by an unfamiliar coachman.

Venetia halted there, debating what to do. The carriage moved forward, and when it halted adjacent to her, she could see inside the lowered window. A smiling Compte de Montreux looked back at her.

Her heart started pounding reflexively, while her thoughts dashed ahead. Perhaps the *compte* was the Paris gamester after all—

"May I offer you a ride, Lady Traherne?"

"Thank you, no. I have my own carriage."

"*Au contraire.* My men have disabled your guards and hidden your carriage." Montreux drew a pistol and aimed it directly at her. "You will please join me."

For an instant, Venetia stood frozen, her heart racing. Her voice sounded faint when she finally managed to respond. "Or what? You will shoot me?"

"If I must, although I would regret acting so precipitously. It is not my intention to harm you just yet."

"But you mean to abduct me?"

"I fear so. Armand, assist her ladyship."

A tall, dark-haired man appeared around the far side of the coach, striding toward her.

One part of Venetia could not believe this was really happening. Montreux sat there, bold as you please, brazenly planning to take her captive in broad daylight.

But she would not go willingly.

Spinning, she ran back inside the gate, toward the house, while footsteps pounded after her in hot pursuit. She was shocked and furious and terrified all at once, but knew she had only a few seconds to provide a clue about her abductors.

Urgently, she dug in her reticule and pulled out a piece of chalk as she sank to her knees. On a paved flagstone, she drew a rough depiction of a frog and a large M—

Before she could write more, Montreux's henchman seized her by the arm and hauled her to her feet.

Venetia gave a shout toward the house, hoping to be heard by her sister or one of the Stratham servants, but fighting Armand was futile, as she was dragged painfully toward the carriage. He was tall and wiry and unbelievably strong.

Hitting him with her reticule had no effect. Desperate to provide another clue to help with a possible rescue, she tore the strings from her wrist and let the cloth purse drop to the pavestones.

At her continued resistance, Armand's arm snaked about her waist, lifting her up. Propelling her the last yard, he forced her inside and slammed the door behind her. She landed on the floor on her hands and knees.

Her pulse pounding from exertion and fear, Venetia struggled to climb onto the seat just as the carriage lunged forward. It was a moment before she gained her balance enough to face her abductor.

Montreux sat across from her, no longer smiling.

Venetia gripped her hands together to keep them from shaking. She could only hope Quinn would come to find her—except that an attempted rescue was doubtless exactly what the *compte* wanted. Suddenly, her own peril was no longer her greatest worry.

Ice filled her veins at the dire threat to Quinn. "*You* were the one who tried to kill my husband," she accused, "and this is your latest endeavor."

His eyes glittering, Montreux nodded with relish. "Alas, my initial efforts failed, but I will not fail again. Having you under my control will lure Traherne to me."

"But *why* do you want him dead?"

"I have my reasons."

A shudder went through her. His tone, like his expression, was cold, remote, implacable. There would be no reasoning with a man like this, she knew instinctively.

Fear gripped her throat and seeped into her bones— *No, stop that!* She could *not* let herself become paralyzed.

Forcibly, Venetia swallowed and tried to summon her courage. Montreux wouldn't succeed in harming Quinn, she vowed. Not if she could help it.

But just at the moment, she couldn't *begin* to think of any way to stop him.

As predicted, the effort to locate Armand Firmin at The Arms in Wapping was unsuccessful. None of the employees could remember serving a Frenchman of his description.

By the time Quinn returned home, it was past five

o'clock. Upon entering, Wilkins greeted him with a grave expression.

"My lord, Lady Traherne's sister, Miss Ophelia Stratham, is awaiting you in the drawing room. She says it is a matter of great urgency."

Before Quinn could hand over his hat and cane, a white-faced Ophelia appeared in the corridor. Evidently she had been listening for his arrival.

"What is amiss?" he asked.

"It is V-Venetia," the girl stammered. "She has been taken."

Quinn felt his heart clench. "What do you mean, taken?"

Ophelia launched into a hurried recitation. "She was leaving our home when a man in a dark cloak forced her into a coach—a footman heard her cry out and opened the front door just in time to see the scuffle—and she left her reticule on the walk, along with a chalk drawing—please, my lord, you must save her—"

By now Ophelia was half sobbing as her words tumbled out.

Quinn grasped her shoulders and demanded she take a deep breath and speak more slowly. With effort he refrained from barking out questions as Ophelia described the sketch of what looked to be a frog and the initial "M."

"For Montreux," he muttered, struggling to quell his own panic. "It has to be."

"I am so afraid for her," Ophelia wailed.

"Don't worry, we will find her," he promised, keeping his own fear to himself. Fury burned hot and bright inside him, as did terror. He could imagine

Venetia shot and bleeding, in great pain. The image turned his blood to ice—and yet at the same time, an unnatural calm settled over him. He would find her and rescue her or die trying.

He ordered Wilkins to summon Hawk to the Stratham home on Henrietta Place, while he accompanied Ophelia there. He wanted to see for himself the sketch Venetia had drawn.

There was still enough daylight to make out the chalk drawing, which convinced Quinn that he was right to suspect Montreux.

The knowledge bolstered his resolve. Remarkably, Venetia had had the presence of mind to leave clues, and he needed to make use of them. She was clever and resourceful, and he had to believe she would continue fighting.

He set his coachmen searching for Venetia's missing guards and carriage, then entered the Stratham house with Ophelia. Inside, the entire household was in chaos, and oddly, Mrs. Stratham seemed even more shaken by Venetia's abduction than her younger daughter.

Hawk arrived some twenty minutes later and listened intently as Quinn shared what he knew.

"If Montreux means to hold her for ransom," Hawk mused, "he will contact you at home—"

"I am not waiting helplessly at home," Quinn insisted.

"I don't mean for you to. It would be far better if we could determine his whereabouts and take the battle to him. No doubt his price will be your head, and he will be lying in wait for you. But the element of surprise can provide us a significant advantage. Where might he have taken her?"

"I haven't the faintest notion."

"It would be some place he knows well and can defend while holding a hostage."

A jolt of recognition ran through Quinn. "I know of one possibility—a country house where he lived while he was in exile, on the outskirts of London, on the road to Kent. New Cross was the village, I believe."

Hawk nodded. "Traveling there now will be a gamble, but that seems a good place to begin our search. If that location proves fruitless, we will rethink our options. We'll set out as soon as I can arrange for reinforcements."

"Ash is in Kent, but I want Jack with me. We will need all the firepower we can muster."

Quinn sent a Stratham footman after his cousin, asking Jack to meet them at Hawk's London home. Just then his coachman returned to report that Venetia's abandoned carriage had been found in a nearby copse of woods, her driver and two guards trussed inside and barely conscious. Quinn took a valuable few minutes to question them, but learned little about their attackers. With renewed urgency, Quinn went home with Hawk to gather weapons and ammunition and round up the earl's available men.

On the carriage ride there, Quinn flayed himself for missing the signs. "I should have suspected Montreux sooner. I feel like a blind, bloody fool. It now seems probable he was behind the attempts on my life all along. But I can't fathom why, unless it was revenge for my father's actions many years ago, for stealing away Montreux's bride-to-be, my mother. But why *now*?"

"With luck, you will have the chance to ask him yourself when we rescue your wife tonight."

Quinn could only pray Hawk was right.

Fear of losing Venetia ripped through him anew, and he found it hard to sustain his former grim determination. Particularly when he was aware of a bitter irony:

If he'd harbored any doubt about his love for Venetia, his visceral response to her abduction would have settled the question. Why only now, when it might be too late, had he come to realize how precious she was to him?

Chapter Nineteen

"*Where are you* taking me?" Venetia asked as the *compte*'s coach rumbled over Westminster Bridge.

"You will learn soon enough."

After crossing the Thames River and traveling another mile or so, she realized their environs were becoming less inhabited. Venetia shivered, unable to control the chills snaking down her spine. Even though she had left clues as to her captor, they were heading beyond the city, where no one would know how to find her.

Yet she couldn't just sit here cowering. Instead, she needed to persuade Montreux to disclose any information she might use to her benefit.

She began by appealing to his vanity, giving him a compliment. "I must commend you on your cleverness, monsieur. You managed to abduct me with very little effort."

Her opening gambit was met by dispiriting silence. "I played directly into your hands, didn't I? By leaving my home to visit my sister, I made your task much easier."

The *compte*'s faint smile made her skin crawl. "You obliged me, yes. Otherwise I would have needed to seize you from your house, and leading you out at gunpoint would have been quite difficult."

"You must have known Traherne was away."

"Certainly I did. I pride myself with my acumen. *You* were the more vulnerable target." Montreux made a scoffing sound. "Did he think I wouldn't deduce his ploy to draw me out? It was much too obvious. I sent my hirelings to divert Traherne while I put *my* plan in motion. And soon enough I will—what is the English phrase?—turn the tables upon him."

Fresh fear swamped Venetia at the reminder that he planned to lure Quinn to his death.

Before she could reply, Montreux cut her off. "Now hold your tongue, *madame*. I have no desire to listen to your babble."

He returned his pistol to the case lying on the seat beside him, which Venetia recognized as a dueling set. Clearly he had great confidence that she was helpless—which indeed she was at the moment. As the coach picked up speed, she had no choice but to obey his command.

They drove for another half hour at least. Venetia alternated between hope and dread that Quinn would somehow divine her location and come after her, for a rescue attempt could prove fatal for him.

By now the road had narrowed to a rural lane. They were in farming country, where houses and cottages were more sparse. Dusk was falling by the time the coach turned onto a badly rutted lane.

When eventually they halted and Montreux handed her down, Venetia took careful note of her surroundings. It appeared to be a farm. Before her stood a two-story, timber-framed cottage, with woods on one side, barns and outbuildings on the other. Perhaps lodging for a tenant farmer and his family.

"I regret the poor accommodations," Montreux said as he took her elbow and led her toward the cottage. "No doubt it is not what you are accustomed to. This was all I could afford when I had to flee France. Fortunately, I recouped many of my lands and possessions, so that I now have significant wealth."

Behind her, a second carriage rolled to a halt and dislodged the henchman called Armand, along with several other grim-faced men. Montreux shook Venetia's arm to prevent her looking over her shoulder, then ushered her inside, where a lamp lit the small entry hall.

"Your room is on the floor above," he said, gesturing at the narrow staircase. "Dinner will be brought to you in a short while, *naturellement*. I am not a savage. I will treat a *comptesse* with the courtesy she deserves."

Venetia quelled a retort. Of course he was a savage, but it would be the height of stupidity to challenge him and let him think her other than a spineless captive.

From his coat pocket Montreux pulled out his fob watch and checked the time. "I expect by now your husband has learned of your disappearance. In the morning I will send a message to Traherne. For now I will permit him to, how do you say it, stew? He will be frantic once he learns of his missing wife."

Unable to imagine Quinn becoming frantic over anything, Venetia again bit her tongue. Somehow she would have to manufacture her own rescue before Montreux had the chance to murder Quinn, but for now she would pretend to go along with her imprisonment.

She was taken by Armand to a bedchamber on the second floor and locked inside. When after a few moments she tried the handle, the door wouldn't budge, but at least she was able to open the window.

Her room faced the rear of the house, she saw in the fading light. There was a vegetable garden below, enclosed by a wall with an iron gate at the rear. If she could manage to climb over the wall, she would seek aid at a neighboring farmhouse. She had to escape, but how?

She waited until full dark, pacing the floor, trying to think of her best course of action. After a quarter hour, she got to work, tearing strips from a bedsheet and knotting them together to make a rope.

Nearly another hour passed—time she spent fretting—before a man delivered a supper tray. He found Venetia sitting meekly in a chair. But as soon as the door closed behind him and the key turned in the lock, she jumped up and began her escape attempt. Now would be the best time to flee, while Montreux and his cohorts were occupied with their own supper.

She secured one end of her sheet rope around the bedpost, then fished the other end out the window. Thankfully, it was long enough to reach the ground.

Now for the difficult part. The drop was only a short distance—perhaps some twenty feet—but she had to complete her feat in silence to avoid alerting her captors. In the hush of the garden, every sound seemed amplified. And the glow of light coming from a window below her would make her more visible as well.

Chiding herself for her faltering courage, Venetia tied up her skirts to free her legs. Then, taking a deep breath, she climbed backward over the ledge and started to lower herself down.

She had miscalculated how taxing it was to hold on to the rope with the friction burning her hands, though. Gritting her teeth, Venetia summoned her last reserves of strength, but after only a few more feet, she lost purchase on the linen fabric and was forced to let go.

Her fall was about ten feet, and she landed mostly on her feet, but the descent jarred her. Feeling a sharp pain in her left ankle, she barely stifled a cry.

Turning awkwardly, Venetia began hobbling toward the rear garden gate, which seemed so far away in the dark. Someone must have heard her fall, for a door opened behind her and a man shouted after her.

Her heart slamming, she tried to sprint along the path, to no avail; moments later she was tackled to the ground, the wind knocked out of her.

Her attacker then rolled her onto her back and wrapped his fingers around her throat. Briefly glimpsing his face in the dim light, Venetia recognized Armand before he shoved her head against the flagstone and tightened his grasp on her throat.

He meant to choke her, she realized. Seeing stars, desperate for air, she struggled to pry his fingers away. She was only vaguely aware of another shout, but then thankfully, Armand's grasp loosened and his weight shifted off her.

Venetia rolled onto her side, gasping and coughing reflexively. She heard Montreux snapping orders in French. Then Armand hauled her to her feet.

Feeling faint and nauseated, she could barely stand, so he half pulled, half carried her into the kitchen and through the house to a small parlor.

Having followed close behind, Montreux was livid—as much at his servant as at her, it seemed. While Armand tied her to a chair, her arms wrenched behind her back, the *compte* let loose a tirade in French at them both, finishing with a final warning to her: "I told you, I don't want you harmed until Traherne can witness it!"

Montreux barked more orders at Armand and sent him back to the kitchen to finish eating, then directed his fury at her again.

"Attempting to escape was extremely foolish, *madame*. Did you not consider that my house is surrounded by my loyal men? Now I shall have to watch you myself."

With a sound of disgust, he drew out both pistols from the dueling case and set them on the tea table in front of him, then settled down to finish his supper while Venetia suffered.

At the completion of his meal, he appeared to have calmed down somewhat. Taking a sip of wine, Montreux glanced across the parlor at her. "A pity you must spend the night here, secured to a chair, when you could have enjoyed a comfortable bed."

Venetia didn't have the heart or the voice to answer. Her misery was complete. The strain on her shoulders was excruciating, the rope cutting into her wrists. Her head and ankle both ached as well. And her throat was raw and dry as dust, which only magnified the pain when she coughed intermittently.

But the chief cause of her discomfort was fear compounded by guilt. She had failed. No doubt the moment Quinn arrived, Montreux would shoot him.

No, Venetia screamed silently. She had to make one last effort to dissuade him from his course.

"*Mon . . . sieur le compte . . .*" The words came out as a broken squawk. Her voice was so hoarse she could barely speak.

Venetia cleared her throat and tried again. "It seems . . . that you mean to . . . kill me in front of my husband," she rasped, "and then kill him."

"*Oui.*"

"The least you can do . . . is tell me why you want him dead."

Montreux took another sip of his wine.

"If I am to die," Venetia pressed, "then it does not . . . matter if I know. Is it for revenge?"

After a moment, he nodded. "In part."

Venetia hoped for a more complete explanation. "I believe I know why. If Quinn's mother, Angelique, had wed you as planned, you would have been an enormously wealthy man, with all the power and legacy her family connections would have brought you."

Montreux's mouth curled with contempt. "Instead I was forced to endure exile and poverty for years, with only scraps from Angelique and her noble husband, Lionel Wilde." A note of bitter hatred laced the *compte*'s voice as he glanced around the small parlor.

"Angelique quite generously provided me with this hovel. Have you any notion how humiliating it is to accept charity from the woman you should have wed?"

She had some inkling, yes, since she'd had to rely on Cleo's generosity for years, even though Cleo was a beloved friend.

Montreux was still spitting venom. "This farm is where I suffered my exile from my country while Angelique lived like a queen at her palace. This is also where her son will meet his demise. There is a measure of poetic justice in choosing this place, would you not say?"

At the relish in his tone, fear squeezed the breath from Venetia's lungs. She closed her eyes, trying to remain calm, and forced herself to continue prodding Montreux for details.

"You owned the ruby pendant, didn't you? You lost it playing cards at a gambling hell in Paris last winter, to an Englishman named Bellamy."

The *compte*'s mouth pursed as he calculated whether to respond. "Lamentably, yes. He played above his skill that evening, and my luck was unusually poor."

"What I don't understand is how you gained possession of the pendant in the first place. Do you have more of the de Chagny jewels as well?"

"If so, I only claimed what should have been mine."

"I think," she said slowly, "you must have stolen the jewels somehow. Is that true? You grew worried when Traherne began inquiries about the pendant and feared he would trace its origins to you and expose you?"

Montreux took a long gulp of his wine, then leaned

forward to refill his glass from a decanter. "That was not my only concern. Your husband sent a man to the south of France to investigate the wreck of Angelique's yacht."

"But I thought there was no excavation of the shipwreck."

A faint smile played on his mouth. "There was no need to excavate. The jewels did not go down with the ship."

Venetia frowned. "We recently learned that in all likelihood, the yacht was not sunk by a storm but an explosion. Did you have a hand in the explosion?"

Montreux scowled and clamped his lips shut, evidently determined to say no more.

Venetia tried another tack. "Surely you realize you won't get away with killing Traherne. Too many people know who you are. He already suspects you since you called at our home this morning. That was not wise, monsieur. Indeed, you should not have come to England at all."

"It could not be helped. Armand failed to do the deed."

"But not for lack of effort. It was Armand who attempted to run Traherne off the road last month, was it not?"

"Yes, by following his curricle from the mews."

"And then Armand stole into the Traherne garden, dressed in the earl's livery colors, in order to shoot him."

Montreux grimaced. "I am extremely disappointed with Armand. He makes an excellent assassin, but in all three instances, luck was smiling on Traherne. At last, I realized I needed to take charge of the problem myself. I could gain access to your home when Armand no longer could. Since the shooting, Traherne has been too well guarded." The *compte* gave a brief chuckle. "In truth, I might have shot him this morning in his very drawing room, but departing afterward would have been difficult, perhaps impossible. A pity. It would have saved me the trouble of abducting you."

Montreux settled back in his chair, looking as if he had begun to enjoy himself. "It is possible I may not need to shoot Traherne, however. If he drinks the cognac I brought him as a gift, he will discover a rude shock."

Venetia's heart lurched. "What do you mean? You poisoned the bottle?"

"Bottles, yes. But I could not rely on that means alone. Success was too uncertain. But no matter. This way is better."

"And you believe you will escape detection," she said shakily.

"Certainly I will. Armand will do the actual killing, so I needn't soil my hands. As you said, my cleverness is to be commended."

His preening revolted Venetia, but she continued to encourage it. "One more layer of concealment to keep your own identity hidden?"

"Precisely. Armand will be blamed for the murder, but he will easily return to France and disappear. There will be nothing to connect me to Traherne's death. I took great care on that score." Montreux turned to stare steadily at Venetia. "You should harbor no doubt, *madame*. You and Traherne will die on the morrow. I cannot allow witnesses."

Finally rendered speechless by his boast, Venetia remained silent, her terror and despair rising in equal measures. She had lost her one chance to stop Quinn's vengeful enemy.

Montreux was no madman, however. He was a cold, calculating, hate-filled man with a great deal to lose, which made him even more dangerous. He was driven not only by revenge but self-preservation—the fear that his entire life would be ruined once his secrets were divulged to the world. And in trying to rescue her, Quinn would be walking directly into his trap.

Quinn neared their destination, beset by doubts. They were indeed taking a risk setting out for New Cross without waiting to be contacted by Montreux to learn his demands. If they were wrong about the location, Venetia would likely suffer for the miscalculation.

But if not, the advantage could prove invaluable, and he had to act. He despised feeling so totally helpless, despised having no control over his destiny, despised even more that he might be powerless to rescue Venetia. If she were to die, he would be to blame— for marrying her and putting her life at risk. A part of him would die as well, he knew with bleak certainty. But as long as he had breath left in his body, he would fight to save her.

Jack had willingly accompanied him, as had Skye and Kate. The ladies refused to be relegated to waiting helplessly at home, arguing that Venetia could need a woman's comforting after what was certain to be a traumatic ordeal. Fully understanding their sentiments, Quinn let them come, as long as they agreed to remain at a nearby inn, out of danger.

His one consolation was knowing of Hawk's vast experience with just this sort of crisis. Montreux's calculations hadn't taken into account Hawk's presence.

Quinn's fear remained at a nerve-wracking level, however. They were literally making a stab in the dark. And time was passing at glacial speed. It took more than two hours to plan for their mission, and another for their procession of carriages to reach the posting inn at the village of New Cross, where they were able to ascertain the exact location of Montreux's former lodgings. Leaving Skye and Kate at the inn, Quinn and Jack proceeded first, with Hawk and his entourage following closely behind. They traveled several more miles and set up a command post in a wooded area, a few hundred yards from the farm cottage where Venetia was possibly being held.

With darkness for cover, Hawk led the effort to scout the premises. Quinn's dread increased with each passing moment until Hawk reported back.

"This must be the right location," Hawk murmured. "Thus far we counted at least four guards stationed around the cottage. We must dispose of them before we can get closer."

Amending his orders, Hawk had his men quietly overpower the exterior guards and drag their inert forms to their camp, while he managed to peer through several windows. Again, Hawk was able to claim a measure of success. In one of the front rooms, Venetia was seated in an armless chair, with her arms tied behind the chair back, attended by a well-garbed gentleman who fit the description of Montreux. And in what appeared to be the kitchens, several men were eating and drinking at a table, including one who might be Armand Firmin.

Quinn's incredible relief was short-lived, for they still had to free Venetia without her being harmed.

After another brief consultation, they decided to act now while they still claimed the advantage, before the missing guards were discovered. Yet if they stormed the house, she could be caught in a crossfire.

Hawk sent his best confederates around back to disable the men in the kitchen while he, Quinn, and Jack secured the front. Although Firmin was likely the more lethal adversary, Montreux was the first priority, and Quinn insisted on being the one to confront him.

The three of them crept up to the cottage. Then Hawk carefully eased open the front door and studied the interior. At his hand signal, they slipped inside, with Quinn bringing up the rear. Keeping an eye out for more guards, they quickly crossed the small entry hall and ducked behind the staircase, where they remained, not daring to breathe, straining to hear.

After a moment, Quinn peered around the corner, down a dimly lit corridor. There was a man posted outside the parlor door, lounging back against the wall in a bored fashion. To lure him away, Quinn called out in a muffled voice, claiming that Firmin wanted him in the kitchens.

Appearing eager to be relieved of his duties, the fellow left his post and strode down the corridor, where

Hawk silently dispatched him by knocking him unconscious.

With the way cleared, Quinn eased from his hiding place. Tightly hugging the wall, he stole forward until he could enter the parlor, holding two pistols at the ready.

His sudden appearance clearly shocked Montreux, who leapt to his feet, brandishing his own pistol as well as a knife. Moving at lightning speed, the *compte* backed away until he stood beside Venetia, with the knife at her throat, his pistol aimed at Quinn. *"Ne t'approche pas ou je vais la tuer!"*

Quinn's heart almost stopped at the vow to kill Venetia if he came any closer, but he struggled to appear calm. "If you harm her, you will be dead an instant later."

He risked a glance at Venetia, who was gazing at him with hope and fear in her eyes. Her hair and clothing were disheveled, her skirts rucked up to expose her stockings and garters.

Quinn returned her gaze, silently offering encouragement even though his own chest was so heavy he could barely breathe. Hawk and Jack were both behind him in the corridor, but could do little good from their position.

"Comment avez-vous me trouvez?" Montreux demanded, asking how he had been found.

"I chanced that you would return to a familiar place," Quinn answered.

The *compte* switched from French to English. "What happened to my men?"

"Incapacitated."

"All of them?"

"Yes."

Montreux cursed vividly in French.

"Release Lady Traherne, and I will let you live," Quinn declared.

"I cannot comply. She is my surety for my freedom. You will permit me to leave with her."

"That will not happen, *Compte*."

"Then she will die."

When the knife blade pressed deeper into her skin, Venetia paled a little but lifted her chin.

It seemed they were at an impasse. Threats would likely not work, Quinn surmised, his desperation mounting. He would offer to take Venetia's place, but Montreux would doubtless see that as a weakness. Judging from the hatred blazing in his eyes, the *compte* was clearly in no mood to give quarter or surrender.

Indeed, his next words conveyed an utter recklessness. "It would give me great pleasure to kill your lady-wife before your very eyes. You will know how it feels to lose the woman you love."

Every muscle in Quinn's body clenched. He had never felt so helpless. Inside he was shaking, yet he forced a scoffing sound. "The woman I love? You overstate the extent of my fondness for her. She was not the bride of my choosing. I was compelled to wed her."

He glimpsed the stricken look in Venetia's eyes, but it couldn't be helped. If Montreux knew how deeply he cared, he would cut her throat on the spot.

"However," Quinn added dispassionately, "she *is* my wife, and it would hardly be honorable for me to leave her at your mercy. I will make a bargain with you." While he spoke, Quinn slowly stepped to one side, hoping to leave a clear line of sight to the doorway.

"What bargain?" Montreux asked suspiciously.

"Release her unharmed and I will let you escape unscathed."

Montreux visibly sneered. "Do you think me a fool?"

"You may be many things, monsieur, but not a fool. You have my solemn word as a gentleman. I will even guarantee your safe passage back to France."

"I must decline."

Crushing his fear, Quinn took another step, meaning to circle the room partway and distract Montreux enough for Hawk to join the fray.

"Stand where you are!" Montreux exclaimed.

The sharp command was enough to halt Quinn in his tracks.

"Now lower your weapons and set them on the table."

Quinn knew better than to comply. As soon as he was unilaterally disarmed, Montreux would shoot him, and perhaps Venetia as well. Quinn would do better to try and provoke the French nobleman.

Changing tactics, Quinn adopted his own sneer. "You are a coward, monsieur, using a woman to shield you."

Montreux reacted with fury. "You dare to call *me* a coward?" Outraged, he took half a step toward Quinn, waving his pistol, which caused his knife to slip a little.

Then three things happened in quick succession:

Clenching her teeth, Venetia braced her feet on the

carpet and pushed sideways so that her chair tipped over, catching Montreux by surprise and throwing him off balance.

The *compte*'s pistol jerked upward, leaving Quinn a clear shot.

And Quinn lunged forward and fired, just as Venetia's cry of pain stabbed through his heart.

Chapter Twenty

The gunshot sounded loud in the small parlor, making Quinn's ears ring as he charged his foe. Evidently he'd hit his target, for Montreux shrieked and staggered backward before falling to the floor.

He was still armed and deadly, however, for he was only wounded in the shoulder, Quinn saw through the haze of powder smoke.

When the *compte* raised the pistol still in his grasp, Quinn brought his booted foot down hard on the Frenchman's wrist, forcing him to release the weapon, which Quinn swiftly kicked away.

Crouching down, he let go a fierce punch to Montreux's jaw, stunning him just as both Hawk and Jack stormed into the room behind them.

Quinn snatched up the *compte*'s fallen knife and hastened to Venetia's side. He used the blade to cut away the ropes binding her hands to the chair, then knelt beside her, urgently searching her pale face.

Her grimace of pain eased when she saw he had come out the victor.

"Are you badly hurt?" he demanded.

"No . . . not badly," she whispered in a rasping voice.

Savage anger filled Quinn. Venetia was alive, but there were visible abrasions on one cheek and dark bruises on her neck.

Wishing his bullet had found Montreux's heart, Quinn carefully eased her from the chair and helped her to stand. He wanted to cradle her in his arms, but the battle with the *compte*'s men was not yet won. He could hear the sounds of a scuffle echoing from the other side of the cottage—thuds and shouts and breaking glass, followed by another gunshot and Hawk speaking abruptly:

"Wilde, if you have Montreux under control, I will see to Firmin."

Jack responded with a curt command. "Go."

Quinn glanced over his shoulder. Montreux lay curled on the carpet, clutching his shoulder and whimpering, with an armed Jack standing guard over him.

Quinn returned his attention to Venetia as she leaned against him for support. His heart still thudding painfully in his chest, he held her away so he could take stock again of her white, battered face, her trembling body. Fresh rage filled him at the cuts and bruises on her cheek and throat—and those were only the wounds he could see. He raised a finger to the abraded skin on her neck. "Montreux did this to you?" he ground out.

"No, it was his hired . . . mercenary, Armand. I tried to . . . escape through the rear garden . . . but

Armand caught me and brought me . . . here so Montreux could watch me."

Quinn clenched his jaw as he marveled at her courage in trying to escape her captors. She must have been shaken from Firmin's brutality, yet she'd had the presence of mind to turn the advantage to him against Montreux, a testament to her mettle. "If you hadn't turned over your chair when you did, I could never have gotten off the shot."

She didn't answer directly. "I knew you would come for me . . . and it terrified me. He meant to kill you." A shudder vibrated through her.

The same shudder swept through Quinn. She had come so close to dying. They both had.

"Can you ever forgive me for putting you in such danger?" he murmured.

She lifted her head to search his face. Her eyes were shadowed and her mouth trembled a little. Then she looked away as if trying to hide her hurt. "It was not your fault . . . that Montreux was so set on revenge."

Now was not the time to profess his love, Quinn knew, but he badly wanted to reassure her.

Before he could, however, she raised a hand to her temple and swayed. "I feel faint. May . . . I sit down?"

"Of course." He helped Venetia to a chair, berating himself for forgetting her injuries.

Just then Hawk returned. "Firmin and his minions are in our custody, and our men suffered no serious injury. What of the *compte*?"

By now the smoke had cleared, but the stench of gunpowder remained. Montreux still lay on the floor, moaning in pain, with blood seeping through his fingers where he clutched his shoulder.

Apparently Jack had examined the wound, for he answered at once. "The ball is lodged inside him, and he is bleeding profusely. He will need a surgeon." Jack glanced between Hawk and Quinn. "What shall we do with him?"

Quinn replied first. "I don't give a bloody damn what happens to him. He abducted and nearly killed my wife."

Venetia spoke up quietly. "That was not his only crime. He admitted . . . that he hired Armand to kill you . . . to prevent you from learning what happened . . . to your parents' ship. I believe he somehow sabotaged . . . the ship so he could claim your mother's jewels. He might even . . . have manufactured the explosion."

A new kind of anger speared through Quinn. "I suspected he might be involved. Nothing else made sense. If so, he caused the murder of my family and the entire crew."

Montreux's gasped reply was defiant. "You have . . . no proof."

His jaw hardening, Quinn gazed contemptuously down at his nemesis. "I will find proof in time. I plan to find the shipwreck to determine if an explosion occurred. But if you wish to have a surgeon remove the ball in your shoulder, you will disclose the part you played. Otherwise your wound will putrefy and rot—if you don't bleed to death first." He smiled coldly. "I prefer you to survive long enough to stand trial and hang, but one way or another, I will discover the truth. You may choose."

Montreux refused to comment. When Jack pulled

him upright, the *compte* groaned and gritted his teeth.

"What is your decision?" Quinn demanded.

Montreux's glare was full of hatred. "Very well, I . . . will . . . reveal to you what happened."

Hawk volunteered his services then. "Traherne, your presence will be required to resolve his fate, as well as that of Firmin and the others. I can deliver them to the authorities tonight. I will find the nearest magistrate and summon a surgeon. But eventually you will have to press charges."

Quinn nodded. He wanted very much to lay charges and to hear Montreux's confession, but he hesitated when Venetia raised her hand to her temple and closed her eyes. No doubt she was suffering from shock as well as physical pain. She needed care and comfort at once.

Bestirring herself, Venetia said in a weak voice, "You ought to go with Lord Hawkhurst. I am well enough."

Again Quinn hesitated. She was pale, frightened, shaky, but also grimly stoic.

He looked at his cousin. "Jack, will you escort her to the posting inn where Skye and Kate are waiting and accompany them home?"

"Of course."

"And fetch Dr. Biddowes to tend to her injuries?"

"I will see to her welfare, Quinn, you needn't worry."

He was immensely worried, and reluctant to give over Venetia's care even to his cousins and sister. Yet she didn't appear to want his company just now.

When he nodded gravely, Jack handed his prisoner

to Hawk, then moved to Venetia's side. "Come with me, my lady."

Although fiercely reluctant to let her out of his sight, Quinn stepped back. He would deal with Montreux as soon as possible, so he could return to Venetia tonight and try to make amends for the trauma he had put her through. He also intended to settle once and for all the question of their marriage.

Jack took her arm and supported her as she rose unsteadily. In that same low voice, Venetia issued a warning. "You must . . . beware, Quinn. Montreux divulged that . . . the cognac he gave . . . you was poisoned."

She left then without another glance or a word of farewell. Quinn watched her go, knowing he would be gnashing his teeth until he could be alone with her.

When Venetia reached the posting inn with Lord Jack, she felt sore in both body and spirit. After battling Armand and the wrenching rope bindings, then being threatened at knifepoint by Montreux, she was still weak and shaking. Additionally, her head throbbed, her throat ached, her shoulder muscles burned, and her hands, which had grown numb, now pulsed with stinging needles.

She was grateful the nightmare had ended, though. Her greatest fear—that Quinn would be killed or hurt—was finally over. Indeed, hope and exultation had filled her at his sudden appearance in the small parlor. Yet his callous disavowal of any affection for her had cut straight into her heart.

Yes, his eyes had blazed with anger when he saw

her physical condition. But his declaration about being forced to wed her had brought all her former doubts and uncertainty rushing to the surface. And when she'd desperately needed him to hold and comfort her, more important matters had demanded his attention—namely dealing with pure evil and the shocking truth that Montreux had likely caused the tragic deaths of his family and the ship's crew.

Quinn's professed indifference had left her with an unmistakable chill—a chill that continued as Lord Jack gently handed her down from his carriage and escorted her inside the inn.

Skye and Katharine were waiting anxiously for them in a private parlor. Visibly grateful that Jack was unharmed, both ladies embraced him warmly, then took custody of Venetia with even greater warmth.

It was comforting to have them fuss over her like protective mother hens—or even sisters—situating her on a sofa and plying her with hot tea and biscuits while Lord Jack quickly recounted the events of the past few hours.

He concluded his tale with the plans to incarcerate Montreux and his minions and added a prediction. "It may take the better part of the night for Quinn and Hawkhurst to complete their task. When you are recovered enough, Lady Traherne, we should be on our way."

Venetia nodded. With sustenance, she felt less faint, although consternation still sat like a leaden weight in the pit of her stomach.

Katharine must have noticed her demeanor, for she asked quietly, "Would you prefer to rest here, my dear, or do you feel well enough to manage the drive home?"

Lord Jack interjected his preference. "It would be best if I deliver you to Berkeley Square and engage Biddowes to tend your injuries."

Katharine agreed. "We can care for you better at home."

"I can manage the drive," Venetia assured them.

"No doubt your sister and parents will wish to see you," Katharine added, "but that can wait until the morning. For now, it should suffice to send them a message saying that you have been found and are well but need to rest after your ordeal."

Lord Jack left to make ready the carriage. Thus, it was not long before Venetia again found herself in his coach, this time with Skye sitting beside her, both of them facing Lord Jack and Katharine.

Once under way, Skye admitted her relief. "I confess I was worried for Hawk, although I know he has often faced similar situations. This will not be the first time he has been away all night, either. The waiting and uncertainty is most difficult to bear."

Venetia agreed in part. Relief still coursed through her now that Quinn was safe, but her apprehension was impossible to deny—which was utterly foolish. She had no rational basis for being so upset. Quinn had only declared what she had always known: that he didn't love her.

She ought to face the fact that he might never love her. Unquestionably his avowal had battered the fragile hope that had begun to blossom over the past few days—that they could have a happy future together.

The memory sent fresh pain lancing through her. When her chin started to quiver, Skye clasped her hand in silent sympathy.

Venetia set her jaw resolutely. She refused to cry. She alone was to blame for her false hopes. She'd spent the past few days deceiving herself, filling her foolish heart with love and dreams, but now she had to face reality.

Perhaps it was time to plan her immediate removal to France. Parting from Quinn would be like cutting out her heart, but plunging in the knife quickly might make the hurt a little less agonizing.

Chapter Twenty-one

The hour was pressing four o'clock in the morning before Quinn at last concluded his business at the jail and climbed into his waiting carriage. Not only was he anxious to see to Venetia's welfare, but an underlying urgency nagged at him. Now that the assassins had been captured, she had no reason to remain in England with him.

On his order, his coachman cracked the whip and sprang the horses. With a rising moon to light the country roads, Quinn made the journey to London in record time. As soon as his carriage delivered him to his Berkeley Square mansion, he bounded up the front steps and let himself in.

The sleepy footman standing duty took his outer garments and answered his rapidly fired questions.

Yes, Lady Traherne had arrived several hours ago, along with the Ladies Skye and Katharine and Lord Jack.

Yes, the doctor had come and gone.

And yes, Lady Traherne had retired upstairs to sleep.

Quinn also learned that much of his family was presently staying at his house. Besides Skye and Kate, Jack had returned with his wife Sophie. And Ash had arrived with his wife Maura and their baby son, having driven through the night from the Beaufort family estate in Kent in response to Quinn's summons. No doubt they all wished to be of service and remain close by rather than repair to their own London homes.

More concerned about Venetia, Quinn took a candle and climbed the stairs. Just as he suspected, she was in her own bedchamber, not theirs.

He quietly opened the door to her room and shut it behind him, then approached her silently, needing to assure himself that she was safe. She was dressed in a long-sleeved nightshift, the covers drawn up under her arms, her dark hair flowing down her back.

As he moved to stand beside her bed, Venetia slowly rolled over to face him. She looked so delicate and vulnerable that Quinn clenched his jaw.

Remorse filled him anew. If she had been killed, if he had lost her . . . a shudder ran through him.

When she blinked at the soft glow of candlelight, he spoke in a murmur. "I didn't mean to wake you."

"I was not asleep. I didn't wish to be drugged with laudanum."

Although her voice was rather toneless, at least it was stronger and less raw than before, Quinn thought. "Did Biddy examine you?"

"Yes. He tended my cuts and bruises and gave me a powder for my headache. I am to rest for a day or two. Skye and Katharine also took excellent care of me, as did Lord Jack."

She sat up slowly, arranging the pillows behind her back. "What did you learn from Montreux?"

The note of interest in her voice encouraged Quinn a small measure. Setting the candle on the nightstand, he drew up a chair beside her bed and sat down. Perhaps it was best to start with something less intimate than the fate of their marriage—the tale of how fourteen years ago, Montreux had carried out his scheme.

"I believe I told you that after the Revolution, the de Chagny family treasure remained hidden for years, and that following the Peace of Amiens, my parents went to France to reclaim it? What I didn't know was that Montreux was a passenger on their return voyage."

Venetia seemed surprised. "He was actually a passenger on the *Zephyr*?"

"Yes. He pretended an eagerness to visit England again, and asked to accompany my parents home."

She frowned, deep in thought. "And all the while he bore them a tremendous hatred. A wolf in sheep's clothing."

"Indeed," Quinn said grimly. "Their gullibility allowed him to carry out his scheme without suspicion. The rumors were true: The yacht's sinking was indeed sabotage. Aided by a trusted cohort, Montreux set fire to a keg of gunpowder and escaped by rowboat with the treasure."

Venetia raised a hand to her mouth in revulsion. "He murdered them for both greed and vengeance," she whispered.

"Yes. He wanted my mother's jewels and sought revenge against my father."

When Venetia stared at Quinn in appalled silence, he continued. "Last night you managed to gain a partial confession from him, or we might never have learned the truth."

"What happened after he escaped the *Zephyr*?"

"He used the treasure to stake his gaming career and rebuild his fortune. Losing the pendant to Bellamy was his first serious mistake, though, for it eventually initiated my investigation. My original letter to Montreux alarmed him. If it came out how he had regained his wealth—by stealing the de Chagny jewels—he would be ruined. Then he learned of my inquiries into the *Zephyr*'s fate and feared I might ferret out the cause. He would hang if his guilt could be proven."

"So he hired Armand Firmin to kill you."

"Yes. Last night Firmin confirmed much of the story in a futile attempt to save his own skin."

Her mouth curled in disgust. "Montreux actually boasted about his plans to murder you. And he was livid that you foiled his henchmen's attempts three times."

Quinn nodded. "After that, Montreux grew desperate. And when I wrote to him a second time, asking questions about Bellamy and the *Zephyr,* he came to England himself to rectify the failures."

"Thank God he failed," Venetia murmured. "But I am so very sorry about your family, Quinn."

"As am I." Remembering the grief he'd felt as a young man, he clenched his jaw. Yet whatever sadness he now felt was overshadowed by the anger that gripped him. "My mother suffered the ultimate betrayal by a man who professed to love her."

After a moment, Quinn added absently, "I may still try to find the shipwreck. Montreux confirmed the general location where the Zephyr went down. Even though he will likely hang for his crimes against me, I want justice for his victims after all these years, and I would derive greater satisfaction if their murders could be acknowledged. He should pay for what he did to you as well."

Quinn eyed the bruises at Venetia's throat and felt his ire rise. "I should have shot him through the heart. I am furious at myself for not figuring out sooner what he intended. When I learned he had taken you, I was terrified."

Venetia looked away. "I knew you would find me."

Her trust moved him, as did her spirit, her fearlessness. But he still couldn't forgive himself. "I am more sorry than I can ever say for what he did to you, Venetia."

Venetia heard the remorse in Quinn's voice and knew it was genuine, yet she couldn't let herself dwell on his feelings.

"Are you in much pain?"

"Not much," she lied. Her heart ached more than her body did, since her fears and doubts had only built over the past few hours. Misery twisted inside her now, knotting her stomach.

She badly wanted Quinn to hold her, but she wouldn't let herself ask for comfort. Not when she would only be prolonging the agony of parting. The reminder sent a fresh wave of loneliness and heartache washing through her.

He must have noted her despair, for he leaned forward and reached out to take her hand, enfolding it in his larger one.

She tried to pull her hand away, but he wouldn't allow it. "Please . . . look at me, Venetia."

She obeyed unwillingly and found him searching her face. He seemed reluctant to speak, though.

Finally, Quinn cleared his throat. "First I need to correct a grave misunderstanding. Last night when I claimed not to love you, it was a bald-faced lie. I didn't want Montreux to know how much you meant to me. I couldn't bear the thought of him harming you. If you had died . . ."

Briefly Quinn shut his eyes before once more focusing on her intently. "I was scared witless, Venetia, but there was a moment when I could only think of the irony. I had finally found love just when I might lose you."

Her lungs gave a hard squeeze. When she stared at Quinn speechlessly, his mouth curled in a humorless smile.

"Believe me, loving you was never my intent. I was determined to master my own fate and never again fall in love as I did in my callow youth. But I couldn't help myself. From the beginning, I saw the great lengths you were willing to go to in order to protect your sister. I wanted that kind of devotion for myself, Venetia. And last night you risked your life to stop Montreux from shooting me." He paused to let his words sink in. "That is exactly the kind of mate I want for my wife, Venetia. A woman of unquenchable spirit and courage."

Venetia felt herself tremble. She closed her eyes, hoping this wasn't a dream, a sheer fantasy.

When she opened them again, Quinn was still watching her earnestly. "I realize that you intend to return to France soon, but I don't want you to go."

Still not trusting what she heard, she looked down at their clasped hands, his long, powerful fingers curling around her smaller ones. His gentle touch made her heart ache with longing, as did his next quiet declaration:

"I know I promised you your independence. And if that is what you truly want, I will honor my word. But I want a real marriage with you, Venetia." He hesitated once more. "If you put your heart in my hands, I swear to cherish it and keep it safe always."

The words bathed her in desperately needed warmth, and when she looked up again, she saw tenderness and love in Quinn's expression, along with an anxiety she never expected to see.

His voice dropped to a pleading murmur. "Stay with me and be my wife, Venetia. Let me be your husband."

Such simple words, such a powerful impact on her heart.

In response, Venetia uttered a small sob and buried her face in her hands.

Voicing an alarmed oath, Quinn stood and pulled down the covers, then scooped her off the bed and sat down in the chair with her on his lap. Cupping her chin, he angled her head so that he could stare into her eyes. He looked dismayed—until he saw that she was smiling through tears she hadn't realized she was crying.

"Are you all right?"

"Yes . . ." She drew a shaky breath. "You just caught me by surprise."

His gaze lingered on her face with an endearing uncertainty. But when she started to speak, he touched his fingers to her lips. "Please, I need to finish. It's true I wed you for honor's sake. I expected to have a union of convenience, nothing more. I was so certain I didn't need anyone, that I would be happy with a solitary existence if you returned to France. I thought I would be content living apart from you, leading separate lives. But my heart will never be content with anyone but you, my darling Venetia."

Venetia searched his face, hardly daring to acknowledge the joyous racing of her own heart. "I can't believe you truly love me."

"You *should* believe it. I love you, Venetia, utterly and completely. And I will love you forever, until my last breath." His thumb brushed across her wet cheek with unbearable tenderness. "The truth is, I was afraid to love but more afraid not to. It wasn't long after our wedding before I realized that I would be the greatest fool in nature if I let you go."

Venetia closed her eyes, savoring this incredible moment. The pain, the sick feeling deep inside her, the fear, all had fled.

But Quinn's fear still seemed to linger. "I collect," he said hoarsely, "that it all comes down to one crucial question. Could you ever love me in return?"

She gave a watery chuckle. "Yes, I could love you, Quinn. I do love you. More than you could ever imagine."

The relief in his expression was priceless. "Thank God."

His forehead pressed against hers. Then shifting, he sank his face into the curve of her neck and wrapped his arms around her in a fervent embrace.

For a long moment they remained that way, with Venetia absorbing his warmth, the steady, soothing beat of his heart. His hold was so incredibly tender. She felt infinitely precious, cradled against him. His hands smoothed over her back, her arms, in an absent, hypnotic caress.

Shortly, however, the heat seeping into her transformed into something more than comfort. She became keenly aware of the muscular hardness of his thighs beneath her, his scent, his increasing pulse rate.

Quinn must have felt her growing tension, for he muttered another quiet oath in her ear. "I want very badly to make love to you. I want to give you the wedding night you never had. But that will have to wait until you are well enough."

Venetia pulled back so that she could see his face. The same longing that gripped her was reflected in his eyes. "I am well enough now," she whispered.

Heat suddenly shimmered between them. And yet he seemed cautious, careful. "I don't want to hurt you ever again."

"You won't. I promise." Caught in the net of his blue gaze, Venetia held her breath.

Drawing her face closer, Quinn kissed her with such amazing gentleness that she wanted to weep. His lips were heartbreakingly soft, as though she were a fragile thing he feared to shatter. When he finished, she took his hand and brought it to her breast.

"Quinn, make love to me now. . . . *Please*."

"Yes."

Between them desire smoldered, flared, in a shock wave of heat. Even so, he drew out his compliance. Rising slowly, he set Venetia on her feet and divested her of her nightshift, not letting her participate. Evidently he intended to provide her solace.

She stood quietly, looking up at him as he shed his own clothes. Candlelight highlighted his hair with gold and illuminated the perfection of his nude, muscular body.

For a moment, Quinn scrutinized her in return, visibly searching for signs of bruising and physical abuse. When finally he stepped closer, a sigh of need whispered from her. She yearned for the physical contact as he reached for her. His hands moved in a light murmur over her skin . . . yet they were strangely dispassionate. He meant only to comfort her, she realized. To remain detached, as if she were an invalid.

But she needed more.

What she needed was his passion. She needed the vital intensity of his lovemaking, the primal expression of life to chase away the threat of death.

"Quinn, make love to me," she repeated, half demand, half plea.

"Hush, angel. Let me take care of you."

His strong fingers cupping her pale breasts, he lowered his face to hers. His kiss was a languid, intimate knowing of her mouth, one that stole her breath away.

Her eyes misted with fresh tears at the healing quality of his kiss, but she still wanted more.

"Please . . . I need you."

He drew her to the bed then and lay down with her, facing her. She could feel his gaze like a tangible caress, drifting over her.

At last he pulled her into his arms and enfolded her in his powerful embrace. Venetia clung to him, absorbing the hard, warm strength of him. She could feel the feather touch of his lips on her hair, her cheek, her throat, searing her, kindling the fires of desire inside her.

How could he be so gentle yet unleash such violent emotions in her? How could he remain so unmoved when she was burning?

Yet he was not as composed as he seemed. When he drew back, she recognized his effort at control in the lines of his handsome face. She wanted him to lose that control, but vexingly, he took his time.

His hand moved down between her legs, seeking and caressing. When he found the wetness there, his fingers stroked her, his touch part solace, part sensual, all magic. But she didn't need arousing. She was already hot and aching for him. His voice was soothing, but she didn't need him to whisper gentle, calming words. She needed *him*. Desperately.

"*Now* Quinn . . . please . . ."

He required no further encouragement. With her plea, he shed his stern control entirely.

His face rigid with desire, he eased between her thighs and buried his hands in her hair. She saw his eyes, fierce with tenderness and intent as slowly he thrust until he was seated deep inside her. The raw need in his eyes was unmistakable. His gaze burning with blue fire, he lowered his head while beginning to move inside her.

The gentle rhythmic movement of his hips was different from his urgent kisses, though. He covered her face and mouth in fiercely loving caresses while whispering beautiful, golden words of love. Her heart soaring, Venetia held on tightly, her fingers feverishly digging into his buttocks, urging him on.

Ultimately he increased his rhythm, sinking into her swiftly, heavy and hard and deep, then withdrawing, only to plunge again. With a moan of pleasure, she responded with equal fervor, trying to melt into him as he surged with her.

Their climax came in moments. She arched in ecstasy, and as the searing sweetness burst upon her senses in a rush of bright light, she felt his body explode inside her, felt his arms tighten fervently around her before he finally collapsed upon her, his chest heaving.

His passion was soul-shattering, as were the pulses of life flowing between them.

After another few heartbeats, he shifted his weight to avoid crushing her and eased to one side with a hoarse sigh.

"You drive me wild, Venetia," he whispered.

She gave a faint smile of contentment. It seemed that Quinn was as shattered as she by what had happened.

In response to her silence, his mouth found hers again. The ripples of passion faded eventually, but the soft mating of their breath continued as his lips lingered on hers.

They lay there kissing and touching for a long time,

the moment indescribably tender and pleasure-hazed. Finally Quinn left off and drew back a space, but only far enough to hold her in a protective grasp.

Venetia opened her eyes to find him watching her earnestly, his face concerned.

"I tell you I am fine," she murmured, longing to reassure him.

His face relaxed a measure, and she was gratified to think that *she* was consoling *him*. Yet she needed reassuring as well.

"I need to hear you say it again, Quinn . . . how you feel about me."

"I love you dearly, sweet Venetia."

Searching his beloved face, she drank him in. He was so beautiful with his tawny hair glazed by candlelight, his gaze so blue and intent. He was so vital, so dear to her.

"I promise we will discuss our future in the morning," Quinn said quietly. "Tomorrow I intend to convince you to believe my vow of fidelity. But for now you should sleep."

"I don't want to sleep," Venetia replied. "I want to stay awake to be certain I am not dreaming."

Perhaps he understood her direst need, for his serious expression turned ardent and tender. "I wouldn't have let you go, you know. If you had left me, I would have followed you to France and somehow persuaded you to love me. Even if it took the rest of my life."

She had no doubt he would have succeeded, either. If she weren't already madly in love with him, he would have worn down her resistance with his relentless charm.

A hint of that provocative charm entered his eyes

now when he added, "I am afraid you are stuck with me, sweeting. It's not merely legend that Wildes marry for life. It is an undisputed fact."

"Is it, now?"

Amusement and affection glimmered in the blue depths of his eyes. "Yes, indeed. As Kate says, you and I were meant to be together."

Venetia answered in kind. "I suppose we could rub along quite tolerably."

"Our union will be vastly better than *tolerable* if I have any say in the matter. I intend to spend the rest of my days striving to make you happy and earning your trust."

Venetia reached up to touch Quinn's mouth with her fingertips. She already was blissfully happy. As for fidelity, she believed him when he vowed he would be faithful.

Trust was a fragile thing; she had learned that painful lesson with her first betrothed. It was sometimes frightening to trust another person with not only your life but your heart.

But this time, with this man . . . with Quinn . . . she was more than willing to make the leap of faith.

"You already have my trust, Quinn," she declared as she raised her lips to his. "But I wouldn't mind a great deal more convincing."

With a soft, loving laugh, he took her mouth and proceeded to fulfill her wishes.

Chapter Twenty-two

Quinn lay there holding a sleeping Venetia in the late morning light, acutely conscious of the moment. He'd made love to many other lovers, but he'd never before felt such a naked awareness of intimacy.

This time was somehow different. This was his wife. The woman he had chosen to be his life's mate.

His hands drifted lazily over her body as he marveled at the profound change in his perspective. Last night he'd been shaken by their joining and the shattering burst of pleasure it had brought him. Yet his feelings went far beyond affection or passion.

This was love.

He had found his match, as if they were incomplete halves now made whole.

Just then Venetia stirred in his arms. Looking down, Quinn found her gazing at him uncertainly.

"I haven't changed my mind," he said at once. "I still love and adore you."

The relief on her beautiful features was unmistakable.

She smiled shyly and raised her lips to his, and they kissed slowly and deeply, cementing the vows they had made to each other.

When finally he broke off, Venetia glanced around her bedchamber. "What time is it?"

"Nearly noon, I suspect."

She stifled a yawn. "I suppose we should rise and dress. Your family is likely waiting downstairs for us to appear."

"My family will forgive us. After your ordeal, you need to rest."

"I am not an invalid, Quinn."

"No, but I require you to remain here with me. I am in great need of succoring—a condition that may last all day and into the night."

Her mouth curved in amusement. "It would be scandalous, staying abed all day."

"Perhaps, but that is what makes you my perfect match. You are willing to be scandalous with me. Isn't that so?"

She laughed softly. "Aren't you hungry?"

"Yes, but not for food—" He caught himself as he remembered the trauma she had endured. "You need sustenance, though, to regain your strength. I will ring for breakfast."

When he started to extricate himself from their embrace, she stayed him with a hand on his bare chest. "Could we wait a moment? This is too enjoyable."

"Yes, of course. Whatever you wish."

Venetia sighed contentedly and laid her head on his shoulder.

Quinn tightened his arm about her, feeling a similar contentment—as well as awe at the drastic nature of his fall. He had guarded his emotions closely for many years, until Venetia had barreled her way into his life. Even when he'd begun succumbing, he'd ignored the danger signs, telling himself he wouldn't burn when the flames touched him.

And her feelings had been even more guarded than his. In the beginning he'd had some thought of healing her wounded heart. Yet he'd freed his own heart in the process. Now he wondered how he ever thought he could live without her.

She gave him joy and delight and pleasure. He wanted to make her happy, to protect her and cherish her always. . . .

If barely a month ago he'd been told he would treasure all these maudlin sentiments, he would have scoffed outright.

Quinn pressed a light kiss against her hair before musing out loud, "I think I loved you from the moment you threatened to shoot me to prevent my courting your sister. I can't imagine my life without you now."

Venetia's muffled spurt of laughter was followed by a note of skepticism in her voice when she asked, "Truly?"

"Yes, truly. Who will argue with me and set me straight when I need it?"

"You have a point."

Another few heartbeats passed before he continued his reflections. "You are more than enough woman for me, Venetia. You are intriguing and challenging and strong and inspiring. You make me want to be a better man. Why would I ever want anyone else?"

He was teasing her lovingly, yet he wanted to make

certain she understood his gravity. Quinn put a finger under her chin and tilted her face up so that he could see her eyes when he repeated his vow of fidelity.

"I swear on my life to be faithful and never betray you, Venetia. Will you believe me?"

"Yes," she answered softly. "I believe you."

Quinn rewarded her reply with another long kiss before he let her rest again. That she'd chosen to trust him filled him with a fierce sense of gratitude.

It was another quarter hour before they stirred again. He wanted to see that she was fed, and she wanted to thank his family for all they had done for her—as did Quinn.

"If I know them, they will be eager for a family conference. Our gatherings became a tradition when our bachelor uncle, Cornelius, tried to raise five unruly orphans."

Still feeling a bit wan, Venetia accepted his help in donning a brocade dressing gown and didn't object when Quinn insisted on giving his arm for support as he escorted her downstairs. On the way there, he directed a footman to have Mrs. Pelfrey deliver breakfast to the drawing room, and in an hour have a warm bath filled for her ladyship in his bedchamber.

When Venetia entered the drawing room with Quinn, Skye was the first to see her. Rising quickly, she crossed to the door and took both of Venetia's hands in a warm greeting. "How are you feeling?"

Venetia returned her smile. "As if I was trampled by a horse."

Skye dimpled. "Don't tell Maura or Hawk that. They both would come to the horse's defense. Come, you must meet Maura and Ash. Their adorable baby is sleeping upstairs in the nursery. By the way, you just missed your parents and sister. They called to make certain that you were all right. And Hawk has brought us up-to-date about that villain Montreux. I cannot believe he got away with multiple murders all these years."

Anger clouded Skye's brow, but she shrugged it off as she shepherded Venetia into the room to join the company. Venetia was indeed glad at last to meet the eldest Wilde cousin and his lovely wife, Maura. Lord Jack and Sophie and Katharine were present also, as was Lord Hawkhurst.

When she was settled comfortably on the sofa, with Quinn sitting beside her, Venetia effusively thanked everyone, especially Hawk, for coming to her rescue last evening.

When he brushed off her gratitude, Skye explained her husband's modesty. "Hawk is accustomed to such heroics. He once rescued our aunt Isabella from a Berber sheik in the Kingdom of Algiers."

An amused Lord Jack chimed in. "The rest of us are not trained in espionage or versed in dangerous enterprises, but we always look after our own."

"Yes," Sophie added fondly. "You are a Wilde now, Venetia."

"Which means," Quinn said with a pointed look at his cousin Kate, "that interference in one another's lives is a given, whether you like it or not. But at least you will never find yourself alone."

The reminder heartened Venetia. "I should like that a great deal."

"I almost regret missing the excitement last evening," Ash jested.

Maura sent him an arch glance before turning to Venetia. "I only regret that we didn't arrive in time to be of help to you."

"Undoubtedly," Katharine interjected, "there will be other occasions in the future. You should prepare yourself to be swept up in all manner of scandals and adventures, Venetia. Perhaps when we are old and gray we can look back on this ordeal as an adventure. Meanwhile, you should have something to eat. Ah, here is Mrs. Pelfrey now."

The housekeeper directed two footmen to deposit laden trays on a side table, then appeared to delight in fussing over her latest patient, Lady Traherne.

Venetia was soon fortified with hot tea and toast, and Quinn a more substantial breakfast. While they ate, she listened as Maura told an amusing tale about their infant son and found herself reveling in the warmth and laughter and familial feelings that pervaded the drawing room. Before this, such a loving family scene would have engendered an unbearable ache of loneliness. Now she was part of it.

Relishing the thought, Venetia let the discussion wash over her while she observed her new family. They were all charismatic, intriguing characters with strong, lively personalities, and she could imagine the pleasure of sculpting each one of them.

The conversation eventually turned to retrieving the remainder of the de Chagny jewels from Montreux and the need to establish ownership. Venetia only half paid attention until someone mentioned that the jewels were not entailed and that Skye was Angelique's heir.

"But Venetia is Quinn's wife now," Skye said hesitantly.

In the pause that followed, Venetia realized that Skye was looking at her questioningly, as if waiting for her to comment.

"You should have your mother's jewels, Skye," Venetia said at once.

"Are you certain?"

"Of course. They rightfully belong to you. You would have inherited them had I not married your brother."

"I confess I would very much like to have them since they were my mother's."

It was only fitting, Venetia thought. She most certainly did not want the pendant that currently belonged to Quinn's former mistress. Admittedly she was still profoundly jealous of the dashing Lady X. Venetia would have liked to be more gracious now that she could claim Quinn as her true husband, her love, but it would probably take a while before she could fully overcome her long-held apprehensions.

When she caught Quinn's eye, she realized he had guessed what she was thinking, for he reached over to take her hand and interlaced his fingers with hers.

Evidently he also approved of her generosity to his sister, for he leaned closer to murmur in her ear, "I will make it up to you. I will buy you a fortune in jewels if you like."

"I don't need jewels to be happy," Venetia whispered back.

His eyes glimmered. "I know. That is one of the many things I love about you."

While he was reassuring her, the subject changed to

the shipwreck that had taken the lives of their parents and the crew.

There was no new information from Macky as to the site of the tragedy, nor was there a legal need to prove sabotage, but if the wreck was ever found, Kate thought they should mount a salvage effort, since she wanted a proper burial for her parents. At the very least, she wanted to journey to France to find her mother's pauper's grave and provide her a decent headstone.

Ash offered to fund the search for the ship's remains, but with his son so young, he preferred to remain at home until the wreck was actually found. Jack, who had been born in Paris and spoke fluent French, was the logical choice to lead an expedition to the southern coast of France, but Sophie was expecting their first child, and he disliked the risk of her sailing abroad.

In Skye's opinion, Hawk had spent too many years living in exile on a Mediterranean island, and she wanted him to come to know his newly reconstructed English home. And Quinn thought Hawk had done more than enough already.

Kate ventured to suggest that Uncle Cornelius might wish to be involved in a salvage endeavor, since Steven Wilde had been his older brother and Lionel Wilde his distant cousin.

As for Quinn's preferences, his steamship was in the final stages of construction, but he promised that after the launch this summer, he would be pleased to help. "For now I mean to take Venetia to Tallis Court to recuperate," Quinn concluded.

Eager to see her new home, Venetia liked that idea

also. But then she recalled her sister. "What about Ophelia?"

"What about her?"

"Until she settles on a suitor, I ought to remain in London, if only to prevent my mother from dictating her life."

Quinn shook his head. "With Kate and Skye to help her marriage prospects, Ophelia can manage on her own. You've done more than enough for her, including risking your life."

"Perhaps so." Just then Venetia also remembered Cleo. "I must tell Cleo she will have to find another companion when she returns to France."

"I predict she will understand."

Venetia arched an eyebrow. "I am not so certain. She is not your most ardent fan . . . although I know she will be happy for me once I persuade her that we have made a love match."

"That should not be difficult. I am really quite humiliatingly in love." A smile lurked about his mouth as he brought Venetia's fingers to his lips. "I had every intention of controlling my own fate, but destiny intervened in my plans."

"And so did I," Kate injected with a self-satisfied smile. "I am glad you finally overcame your cynicism, cousin."

Quinn amiably acknowledged her aid. "Although I am loath to admit it, I am supremely grateful for your persistence, Kate. If not for you, I would have missed the love of my life."

"Oh?" she said archly. "Do tell. I was right, wasn't I?"

"Yes, you were right." Venetia saw the self-mockery in Quinn's beautiful blue eyes, the suppressed laughter, yet he seemed entirely serious when he declared, "The truth is, love can readily be denied, until you meet one person who changes your life forever."

Venetia gazed back at him adoringly, happiness welling inside her. With every word he bound himself more firmly in her heart.

Quinn turned back to his cousin. "But you should not be so smug, sweet Kate. Your turn is next. You are the only unattached Wilde left."

When she wrinkled her nose, Ash threw a fond glance at his sister. "It is easy to advocate for a love match when someone else is your victim."

Quinn chuckled, and Jack joined the teasing against her. "Yes, it is your turn to be tortured, my scheming Kate."

Skye took Kate's side, however. "Your future soulmate is somewhere out there waiting for you."

Amazingly, Kate looked uncertain, perhaps even concerned. "I once thought so, but now I'm not sure I believe that any longer."

Sophie also expressed her support. "If your legendary lovers theory is correct, Kate, your story will be Pygmalion."

"I sincerely hope you are wrong." A frown turned down her mouth. "Yesterday I received a letter from Aunt Bella with a request on behalf of a friend who recently inherited a barony. She wants my help in turning him into a proper English lord."

"Who is it?" Skye asked curiously.

"Mr. Brandon Deverill . . . The American cousin of Trey Deverill, one of Hawk's former colleagues, I believe."

Hawk nodded. "I know both Deverills well. I served

with them in the British Foreign Office. We were fortunate to have Brandon's contributions for several years, despite his American citizenship."

"Is Brandon Deverill such a heathen, then?" Skye wondered.

Kate winced and continued her lament. "I suppose he is a gentleman—of sorts. Appallingly, he turned to privateering and fought against England when hostilities broke out between our countries some years ago. But Aunt Bella asked me to put my matchmaking talents to good use and find a bride for him. Believe me, I am not happy about the prospect. But for our aunt, I would do anything."

Venetia wondered if Mr. Deverill was the same American who had humiliated Kate years before by rejecting her. If so, there was bound to be conflict between them, which would not auger well for a legendary romance.

Then Kate shrugged off her unease and smiled at Venetia. "At least *your* story was a grand success. You have tamed your rake."

"It would be nice to think so."

Maura spoke then. "Take it from me, a reformed rake makes the most devoted of mates."

Ash laughed, and Venetia looked up at Quinn thoughtfully. "Perhaps I was wrong. You are not so much a rake after all."

The glint in his eyes was full of affection. "Thank the saints. I have endeavored to convince you of that for weeks now, and you are finally coming to agree."

When his arm slipped around her, Venetia laid her head on his shoulder. She felt cloaked in warmth and safety. She felt cherished. She felt raw with love for him—and gratitude as well. Quinn filled the aching emptiness that had plagued her for so long.

Her fears had dissipated also, yet she would not leave her future to mercurial fate. She would love Quinn so much he would never give a single thought to another woman.

After a while longer, he tugged on her hand. "Come, darling. I will escort you upstairs. You need proper rest."

Once they said their farewells, Quinn ushered her from the drawing room and upstairs to his bedchamber, where a copper tub filled with steaming water stood in one corner.

As soon as he shut the door behind them, Quinn turned and gathered her close. "I have wanted to hold you like this for hours."

She laughed softly. "It has not been that long."

"It feels like an eternity." His arms wrapped around her in warmth as he gazed down at her. "I shall take great pleasure in helping you bathe and soothing your injuries. I plan to kiss every delectable inch of your naked body. And afterward, I intend to take you back to bed."

A smile curved her mouth. "I thought you said I needed proper rest. If we retire to bed, we are unlikely to get any rest."

"Which is exactly how it should be. We are newly-weds. Since our marriage vows, we've had little opportunity to enjoy the nuptial bed and need to make up for all the lost time. Besides, you are still in need of reassurance, my love."

"Indeed, I am."

The tender heat in his voice warmed her skin, as

did the fire in his eyes. Venetia felt another powerful rush of love for him, a love that she knew was wholly reciprocated.

When Quinn lowered his head, she opened her mouth to him, her invitation wanton and inflaming. He responded by kissing her with a fierceness that stopped her breath—which, as he'd said, was exactly as it should be.

Read on for a sneak peek
of the next Legendary Lovers book

My Fair Lover

by Nicole Jordan

Chapter One

The last time she'd visited Brandon Deverill in his hotel rooms, she had climbed into his bed naked—a foolhardy scheme that ended in utter disaster.

Wincing at the scalding memory, Lady Katharine Wilde raised her hand to knock on the door to room number 7, then promptly lowered it again as the swarm of butterflies resumed dancing in her stomach.

Gaining access to the second floor of Fenton's Hotel this afternoon was the easiest phase of her clandestine mission. Disguised as a nobleman's liveried male servant, she didn't fear recognition. No, her anxiety stemmed from having to face Deverill again after six long years.

She fervently hoped that history wouldn't repeat itself today. Before, when she'd brazenly thrown herself at his head, he had rebuffed her offer, gently but firmly.

"What kind of man would I be if I took your in-

nocence and then sailed away to fight a war, perhaps never to return?"

Her subsequent pleas had not affected Deverill, either. Remembering her abject humiliation that night, Kate bit her lower lip and stepped back from his door. How she had longed to crawl into a hole and die! Maddeningly, her wounded pride still stung all these years later, as did her foolish heart.

Turning, she paced the corridor in an effort to drum up her courage. Unmarried young ladies simply did not visit gentlemen's hotel rooms unaccompanied— although at four-and-twenty, she was hardly *young.* And Brandon Deverill—an American merchant and former privateer whose fleet of ships had battled the British Navy—was barely considered a gentleman, even if he *had* recently inherited the title to an ancient English barony.

Yet she had numerous reasons for risking scandal today: To prove she had recovered from her hurt and show him she was not still nursing a broken heart. To test her fortitude and confirm that she could handle meeting him alone. To deal with her certain embarrassment out of the public eye. And to make her unusual proposition in private.

She'd vowed to have nothing more to do with Deverill, but her aunt by marriage, Lady Isabella Wilde, had asked her help in turning him into a proper English lord. Since Aunt Bella was her dear confidant and the prime motherly figure in her life, Kate felt she could not possibly refuse. Not at least without good reason.

Which would mean confessing the mortifying details of the most lowering experience of her life, when she'd pursued Deverill like the lovesick, starry-eyed, half-witted females she deplored.

Scolding herself for her cravenness, Kate returned to his door and managed to subdue the violent flutters raging in her stomach long enough to rap lightly. Last time Deverill had unequivocally rejected her amorous advances. This time, however, she had something he wanted.

When eventually the door swung open, the first thing that struck her was his bold, dark eyes. They were much as she remembered—deep, penetrating, black-fringed. His arresting eyes had always matched his daring demeanor and actions, she thought in bemusement.

In their dark depths she saw his instant recognition of her, even though she was garbed in her noble family's livery, complete with silvery powdered wig covering her auburn hair.

She had clearly taken him by surprise. Kate herself was startled by the sight of Deverill wearing only breeches. He was bare-chested and bare-footed, while his overly long raven hair was damp and curling. Apparently he had just bathed and was about to shave, for he held a razor in one hand.

A stubble of beard shadowed his strong jaw, a raffish look that only accentuated his appeal, much to her vexation. A ruffian—a pirate, at that—should not look so blasted appealing. He smelled delicious, as well, deuce take him.

Confounded by his unwanted impact on her senses, Kate stood staring back at him speechlessly, much to her dismay.

When his gaze drifted down over her attire, one

eyebrow lifted and she could see amusement spark in his beautiful eyes.

"I should have expected you to act unconventionally," he remarked in that rough-velvet voice that never failed to rake her feminine nerve endings.

She could say the same of him. He didn't seem at all nonplussed to be caught in a state of near undress. But then Brandon Deverill was the most infamous man of her acquaintance, which was saying a great deal, considering that she hailed from the passionate, scandalous Wilde family, who could boast centuries of notorious ancestors.

There were lines on Deverill's face now that made his striking features more mature. But shirtless, with his sun-bronzed, muscular torso exposed, he was even more devastatingly handsome than she recalled. His masculine beauty put classical statues to shame—

Oh, merciful heavens, gain hold of yourself, you moonling.

She was badly mistaken about having conquered her vulnerability, though. She most certainly was *not* over him. Deverill still had the power to make her knees weak. And she was still swamped by the undeniable, unquenchable attraction that had hit her the first moment upon meeting him so long ago.

Kate gave herself a violent mental shake. She would be in deep, deep trouble if she couldn't contain her captivation.

Thankfully Deverill interrupted her muddled ruminations. "How did you find me?" he asked with a note of curiosity.

"At my request, the harbormaster was on the lookout for your ship and alerted me when you docked. I sent a servant to question him about where you were lodging."

"I admire your resourcefulness, if not your prudence. What the devil are you doing here?"

"May I come in?" Kate pressed. "I wish to speak to you, and I would rather not hold our conversation out here in the corridor."

After a moment's hesitation, he stepped back to allow her entrance and closed the door behind her, although he didn't appear elated by her presence. "Could you not have waited until I called on you tomorrow?"

"I felt sure there would be awkwardness between us, and thought it best to deal with it in private."

"Will you be seated?"

Glancing around the small chamber, she saw a table and two chairs, a washstand, and a bed, which reminded her uncomfortably of their last ignominious encounter. Kate smiled amiably to cover her discomfort. "I will stand, thank you. This should not take long."

"Good. It would be best if you weren't seen visiting my bedchamber. Does your brother know of your whereabouts?"

"No, and I don't intend for him to find out."

"Beaufort would have my head if he knew you were in my room."

"You needn't worry. Ash is in the country and is not expected to arrive in London until tomorrow."

Deverill scrutinized her costume. "You aren't concerned that someone might recognize the beautiful Lady Katharine Wilde?"

"No one looks twice at a footman."

"Thus the disguise. You make a fetching lad."

His compliment flustered her, but he followed it with a censorious remark. "Evidently you haven't changed. You make a habit of frequenting gentlemen's hotel rooms."

"Not all gentlemen," she returned archly. "Only yours."

"Should I be flattered?"

She sent him her most charming smile. "Indeed, you should," she quipped before catching herself. She had no business engaging in spirited repartee with Deverill as they'd enjoyed in the past.

Fortunately, he changed the subject by rubbing the stubble on his jaw. "Would you object if I continue shaving while we talk? My cousin Trey should arrive shortly to convey me about town. I have business with my solicitor regarding issues of the inheritance, and then plan to dine with Trey and his wife, Antonia, this evening."

Kate had met Brandon's distant English cousin, Trey Deverill, years ago, although she had not seen him recently and had never met his new wife. "No, I wouldn't object."

Deverill went to the washstand and picked up a cake of soap. "It has been a while since I last saw you," he mused aloud as he began making a lather.

Six years, two months, and nine days. With another mental shake, Kate focused her thoughts on the future, not the past. "Aunt Bella has generally kept me abreast of your situation. I was sorry to hear of your uncle's passing."

Deverill nodded solemnly. "Reportedly Valmere was in a great deal of pain, so perhaps it was a blessing. I plan to travel to Kent this week to pay my respects to his remaining kin and make arrangements to provide for them."

Kate was aware of Deverill's lineage. His late grandfather, a younger son of a British baron, had emigrated to Virginia in America decades ago and married into a prominent merchant family who owned a fleet of sailing ships. This past January the current Baron Valmere—Augustus Deverill—had succumbed to a lingering illness, leaving behind a widowed daughter and two young granddaughters. The title and entailed properties had devolved to Brandon as the closest male relation.

For a moment, silence reigned as he lathered his face with soap. Watching, Kate found herself distracted by the sheer allure of his bare torso. Without volition her gaze skimmed over his wide shoulders and followed his tapered back to his lean waist, then lower to his tight buttocks and powerful thighs encased in buff knit breeches—

She looked away quickly so Deverill wouldn't catch her admiring his lamentably impressive body. "Would you mind donning a dressing gown?"

"Regrettably, I don't have one with me."

"A shirt then?"

He hesitated. "I will when I finish shaving." Deverill glanced over his shoulder at her. "Have you turned missish all of a sudden?"

That tender, amused light that she'd loved so well had returned to fill his eyes. Seeing it, Kate remembered another provoking quality of his: No other man could make her blush as he could. She always felt as if he knew what she was thinking. And sometimes he seemed to be laughing at her—or at himself—inviting her to share a private jest.

It had been that way from the very first. He'd always taken vast liberties with her and never stood on formality. On the contrary, he'd teased her intimately, the way her brothers and cousins did. She could also count on Deverill to be candid, even brutally honest.

She had never minded his casual familiarity before, for it felt amiable, comfortable. Indeed, she had prized his frankness after all the sycophants who had toadied to her all her life as a wealthy, noble heiress.

They had met seven years ago when Deverill was visiting his uncle in Kent, the introduction made by Lady Isabella, who knew him from the days when he worked for the British Foreign Office. It was an unusual occupation for an American—a career that had originated because of his cousin, Trey Deverill, and was cut short when war broke out between their countries.

"I have not been completely sheltered," Kate answered lightly. "I grew up with male relatives, so I've seen partially unclothed men. But you and I are not at all related. Just because I dared call at your room twice does not mean I am unaware of the impropriety."

"You forget I've seen your charms as well," he murmured.

Her face flaming, she ducked her head. "You needn't remind me," she said in a low voice. "I once felt a foolish infatuation for you, but that is long over."

Realizing how faint-hearted she sounded, Kate raised her chin and met his gaze bravely. It was best to confront her embarrassment head-on.

Deverill was regarding her with that penetrating look, as if he knew all her secrets. Defensively, she flashed him her most winsome smile. "Never fear, Mr. Deverill. I am not here to throw myself at you again. I promise I won't accost you or try to sneak into your bed."

He looked as if he might reply, for his mouth curved for a moment, but he only shook his head and commenced shaving.

When he turned his back to her again, she noticed a wicked-looking scar beneath his right shoulder blade, perhaps three inches long, as if a knife or bayonet had speared his flesh. It must have hurt dreadfully, Kate thought, biting her lip in sympathy. She started to ask how he had come by the scar but stopped herself. The condition of his body was far too personal a matter for her to contemplate.

She changed her mind about taking a seat, however. Pointedly ignoring the bed, Kate crossed the small chamber to one of the chairs and sat down so she wouldn't have to gawk at him directly. Deverill was pure physical temptation. More than that, he possessed the type of raw, vital presence that was supremely dangerous to any woman's virtue. *Any woman's but mine,* she amended. *Her* virtue had been perfectly safe in his hands, to her immense regret.

Kate cleared her throat. "Aunt Bella wishes she could be here to greet you, but she recently travelled to Cornwall to attend the lying-in of a friend's daughter and needs to remain there a while longer. Meanwhile, she solicited my aid in her absence. I don't know all the particulars of your correspondence with her, but I understand you intend to fully assume your role as Baron Valmere?"

"Yes."

"I would like to hear from you what your aim is."

He complied as he scraped off his whiskers. "You know that when the conflict escalated, my father requested I come home? When he died a year later, I assumed the reins of our shipping company. I've spent the past several years rebuilding, since commerce suffered significantly during your British blockades of our harbors, and a portion of our fleet was depleted. Now we are finally on solid enough footing that I can turn the enterprise over to my younger brother and fulfill my duties here."

Kate eyed him inquiringly. "You actually mean to settle here in England?"

"In all likelihood, although my mother is not happy about it," Deverill said dryly.

"I find it surprising that you would even consider it, given where your loyalties lie."

"My loyalties?"

"To America. It is no secret that you were devotedly engaged in privateering."

When his gaze sharpened at her disapproving tone, Kate pressed her lips together. There was no point in arguing the past with Deverill. The fact remained: He was the bold American seafarer who had stolen her heart and left her pining, which was his greatest offense.

She'd thought he could be her perfect mate, but he'd spurned her in order to go fight a war against her countrymen and thus had become her enemy. Now, not only was he back in England but she had promised to consider helping him.

"What do you wish of me?" she finally said.

"To start, I need an introduction to society. The enchanting Lady Katharine is the toast of the polite world. Who better than you to help pave my way? From what I hear, you rule the ton with your charm and wit."

Kate laughed. "Hardly. But with Ash being a marquess and my cousin Quinn an earl, I do have noble family connections that might benefit you." Her expression sobered. "Aunt Bella also mentioned that you are looking to wed."

Deverill nodded. "I am three-and-thirty. It's time I settled down and took a wife."

Hearing him confirm what she already knew—that he wanted to marry—affected her oddly. But she had vowed to repress any rebellious pangs of jealousy and turn his need to her advantage. "Are you interested in making a marriage of convenience? Or something deeper?"

He cast her a swift glance, although his expression was inscrutable. "Nothing deeper. Isabella claims that you can find me a suitable bride. She says you are a matchmaker at heart, and that your past endeavors have been highly successful."

"I have developed something of an expertise at matchmaking, true," Kate admitted. "Not to boast, but I aided most of my family in finding their ideal mates. I am willing to advise you as a favor to Aunt Bella, but I would like to make a bargain with you in exchange."

"What sort of bargain?"

She took a deep breath. "If I find you a bride, you must escort me to France at the end of the Season."

Deverill rinsed his face with water from the wash-basin and began drying it with a towel. "Why do you wish to go to France?"

"I believe you know how my parents were killed?"

"They perished at sea when their ship sank in a storm."

"So we thought." Kate frowned. "It is rather a long story, but to be brief. . . . You may remember that my Aunt Angelique was French—the daughter of the Duc and Duchesse de Chagny, who were guillotined during the Revolution."

"Your cousins Quinn and Skye's mother?"

"Yes. Angelique wed my uncle, Lionel Wilde, Earl of Traherne. Their branch of the Wilde family is some-what distant from ours . . . At any event, the priceless de Chagny jewels were hidden while Britain was at war with Napoleon's armies. Then during the Peace of Amiens, my parents travelled with Angelique and Lionel to southern France to recover the treasure, and on their return, their ship sank just off the coast. For years we believed everyone on board perished, but recently we learned that their ship was actually sabo-taged. Not only that, but my mother made it to shore and survived a short time before succumbing to her injuries."

Falling silent, Kate stared down at her hands as she recalled the shock and pain of discovering the truth about the shipwreck. She'd been twelve when she lost her mother and father to the tragedy, and with the new revelations, she had relived her grief all over again.

Moreover, imagining the suffering her mother had endured, picturing her father's watery grave beneath the sea, had only added to the persistent nightmares she'd had since childhood.

Kate twisted her fingers together as her voice dropped to a murmur. "Mama had a pauper's burial, and Papa and my aunt and uncle had no burial at all. I would like to visit Mama's resting place to put a headstone on her grave, and search for the shipwreck while I am there." She gave a faint, apologetic smile. "I confess, it has become an obsession of mine. Perhaps I am foolish, but I want them to have a decent burial."

"I would not call you foolish."

She lifted her gaze to find Deverill watching her, a gentle look in his eyes, as if he understood her need. She was grateful that he wasn't teasing her about an uncertain—perhaps perilous—undertaking that was so close to her heart.

"Anyway," she went on, "the saboteur was brought to justice and most of the treasure recovered, although some of the jewels sank with the Zephyr."

"And you wish to salvage the rest?"

Kate hesitated. "I doubt that is possible. It has been twelve years. But I hope at least to locate the ship's remains. We can guess at the general site based on reports from that night and where pieces of wreckage washed ashore. The Zephyr was rocked by an explosion and caught fire. Although it attempted to limp back to port, it only came close to shore. It may have sunk in shallow water, though. The problem is, there are pirates inhabiting the nearest villages along the coast."

"You seem to know a great deal about the circumstances. How did you obtain your information?"

"I believe you know Beau Macklin? He was a colleague of yours in the Foreign Office, along with Skye's new husband, the Earl of Hawkhurst."

"I know Macky."

"Well, some months ago, he went to France to investigate for my family."

"So why do you need my escort? Why can't you call on Macky?"

"He has done enough already. But mainly, I need an experienced sailor. Someone I can trust."

Deverill's mouth curved. "And you trust me?"

She suspected he was trying to lighten the moment by provoking her, so she answered in the same vein. "Amazingly enough, yes. You know more about the sea than anyone of my acquaintance. In fact, you own an entire fleet of ships, and now you have your own right here in London."

"I had planned for my ship to return to America in a week or two."

Kate felt her heart sink. "Oh. Well, perhaps I could make it worth your while. I can afford to pay a great deal."

"You have your own extensive fortune, I know."

She ignored his amused drawl. "I could hire a ship and captain, perhaps, but I would rather not depend on strangers in this endeavor. You see . . . I am not very fond of sailing."

A vast understatement, Kate reflected. In fact she had a base fear of ships, considering how her parents had perished. "I can swim quite well," she explained.

"You will recall the lake at Beauvoir where I grew up? But I have a morbid fear of drowning at sea."

"And you need someone to cosset your sensibilities."

Certain now that he was ragging her, Kate smiled. "Alas, yes. I concede that I am craven. But there are other reasons you would be a better choice. Even if I could employ men to search for the wreck, I might have to deal with the pirates. I am English. After decades of war, the French are not exactly our bosom friends. I suspect pirates are much fonder of you Americans, since many of them aided you during the war."

Deverill frowned as he pulled on a linen shirt and began tucking the hem into his breeches. A pity to cover all that bare flesh, Kate thought before scolding herself and concentrating on what he was saying.

". . . it could be dangerous."

"Perhaps, but pirates are unlikely to threaten *you*."

He cast her a wry glance. "I am not concerned about my own skin, but yours. A young lady travelling along the coast needs protection."

"Which is why I am asking you."

"What about your family? Will they be accompanying you?"

"Although they would all very much like a resolution, they are not as adamant as I am. And they are all busy starting their own families."

Kate watched as Deverill wrapped a length of cambric around his neck and began tying a cravat in a plain knot. The white fabric contrasted appealingly with his tanned skin. Indeed, clean-shaven, he was even more attractive—*Stop that, you ninny.*

She drew a steadying breath. "So you see, I want to lay my loved ones to rest. That is my one condition. I will help you find a bride if you will help me by taking me to France afterward."

Deverill hesitated while he donned a coat of serviceable brown kerseymere. "Very well. I agree."

Her eyebrow rose skeptically. "You do?"

"Why do you seem so surprised?"

"I thought it would require more effort to convince you."

"But you are Princess Katharine. You have always been able to wrap men around your finger and persuade them to do your bidding."

She gave him an arch look. "Some men, perhaps, but not *you*. And you oughtn't call me princess since I am not of royal blood. You clearly have a great deal to learn about British customs, along with any number of other matters." She paused as the urgency occurred to her. "We have very little time—merely a month till the end of the Season. We should begin working on a plan at once."

Fetching his stockings and boots, Deverill crossed the room and sat down in the adjacent chair to put them on.

Kate disliked his proximity but forced herself to remain seated as she studied his attire. His coat fit his muscular physique well enough, but the style screamed "provincial."

"Our first order of business," she said, "should be to find you a good tailor. You don't want to look like a backwoods colonial, Mr. Deverill—Lord Valmere, I mean. I suppose I should address you by your new title."

"Pray don't. I prefer you call me Brandon as you once did."

"You must grow accustomed to it, my lord."

He grimaced. "I will have a difficult time."

"It will become easier with practice. I, however, will have my work cut out for me if I hope to turn a brash American merchant into an acceptable English nobleman."

An amused gleam reentered his eyes. "I am part English. My paternal bloodline should count in my favor."

"But you are a scandalous privateer," she said sweetly.

"Says the lady shockingly dressed as a lad. You've never objected much to scandal before, if I recall. None of your family has. With you advising me, I should fit into the ton well."

His retort was reminiscent of the sparring they'd done when they were both younger, but as pleasant as it was, Kate knew she would be unwise to encourage him. "I have had to curtail my scandalous inclinations of late, and I trust you will do the same if you wish to attract a genteel bride. We should begin as soon as possible. Are you free tomorrow morning?"

"As far as I know. I won't be leaving for Kent for another day or two to see my Valmere relatives."

"Could you call at my house at eleven tomorrow?"

"Why so late?"

"Usually I ride in the park in the mornings."

"I could accompany you. I haven't stretched my legs on a horse since leaving Virginia several weeks ago."

Consorting with Deverill in their old haunts would

definitely be unwise, Kate realized. At least until she had more control of her feelings. She would do better to face him on her own grounds with her companion present to preclude any chance of intimacy. "No, you cannot be seen in public looking like that. And it will be more appropriate if we have a proper chaperone."

Her comment made *his* brow rise. "You can't be serious."

"Indeed I am. When my brother married last year, I hired a companion . . . a middle-aged widow . . . although she will be marrying soon so I must seek another. I recently found an ideal match for her also, by the way."

"Do you truly need a chaperone at your advanced age?"

Deverill was roasting her again, but his teasing stung a bit, since *he* was chiefly the reason she was still unattached, drat him.

She forced herself to answer lightly. "Sadly, it is one of the frustrations of being a single lady living alone in London. I am old enough to wear caps, but Ash and his new wife, Maura, prefer the country, especially since they recently had a son. If I hoped to remain here to enjoy the Season, I was required to bow to propriety. I will ask Mrs. Cuthbert to join us tomorrow when you call."

Deverill studied her thoughtfully. "If you are such an expert at matchmaking, why have you never made a match for yourself?"

Because no one lived up to my memories of you. "I never found the right match. I have no intention of marrying without true love."

His dark gaze moved over her with more intensity. "By all reports you've rejected countless suitors. And I know for a fact you've always had a bevy of swains at your beck and call."

It was true. As a wealthy, noble heiress, she'd been sought by numerous men, from awkward lads to hardened rakes. Her appearance, too, tended to attract male attention. With her dark red hair, she stood out among the fair young ladies making their debuts.

At eighteen, however, she had been brought up short by Deverill. For the first time in her life, she'd felt vulnerable to a man and uncertain of her powers. She had learned a valuable lesson in humility then. As a result she'd resolved to be kinder to her lovelorn suitors and let them down gently, settling into an amiable friendship with most.

But this conversation was growing far too personal for her comfort. Striving for casualness, Kate rose to her feet. "If your cousin Trey is arriving shortly, I had best go. Tomorrow morning we can discuss our plan and review exactly what sort of bride you are seeking. Meanwhile, I will begin thinking of possible candidates. I have enlisted Ash's aid as well—to advise you on government and legal matters and the like. In truth, that is primarily why he is coming to town tomorrow."

Deverill's eyes narrowed, but she could see amusement there. "You were certain of my agreement, weren't you? But then you usually manage to get your way."

She smiled ruefully. "I could never count on getting my way where you are concerned." When Deverill stood as well, she gazed up at him. "I trust you won't mention my visit here to your cousin Trey?"

"Your secret is safe with me."

"It is your secret as well. I could be ruined, but if you are complicit in my downfall, your plans to take a genteel bride would surely suffer."

His teeth flashed white in his tanned face. "I seem to recall you instigated both trysts."

"This time was not a tryst . . . and neither was the last time, actually—or at least, not entirely. True, I was enamored of you. I have always been overly romantic. It is my worst failing—or among my worst. But my main purpose that night was not to seduce you. I had convinced myself that I could persuade you to stay in England."

"I explained to you at the ball why I could not."

"So you did." Kate managed a careless laugh. "Forgive me, but I had some thought of trying to save your life."

"My worthless hide, you mean?"

She dimpled. "I did not say that. I did not even think it."

"I imagine you were angry with me."

She had been furious and heartbroken and afraid for him. Deverill had hurt her, although it was not wholly his fault. Apparently he had never harbored the same feelings for her that she had felt for him.

"I have forgotten all about that unfortunate incident," she lied. "A true gentleman would endeavor to do the same."

His smile was wry. "That is one event I could *never* forget."

"Well, *I* distinctly recall my mortification."

The laughter left his eyes. "I admit, I was greatly to blame. I led you on by kissing you. But refusing you was my only honorable course."

She lowered her gaze to a button on Deverill's coat. "So you said at the time."

"My duty was to my country. I had to leave, and I didn't know if or when I would ever return."

"If you would be killed in battle, you mean."

"Yes. If I had taken you, I would have been obliged to stay."

That had been her goal, persuading him to stay instead of sailing off to fight a war against her own countrymen.

In her defense, she had thought she stood a chance. The night before, at a ball, Deverill had given her a stunning farewell kiss, meant as goodbye. That thrilling, stolen embrace had shaken her down to her satin slippers and set her world askew. Worse, it had started her dreaming.

She'd wanted to tell him how she felt as well as to beg him not to leave England. So she went to his hotel room and waited for him to return. Her scheme to seduce him was not premeditated, however. The longer she waited, the greater the temptation to use her budding feminine wiles, which had served her well in the past. Impulsively she'd undressed and climbed into his bed . . .

Memory descended in vivid detail: The flaming embarrassment flooding her body, the hurt stabbing her heart at his unceremonious rejection. She had never behaved so wantonly—and ardently hoped never to do so again.

Raising her gaze to his once more, Kate smiled

brightly. "You will be pleased to know I have conquered my obsession with you. I will not make a fool of myself a second time."

When he didn't answer, she searched his face. "Surely you are relieved, my lord. You won't have to send me packing as you did the last time. You needn't fear my unwanted attentions."

"A pity," he murmured.

His comment confused her. "What did you say?"

"Nothing of consequence." Oddly, his gaze softened. "If it is any consolation, I was extremely flattered by your offer. I was wildly attracted to you. I simply couldn't act on my desire."

His casual admission drew her rapt attention. "You desired me?"

His faint chuckle was self-deprecating. "Of course I desired you, along with countless other hapless males."

His confession was a sop to her pride perhaps, but it was gratifying to think her own wild attraction then had not been one-sided. As foolish as it was, beneath her surface confidence, doubt had been eating away at her all these years since.

Kate gave a light shrug of her shoulders. "It doesn't matter now. It happened a long time ago. I was a mere girl then. Girls are inclined to do idiotic things."

"And now you are a beautiful woman."

"Your flattery is unnecessary."

"It is not mere flattery." To her surprise, Deverill reached up to finger a stray tendril that had escaped her wig and brushed it back from her face. "I am glad you have not taken to wearing caps. It would be a shame to cover your lovely hair."

That brief gesture sparked a fiery awareness in Kate and caused her to take an involuntary step backward. If he was attempting to keep her off-balance, he was succeeding. And strangely, his scrutiny only grew more intense.

"What if I wanted to claim another kiss?" he murmured.

His unexpected response made her inhale sharply. "That would be entirely inappropriate."

"Aren't you curious?"

"Curious?" she repeated breathlessly.

"Wouldn't you care to see if there is still any attraction between us?"

The notion was absurd. Of course there was still an attraction between them. A potent one. At least on her part.

"No, I don't want to know. I mean . . . there is nothing on my side. I don't need to kiss you to know how I feel."

"Perhaps I do."

When he stepped closer, Kate felt her heart leap, whether in alarm or anticipation, she wasn't certain.

"What are you about, Deverill?"

"Answering a question."

His gaze captured hers, making her heart pound. His mouth was close, his body closer . . .